Y0-BGG-568

Books by Norman Keifetz

THE SENSATION (1975)

A JACK IS A KING (1962)

The Sensation

THE SENSATION

Norman Keifetz

New York ATHENEUM *1975*

This is a work of the imagination. It is not intended to portray the life or problems of any person, living or dead. If there are similarities to real people, they are coincidental. NK

"Try to hold 'em for four innings
or nine runs, whichever comes first. . . ."

> —DANNY MURTAUGH, *as Manager*
> *Pittsburgh Pirates*

"Years ago, you gave a guy a bat and a glove and he played.
. . . You have to be more of a psychologist today. . . . I can't
condemn a guy if he's doing what he feels inside. . . ."

> —DOC EDWARDS, *as Coach*
> *Philadelphia Phillies*

For Brom and Amanda

The Sensation

Chapter One

Nobody remembered that Potter Cindy made the "Faces in the Crowd" column of *Sports Illustrated* at age 12, when in Albuquerque, New Mexico, Little League championship play, he cracked eight consecutive home runs—four measured at over three hundred feet. That year, the boy batted .625, a feat he was to outdo twice in his career—his senior year at the University of Arizona (.647) and at rookie instruction camp for the Redbirds (.665).

Potter Cindy was a sensation. The Redbird fantasy was that Mays, Mantle, and even Musial would eventually be considered mere banjo hitters compared with Potter. The team even had mad visions that Ruth and Aaron were mere lollipops to Potter's all-day sucker. Even the great DiMaggio would have had to move to right field if Potter Cindy had played on the same team. It was said the boy could be the greatest ballplayer that ever lived.

With the Redbird press corps and publicity men very nearly daring to mouth such hopes and fantasies, Potter Cindy came to spring training certain to make the majors. It was in the cards. Potter had hit .414, belted 43 homers, 19 triples, 28 doubles for the Bougainvilla Burros in his first and only minor league season.

I

His autograph was already a consideration, rapidly being imprinted by Wilson as well as Japanese glove manufacturers on thousands of baseball mitts and Louisville sluggers. His face was to smile later in the season on six million tee shirts. Only once during the year that he played minor league ball was Potter Cindy not the most talked about person in Bougainvilla. He was jumped off the lips and front page of the *Bougainvilla Beacon* on a fuggy July day when some lunatic sexually molested or harassed a ten-year-old girl in nearby Selhurst, a town of some four thousand people, most of them Bougainvilla Burros rooters.

With that in the news it was natural that fewer people than usual noticed that Potter Cindy went 4 for 4, all home runs, especially the poor little victim and her parents. But, if they did not have time for Potter's exploits, Potter had time for them. He actually gave more than passing thought to going to see the people and telling them how sorry he felt for the little girl and her family. But he had heard the folks were in something of a state of shock. So instead, he privately devoted the next home run he hit to the family.

Potter was good. Potter was considerate. He was pleasant and friendly. He spoke to reporters and did not sound like a dunderhead or a phys ed major. The Redbirds had a winner. He was only twenty-three, had a cannon for an arm and a vacuum cleaner for a glove. He ran like an antelope and knew how to slide. It was going to be a beautiful summer for the Redbirds.

The owner of the big team, F. M. Heller, a pretzel baron, was delighted. He would fill Heller Park with thousands upon thousands of pretzel eaters—all come to sink their superstar-loving teeth into this new salty bagel in spiked shoes. "Number 49 . . . . " And then only the deafening roar, as Potter Cindy was introduced to the big leagues, that sensational center-fielder from 49 Barcella Lane, Albuquerque. He was, Mr. Heller said, warehouses full of giant bags of pretzels all by himself. By that he meant that Potter alone would help sell several warehouses full of pretzels. Mr. Heller assigned warehouses or parts of warehouses to all his ballplayers—their value measured in cases of pretzels consumed by middlemen as well as eaters. To those who had served him faithfully, he gave a Heller Pretzel distributorship when they retired.

Ironically, Potter Cindy did make the cover of *Sports Illustrated* the year he broke into the majors, not especially for being a spring training sensation, which he was, not for living up to his press notices, which he did, but for marrying Sissy Lindmore, a painfully thin little Hollywood personality, a well-publicized swinger who everybody thought was just a delightful little cunt, Potter Cindy's diversion from the great game of baseball. But no. They were in love. F. M. Heller hoped it would not interfere with his hitting. Some suspected *Sports Illustrated* had the same notion. When the article appeared on the newsstands, it carried the title, "Rookie Sensation with Energy to Burn." It never mentioned that Potter had been that kid "face in the crowd" some eleven years before. Instead, it revealed that both he and his wife slept nude and that "to the non-mind's eye, Potter's chest was a hell of lot better developed than Sissy's." The piece dwelled on the implication that night games would be more tightly played than the day-time exhibition events, as Potter and Sissy got to know more about each other. Mr. Heller took some comfort in the fact that the team did not allow wives on the road and that the 11:00 P.M. curfew was supposedly strictly enforced.

Mr. Heller did not have to worry about it, really. Screwing had nothing to do with a slugging average to Potter. Besides good luck, the key to success, Potter used to say, was total confidence.

"I go up to the plate thinking I'm going to belt a home run every time up. That's the only way to do it. You can't take a bat to the plate and think about how many strikeouts the pitcher has, or his earned run average. I don't think about curve balls or sliders or smoke. I just think 'that's my pitch.' I don't care what the guy throws. I hate to say this, because it sounds like boasting, but it surprises me when they get me out."

It was said by "intimates" that it took that kind of confidence to marry Sissy Lindmore. Potter, of course, was not the first to blast a shot into the hole. Sissy was rumored to have been a vulnerable opening to swinging producers, directors, movie stars, screenwriters with some clout, and not one of them could hold a bat properly, no less hit with it.

"So what," Potter would argue, if the suggestion were to be posed, "just because the ball has been fouled off a few times, doesn't mean you can't win a game with it. Besides, if it's all right to put pine tar and rosin on a bat, I don't see why I should bitch about hitting a ball that's been tagged a few times."

You can say what you want about him, Sissy once pointed out, Potter never insisted on the double standard.

Sissy did not let marriage change her, either. She remained as thin as a baseball contract, topped by a dirty-blond boy's haircut, and a childlike face. Her turn of speech still whirled with suggestions of conquests and availability. She spoke of sex perhaps as freely as she had given it. Of Potter, she was quoted as saying, "he's got a terrific bat."

On their wedding day, she was asked by a *Kansas City Star* sports writer how she would enjoy being a baseball widow when Potter was on the road. "I've gone for eight and sometimes ten days without a hit," she answered. "The nicest thing about being in a slump is when you come out of it," Sissy beamed. "That's basic baseball, mister."

Potter was attracted to Sissy's baby looks and whorey mouth. He found it cute, inviting. He found that he needed that kind of woman—someone who seemed less a grownup than a naughty, maybe silly kid. He remembered that little girl in Selhurst when he was on the Bougainvilla team. The

4

kid didn't look unlike Sissy. He was glad he socked a homer for the kid. He felt he had to do that. But if he had to say who Sissy reminded him of most, it was probably the girl who played Lolita in the movie of the same name. It might have been Merv Griffin or Dick Cavett who first told him that the book was even better than the movie. Potter later tried reading the book. It was, as he put it, "okay." But he had always been more of a moviegoer than a reader. "A book's a pitcher's duel," he once said, "a movie's more like a home run."

Sissy liked Potter because he was beautiful—jet-black hair, bright blue eyes, topping a beautifully muscled body, which actually seemed to be fatless. He was strong and graceful, tall and handsome. It had to be considered a bonus that every time Potter got ink, Sissy got publicity, too.

They met each other on the Johnny Carson Show, introduced as the two most talked about young people in America. Potter was the most heavily inked young minor league ballplayer since Mickey Mantle played for a Yankee farm team. Potter was asked how many home runs he had hit in his lifetime, and he mildly complained that he could not say "because he just started hitting them." When pressed to estimate, he answered, "about 712," knowing full well that Ruth had hit 714, and that Hank Aaron had hit even more than that. Potter only toyed with arrogance. "I don't expect to hit that many in the majors, though I sure wish I could."

As a gag, Sissy was asked how many homers she had hit, the inquiry clearly implying sexual experience, and she answered, "Not as many as Potter Cindy, but when I hit them they travel farther."

Except for the commercials—do you believe Heller pretzels—and a smooth nightclub singer, very nearly the entire show was about baseball and sex. It rocked the seismograph that measures television audience rumblings for the week, or month. The low point of the show came, apparently, when they had a brief interval, free of baseball and sex innuendo, describing the background of the two main guests. Potter and Sissy were surprised to learn that both their forebears, grandparents, had been migrant agricultural workers, Okies, who left Oklahoma like many in the thirties, for a fresh start in old Calliefornayay. Potter's granddaddy did not get as far as Sissy's, California, that is, as he took an unorthodox turn and his old junk-box of a car just obstinately stopped in Albuquerque, Tijeras to be precise. Grandpa Cindy started looking for work the moment he realized it was the end of the line. He found work, Potter said, "laboring work, hard work, the kind he knew, all he knew. And that's how I happened to grow up in New Mexico. I don't think of myself as an Okie, and I don't think my dad does either, though he grew up more in Oklahoma than New Mexico. Still, I suppose there is no denying our roots."

Sissy did not think of herself as an Okie, either. She was every bit a California girl. She sounded like a Californian, acted like a Hollywood brat, and was "one little sweet, tasty, sunkissed California tomato"—that was Johnny Carson's description.

Potter did not know Sissy by any other name. Even the preacher at the Assembly of God church who married them said, "Do you, Sissy," etcetera. Her Christian name was Suelee, but even the Okies had called her Sissy, as she was the sister, or sissy, in a family of five brothers, two of them California state troopers, the other three owners of a garage and filling station in San Diego.

Potter had asked her out after the show, and she quickly accepted. They ate in a celebrity-filled Mexican restaurant, and Potter ordered, as he was familiar with the cuisine, being from New Mexico, a state that is believed to have some of the finest Mexican eateries in the country. Potter made that claim to Sissy as part of his worldliness and early flirtation; he did not know all that much about eating "Mexican."

6

She invited him back to her place after dinner, and Potter quickly accepted. He did not expect to be served flan, a Spanish custard, and Sissy did not offer real dessert. She was out of her clothes very nearly before you could say Jackie Robinson, and Potter had not even said it. He took off his clothes, too, to be sociable. Sissy watched.

"Oh, wow, you don't wear any underwear," she observed. "Not even jockey shorts."

Lest she think foul of it, Potter explained, "I take a lot of showers." Sissy did not mind. She thought it was cool, and said so, a description she also gave to Potter's washboard stomach.

"How do you get a stomach that great-looking? Do you lift weights?"

Potter told her he suspected weight-lifting and isometric exercises were not good for a baseball player because he had known lots of guys who did them and they not only looked like apes but, and this the greatest of condemnations, "they couldn't hit the side of a barn from inside it." He confessed that he ran more than seven miles a day and did fourteen hundred sit-ups and leg lifts each week.

Sissy was impressed because even Potter's ass had muscles. There had to be something to exercise, she reasoned.

"You don't have an ounce of fat on you."

Potter studied her in turn, carefully. "Except for those little bitty titties, you don't either," he observed.

"Those 'little bitty titties' are fashionable," she argued.

"I wasn't complaining," Potter told her, straightening things out.

She threw him when she leaped on him, hitting Potter with her bony shoulder, momentarily catching him off balance, knocking him to the bed. She was on top of Potter and the young man, figuring it was fashionable, rose to meet her. She bounced, or found some way to bounce, looking, Potter thought, like a child thrilled with the free spring and push

7

of a trampoline. Her eyes were closed and she was smiling.

It was very much later when Sissy asked, "How many push-ups did you say you did?"

"I never do push-ups. Someone told me it thickens the muscles. I like my muscles long."

"Mmmmmmmm," she said, or uttered.

"For a little bit of a thing," Potter said, "you sure like to keep busy." He thought, *Here is a girl serving up these sexy pitches, and I don't even want to, or feel the need to swing.* But, as he had already unloaded his shot and was somewhat in the lead, he did not want to be bush-league. You could win by one run. You don't have to win by ten.

Sissy offered up a hanging curve ball again in the morning, charging into the shower with Potter, soaping, rubbing against him, finally luring him out. He had to take another shower, but Sissy could not feel guilty. After all, Potter said he took a lot of showers.

Showered, Potter reported to the Redbird camp in Venice, Florida, two days later and without Sissy Lindmore. Potter told her he hated to leave, but he had to start concentrating on making the team. Sissy promised to join him in a few weeks. He urged, "Make it three weeks. By then, I'll know if they are taking me north. And, if they are, we'll have some fun." She thought Potter was being sweet. She made no plans to visit Florida. She did not know that in three weeks she would miss him in the head and toes, both mind and body.

Potter was already missed by Whitey Knocthofer, the Redbird manager, who had expected his minor league sensation the day before. When Potter gave the gatekeeper at Nap Reyes Field his name, the old man nervously rushed him into a side office in the clubhouse, where Whitey sat, as if he'd been sitting there since the day before growling, "Where the fuck's that kid?"

"This here's Potter Cindy, Mr. Knocthofer."

"I know who he is," Whitey said bitterly, "I saw him on television."

8

Then to Potter. Whitey laid out the cards: "Well, if you're half as good as you were in Bougainvilla last year, you'll make the majors and we'll be damn pleased to have you. I don't have to tell you we're weak in the outfield, and we need some punch, muscle, at bat. We hope you can provide it."

Whitey had been a Redbird outfielder himself in his playing days and it was said that he had "softer hands" than Terry Moore, a man who knew how to catch a fly ball like it was landing in cotton. Potter did not answer his manager.

Whitey, via the fabulous underground baseball-snitchers network (usually coaches and sports writers and front office personnel), knew all about Sissy and Potter. "I don't like to tell a man what to do with his pecker. That's your business. But, until you make this team, I think you ought to lay off the cunt."

Potter still did not speak, an invitation not forthcoming.

"I'm going to room you with Bobby Hartman. He's been with us three years and he knows the score. He'll help you feel your way."

Potter remained silent. Bobby Hartman was a tidy-fielding second-baseman, a good bunter, with lightning speed. He rarely hit the long ball. His Texas Leaguers were a menace.

"You're not prejudiced, are you?"

"I thought Hartman was white," Potter responded finally. He was asked a direct question and he could hardly not answer it. Potter wanted to say that if Whitey bothered to check he could have easily learned that Potter Cindy got along with all the guys at Bougainvilla—white, black, Latin American, even an albino—but he did not. The best way not to say things, to keep control, was to just keep cool.

"Yeah, he is. But he's a Jew. We're not bigoted on this club."

Potter nodded.

"Well," Whitey pressed, "you have nothing against Jews?"

"Does he have anything against the Assembly of God?"

"What is *that*?" Knocthofer wanted to know.

9

"That's my church," Potter said, "when I go to it."

"I never met anyone who belonged to that church," said Whitey. "And I don't think Hartman has, either. Hartman's not against churches as far as I can tell."

"In that case," said Potter amiably, "I'm not against Bobby Hartman."

Potter appreciated being assigned number 49, and said so to Whitey later on. Other rookies that season did not get preferred numbers, or the chance to room with any regulars, whether Jewish, black, or yankee doodle dandies. The equipment man told Potter, "Everybody kids me about brownnosing you because I know you'll make the team." Potter had been signed for a $40,000 bonus, cold cash. The figure was well publicized; there were no strings attached to it. It was just nice currency handed to a damn good prospect. Potter was not looking for special attention, but at Bougainvilla he had gotten used to getting it as a big bonus baby, and he had learned to accept it gracefully, politely. Potter gave to flatterers and to genuine admirers alike just the proper amount of gratefulness and warmth. Therefore, no one felt embarrassed or uncomfortable with him, and it showed in his relationships, and in the press. He was polite and respectful, though given to an occasional bit of mischief, harmless stuff. For example, when the trainer gave him a medical application to complete, he filled in his name, age, religion, and blood type, and across a very long checklist of ailments and disorders, including hemorrhoids and nervousness, he wrote in block letters, HEALTHY. Potter had observed that that statement was a good deal more than could be said for the rest of the club, which seemed to contain all of the feeble, lame, moribund, hypochondriacal crybabies in the league, who complained of everything from sinus trouble to water-on-the-knee. Everybody seemed to suffer some sort of muscle spasm, pulled tendon, stretched ligament for which they were all being ministered to in the treatment room with combinations of heat, ice, diathermy, whirlpool, painkillers, even Sloane's liniment. Six regulars had to see the doctor periodically to have fluid drained from somewhere or another. One fellow had a hydrocele, which is excess water in the testicle, another a pilonidal cyst, still others were suffering from chronic headaches, backaches. One guy had Bell's palsy, someone else was laid up with sun exposure. The third-baseman clumped around the clubhouse in a fifty-pound shoe, looking like a one-footed Frankenstein. He claimed to be recovering from knee surgery, and was using the heavy shoe to build up the muscles around his knee. Seeing them, the barely crawling wounded, Potter understood for the first time how the Redbirds blew a nine-game lead and the division championship the previous season. They were a team of cripples. They needed amphetamines—"ups, pep pills, little greenies"—to build up enough energy to get themselves to the treatment room. One newspaperman serving a paper in a rival city summed up the Redbirds' chances for his readers back home. "Their best guys seem to be a good-looking rookie named Potter Cindy who knocks the cover off the ball, and the team physician. But this club will need a trip to Lourdes to get ready."

It was more than a miracle that in three weeks these same cripples were playing like champions. Potter helped; he had hit 7 homers, 3 doubles, 1 triple, fielded flawlessly, effortlessly on tough chances, threw out two runners trying to stretch, and stole four bases. "Jesus Christ," glowed Whitey, "I still don't believe it. This kid's a fuckin' sensation, ain't he?"

The team would clobber somebody in an exhibition game, and the next morning a rival sports reporter, maybe green with disbelief, would see a long line of enfeebled ballplayers queuing up for the treatment room. The team doctor, Jethro Hardy, a battlefield surgeon during World War II, taxed all of his expertise, obviously, to get this team moving.

Indeed, they would seem semi-comatose till some team rolled into Nap Reyes Field and then, as though a rival uniform were a blood transfusion, they woke up and slaughtered the intruders. Hank Mayknoll, the Redbird pitcher who had won twenty-one games the year before, for example, would very nearly spend his entire day soaking his beautiful black arm in everything from camomile tea to ice water, and then he would go out to the mound, and promptly shoot holes through nine consecutive Texas Rustlers, wincing through every pitch of the massacre. This even puzzled Potter, who had clobbered Mayknoll all over the lot in practice.

After a typical shootout, Potter asked Mayknoll, "Henry, how come I slam the heck out of your pitches in intersquad games and you get so tough against those other cowboys in a real game?"

Mayknoll, who was rubbing some kind of highly touted horse liniment into his sore arm, said, "They ain't in your league, Potter."

"Come on, Mayknoll," Potter said, "you don't give it your best against me."

"I'm not paid to get you out, slugger."

"You think you could, if you were?" Potter asked pleasantly. It was not a challenge.

Mayknoll was intelligent. He answered in kind. "I guess I'd have to, rookie. Lucky for both of us, right, that we don't have to do that number now? You'll probably be traded or run out of steam in a couple of years and I'll be ready to retire and wait till they elect me to the Hall of Fame."

Potter let it be. Mayknoll must have had something to win twenty-one games.

Whatever he had, it was not conditioning. Potter heard Mayknoll and nearly the entire squad grunting and groaning each morning, as they were put through an hour of hellish exercises by Dr. Hans Knauerhase, a workout specialist, deputy director of phys ed at De Paul University, hired for training season to scientifically toughen the Redbirds.

Dr. Knauerhase claimed to be able to systematically work every conceivable tendon and muscle in a series of specially designed exercises, resembling the usual toe-touching and back-arching. The only workout Potter had not seen before was a thing called the log roll, in which Bobby Hartman, Potter's roomie, stretched himself rigid in the center of a circle of seated Redbirds and was passed from one player to the next. Dr. Knauerhase, who labeled the Redbirds after things by the way they went through the exercises, thought Hartman and Potter were the best-conditioned people in the camp. "Hartman is a sapling. Potter Cindy is a ballet dancer. Mayknoll is my oak tree, Brossi is a listing sailboat." Phil Brossi was the player who wore the heavy shoe to build up his quadricep muscles.

The team medical man, like Dr. Knauerhase and most everyone else in the Redbird organization loosely connected with management, or Mr. Heller, developed a fondness for Potter. During one of his famous "bedside chats"—informal discussions on personal pathologies discovered in a player, whether physical or emotional (one player was told he had TB, another that he was throwing too hard and too often with an elbow that was traumatically osteoarthritic, still another that he was too anxious)—Dr. Hardy revealed to Potter, "I've gotten word the team is taking you back with us when we break camp. You've made it."

Potter could not imagine what confidence the doctor would reveal next, as there was never any doubt of Potter making the team if he performed at all well. Right from the start, they had traded their rightfielder and moved Peeve Borkowski, their former centerfielder, to right. If Potter did not go north with the big club, it would have a gaping hole up the middle that nobody was practicing to fill. They would also need someone to hit third in the lineup.

Potter said nothing, just looked the doctor in the eye, examining him. He blinked every now and then to let Dr. Hardy know he was conscious.

The doctor said, "You seem to be in terrific shape. One of those perfect specimens."

13

Potter made no reply. He could not tell him about his sudden affection for that little girl in Selhurst or the dozens of other little girls he had wanted to hit homers for.

"I know this is going to seem odd. You never filled out a medical form and I'd like to have a history on you—for the records. You remember that you gagged up the official form by writing 'healthy' across it. After seeing you and examining you, I cannot dispute your diagnosis, Potter. But I'd still like to know more about you. You know, stuff like what diseases you've had in the past, drug sensitivities, any allergies, stuff like that."

"Oh, sure," Potter said. He told the doctor that he had no allergies, was sensitive to nothing he knew about, never had piles, syph, or long-lasting diarrhea, constipation, or stomach aches. He had an occasional headache, suffered from influenza once. He could not remember ever having had to sneeze before or after that bad cold. If he had to say, he would think he sneezed on the average of once a year. He knew most people sneezed a lot more. He had had one undescended testicle as a child which was surgically corrected. The doctor thanked him. Then, "How do you feel now?" Dr. Hardy said, "I know you must be under a lot of pressure, trying to make the squad."

"I thought you said I made the squad," Potter pointed out.

"Oh, yes. That's unofficial, of course. Whitey will be the final word. I was just asking if you are undergoing any emotional strain."

"No," Potter said, simply, eloquently.

Dr. Hardy considered. "Someone who knew you in the minors said you sometimes seemed unhappy, even depressed." Nobody had really said that. It was just a technique Dr. Hardy used. He fancied himself a bit of a psychiatrist, too.

Potter asked, "Who said that?"

"I can't say," the doctor answered, sagely.

"Well, it's not true," Potter said.

"What's not?"

"That I have problems. That's a lie." Potter felt like telling him to take his dumb guesses and rumors about his unhappiness and depression and shove them up his ass. What right did the doctor have to pry, to look for scandal? He decided to hold on, to tell nothing, to control himself, to be cool.

The doctor put his arm around Potter. The boy looked upset.

"Nobody said anything, Potter. I was just checking. Mr. Heller likes me to check the head as well as the body."

"I was depressed because I thought I was good enough for the big leagues last year. That's why I was unhappy."

Dr. Hardy did not want to create troubles. He was sorry. He knew these kids were under great strain to perform well. He knew they worried about slumping at the wrong time, when everybody was looking.

"I know, Potter. Forget it."

Bobby Hartman later explained, when Potter claimed with a measure of irritation that the doctor thought he had a degree in head shrinking, not to take it personally because Dr. Hardy had gotten burned pretty badly when he misdiagnosed a serious case of manic depression in a player the organization had signed for big money on Dr. Hardy's "clean bill of health."

"Now the doctor thinks every new guy is a lunatic until proven sane," Hartman said. "You'll be under observation for a while. But, by now, you should be used to it. Nobody thinks you're for real. You've been too perfect. You can run, hit, field. You never get hurt, never complain. I don't even think you've been struck out yet. You can't be that good. So everybody must be figuring you're fucked up in some other way. I think you worry them."

Potter released a wan smile; it certainly was not a beam of joy—perhaps six watts at best. "Wait till Sissy Lindmore gets here. That'll give'em heart failure, I guess."

"I heard you were going with her. Is that true?"

"Yes."

"I once went out with a skinny girl. When I brought her home my grandfather took one look at her—a good look—and I could see he really felt sorry for me. 'Nothing to feel,' he explained later in Yiddish, under his breath. But I liked her a lot. And she was one of the best lays I've ever had."

"So's Sissy," Potter volunteered, though he had only slept with her a couple of times, and the sex part, he felt, was not as much fun as the kidding around. "I might marry her."

"You might—?" Hartman, who had taken on more of his grandfather's values now that he was older, in his mid-twenties, was thinking, *But there's nothing to feel, man.* Then, *Holy smokes, this guy must be fucked up. He's going to marry that skinny cunt.* Still, even Dr. Hardy would agree that it was better than manic depression.

Talk about ups and downs, one somehow always gets back to Sissy Lindmore. When she showed up at the Redbird spring-training camp in Florida, Whitey, his coaching staff, Dr. Hardy, Mr. Heller's representatives from the front office came down with an outbreak of depression. They all feared at once, as though a rash suddenly erupted, as though it were part of the syndrome, *Shit! There goes our sensation.*

Chapter Two

For the first eight days that Sissy was in Florida—four exhibition games—Potter went 1 for 14 against the generally anemic pitching of the Phils, White Sox, Indians, and Cardinals. His only hit in that brief slump was an example of what came to be known for the rest of the spring and into the regular season by friendly reporters as "Potter's Poke." This was a tracerlike shot that zoomed out of the batter's box like the beginnings of a low liner and rose gradually to clear the fielders and the fence. Unlike many big home-run hitters, Potter never hit those high, lofty, mortar-type shots—those long fly balls, really—that somehow travel too far for the outfielder to get under. Potter's Poke went out like a sidewinder missile, exploding into the stands.

Predictably, Whitey asked the "slumping" Potter, "What's wrong?"

"Not a thing, Whitey. Everything's just fine."

"You call 1 for 14 fine?"

"Jeez, I've hit about 7 homers, haven't I? That isn't exactly a slump for spring training. Look at the other guys' stats. You know, Hartman isn't so famous for a long ball, and he's the only other guy on the team who's hit a homer." Potter did not like the sound of his own voice. It seemed to him that he was whining. He wanted to give a different impression. He continued more evenly, calmly, flat-voiced. "All the power on this team has come from one little room in the motel."

"Yeah," Whitey paused. "Yeah, well keep it up." He was frustrated that he could not find a way in this exchange to condemn Sissy for weakening his best hitter. Unyielding, he pressed the pitching coach into secret service duty for the good of the great and wonderful tradition-filled, Hall of Fame-filled Redbirds. The coach, who made his living strictly on allegiance to Knocthofer and the flag—Mayknoll said he was a lousy pitching coach and that he was stupid—showed up at Potter's room about 12:15 A.M. to see if he could catch Potter sabotaging the pennant in sprint training. The coach, who hunted different birds on the off-season, at a more civil hour—6:00 A.M. —unsubtly pounded on the door, presumably to set these birds to flight.

Yawning, Hartman finally surrendered to the pounding, and answered the door.

"Where's Potter Cindy?"

"He's asleep, Coach. Why?"

"Bullshit! He's in there with that cunt." He pushed by Hartman to find Potter in bed nude and sound asleep. There was no Sissy at his side, not in the closet or bathroom. The coach checked.

"Why isn't he wearing pajamas or underwear?" he asked sagely, proving his point that Potter had been banging someone in the room.

"I'll ask him in the morning," said Hartman, bitterly.

"Never mind. Just answer one thing. Is he humping that skinny dame?"

"You see he's asleep. You wanna check to see if he had a wet dream?"

"Shut up, you fuck! Or we'll trade you." The embarrassed bird hunter stormed out. Then, in a sudden, brilliant second thought from the hallway he called out at 12:30 in the morning,

"You knew what I meant, you prick, Hartman."

The next morning at the field, Mr. Heller's general manager, Herbert Zarember, appeared at the foot of the dugout, looking dyspeptic, the ulcerous state undoubtedly triggered by Mr. Heller's inquiry into the problem of Potter Cindy's "slump." The sensation jogged by on his way to the outfield and blithely called out, "Well, howdydo, Mr. Zarember. You're looking dreamy."

"Huh," Mr. Zarember recovered momentarily, but not brilliantly. "Oh, hi there, son. You going to poke one today, I hope."

"It's all in the stars, Mr. Zarember. Who knows?" Potter called over his shoulder. It was quite a witty comment that completely escaped Mr. Zarember. He did not remember that they were playing the Astros that day, that Sissy was a young Hollywood character, or that Potter was already regarded as a star, albeit a rookie. All Mr. Zarember could think, belching, was *Shit, let's hope it's something more substantial than astrology. Mr. Heller's not too crazy about eccentrics.*

Dr. Hardy, who was not far away, spotted the sensation and called him over. The doctor knew everyone had a stake in this boy. He was not just any rookie. This one hit home runs, caught the ball, ran. If, as he observed, Mr. Zarember bothered to talk to him about something other than money—which was the general manager's main and often exclusive topic—he knew it made sense, retainer-wise, to show concern for Potter.

The outfielder jogged over to the doctor.

"How you feeling, Potter?"

"Strong as a horse," Potter said pointedly. "I'm going to hit 6 homers today."

"Take it easy, old boy. Whitey tells me homers are like orgasms. You run out of them after a time."

"What do you think of that as a doctor?"

"It's not the latest medical thinking, I'll admit. But I don't speak for baseball lore."

"Me neither," Potter said. He tipped his cap and, smiling, ran out to shag some flies.

During the first inning of the game with the Astros, Hartman bunted for a base hit to open the game. The next hitter fouled out, bringing up Potter as the third hitter. Sissy was in the stands just above the Redbird dugout, which seated Whitey, Mr. Zarember, Dr. Hardy, Mr. Heller, and some other players who filled out the remaining space left on the bench.

Potter stepped to the plate. He did not need to look for a sign. He looked to the four nervous great stone Mt. Rushmore faces on the bench. The first pitch was low and Potter, who swung lefty, drove it in his typical rocketlike fashion in the direction of South Dakota, far over the right-field wall.

With the score 2-0 Redbirds, Mr. Heller left the dugout trailed by Mr. Zarember. It was said they flew home to draw plans, and a contract, for the approval of a certain young power hitter from Albuquerque. The newspapers later reported that Potter had signed for $300,000, an unbelievable figure, even granting the rookie his full potential. He was, after all, only a rookie.

Potter confided to Hank Mayknoll, who was reportedly making $90,000 a year, that the money was contingent on his making himself available for Heller promotional activities on the off-season and that he play at least 100 games during the season. In other words, if he was taken out for a minor injury or a slump it would count against him, or if the manager had a bug up his ass about him and benched him, it would also go against him. If he played fewer than 100 games, for whatever reason, he would be paid $25,000 a year and still have to fulfill the promotional aspects of the contract at the management's discretion. At the end of the third year, if he played 300 games and if he otherwise satisfactorily fulfilled the terms of the contract, he would be paid $150,000. So, at best, he'd get it all. At the worst, he'd get $75,000 at the end of three years.

"You're a dummy, Potter," said Mayknoll. "I get $90,000 each year—outright—and I'm paid extra for any promotions. I don't get a lot of promotions from Heller because, the truth is, I'm too fat and too black to be eating lily-white pretzels, even though the pretzels, themselves, are more my color. But, Potter, it is not hard to see that you need my lawyer. He's black, too, and I'm certain he's smarter than yours."

"Maybe so, Hank." Potter was not an envious or avaricious young man. He was not brought up to complain. He knew that he'd be making more money than most Americans. Potter knew nothing about business. He did not even think baseball was a business.

Potter was thinking about slumps—not money—when he drove to Miami in a rented car to play the Bucs. The only thing different about Potter Cindy that day was that he felt tight, uneasy, uncomfortable. Sissy had stayed behind in Venice, Fla. "It's too boring to sit in a car," she said. "You don't mind if I don't make the trip?"

Potter did not care. He did not want company, anyway. That's why he asked permission to drive to the Bucs game rather than go in the team bus. He wanted to be alone for a few hours—away from reporters, fans, baseball players, people. He did not like himself this way. It was not natural. There was a hitch in his emotional swing and he had to shake it the only way he knew how. He'd had the feeling before. It was maddening. It drove him crazy for a while.

Then, zipping along the Florida causeway, he felt he would come out of it. Just before the horizon was a ballfield, a big schoolyard, really, nearly deserted, as schoolyards are on early Sunday mornings everywhere. Potter drove up along the wire fence of the yard, and there on the tennis court, a kid racqueted a ball against a brick wall behind the courts.

Potter got out of the car and watched. A ball broke loose and bounded toward Potter. He scooped it up and tossed it back.

"Wanna play, mister?"

Potter said, "I'll just watch you for a while, if you don't mind. I don't have a racquet."

"Well, okay." Then, another thought occurred to the child, "Would you throw them to me so's that I can hit 'em back to you?"

Potter agreed. The child had good form, moved gracefully, and had a strong swing. He saw she would be a good player someday, if she practiced. Maybe another Chris Evert. She looked a little like a twelve-year-old version of her, he saw.

"Do you live around here?" she asked.

"No. I'm just a visitor."

"There are a lot of visitors in Florida," she said, as she drove one that took off like a Potter Poke and sailed over the ten-foot brick wall of the building behind Potter.

"Well, there goes the game," she said. "That's my only ball." Little Chris Evert had another thought, "Could you boost me over, mister? I don't want to lose it."

Potter boosted. He accidentally saw she was wearing little blue panties under her white tennis outfit. Perhaps he had imagined that she intentionally rubbed against his body when he helped her. He did not remember how she came to be sitting next to him in the car, or why she kissed him on the cheek, or why she did not run away when he zipped down his fly and revealed his tumescence. He did not even remember if she touched it or not. She probably had, because he had to clean himself after she was gone. She said her name was Nicole or Nancy. She had had, presumably, a new experience. If she told her parents, they would probably think she was imagining things. He had only touched her fine blond hair, her warm face and her budding breasts. He did not hurt her.

22

There was, of course, no one who knew that the season, career, and maybe even the life of the Redbird sensation was a split second short of having violently ended only moments after he had taken his enjoyment from the little girl.

There was a growing awareness on the part of the young outfielder that his personal madness was getting out of control. He saw that this was not one of those crazy things a person does one time out of curiosity and then never does again. He saw he had become like a wild animal that once having tasted blood, must do it again and again. Nobody would be able to understand or accept that while he liked little girls to kiss his penis, or touch it, or press their little fannies against it or sit in his lap, he did not want to hurt them. Who would believe that he felt more affectionate toward the children, paternal even? He had played with many little girls before, and he knew that the feeling satisfied him only temporarily.

The remembrance of this time, like the others, would wear off, he knew as he sat behind the steering wheel of his rented car. There were tears on his cheeks and sadness on his face and grief and contempt and shame in his thoughts. He felt helpless, trapped, alone. He saw himself as a criminal, a violator of the law of the worst order. The vision, the thrill of the moments just past with the little tennis player, would wear off sometime and he would have to find another. "It's destroying me," he screamed behind clenched teeth to the windshield.

He was only going about thirty miles an hour when he saw the big trailer truck suddenly turn onto the road he was traveling. Potter meant to hit the brake, but something inside of him, the shame, the guilt, the sorrow for all the little girls he had played with—no, MOLESTED, that was the word they used in the papers—forced his foot to the accelerator. He saw the truck was huge as he came closer. The impact would hardly budge it. The driver would be safe and he, Potter Cindy, ballplayer and freak, sex maniac and criminal, would have ended the suffering, the agony, the torment, the fear of hurting some kid accidentally forever. At the last moment, when he saw that his course would impale his car and himself on the end of the steel construction beams which overhung the back of the truck, Potter promised himself, swore to avoid children forever, never allow himself to be near them alone, and he turned abruptly, just barely missing the giant vehicle.

Potter came to a halt on the service road beside the highway. He was unhurt physically. He thought carefully, *Hell, I'm practically a major leaguer. I've made it! How many guys make the majors? And of those that do, how many have a chance to star in the bigs? All I have to do is avoid little girls, because that's my bean ball sure as hell. I've come all this way to the big time. If I can manage to leave the children alone, I'll be okay. It sounds so simple a thing to do. But I know it isn't. I'm like a drunk, and it's time to dry up and get on the wagon.* Potter Cindy made a vow: "There is no way that I'm ever going to do that again. I'm all done molesting. Yes, molesting! Let's call it by its name because that is what it is. I can only thank God that I never hurt any of those children."

Potter knew that while he would no longer molest little girls, he was not really free. Something might come out in the papers. One of his past misadventures might be accidentally revealed in some way.

But he was on the right track now. And that was important. He had suffered personally for past transgressions. And if that could serve as justice enough, then he'd be okay from now on. He had the determination. All he needed was a little luck.

Potter drove on to the Bucs exhibition game. He went 3 for 5 at the plate, one hit a homer.

He married Sissy Lindmore three days later.

Chapter Three

As spring training began to wind down, the Redbirds were showing signs of improved health. The lines were shorter at the treatment room. Not so many players were complaining of aching muscles and tenuous tendons; there was less of a call for the whirlpool bath and the diathermy and painkillers.

Now the daily call for the wounded and the weary brought out more kibitzers than patients—guys joined a teammate or a roommate, the legitimate patient, just to kid around or to ask Doc Hardy to resolve a medical argument.

Ballplayers, like most young men outside of baseball, got into disagreements that only the knowledge of an experienced physician and surgeon could solve. Hartman, for example, had to prove to his shortstop, Dick Condon, that there was no such thing as a straight pubic hair. Hank Mayknoll had to convince his battery mate, Jake Minbar, and first-baseman Jim Domijo that a eunuch could indeed get an erection, "even though he didn't have any nuts or jizum." Other guys had questions about the potency of aphrodisiacs, particularly pot, Spanish fly, the inscrutable ginseng and other assorted herbs and roots. One player wanted to know if it was true that an orgasm could be heightened and prolonged by sniffing a drug that expanded the blood vessels at the key moment.

Dr. Hardy answered most things very professionally. He gave scientific explanations to maintain dignity when the question was clearly not designed to elicit an answer out of a medical textbook. Still, Dr. Hardy had his lapses from tongue-twisting, incomprehensible medical jargon and that was what probably kept the players coming back with their "scientific" inquiries (most of the questions were about sex).

One such lapse involved Potter as an innocent bystander. The rookie outfielder was at the time briefly nicknamed Big Bat for his spring-training slugging.He was sitting on a table chatting with Mayknoll, who was immersed in the whirlpool bath, when outfielder Borkowski, another non-patient hanger-on, asked the team physician aloud, "Doc, what's the biggest wang ever recorded in medical history?" Dr. Hardy looked up from his patient with a smile. He had been holding a tape measure to record the leg muscle atrophy of Jake Minbar, whose mended limb had recently been freed from its plaster cast. The doctor, to Potter's surprise, walked over to him, stuck one end of the tape measure at his crotch, and drew the tape down to Potter's knee. "About the size of Big Bat's here," Dr. Hardy said, holding up the outstretched tape. It triggered an explosion of laughter in the treatment room.

Potter liked it, too, for other reasons. It was important in his new determination to "go straight" that he be endowed with nicknames of sexual prowess, like Big Bat, and be chosen to symbolize the "great wang," even in jest. It did not matter that in the shower he was only average. What could they know, his teammates, of the kind of hell he had gone through to make it all work? Their dreams were not filled with the horror of being locked in a room, unclothed, with a little girl. Were they haunted by dreams in which they could not control their bladder in public? Did they wake up thinking that they had befouled their baseball uniform in full view of thirty thousand fans? Did they worry themselves sick thinking that the little girl who stood horrified by his nakedness might actually be another victim and not the nighttime torment of the past?

Yes, Big Bat. Big Bat! I cannot thank you all enough for that. "I am the Big Bat," said Potter, jumping off the table and standing to his full height. Then, he pinched both of the doctor's cheeks and walked out of the treatment room, listing to one side, as though the weight of his immense organ was so great it very nearly tipped him over. Laughter followed him and Potter was pleased.

He saw the team growing fonder of him, accepting him. Potter really worked at making it, not only at bat and in the field and on the bases, but also in staying cool. It meant taking part in high jinks, a role Potter was not really comfortable with.

The key to staying in the saddle, he knew, was a minimum of slip-ups. He had to make certain not to give anyone any reason to link him to the events of the past. He had to make people like him, and that meant no whining and not being ornery or resistant to the management's suggestions; he had to go along and get along; he also had to be amiable and cooperative to newsmen. This would not be hard; he had never been a prankster or a horseplay artist, even though he liked rambunctiousness in others. It was fun observing silliness; he appreciated it in others. And then, thinking of his fondness for the carefreeness of youth, he shuddered in fear and disgust; it seemed that this was, after all, the heart of the problem. *Jesus*.

Potter took a moment of peace in the thought that some of the fellows on the team were laughing with him, admiring him, believing more each day that he was no different from them, and that, best of all, he belonged.

When he was in the minors, with the Burros at Bougainvilla, that is, when he was comfortably entrenched as a regular and a superstar, he must have taken more liberties as a locker room leg-puller or clubhouse comic than he believed he had.

He remembered that he hardly recognized the picture of himself, described by a young woman writer for a national teen-age magazine, *Seventeen*, or one of the others, under the overall suggestive title of "Prospects—An Intimate Look at the Swingingest Jocks in America." The author of the article portrayed him as "a cross between Gregory Peck and Clint Eastwood with a locker room personality of the Katzenjammer Kids. Potter Cindy is nice, dreamy, fun to talk to, sexy, understanding, pleasant. He makes a lot of behind-the-scenes wisecracks, but that's part of the game the boys play without a ball and a bat. His only weakness seems to be an occasional madness for dumping the contents of a goldfish bowl down somebody's trousers. ..." Potter never remembered having surrendered to such madnesses; in fact, he never did dump any goldfish bowls down anyone's pants, but he may have told the writer that he had done so when she was eagerly looking for material on what she called the "smell of the locker room" or "bachelors at play."

The writer's description of him never hurt him, however. Maybe it was an image to shoot for.

Chapter Four

It had been raining all night and morning. The game would be washed away. She had been expecting her favorite outfielder for hours.

Sissy, clothesless, walked around her motel room, a cup of coffee in one hand, a Deringer cigarillo in the other. She was thinking that Potter reminded her of someone she had known long ago: a boy who had died, she had heard, in Vietnam. They had never slept together, though until she was launched into her career as a *fahbrenteh pushka*, a Hollywood expression for ardent vagina, or hot box (she never bothered to get the King James translation), every man or boy that she had ever slept with was that dead GI.

The trooper was seven when she first saw him looking at her with his big blue eyes, bugged out by what was being done to her in the park by the other kids. They were playing doctor, the children, using a wooden thermometer to take her temperature vaginally. She saw in the way he could not help staring that he was fascinated by it and troubled, too.

They knew each other through elementary and high school, paralleled each other, really, because whenever one was free the other was engaged or "pinned." Sissy did manage to corner the boy once, all but undressed him, but he was so sweet

29

or sentimental or full of nostalgia that all he managed was to get a fast reading of her temperature with his finger. Sissy felt frustrated, angered, and let some other Los Angeles dudes spur her just to show him. She showed twenty-one other dudes on a rough count that that boy was not the only man in the world.

When she became the sweetheart of Hollywood and Vine or Palm Springs, she no longer saw the boy behind every non-wooden thermometer. "The seduced" only gave herself to important or distinguished or classy seducers. She had been "honey galored"—another one of those super-duper, marvelous, inside Southern California euphemisms for civilized carnality—by high-profile functionaries in the world of Art, Business, Government, and Crime. "You notice," said one Hollywood smartass, "Sissy Lindmore only sleeps with philosophers and kingpins." Indeed, she had slept with a fat steel executive, a skinny playwright, a high-strung film-maker, a low-key baritone, a nondescript odds-maker, and a political pollster. Her favorite criminal was a winsome imp, one Marvin "Scruffy" Levinson of Atlanta football, prostitution, numbers, and assorted real estate hustles. Nobody ever explained how he got nicked with the name Scruffy; he was actually pathologically fastidious and tidy. Ever since he'd become a big shot, Scruffy never wore the same underwear or pair of socks twice. Sissy estimated that he threw out 180 pairs of socks and shorts in the some six months she knew him.

Sissy had a lot of oddballs in her time, not that she thought Potter was one. He was more willing than the boy of her childhood (bless his soul), but full of the same innocence and sweetness, puzzlement, admiration, and caution. He did look at her the way her childhood "crush" had, both kindly and curious at once, attracted on the one hand, hesitant on the other, she guessed.

A girl never quite knew how much to lead a man like Potter. There was always that possibility that if you undressed him, which, considering his underwear situation, was something even a girl with St. Vitus' dance could do, he might shy, rear up, back off. And where would she be? Thrown for a damn loop. Poor old Sissy. She laughed. She remembered that someone once told her that when a high-strung thoroughbred is standing in stud, it sometimes has to be brought a cold mare, to test the temperature, so to speak. She would have to work out a device, a cold mare, for Potter. He was a willing lover, or more precisely, willing to experiment. But he had to be settled down first. He always came back from the ballfield turned tighter than the bolts on an automobile tire by that jack-handle known as "being a pro."

There had been nothing more important in Potter's life, as far as Sissy knew, than playing ball and being a professional.

When she came to learn more about him, about how very much of himself he gave to improving his skills and being "great," she felt gloriously flattered that he would marry her and be her husband at this stage of his career. Potter was the kind of man who married, she knew, but for his primary life and love—baseball—he would have been better off marrying later in his career than at the beginning of it.

He was strikingly handsome, tall, the all-American boy, at first glance, save for his black hair. The second closer look showed a face that bore some suffering, or had known grief, and for Sissy that cut him out of the wolf pack, touched the mother in her, and made him irresistible, both puppy to be nursed and lover to take in her mouth.

There were those days when Potter came home without needing to be unwound or cold-mared. They were so few they could be counted on two fingers.

Potter came into the motel room on one of those days, picked her up like a loaf of French bread, put her under his arm, and all but ate every last crust of her. He had had a thing for her that day that refused to be diminished.

"Potter, you must have hit four homers today."

"I love you, Sissy," he said.

She was flabbergasted, delighted, all-accepting.

"Potter, you're a major leaguer." She told Potter that during spring training when he was still officially a minor leaguer.

"Never mind that. I'm the whole team so far. Do you love me?"

"Of course. You're my whole team, too. I not only love you. I need you."

He was a treat. She never had a boy as good as him. Oh, she'd been with cooler, more experienced lovers, guys that would make your teeth rattle, but they weren't as genuine as old Potter, could never be, because she did not love them.

The other time Sissy remembered Potter slugging with such authority on the field of the mattress was the day he got back from a rained-out game early. He caught her nude, as usual; she was standing there on the bed, her legs crossed like a little girl with a full bladder. Old Potter just moved in for the kill, or whatever it's called. Man, the little girl didn't even have time to empty her bladder, or prepare. Thank goodness for contraceptive pills, she thought, even if they do cause blood clots. It's better than having an acting career blow up in nine months, like a uterus.

The pill, for all its faults, Sissy knew, was her best defense, especially that day. The young slugger came to plate wielding a hot bat. His wife had seen him hit before, but that day, with the rain pelting down and not even the groundkeepers left at the ballpark, he was on fire. Sissy thought afterward, *Mmmmmmm. I'll have to walk around like that more often. It turns Potter on.*

"You nearly tore my head off. That's not like you."

"I'm sorry."

"Don't be, Potter love. It's a nice change of pace." Sissy was special. She took things in stride. Though often mocked, passed over, maligned, she was better than a politician in fielding slams, damns, hecklers. Perhaps it was because she just saw things simply and cleanly, the way she'd been taught, by experience. She was not one of the world's great thinkers.

When she gave an idea some time, it was spent positively and with a purpose—for enjoyment. So when Potter said, "You know, Sissy, everybody thinks that all we do is screw, that our whole lives are a wang and giney. They don't want to realize that we are fond of each other, close to each other in different ways."

"That's good, Potts. Let them think that. It helps the rep."

"Whose?" Potter wanted to know.

"Don't you want a big rep as a marvelous lover?"

"Not if I haven't earned it. I'm not all that sexy. In fact, I'm going to tell you something, which isn't easy to admit or talk about. But, Sissy, I never really enjoyed sexual intercourse before I knew you. I got a bigger kick jacking off with a fantasy."

Sissy touched her young slugger's cheek tenderly. She said, "Well, who said being sexy is so great?"

"Didn't you just say it?"

"No, sweet Potter. I was talking about people thinking you're great in bed. That's what counts. The truth never helped anyone. If enough people believe you're the cat's pajamas, then you're everything they say. Truth is horse shit."

"Suppose they start saying things you don't want to hear or can't put to your advantage. Or suppose they tell a lie that isn't good for your rep..."

"You just ignore it," Sissy said. "Or tell them to kiss your ass." She was a girl with a lot of confidence, Potter thought, not dumb, either. He was glad he had married her. Potter studied Sissy, this beanpole little girl, this naughty emaciated thing, in her bathtub clothes, nakeder than a jaybird, looking like everybody's vision of America's underdeveloped fourteen-year-old, hot-to-trot sister. She was haystack blond and cute, with a small, straight nose, slightly turned upward, and full, sensuous lips. She constantly wore an inviting, if not seductive smile, which offered sexual enthusiasm if not innocence. She was not now, and maybe never had been, "full with virginity."

She was always bawdy, Elizabethan, which bordered on what had been described as "sewer-mouthed" by a California legislator, an upstater, who once actually proposed, without a touch of whimsy, that a tax be imposed on every act of sexual intercourse to help put the state in the black. The legislator actually called Sissy "a bed-hopping toothpick with a mouth like a sewer." Sissy did not mind, really. She claimed it was good publicity, brought her air time on local radio and TV stations. She sued the prude anyway, for increased publicity mileage, and it got her on network television, where she met Potter Cindy, the big poker or little poker or whatever.

Potter had never been a big C-man, or marvelously aggressive with women. Though clearly picture-book handsome, he had not chased tail. They had chased him, and occasionally he stopped running wind sprints in the outfield to be caught on the right field on a balmy night, with the stars and the moon in the right position. He would reap a harvest, tire them out. He had a low libido or a slow trigger, and many a lass would exclaim "Whew!" before the gun went off. But, for Potter, it was firing without a full musket. He got the thing loaded up so he might just as well let it go—that was, more or less, the way he looked at it.

What was special about Sissy? It was, he had to admit with some pain, that she was childlike. Even her mouth, which wasn't always pleasant, was more like a child raising hell, looking for attention, rather than a tough, vulgar broad. Nobody really minded the times Sissy said all those "fucks" and "shits" and "cocksuckers" because, while the words were there, the anger, rage, or frustration was not. For example, in describing to the press how popular she was on a TV show, Sissy said, "I knocked them for a row of shithouses." Nobody reported the actual words, even if the city editor said it was okay, because it was just typical Sissy Lindmore, playing for the boys in the back of the burlesque house. The press would actually feel let down if Sissy didn't swear at least once.

34

Sissy never seemed to mind that Potter was not a big screwer. She'd take what was up for grabs because she enjoyed sex when she enjoyed it. But she did not push for it, or demand to be serviced. And that's what she liked about Potter, too. He was not the kind of man who led with his genitalia. He was more fun to be with and look at than to sleep with. Maybe. If there were those times she was caught by surprise by Potter, it was pure joy because she did not resent her slugger, she loved him. "Shit," she consoled herself, "Pottsie's a long-ball hitter, you've got to expect that he's going to poke one on you when you're not expecting it."

·One of the things Sissy loved best about Potter, besides his poking one on her when she wasn't expecting it, was his devotion to the game of baseball. Even when it rained cats and dogs he would be out there with them, training. And sometimes Sissy would get behind the wheel of the car and creep along behind him while he ran. She loved to watch him run, never breaking stride, leaping over boulders, shrubs, pits. He was the picture of unfaultable grace and endurance. He would stop finally after miles and miles, with his gray sweatshirt blackened by perspiration, reaching for breath, a smile on his face. He loved to run. Sissy once followed him in a car for seven miles, and estimated that he was breathing no heavier two minutes after he had stopped than a man out walking his dog. It was said that there were major leaguers who were faster than Potter going down the first-base line, but nobody in either league circled the bases faster and nobody could leap higher against a fence.

In the minors, before Sissy knew him but with Mr. Heller's $40,000 in bonus in his bank account, he went after a well-hit ball that would have gone over most outfielders' heads, but Potter turned the speed on, caught the ball about seven feet from the fence, over his shoulder, and then just leaped over the wall. The fence was about six feet high.

They showed that very film clip on television the night Sissy first met Potter. The outfielder told the interviewer

35

who asked, "Did you think you were going to catch it?" that there was no doubt in his mind that he'd catch it because he had it lined up. "The only thing that worried me was whether it would come down before I ran out of ballpark." Potter had said that so sincerely and so modestly and so sweetly that Sissy jumped right up and in full view of the network audience everywhere, she kissed Potter full on the mouth. It was not just a peck, either. She held herself there for about ten seconds. Somebody estimated that the kiss was worth about $135,000 in advertising time—that is, if the kiss had been Hershey milk chocolate. Potter blushed and smiled and was pleased. And Sissy grew mad about him because he said with his usual chocolate kiss reserve, "If I thought that catching a fly ball like that would get me this close to you, I would have done that years ago."

That night on the TV show Sissy was asked by Johnny Carson why she let fly so often with those choice homilies of hers (by now, her mouth was famous) and Sissy must have surprised her interviewer when she said that Mark Twain once pronounced that "in certain trying circumstances, urgent circumstances, desperate circumstances profanity furnishes a relief denied even to prayer." Sissy was no great brain and a cross-country run away from a bluestocking gal, but she had a way of absorbing from shrewd studio publicity men little force-fed bits of information which she was able to recall and publicly expose at the most opportune and precise occasions. Potter was one of the flock of the Assembly of God church, a fundamentalist sect, and while he may not have cherished Mark Twain's commandments, he did not regard swearing as blasphemy. If you think about it, Potter was sort of a black sheep, or spotted sheep.

He did not believe Sissy would actually marry him. When he asked her he had expected that she would tell him that she had a career to follow, as he had, and that they should be "just good fuckin' friends" for a while, rather than jump into marriage. That's not, as it turned out, what she said, though it was fair, knowing Sissy's partiality for a blistering mouthful, to expect that she might have said that.

"Are you serious, Potter love? You know, we have not even . . . how shall I put it? . . . swung much together yet."

"The best baseball scouts and reporters have always said that I only swing at pitches I think I can hit. That's actually been recorded, written into a scouting report or two. Honest."

"Shit. You are serious? You want to marry me? You don't know anything about me."

"All I need to know, Sissy, is that I like being with you. I've never liked being with any other woman. And I told myself once that if I ever find a woman I want to be with, I'd ask her to marry me."

"Wow!"

"Does that mean yes or no?"

"You realize, Potter, that I have a reputation that would knock the wax out of your ears."

"I don't put very much weight on reputations."

"Why don't you just take me to bed again and get the wax knocked out of your ears?"

"Don't be silly now, Sissy. I mean it!"

He meant it, she knew. She saw what it could do for her career. It would be stupid to turn him down. She was only a small-time actress, a small-time mouth, who had already used it to excellent advantage. Potter Cindy was going to be the greatest baseball player that ever lived. That's what everybody said. The scouting reports on the outfielder were public knowledge: "You see this Potter Cindy on the hook, just hanging there, and he looks like the greatest. He's got a very good temperament. He's big enough and certainly fast enough. He has desire. He'll sacrifice himself. Put it this way, everybody shows up for games. This guy shows up even if he's got the day off. He can knock the damn cover off the ball."

"You've got me, slugger." Sissy was always influenced by press notices.

"For keeps?" Potter asked.

"I sure hope so."

They finally honeymooned in the Organ Mountains of New Mexico, when they found the time, via Palm Springs, California, as Sissy had to collect "some of her crap"—she meant clothes—she had stashed away in the house of a lover, Potter's most recent predecessor. New Mexico was Potter's idea. He wanted to show her his turf. To a New Mexican all of the vast state is hunting ground, whether he lives north or south, east or west.

"Can you ride a horse, Sissy?"

"That would be a great straight line for me if we were on television. Bring that up the next time we're on TV together, okay?"

Potter smiled an okay, imagining what she could do with that line. He was a pretty sophisticated boy for a fundamentalist. He did not, he insisted, resent Sissy's former adventures, or her self-mockery about them, or her exploitation of sex, or her offering a picture of her many bedrooms for public consumption.

"No, really, can you ride a horse?"

"Shit," Sissy said. "Don't tell me you're taking me to a dude ranch for our honeymoon."

"No, I thought we'd get ourselves a couple of packs, climbing ropes, and horses and camp out in the mountains for a couple of days."

"You mean just the two of us in the damn wilderness?" It horrified her to think about it, but as she considered it the idea began to appeal to her. She confessed she could ride. "I took sixty-eight riding lessons, I'll have you know. I ride better than the jockeys at your La Mesa racetrack. At least that's what Scruffy Levinson, a former admirer of mine, once said. Scruffy knew, too. On the strength of one phone call, he could lay off half a million dollars in bets."

38

Potter knew it would be a different kind of riding in the Organ Mountains. They'd only be able to ride part of the way up. The rest would be rougher terrain. He would see how much he could reasonably expect her to handle. Maybe they wouldn't climb very far.

"Okay," he said, "I think we'll have some fun up there. We're not likely to run into anyone. We can pretty much do what we want."

"You'll be giving me lesson number sixty-nine," she pointed out with mock-wantonness.

"They hang you in the hills of New Mexico for doing that. It's the only crime worse than stealing horses or chili peppers in the state."

Sissy didn't need any lessons, Potter remembered. They camped out in the same bedroll because it was chilly. Potter claimed not to have remembered if they actually slept together that night.

Sissy heard the key in the door. She knew it was Potter. She dropped her Deringer into the ashtray, placed her coffee cup down beside it. Then she rushed up to the door, stood in front of it, adopting the most playfully lewd pose she could think of on short notice. She had some unhappy news to report. The pose was to relax him. Sissy made certain he would be seeing her rear end and everything else there was to see in looking at a girl whose skinny butt was the very top of her, bent over as she was. It was the best position from which to kick or goose her, whichever Potter would choose.

"Holy smokes!" He chose neither, apparently.

"That's my ass and you can kick it."

"Did you say kick or kiss?" He gave it a smack, not hard. Sissy straightened up. "How you doing, slugger?"

"It's raining."

"Poor Potter. No hits, no runs, no errors."

"No perfect game," he added.

"No perfect wife, either, I think I fucked up."

"How's that?" He took his wife's swearing for granted.

Sissy took a deep breath, then plunged into the monologue of her naughtiness. "Mrs. Whitey Knocthofer called. She was having some of the players' wives for cocktails. Just the girls. And I turned her down. I didn't want to have cocktails with those dumb fuckin' broads in hair rollers. I said, quite pleasantly, that I had a previous engagement, but she persisted, said the ladies wanted very much to meet me. They had heard I was so amusing. I told her I was sorry but I had to see some friends and I wouldn't be able to. She asked, this cunty baseball Empress, if there was something she could tell the others. Well, you know, Potter, she acted like I was obligated to come and if I couldn't, well, by God, I had better make some damn good apology to the fuckin' ladies. I asked her what she meant, just to be bitchy. And the Empress answered that she'd have to tell the baseball twats something more substantial than that I had a prior engagement because she had promised them that I'd be there. You know that urinated me off. I told her 'Listen, Mrs. Knockhockey (I said Knockhockey deliberately so that she would know I knew her stupid name), tell the ladies this funny baseball yarn I heard about a team manager and his third-base coach who were out hunting in the woods. They come across a nude woman, the kind men find irresistibly sexy. The nudie asked the manager and coach what they were doing in the woods. 'Hunting game,' the jerks say. So the girl says, 'I'm game.' And the manager and coach shoot her. That's what is known as baseball genius,' I explained, in case she didn't get it.

"Well, Potter, Mrs. Knockhockey said I was vile, vulgar, a terrible young woman and she was pleased that I was not coming to cocktails after all because I was not the sort of person who was welcome. Of course, I told her to go take a flying hump for herself. I could not resist.

"Will it hurt you, you know, go against you?"

"It's not going to help. That's Whitey's wife."

40

"Maybe he doesn't like her, either," Sissy offered.

"Shhhhhhhhhh . . . sugar! You keep swearing to the manager's wife and I'm going to have to break Ruth and Maris' records before the All-Star break."

"Did I screw it up for you?"

"I'll let you know when I hit my first real slump."

"The baseball wives are lucky I didn't go. I was going to suggest that they rate their own looks and sexual appetites on a scale of $10 to $100, collect the money in a paper bag, and give it to the first unhappy baseball wife whose husband comes down with a case of the clap."

"Don't ever do anything like that."

"Like what? Get the clap?" He ignored her wit.

"I'll be sent down to Bougainvilla—if I'm lucky—if you ever start suggesting that the fellows have broadies on the side. That would be an unpardonable sin. Don't ever suggest anything like that."

"Why? Do they?"

"Of course. You just ain't a baseball player if you don't chase tail."

"Do you? Will you?"

He said *no* after a moment, stopping to consider painfully if his special misdeeds, which he liked to keep out of sight and mind, would fall into the category of "broadies on the side."

"Why'd you take so much time to answer?" she wanted to know.

"I took some time to think about it, that's all."

Sissy accepted. "I've known lots of guys and I can't say that I was what you'd call very faithful to any of them. But I won't be unfaithful to you, if you're not to me, I promise."

Potter smiled. He was pleased. The thing about Potter's "duster" was that once the deed, the separate adventure, was done he truly believed it would never happen again. He promised himself to see to it. So it was not dishonest when he said, "I'll tell you what, Sissy. I have a feeling you're going

41

to play second fiddle to baseball, but to no one else."

"You promise?"

"Well, I just can't manage to devote so much of myself to the game and have all that left over for screwing around."

"Good. I bet you never thought you'd find a gal who loves you down to her toes and could still manage to say *good* that baseball's burned the fire out of your wang."

Potter laughed; it was somewhat forced.

Sissy wondered if she should confess that she had only enjoyed sleeping with a beau for a short period of time, anyway—say two months at the very outside. Once she had snuggled with a guy about fifteen or twenty times, she knew everything about him and the only thrill for herself beyond that was learning to relax more.

Sissy was a "looker." In the language of sexual encounter, California-style, a looker did not mean good-looking. It meant she was a girl who looked a fellow over more closely than a county coroner did a corpse. The other kinds of women, the "non-lookers," either kept their eyes closed, or worked in the dark, relying strictly on imagination and tactile sensations. Sissy did her share of feeling, too, but when she got her hands on a man, she studied him—front, back, top, bottom, orifices, body humors (some of them, at least). Her clinical observations were thorough. She kept her eyes open. She looked a phallus over so closely, she could probably give you the size of a urethra within a millimeter.

So what had she discovered about Potter? He was one person who actually derived enjoyment from her microscopic investigations of his privates. Other lovers usually did not make a fuss one way or the other. If her examination was excessively slow, or if they grew impatient as patients, they would grumble, "Hey, enough of that kidding around, baby. Let's get rolling." Potter was different. He would ask a series of questions designed to uncover all about the specimen, like the head of a medical department to his younger associate. "What's there, Sissy? How does it look to you? How does it compare, would you guess, with Babe Ruth, Lou Gehrig, Jimmy Foxx? Describe possible differences. Anything unusual about size or shape?" At first Sissy thought he was trying to embarrass her and discourage her from looking so closely.

"Don't you like me to look, Potts? Does it upset you?"

"Heck, no. I like it. I do. I just want you to share what you see with me."

"But it's your own thing. You know it."

"Sure, but I like to know what you see."

"You mean what I *really* see or what I think when I look at it?"

"Both, I guess."

"You're weird, you know that? I don't object. I think it's cute."

She told him what she saw and thought and she could tell it pleased him. She felt it. To please him and for fun she would describe, as she fondly scrutinized, a batter stepping to the plate, taking a toehold, fouling off pitches, and finally reaching, reaching, reaching for the pitch that always exploded into a homer at precisely the proper moment.

How could she ever believe that such good fun was part of the problem? Who could have known that all the descriptions—in jest or real—all the retelling of her clinical observations were needed to keep Potter going? She was only a little girl from California, innocent in spite of her willingnesses and experiences.

Chapter Five

It was the next to the last day of spring training and the Redbirds were happy. They had just been told by Whitey that the team had had a real good spring and that he felt he was taking the best twenty-five men he ever had managed north to open the season. "I think we'll be a contender if you guys don't whore around too much or get zonked on grass or looped on speed. What more can I tellya? You're pros, not a bunch of jerk-offs or bushies. Go and do what you get paid for. I mean, I'm not going to tellya to read a book when you got a lot of lead in your pencil, am I? I once had a manager who told us to read books instead of boozing and looking for ass. He caught one of the guys with his pants down and when the manager asked him why he wasn't reading a book, the guy told him he was allergic to them. The funny thing was the guy was really allergic to the dust or the molds in old books. He even produced a letter from some crackpot doctor who swore the player was telling the truth and that if he ever read a book, especially an old dirty one, he might stop breathing. So don't wear out your peckers; we got a long season ahead of us."

Whitey delivered the modern version of the famous Knute Rockne pep talk; it was more bearable to the Redbirds to be sent out there to win one for their peckers than for the Gipper.

Whitey also announced the unstartling news that Potter Cindy was the only rookie who had made the squad this season, but he stressed that none of the veterans would be affected because he had sold a starting outfielder over the winter with the hope that Potter would come through. "I'm telling you this because I don't want any of you prima donnas worrying about Potter stealing your place in my heart. I love ya all, okay? And you can show your appreciation by winning a couple of games when we play them for real."

Potter was not present at the time and it was the consensus in the locker room afterward that Whitey did not want Potter to hear because he did not think it good managing to single anyone out, good or bad, before his teammates. Whitey would tell anyone off or pump him full of hot air, but he liked to do it in one-to-one situations if it was possible. When Whitey left the clubhouse, the veterans jointly considered Potter; they evaluated him, assessed just how much of Whitey's heart he had won.

"He'll run out of gas," Jake Minbar predicted.

"Bullshit, he will. I was talking to one of the kids they cut from the squad. The guy played with him last season at Bougainvilla. He said that fuckin' Potter never stops. You can't tire him out. He's like an animal or a man from another planet. The kid told me he couldn't remember Potter Cindy having a serious slump. You know, he might go hitless in a game or two, but nothing that might really be called a slump, like normal ballplayers get. The kid said he was kind of quiet and kept pretty much to himself. And we all know he's right there." The speaker was Peeve Borkowski, now the Redbird rightfielder, the guy Potter bumped from his original center-field position.

"That's not what I heard," said Jim Domijo, the first-baseman. "I heard from another rookie who played with him that he started off real quiet but became a cutup and a clown by the end of the season. I heard he was well liked by the Burros."

"Aaah, whaddya know? Let's ask Bobby Hartman. He lives with the guy. Whaddya think, Bobby?"

"He seems all right to me. I suppose he'll get into slumps just like us. He had a little one this spring, didn't he, when he went one for fourteen or something like that? He seemed very uptight about it, nervous, like any rookie, or veteran for that matter." Hartman spoke cautiously to his teammates just in case tomorrow he, Bobby Hartman, would be singled out for some reason—like being a man from Mars, or Israel. He wasn't going to tell them he thought Potter was like a circus act: he could hang by one hand and piss two miles while smoking a cigar with his ass. *It's not for me, the house Jew, to look for flaws in Potter that I want to make public. I'm not in my rookie season, but I get along best psyching myself up that I've got to make it each year. "You can't win them all," these guys tellya. But when you're a Jew you better win most of them.*

"Yeah, well that kid who played with him in the minors said the rival teams called him 'The Beast of Bougainvilla.'"

"Where'd they get that name from?" Mayknoll asked.

"Because he was scary, creepy, and unbelievable," Borkowski conjectured.

"That's not where they got the name from," said shortstop Dick Condon. "I gotta relative who lives in a town near Bougainvilla, in Selhurst. My cousin. He was telling me that Potter Cindy was a real good ballplayer and a nice guy. They just tagged him with that name because the papers were full of stories over the summer about some Jack the Ripper type in the area who they called the Beast of Bougainvilla. The beast killed kids or fucked little girls; I can't remember. Anyway, they tagged Potter with the name because he killed or fucked rival teams with his bat. That's how the name came about. My cousin told me."

46

"All I can say," said Mayknoll, "is that I'd rather have the guy hitting for us than me having to pitch against him. There's no way in the world to figure out the strike zone on a beast."

"Yeah, but he's getting too much ink and too much attention from the management," Minbar put in.

"Lissen," said Phil Brossi, "you guys complain about his getting too much attention, but here we all are sitting around jawing about him. He hasn't played one major league game yet and we've made a fuckin' legend out of him—like Viva Zapata, that old Brando movie I saw the other night on TV, or like Billy the Kid, or Casey at the Bat. Look, we call him 'Big Bat,' the newspaper guys describe his home runs as 'Potter's Pokes,' in the minors he was so scary to the other teams they called him the 'Beast of Bougainvilla.'"

"So what point are you making?" Dick Condon wanted some clarification.

"Why don't we just treat him like any other guy breaking his ass to make it and drop all this other crap. He's one of us now, right?"

Mayknoll bugged out his eyes, exaggerated his teeth, stiffened his arms and fingers, like outstretched monster claws, and walked stiff-legged, making horrible sounds. "No," he said with his fangs showing, "I'm the Beast of Bougainvilla and I'm going to eat you for lunch."

It was on this scene that Potter walked into the clubhouse.

"AHHH," screamed Mayknoll, spotting him, pointing over the rest of the players' heads, "there he is!"

The players turned to look, and seeing Potter, they slowly, silently, gracelessly broke up the meeting, leaving Brossi and Mayknoll to explain.

"We were just having a little fun," Phil Brossi said with embarrassment.

Potter was anxious, stunned. He could not speak because he had heard them say "Beast of Bougainvilla" and he knew that it was the newspaper name given to the "unidentified" man who had exposed his genitals last summer before three little girls—in Gurney, Larnesa, and Selhurst. It was the name of his villainy.

Potter closed his eyes in pain and repentance. He had been exposed by someone. He was caught, as he knew he would be one day. That was it. This was their way of informing him. What should he tell them, these two, obviously left as spokesmen? Would they believe that it was all in the past now? Would they accept that it was a sickness that he had gotten on top of and could lick? Would they forgive him? How could he convince them that it was over, that he had made a resolution, a sworn promise never to have anything to do with little girls?

"Shit, don't take it so bad, man. We were only kidding. We don't talk about you behind your back all that much. One of the rookies that was cut told Borkowski you were such a terror to the rival minor league teams that they called you that," Mayknoll explained.

"Yeah," said Brossi, "you're kind of overreacting, aren't you? If this flaw in your character gets out, the guys are going to lower the boom on you, like they've done to every rookie that ever joined this team."

"What do you mean, flaw in my character?" Potter asked nervously.

"I mean being sensitive to jokes about you. If the animals on this club find that out, they'll be brutal and unmerciful. I can tellya that."

"Find out about what?"

"Whaddya have, sunstroke or something?" Mayknoll said. "Just because we've been having a little fun at your expense, you don't have to get that long face, that suffering look, like we hurt you or something."

Potter smiled. He had come out of the heat of fear into the nice cold reality of locker-room joshing and bullshit. *Thank*

48

God! They know nothing. It's going to be okay. Potter was happy to have another chance.

"Whitey told us you made the team. Congratulations. And best of luck. From all of us," Mayknoll said.

"Thanks, I'm really going to need it."

"The Beast of Bougainvilla. That's no name for a major leaguer," Brossi offered, like he was saying "no hard feelings."

On the sound of the name Potter felt a stab of adrenalin or guilt, but he managed another smile.

Chapter Six

"Honk! If you love Jesus." On the third day of the season, Potter Cindy bought himself a new little Gremlin in Atlanta and promptly put the "Honk" sticker on his back bumper. He had struck his third home run in three days and, perhaps, feeling a flush of confidence or Evangelism, went right out and bought himself a new car. The players verbally pulverized him on his purchase. "Sheeeeeit," said Hartman, his roommate, "you're a real big spender. You open the first series of the season with a home-run spree. You got a headlock on organized baseball, the batting crown, RBIs, and you buy yourself a little Gremlin. When you break Hank Aaron's record, maybe you'll go to hell with yourself and buy a Jeep."

Hank Mayknoll put it simply, "You ain't got class, Potter." He should have been kinder because Mayknoll, struggling on the mound on opening day, was suddenly saved from certain defeat by Potter's three-run homer in the fourth inning. The Redbirds were trailing 4-1 when Potter poked one out of sight.

At first everybody just laughed, thinking Potter must be a great guy to buy a car just for the gag of putting on that bumper sticker. It was Herbert Zarember, the nervous general manager of the team—known unaffectionately by the players as Remember Zarember—who accidentally uncovered the fact that Potter was not given to such frivolous excesses. He pulled the young outfielder aside and said, "We're playing in Atlanta, son. This is Baptist country. These folks take religion seriously. You go parading around town with a sticker like that and you'll upset people. It doesn't speak well for yourself, the team, or the whole league."

Potter stood there, staring at Zarember, chomping on his bubble gum. He blew a bubble, popped it, and said softly, "It was church people who gave me that sticker."

"It was? Well, why in hell did they do that?"

"Because I saw a sticker on a car outside a church and I went in and asked them if they had another."

"Well," said Zarember, obviously thinking *Who the hell is he trying to kid, married to that cunt and pulling this religious shit?* What Zarember thought was stamped on his face like a map, like the boot of Italy. "When'd you suddenly get so holy?"

Potter could feel rage beginning to spread, from wherever rage comes, throughout his body. He felt like telling Zarember to shut the fuck up or he would knock him, like a bad pitch, out of the park. But he had to watch it. He could not afford to get a reputation as a foul ball.

"I was brought up in a Fundamentalist church."

"Yeah, you and the Marquis de Sade."

Potter missed the reference, but he could tell from Zarember's face that it was unkind.

He was not a religious person, though his folks had been zealous. They dragged him to revival meetings so that they could all get saved. Maybe they would be saved someday. He did not feel saved himself, but then he was not as deeply religious as they were, and probably not religious at all. He did believe, however, that a person should be polite, respectful, and as unmean as he could possibly make himself, or keep himself. That was not religion, he knew, or godliness, but it was behavior he learned from the religious people and it seemed to suit him.

"Mr. Zarember, I'd be pleased if we could drop the discussion. It doesn't seem all that important. I put the sticker on because I like to kind of christen new things. It's something from my past. I don't do it to sanctify the things, actually, but more to give thanks for the reward. By now it has become a habit. I gave Sissy a Star of David on a chain when we got married. A fan had sent that to me for luck when I played at Bougainvilla."

Zarember had a this-guy's-too-good-to-be-true look on his face. On his mind was a nifty promotional idea. He released to the press the news that Potter Cindy bought a new Gremlin—a humble symbol—and rides around with a bumper sticker that reads, "Honk! If you love Jesus." Everybody was told that Potter was a Fundamentalist, a deeply religious man, a church-going good guy. His marriage to Sissy Lindmore was the beginning of her salvation, praise be the Lord, so sayeth Zarember.

Remember Zarember. The players gave him that name because he was treacherous, sneaky; he hit you from behind. It came from Remember Pearl Harbor, via their ex-GI fathers.

When Whitey Knocthofer saw the sign, he ignored it. What the hell! Potter had hit three homers. What did the guys without religious bumper stickers do for him? Managing is not easy if you don't have home-run hitters. He made a note to talk to Potter about buying that Gremlin. It wasn't a major leaguer's car.

Phil Brossi, the third-baseman, who was not a manager and had no ambitions in that direction, told Potter when he saw the sign, "If everybody paid attention to that sign, you'd have a country full of deaf people. Didn't you ever hear of noise pollution?"

Phil was the team radical. He took every politically left position which, of course, got him tagged with the name Lefty, even though he had always batted and thrown right-handed. Phil had been against pollution, the War, bigotry, the director of the FBI, racists, the Conservative party, Henry Kissinger, the Italian Anti-Defamation League, the Rifle and Gun Association, offshore oil drilling, and Richard M. Nixon. Brossi was balding or he would have had the longest hair on the team.

Potter Cindy, who was neither right nor left nor center nor political, simply told Brossi, "Praise be to Jesus." Brossi, who did not know if Potter was kidding, winked. Potter winked back.

To Zarember, whom Potter cornered in the hotel lobby of the Regency Hyatt House, the sensation said, "I see the papers are chock-full of my religious zeal, thanks to you."

"Yeah, well, you're so religious, live with it. Billy Graham. Big deal!"

Potter grabbed him by the shirt front and lifted him in the air. "I'd appreciate it," Potter warned, "if you cleared future press notices about me with me. I make myself available for interviews. So let me tell the story to the reporters myself." Potter had learned not to object to the press running stories. He had taken a course on the History of Journalism one year at the University of Arizona. He knew that reporters had stories to file, the paper had to fill space, and editors were surly, sassy, hard-drinking slobs with pencils who had to get those columns filled with scores and sports human-interest yarns.

"Put me down!" Zarember ordered. He paraphrased and misquoted the former great New York Giants football coach, Steve Owen. "You ballplayers meet the same general managers on the way up as you do on the way down. You're just a bunch of monkeys." The real Owen quote was, "Coaching is like a monkey on a stick. You pass the same fellows on your way down as you passed on the way up."

"Praise be to Jesus. Say, 'Praise be to Jesus,' Mr. Zarember."

"Okay, Praise be to Jesus. Put me down!"

Potter obliged.

"You keep that up and you're not going to last with this club, Cindy, I'll see to it." Zarember was walking away before he challenged Potter. "You evangelist phoney! Why the hell didn't you buy a real car instead of a Gremlin? All the guys think you're like Li'l Abner, for crying out loud. Get yourself educated. You ought to be ashamed of yourself. A big hotshot star with a nice little Gremlin. That ain't humility, Cindy, that's strictly from Dogpatch."

Potter felt pained. They thought he was a yokel. So that was part of it. If he had put his bumper sticker on a Mercedes-Benz or a Jaguar or a violet Cadillac, it would have taken the curse off of it. The bumper sticker could have said "Horseshit," and it would not have troubled anyone one tiny bit. He bought the Gremlin because, despite all the rave notices he was receiving, he did not have all that much money in hand. But he bought it mainly because he did not want to spend a great deal of money on a big car when that little one was all he would need. What was so Dogpatch about that? Besides, he wanted to lend some of his money to his father, who was planning to go into a business of producing or gathering farm effluent that could be fed to other animals. Basically, his father was going into the chicken business more to raise chickens for their excrement than their food value, as Potter understood it. It sounded like a good idea to the outfielder, who had punched cattle two years before and had observed, to his surprise, that the animals were fed on pellets of chicken dung. Would Li'l Abner have noticed that? Would he have invested in a business, even if the end product was a lot of shit?

Later that day, in the locker room at Atlanta Stadium, the outfielder had his jaws clamped shut as he dressed for the final game of the series. Someone had scrawled "Home run for Jesus" on his locker in chalk. Potter was solemn, grim. His name was listed third in the batting order on the blackboard, and beside it, somebody had written, "Honk! If you love little Gremlins."

Before the final game in Atlanta Hank Mayknoll came up and stood before Potter. The outfielder looked at him. "You're going to have to be good today, son," he said softly. "You've taken jobs, headlines, attention away from these halfasses, these crybabies, your teammates, and they'd like to torture you for it. So today be special, Potter. Don't let them eat you. Don't let them get to you." The pitcher walked away. He was fond of Potter because he gave one hundred percent. Mayknoll was a one hundred percenter when the games were official. He was not big on killing himself in practice, but when he first broke in he lived and died with every victory and loss. The only other time in Mayknoll's life that he didn't practice was when he took piano lessons, and he still regretted it. He was pulling for Potter, hoping the vultures would not get him.

Potter did not acknowledge Mayknoll. The sensation rose from his seat on the bench in the locker room and slowly walked out to the field to shag flies and take batting practice. When the public address announcer read the lineups, the stadium caved in when he said, "Batting third and playing centerfield, Number 49, Potter Cindy." The fans had read the articles about him in the Atlanta papers. He was a big favorite in Atlanta already, even though he killed their hometown club. No Atlanta player that day got the kind of decibels in applause given to Potter. There was a banner unfolded in the stands bidding the Atlanta management to TRADE FOR POTTER CINDY. While the noise still reverberated in the ballpark for Potter, Phil Brossi whispered in his teammate's ear, "Applaud, if you love Jesus."

Potter was still laughing when he stepped to the plate for the first time. He was having trouble controlling himself. He had to step out of the box four times to restrain his hilarity.

55

Hartman, the leadoff man, had walked. He was sacrificed to second by the shortstop, Dick Condon. When Potter finally got hold of himself, all he could manage was a bunt. He caught everybody on the field out of position, looking for a big hit. Hartman raced to third. He called time out to get some dirt out of his eye. But, really, it was to laugh.

"What the hell's going on?" Whitey Knocthofer demanded. "Who gave Potter the bunt sign?"

"Jesus," Mayknoll said.

Whitey missed the point. "Jesus Christ! That's right. How we going to win when the best hitter bunts? This is such a screwed-up team! Are they all going to bunt with the hit-away sign on?"

Potter stole second on the next pitch. And came flying home right behind Hartman on a base hit by Brossi. Potter didn't get a steal sign, either, but Whitey forgave him. "I'll just go home," the manager growled happily, "and let you creeps run the club. It'll be easier on my blood pressure."

Lest they missed the sarcasm and only heard the goodwill in his voice, Whitey got up and walked to the water cooler. He drank, yelled, "Let's get together out there, you fuckin' monkeys!"

Hartman and Potter got together in the eighth inning when Atlanta loaded the bases with two out. Those two runs scored by the Redbirds in the first inning were the only runs scored up to that point. The next Brave batter was the team's big slugger. Potter was moved back a few steps by Whitey. The hitter swung with all his might but didn't get all of it. The ball was lifted into the air in short right-center field and was coming down, seemingly between the flying Potter coming in and the scampering Hartman going back. The players were going to collide if they reached the ball. Whitey was already wincing. But Hartman caught up to the ball, snared it, and waited to be belted by the charging centerfielder. It was going to be a bone-shattering meeting. But the only pain Hartman heard was the deafening roar of the crowd. His eyes were closed and he just did not see Potter make that beautiful high jump right over him. They talked about that leap in Atlanta for months.

"Oh, yes, Potter, even-Steven, Peter and Paul, share the wealth," said Whitey. The manager wasn't name-dropping, of course. He simply took a whole lot of clichés, cut them up, and pasted them together. There is a point at which one can be so elliptical as to be illiterate.

"What's that?" Potter asked.

"He forgives you for bunting in the first inning," Brossi explained. "Your leap in the eighth inning made up for your bunting without a sign."

"Leap! if you love Jesus," Hartman added, smiling.

"I spared your thin little frame, Bobby," Potter pointed out.

Hartman applauded. In the ninth inning, Hartman singled. Dick Condon bunted him to second. The Redbirds were playing for an insurance run. The All-State Insurance Company, also known as Potter Cindy, singled Hartman home.

"How'd I do, Mayknoll?" Potter asked privately, in the locker room.

"You rammed it up their ass, boy. I'm proud of you."

"I appreciate your taking an interest," Potter said humbly.

"Well, if you really do, I'll tell you who scrawled with that poisoned chalk on your locker and on the blackboard."

"I don't want to know. It doesn't matter. It's over with now."

Mayknoll ignored him. "It was me, Potter."

"You?" The outfielder was stunned. "I don't believe it."

"Look, Potter, I did it for you. If I didn't get it all said, the guys would be doing it over and over in little ways and it would never end. Do you get the point?"

Potter said, "Yep. I suppose." But he was thinking that it was too bad he was a rookie. He would have liked to punch

Mayknoll in the mouth. Mayknoll, he saw, was behind some of the guys laying all that pressure on him. They were shitty people, these major leaguers. He remembered that the guys in the minors never worked on you in that way.

"Well, I can tell you, man, that you won over the blacks on this club," Mayknoll said as Hartman passed by.

"The Jews, too," Hartman added, "Now all you have to do is win over the *goyim*."

"Who's that?" Potter wanted to know.

"*Goyim*? Oh, that's all the rest of the world," Hartman explained.

"That one word takes in a lot of folks, doesn't it?"

"Yeah, we're an outnumbered people, we Jews."

"God's chosen people. That's what I was taught," Potter said.

"Bullshit," said Mayknoll. "If you judge by suffering, the blacks are in the running for that title."

"If you judge by suffering," Potter said, "I guess we're all in the running."

"You're a regular little philosopher, Potter," added Brossi, who was now listening.

"Well, thank you, Mr. Brossi. If you say so, it must be true."

The one thing about baseball players' discussions is that nothing of import is ever really said, except if they are talking about baseball or women. Every now and again a nice home-spun little homily babbles from their lips, and if a newspaper-man is in earshot, the whole world gets to know that so-and-so is the Mark Twain of the Yankees or who's-it is the William Faulkner of the Texas Rustlers. Some players got reputations for being geniuses who never got past the third year of high school. That year, the season Potter Cindy broke in, the Red-birds had a collection of geniuses, if you believed what you read in the press. They were the Harvard College of baseball, or "birdbrains," if you listened to the rest of the ballplayers, especially Whitey Knocthofer: "There's one guy on this team that goes out with broads, gets them to go to bed with him, and then kicks the shit out of them. If I catch the sonofabitch, he's going down so deep in the minors, he's going to look like a coal miner. You gotta be a moron to do something like that. I'll bet he can't hit, either."

Another Redbird of Harvard Yard wrote poetry. Muhammad Ali was a heck of a lot better. The player's poetry was nauseating. It was absolutely illiterate and musically hopeless. He was, it was rumored, an assman—men or women—for whoever was available. Nice person.

One guy read *The Three Musketeers* in the sixth grade, *The Old Man and the Sea* as a senior in high school. He named his two sons D'Artagnan and Hemingway. Everybody thought he was literary. Insiders knew the only other books he ever read in his life were the stories of Ted Williams and Jackie Robinson.

It was sort of a relief to the press to have a natural talent like Potter Cindy around. They could finally settle down and write real baseball stories every now and again. Potter provided the material with his extremely gifted ballplaying, his dozens of skills.

"How'd you manage that leap so perfectly? It looked like you were going to cream Bobby Hartman," one reporter asked.

"He's my roommate," Potter joked, "I had to do something or I would have hurt him."

"Could you make that play again?"

"Only if Hartman was in the way."

"How many home runs you expect to hit this year?"

"Well, I've already hit three. So I guess I'll hit at least four or five."

"How does it feel to hit a home run in the majors? I'll bet the feeling is indescribable."

"No. I think I can describe it. It feels better than hitting a home run in the minors."

"If I remember correctly, you leaped over the outfield wall in the minors, didn't you?"

"Caught the ball that time, though."

"Did you ever do any high jumping in college?"

"No. I only played baseball. But I practice jumping over obstacles that would be natural to baseball—fences, roommates, things like that." Potter told them that he loved to run and on days off or rained-out games he ran on streets and along the roadways.

"They used to say of Willie Mays that he was perfectly built, so free of fat, you could scratch a match on him. You're the same way. I guess you have to work at having such a beautiful build. You agree?"

"I guess so. I don't consider it hard work. You can't think of it as hard if you love to run and exercise."

"How many miles can you run?"

"I'm not sure. I think Sissy once followed me in a car for seven miles."

"Is that a fact?"

"Well, maybe it was six and one-half or eight miles. I don't remember exactly."

It would be hard to pinpoint the moment a rookie becomes an integral member of the squad, important to it, a part of its biology, its life, its function. It was probably during the Atlanta series that Potter was, like a kidney transplant, attached to the body of the Redbirds. Reporters who claim to understand some of the small but special points of the game have said that a rookie becomes a full-fledged member of his team not when he drives in his first run, or makes his first game-saving catch, but when veterans, the team's established stars, find that he is the subject of an argument.

"I think the whole thing about the car and the sticker was a dumb thing to pull on Potter. Whoever dreamt it up was an asshole," Brossi told Mayknoll.

"He took it all right," Mayknoll said, "it didn't seem to hurt him none."

60

"Well, what does that have to do with it?" the team radical said. "I mean we take high prices, inflation, war. It doesn't mean it's right."

"Oh, bullshit, man. Don't get into your wild-eyed radical routine."

"What's wrong with radicals?"

"Nothing," Mayknoll said, "let's forget it. I've got to run wind sprints and get the fat off my ass."

"No, wait, I want to know. It's probably the same thinking that makes you dislike radicals that lets you think what you did to Potter was okay. Making fun of him like that, of his religion, was wrong."

"Cool it, man. Be like Potter. Nothing bothers old brother Potter. You should be more like him. He never blows up. He's cool. I mean, man, we could of tied a tin can to his ass, and you know what he would have done?"

"No, but I know you're going to tell me."

"For your own good, Brossi, I'm going to tell you. Old Potter would simply have taken the can off his ass, set it down near his locker, taken a deep breath and carried on same as ever."

"Everybody doesn't have to scream to be heard."

"A man's got to scream, Brossi. You know that best of all. That's all you do is scream and complain."

"Bullshit. I scream about important things—about issues that have some meaning."

"Don't give me that horseshit. You collect your check from Mr. Heller same as all of us—"

"Yeah, well I'm not happy about it. It's not my favorite thing in the world to do."

"It ain't? Well, how come you sign your contract and show up for spring training each year? You don't say screw it and get in with a protest against Mr. Heller or on the White House lawn."

"I serve in my own way."

"That's good, man."

"How can you be so sure about what I do on the off-season?"

"I know what you do and I know what Potter does."

"Yeah, what do I do?" Brossi challenged.

"You drink wine, eat spaghetti, and hump them little hippies in the communes."

"Aw, fuck off!"

"And Potter, he stays in shape. He runs, man. He sweats. He hones himself down sharper than a Gillette blade. That's how he stays on top of the situation."

"What situation?"

"Who knows? Baseball, the whammy?"

"Somebody said he punches cattle on the off-season."

"That's good," Mayknoll said, " 'cause now we know he punches something. Besides, I hear you got to yell at them cows to keep them in line."

"You're a real prick, you know that?"

"I've been called a lot worse."

"Yeah."

Chapter Seven

If charm was of any value in baseball, and there were and still are those newsmen and publicity guys who insist that "good copy" helps make a mediocre ballplayer better than his gifts, Potter Cindy would have made the Hall of Fame after spring training. The youngster from New Mexico knew when to smile. He was rarely sullen or difficult or unreasonable. He was good copy.

The outfielder had a way of turning up the corner of his mouth in an embarrassed smile if someone asked him an idiotic question, one that he knew you should not have asked. It told you all at once, *Passed ball*. He was a man who seemed to be without meanness and he could therefore be amusing at someone's expense, usually accidentally. The governor of a large southwestern state once asked him to autograph a baseball for his grandson. Potter obliged gracefully. "I know my grandson will cherish this, Potter."

"It's okay, Governor," Potter whispered. "I know you really wanted it for yourself." Potter signed it to both of them at once. "To Governor _____'s Grandson Billy."

The governor was so impressed with Potter he actually ordered one of his top aides to call the owner of the state's major league franchise to urge that the team trade for Potter

Cindy. The inside report, and it might all be hogwash, was that the owner of the team was supposed to have said, "Even Potter Cindy would not help our club, that is, if F. M. Heller is fool enough to give him up." As wrong would have it, Potter was to eventually wind up on that club in that governor's state, where exhibitory sexual eccentricities are punishable by ten years to life in prison.

With the Atlanta series won in full, and with a weak Philadelphia team on the schedule next, Potter got behind the wheel of his Gremlin, honked once for Jesus, and set out for points north, leaving his teammates to shake their heads in admiration or contempt.

Potter may have still been legally within the city limits of Atlanta when the rubber ball came bouncing across the road, bringing Potter and his Gremlin to a screeching, jarring halt. He was glad he had honked for Jesus and gladder still that he had fastened the seat belt and shoulder harness. Behind bouncing rubber balls, children bound. And this time it was no different. There, trailing the ball, was a little girl. She had been spared by Potter's reflexes. Had a Redbird of duller learned movements been behind that wheel, the child might have been no more. The child's knees were scabbed over from earlier mishaps, perhaps related in some way to her forever bouncing ball.

Potter looked around. There was no school, no houses, no cars, no people. Only trees on both sides. Where had the little girl come from? It is hard to play ball in the woods. He drove on slowly, the child safe now, ball in hand, watching her through the rearview mirror. He saw that she had disappeared in the woods to the right, from where she had come in pursuit of the bouncing ball. Was she merely a woodland creature with a ball and scraped knees? He knew he should just step on the gas and get out of there. This was going to be his test. A promise, a resolution, a man's determination had to be tested for truth and for strength. He considered, made up his mind to leave. Yet what kind of a test is it to run? He found himself circling around and around several times and coming back to that spot where the ball had bounded out. He saw the child at the edge of the road again. She had no ball. He stopped. If he drove off at that moment he could never be sure. Potter called out the window, "Where's your ball, honey?"

She pointed. And then he saw the opening in the bushes. It was a very narrow path, hardly big enough to contain a Gremlin.

"What's in there?" he asked, getting out of the car.

"That's the back of the school," she told him.

He looked in; he saw nothing. "I don't see any school."

"It winds 'round. If you go in further you can see the roof of the schoolhouse."

He took her hand tenderly. Still testing. "Show me." They walked into the greenery together. Potter was beginning to get interested in the challenge. He did not ask her name. He did not offer his. Yet he was not without conflict. When, at what point, should he deem the test sufficient? Surely men, even freaks, have a breaking point. He pushed himself to greater challenge.

"How far does this path wind?"

"It's only a little way now," she encouraged.

He saw the school around the next turn; it was thirty yards away opening on a field, a ballfield, beyond that another field, a farm, and beyond that more hills and wooded area.

"You want to see something?" he asked the child. Perhaps she was about nine years old.

"Wha?"

Man is weak and a sinner. He had been taught that and had always known that.

"What I've got in my pants?" Potter had stiffened.

"Aw, my brother and Daddy's got the same thing. That ain't nothin'."

"Take a look anyway, okay?"

The child seemed slightly put upon. "Aw, all right." The little girl was not uncomfortable. Perhaps she was stupid; she was certainly not jaded at age eight or nine.

Potter was very excited. He considered the possibility that it was a dream but knew better. He had a little trouble with the front clasp of his trousers, but he managed to lower them.

Can the sound of a voice hurt? It struck, like the damnation of Zeus, into the heart of the little girl's friend. "Hey! You there!" was all it said at first, but it drove poor Potter to his knees. He was not going to hurt the girl. All he wanted to do was show her his organ and testicles. He wanted her approval, her acknowledgment, or her reaction. Maybe all three. He did not turn to look at Zeus. He heard him coming; Potter rose from the ground, got his pants clasped and started to run. The man had nearly been on him, in fact, missed him by the length of three outstretched arms. Had he really been Zeus, Potter would have been destroyed forever, his brain burned by a lightning bolt.

The man was a strong runner. "Stop! You sonofabitch pervert. You hear me?"

Potter increased his lead across the baseball field. The man pursued, though he must have known it was hopeless. With each stride, Potter drew farther away. Zeus could not catch Mercury, especially on a baseball field. The outfielder was flying across centerfield, the man only at the pitcher's mound, and laboring. And even farther away now, the outfielder increased his lead with those long, graceful strides. Potter took a quick look over his shoulder. The man had given up the run, but not the chase. Zeus had summoned a chariot from the heavens because Potter was now being pursued by a small white car. Potter had about sixty yards on the car

66

with forty more yards to go to the fence. If he could beat the car to the fence, it would have to stop and he could outrun the passengers, he felt. The car was closing ground fast.

"Overtake that fucker, Billy. I want his ass."

"I'm down to the floor now."

"Keep going, man. I think we got the sonofabitch. He runs faster than a racehorse, don't he?"

"I'm doin' sixty-five miles an hour."

"Get him. Get him!"

Potter was fifteen yards from the fence. He saw it was higher than he thought and hoped. Was it too high to leap? How long would it take to get over it? They were practically on him. It was Potter Cindy against American Motors.

"Ram him! Ram his ass!"

"We gotta be crazy. But hang on!"

"Ram his ass to the fence!"

There was a sickening sound as the car struck. And human beings screamed in pain and fear. Glass shattered. The fence came down. Blood came in spurts from cut and crushed legs. The car rolled over on its side. The men inside, hurt and bleeding, probably still do not believe that the man they had chased in a car not only beat them to the fence but leaped it. They saw him fly over the six feet of wire fence. And even if they were not dazed, nobody could blame them when they claimed that they had chased a sex pervert with a built-in helicopter.

Potter waited some thirty yards away, wanting to run, needing to stay, at least long enough to see the passengers come out of the disabled vehicle. Thank God! They were not dead.

Others—men, women, and children—were running toward them. They would see that the men got to a hospital, Potter reasoned. He had to leave. As he turned to run he saw a truck parked on a street across from where he had paused in his flight. Shit. The driver had seen him. He ran away from the people and the truck driver. He loped across a field and sailed over a small wire fence into a farm. By circling around full left he reasoned he would come eventually to his car. And he was right. Potter had good animal instincts for survival. Perhaps in some other life he had been a fox.

For a moment he had forgotten he was being chased. He felt he was moving smoothly across the newly planted farm. He was for that moment as free as a fox that had turned the hunt. And then, in the distance, he saw them. Three dogs, he estimated, in full pursuit. God. He was suddenly tired. They were far away but coming at a dead run.

In the insanity of fatigue, he thought perhaps he could outrun the dogs. He would not let them tree him, figuratively, that is, for there were no trees to climb. Potter could hear their barking more clearly now. He knew he must not stop running. Or they would have him. He wished there was another fence, something to race to, an obstacle to leap over, before the dogs sunk their teeth into him. There was nothing but a shed about one hundred yards away, in the direction he was moving. The sounds of the dogs grew louder, more menacing. He knew he would get to the shed before them if he did not fall. But then what? How many seconds would he have to set up a defense against the hounds? He took a quick look. God! The dogs were closer than he had thought. They were about the size of collies or shepherds, but not pedigreed. He estimated, from the distance they had made up, that he would reach the shed perhaps ten or twenty seconds before them.

It was an underestimate, for Potter could not know how fast he was flying. He actually had thirty seconds. In that time he found an ax handle and had taken up a batting position just in front of the shed. How could the poor dogs have known they would be facing one of the acknowledged wickedest swings in baseball?

They came, the dogs, like three mean pitches, rising, buzzing, snarling to kill the batsman. They showed their menacing fangs and Potter swung, shattering the skull of the first animal, splattering blood across his baby-blue sports shirt. He recocked the bat for the second dog and drove it with all his might into the animal's neck. It flew back, sucking for breath, its head painfully lowered and turned to one side, uselessly seeking air from somewhere. It made one horrible gasp before it fell over, dead. The force of Potter's home-run swing fractured the hind quarters of the last animal, who managed to get Potter's thigh before he silenced it with a clout that, had the dog's head been a ball, would have been a certain base hit. When the inning ended, Potter dropped to the ground on his knees and sobbed. There were no feelings of relief, freedom, or victory in his tears. He was exhausted and he had failed. He had flunked the test.

In an unreal state as though he were not himself, he made his way back to the Gremlin, uninterrupted, somehow, by man or beast, though he had heard police or ambulance sirens. He started back to the hotel in Atlanta. Potter had decided not to drive to Philadelphia, as planned, where his team had a series coming up with the Phillies, but to take the car back to the dealer and accept his original offer to ship the Gremlin home for Potter free of cost.

In the hotel he showered and changed and cleaned up his superficial dog bite (it was more of a deep scratch than a bite). He considered that he might possibly get tetanus. Then, he remembered that he had gotten a shot for "lockjaw" at the ranch in New Mexico, six months back, when he cut his shoulder on some barbed wire. He hoped the shot was still good. Then, he chuckled at the stupidity of it all. He had at that moment not quite made up his mind whether or not to kill himself.

He lay on the bed then, his body suddenly very cold. He pulled the covers up. In a few minutes he began to perspire and pushed the covers off, only to grow cold again. Tears came to his eyes when he thought about the men who had been hurt chasing him. He sobbed when he thought about the dogs he had slain. He thanked God that he had not had the chance to do anything unnatural to the child, the little girl. He hated himself when it occurred to him that "had the chance" was the very kindest way of putting what he had not done to the child. "Prevented" is what had happened. He was prevented. That was the truth.

He took solace (while he cried and felt sorry and hated himself) that his problem was beyond his control, like a knock-down pitch. He remembered that he had fought to control the urge; he had tried to leave the child to start with, but she was suddenly there at his head, like a duster.

Potter sobbed or laughed, he was not quite sure (he could see only that his body heaved). He got up and rushed to the bathroom. His stomach did what his body and soul did. He heaved.

He took another shower and he thought with the water pounding his head that for a moment, just a moment, he could remember back all those years, more than twenty, when he was not a real person but an infant being baptized.

It was only when Potter took the decision to commit suicide a step further—he looked up the address of a firearms store close to the hotel—that it occurred to him quite clearly that while he had flunked the test with the little girl hours before, struck out (there could be no denying that he could not resist revealing himself to the child), it was really the first time that he had tried to resist at all. Hadn't he driven around and away more than once? If, during one of those circlings around he had driven on, he would now not be thinking about killing himself; instead he would be pleased and proud of his strength. He had tried but wasn't able to make it. That's not anything to be proud of, but it was hardly reason to hang up your spikes. How many times had he failed as a ballplayer to deliver in the clutch? Did he think of killing himself for that? No. He just tried to do better the next time. He was down on himself; that was for sure.

This was not baseball, of course. It was a crime! A criminal act. "Disgusting and Terrifying" one newspaper called it. It was a hell of a lot worse than popping up with two down and runners on in the ninth. But the best advice for life he had ever heard was from his high school baseball coach, who was also a Sunday-school teacher. "Potter," the coach had told him, after he wiffed in a key spot during a game, when the team had been counting on him to be the crowd-pleaser again, "don't ever give up on yourself, wait until you are going real good to do it. Then, if you still think everything is hopeless, well, then, pray to God and pack it in. I guarantee you, you'll live to be one hundred."

The wisdom had carried him to the major leagues. Maybe, applied to his problem, it would carry him to some kind of non-freakiness. Next time he would not only avoid children, he'd just run if he felt himself getting funny, just put distance between himself and the damn duster.

Before checking out of the hotel Potter considered if he was just making excuses for himself. He pondered whether or not he had the courage to kill himself, and recognizing that he did indeed, he decided to give himself one more chance. It was clear to him that he just couldn't let that kind of thing happen again.

At the car agency, the dealer said, "Listen, Potter, I got a better deal for you. How would you like to drive a new Mercedes each year?" He had already ordered one of his employees to rev up a Mercedes and take Potter Cindy to the airport.

"A Gremlin's good enough for me." He had asked the car dealer if he'd just be kind enough to ship the Gremlin up north when he proposed the Mercedes deal.

The average man, like Potter, considered the offer made by the car dealer to be nice—a good gesture. However, there are some in, out, and around baseball, whether big, popular, or ignored, who've been stung too often by lies, tricks, and broken promises and therefore hold the view that "nobody does nothing for nothing" in business. America was made great, at least American business, including baseball, by there being a percentage in it for someone. Big deal. Potter was flattered that the car dealer told everyone that the rookie sensation had bought a car from him because he, the dealer, had the best darn American and foreign motor agency in the south. Potter was pleased that the guy went to the trouble of having a banner put up outside his agency reading, "Potter Cindy Bought His Car Here!!!" with three exclamation points. That was a real honor. Potter was not an Atlanta player. He was not even a home-town boy.

"I don't have to be chauffeured to the airport. It's real nice of you, but I'd just as soon catch a cab."

"Nothing doing. We'll see you out there." Then, he yelled out to one of his men, "Tell Buck to get on up here with Potter Cindy's transportation."

He turned back to Potter. "Well, if you like the Gremlin so much, why don't I give you a new one free each baseball season? And I'll present it to you when you come down here to play Atlanta the first time each year, whenever that happens to be."

"Why do you want to do that?" Potter asked.

"Well, I'll tellya. Just because you were so nice about puttin' up the sign out front." The dealer's accent grew more backwoods southern with each new little gesture of hospitality and generosity.

"I don't know," Potter said. "It just doesn't seem right, somehow."

"Oh, hell, man. It's perfectly legal. We give cars away to lots of professional athletes in Atlanta."

"Each year? You'll give me a new car every baseball season?" Somehow the notion of institutionalizing the gift upset Potter.

"Sho' enof. Wun cost you a wooden nickel." Then, the car dealer chuckled. "Course you'll have to pay for the gas 'n oil and for servicin'. But I reckon somebody with all your talent could cook up a deal on that somewhere, if you know what I'm drivin' at."

Though it is said by wise men that man resembles the pig in size, metabolism, and physiology, if not in other ways, one could not use Potter Cindy to represent the breed.

"What do you mean by my talent?" Potter wanted to know.

"Oh, I don't mean anything unkind. I mean, most businessmen who know anything about business would be breaking their little hairy nookies just to know you and have you on their team. A big star like you can get favors done, is all I mean."

Potter considered. He managed a smile. "I'll stick with the car I bought. You've got to drive a car for a year before it's any good anyway. No point in trading it in once you've got it running your way. Besides, where I come from, you don't trade a horse that easy, not after you wore out your jeans breaking it."

"Well, suit yourself," the car dealer said. He was stunned, thought Potter was a numbskull. "I don't mean any discourtesy, Mr. Cindy, but if I were you, I'd look into some of the advantages of being a big league ballplayer. You know, they say you fellers only got about ten years to make it, that is, if you're good. Heck, if I was you, I would not back away from an easy buck, or look a gift horse in the mouth."

Potter smiled and got into the car the dealer had provided for his trip to the airport. "I appreciate your advice and your help in shipping that Gremlin I bought."

"Anytime," the dealer said. "I'm willin' to return your check whenever you say."

"Why? Is there something wrong with the car I bought?"

"No. That's a darn good runnin' li'l car."

"Okay, then, let the deal stand."

Potter waved to the driver, a little arch of a wave that told him to accelerate the engine. The driver pulled away smoothly in a shiny, temperature-controlled (air-conditioned) lavender Mercedes. The radio was on and the fidelity was excellent. The sound came from at least three speakers. One would have to imagine that the car dealer thought automotive finery would seduce Potter into accepting his yearly token of appreciation, so to speak. But, there was something hotter in the kiln that required Potter's attention. It came over the car radio as five-minutes-before-the-hour news, a repose from hot rock music, over station WBDK, Atlanta:

"Two men are in Emory Hospital and three dogs have been beaten to death in a bizarre series of events that took place just hours ago in De Kalb County.

"The injured men said they had run their car into a school fence in an attempt to capture a man who had made obscene overtures to an eight-year-old girl. The subject escaped by leaping the school fence. The fence was six feet high.

"The man apparently continued his escape through the nearby Abery Farm. He was pursued by three large dogs that guard the property. The man somehow got hold of an ax handle and slaughtered the animals, according to Lieutenant Craig ("Feets") Patrick of the De Kalb County Police Department. The man is still at large. He was described as white and tall with longish black hair. His face was seen only by the would-be victim, who described him as 'very handsome'.

"The two hospitalized men suffered fractures and deep lacerations of the limbs and superficial cuts on the face. They were treated and discharged from the hospital. The little girl was 'unharmed.

"Police are looking for an athletic man, perhaps under twenty-five years, probably a former track star, specifically a hurdler."

"You reckon somebody could jump a fence that high?" the chauffeur asked Potter.

"I guess so," Potter said softly.

"I wouldn't have thought it possible. What do you think that fella had in mind with that little girl?"

74

Potter didn't answer. His driver asked again.

"Nothing much," Potter said softly, almost inaudibly.

"*Nothing much?* Why, that fucker was goin' to split that li'l girl wide open. Don't you think?"

"No! And don't ask me any more questions. Just drive the damn car. Okay?"

"Well, okay. I was just making conversation."

"I'd appreciate it very much if you kept quiet."

Potter felt he was blaming the poor fellow when he was really angry with himself.

"Listen, I don't mean to snap at you. I'm sorry. But I've had a rough weekend."

"Is ballplaying all that hard?" said the dense chauffeur. "I wouldn't of thought it was."

"There are pressures."

"Oh, pressures. Never thought of that."

"What is your work, when you're not making conversation?"

"I service the cars. I'm sort of a mechanic."

"Did you ever fill tires?"

"Yep. Millions of 'em."

"Well, you must know then that if you put too much air in they'll blow up, but if you fill them under less pressure, they'll be okay. That's what I meant when I said there were pressures." Potter could not be certain if the driver understood. At least he could see that the man took it as an apology, if not an explanation. Potter gave the driver a ten-dollar tip at the end of the trip.

"My boss wouldn't want me to accept this —"

"Tell him I pressured you." Potter walked away.

Chapter Eight

They say Police Lieutenant Craig "Feets" Patrick's kin were Irish who came to the south, long after General Sherman, in the very early 1940's in fact, to escape the depression in New York. They say the family's name was originally Fitzpatrick, but Craig's father got sick of southerners calling him "Feets" for Fitz, so he just dropped the Fitz altogether. He moved from Birmingham, Alabama, where he was supposed to have had work as a railroad dick, up the road to the New York of the south, Atlanta, where he was hired by Coca Cola as a guard in the company's security department. He was assigned to the "patrol," which meant the entire plant property was his to oversee, which is sort of like guarding Atlanta itself. Nearly everybody in Atlanta recognizes that Coca Cola owns it or, at least did, in the forties.

If the story was true, and you cannot ever tell in the south what is real or false with new southerners, like Craig's folks, it was Mr. Patrick's ill luck to have a son who was a track star in high school, who could run like a frightened leprechaun, or a British Tommy with an IRA man waving a hot Shavian preface at him. At any rate, Craig ran so well that they began calling him "Foot." It's sad, but in the south they never let well enough alone when it comes to language or nicknames.

Alas, "Foot" became "Feet" and finally "Feets." Old Mr. Patrick used to shudder when he heard Craig's friends call his son "Feets" Patrick. He was rarely just called Feets or Craig or Patrick. Usually Feets Patrick. Even his wife called him Feets Patrick sometimes.

He followed in his father's footsteps, only faster, of course; he became a military policeman during the Korean War, and after that, at age twenty-two, he became an officer in the Georgia Department of Correction. He switched to the De Kalb County Police Department in the sixties and quickly worked his way up to lieutenant. He was a smart cop who thought well on his feet.

There were several things that interested Feets Patrick (may old Mr. Patrick forgive those who take his name in vain) about the events that took place at the Briar Vista School in De Kalb County. For one, a good friend of his was hurt in the crash of car against school fence. His name was Dave Skipton, a gym teacher at the local Briar Vista School and an old teammate of Feets' on their high school track team. Feets Patrick also owned an offspring—a bitch called Maxalene—of one of the dogs that had been killed at the Abery Farm. Finally, Feets Patrick was intrigued by the fact that Dave Skipton had said the man jumped the six-foot fence. As a man who had made his name and earliest reputation on the track and who had even tried high-jumping in his time, Feets Patrick knew that a person would really have to be able to jump to get over a six-foot fence. More than that, he'd have had to be in shape, and young enough to get his body up that high.

He thought it was kind of stupid of Dave to plow into that fence. He had always been an impulsive type with a disregard for consequences. But Dave knew the difference between a fellow who jumped six feet and one who just looked like a fellow who jumped six feet.

"Did you get a look at the man, Dave?"

"Only his ass. And I saw that raw."

"You mean he had his pants down and you couldn't catch him?"

"Feets Patrick, that man flew like greased shit. I dare say he could have licked you, even you, in your prime. That man was a track star, a runner, or a high-jumper, and if he wasn't I'll eat my cast here." The man pointed to his leg, the one that had been fractured and set in plaster.

"I need a description, Dave."

"Well, like I've been tellin' you, I only saw his backside."

"His hair was dark?"

"Yep. More black than dark brown."

"About how tall was he?"

"Well, he was taller than me. About six-two or so."

"How much you figure he weighed?"

"Well, he was smaller than both of us. About one-eighty-five. Something like that."

"Would you say he was lean or broad?"

"He wasn't lean or broad. He was evenly built. It's kind of hard to say because he was just built sort of perfect."

"Did you hear him speak?"

"Nope. Mostly he was running like the daylights. Seemed like he wasn't moving all that fast to look at him, but he just kept putting acreage between us. If you were watching it would look like I was standing still."

"Did he have any characteristics that you could remember?"

"Nope. Just kind of longish black hair. Not very long like a hippie. Sort of long but not like a hippie, if you know what I mean. I wouldn't be upset if a kid of mine had hair like that. You know what I mean, Feets Patrick. The day of the clean bean is gone."

"You know, Dave, these little side comments of yours aren't helping me all that much. I need characteristics. Something about the guy that would make you recognize him. No offense. But it isn't important what length hair you would accept in your children."

"Yeah, well, all right, then."

"Did he jump the fence like a hurdler or a high-jumper? Did he take it in one leap?"

"Man, I don't mind tellin' you, you forgot your track. There's no man who can hurdle a six-foot fence. He went up like a high-jumper. And it only took him one leap."

"That's a good jump."

"That's what I've been telling you! Now, the little girl he was after saw him. I'll just bet she'll be able to give you some of your 'characteristics' you've been looking for. You can bet your life she got a look at his wang."

"Dave, shit! I can't make an arrest on the size of a man's genitalia. Besides, it's not the kind of thing you can ask an eight-year-old who was very nearly abused."

"Well, maybe she could tell you what he looked like."

"She already did. He's handsome. Period. She said he looks like her Daddy. The little girl's Daddy is about five-foot-nine, and blonder than you are, Dave."

"Looks like you got your work cut out for you, Lt. Feets Patrick."

"That's right. Question is, is it worth it?"

"Why, of course it's worth it. Look at my darn head and arms and legs."

"You've done that to yourself, Dave."

"Still, he was going to molest that little girl. Maybe rape her."

"I doubt it," Feets Patrick said. "They don't do a heck of a lot more than just show their peckers, guys like that."

"Well, what about them Abery dogs? One of them was your Maxalene's momma."

Feets Patrick considered. "Yah. Yep. Umm. Er," were the sounds he made, thinking. "They're just dogs, after all."

"Dogs. Why if they were people who guarded Abery's land, you'd be huntin' that fellow in fifty states. Why, suppose that fellow ran into the Coca Cola factory and it was your Daddy on guard instead of the dogs?"

"My Daddy would have blown that poor bastard's head off. You know, those Abery dogs aren't exactly friendly."

"Well, I'm going to press charges, Feets Patrick. An' I want you to find him. We got us a wrecked car, a busted-down fence, and two bodies all broken up, to say nothing of Abery's dogs."

Feets Patrick was hardly listening to his friend's complaints. He was thinking that a person who can run all that distance and still have the strength to clobber three fairly vicious dogs, and not get himself all chewed up in the process, would have to be something special. There were no traces of human blood where the dog fight took place, so they were dealing with a man of almost inexhaustible endurance and strength.

"Our man," Feets Patrick told Dave, "wields a mighty powerful ax handle. It would take some doing to kill those Abery dogs. From the look of it, those dogs didn't get very much of him."

"Maybe he's some kind of animal trainer," Dave Skipton suggested.

"No. He's a young, powerful man. I wouldn't be all that shocked if he turned out to be one of our top athletes at the University of Georgia or Georgia Tech or Emory University."

"Tech or Emory'd be more like it because they're nearby," Dave offered. "The other school is out of town, as you know."

"Dave, it's Easter vacation. You ought to know that. You're a teacher. Besides, Emory doesn't have a sensational athletic program."

"Well, Tech, then. But don't forget that a lot of athletes hang around on Easter holiday to practice. I was headed toward the school to coach our baseball team when I ran into that friend of ours."

"You got something there, Dave. He might just be a local fellow even though the little girl did not recognize him from anywhere. I asked her. She's never seen him before."

"You reckon he's an Atlanta boy?"

"I don't know. Seems so. At least he had some business in Atlanta or why else would he be here? I asked the little girl if he had an accent—you know, who he sounded like—and she said like her Daddy. But you know how reliable that is."

"Maybe he was just passing through."

"It's possible."

"Feets Patrick, I don't think you got a prayer of catching him."

"Well, if I don't, Dave, you're going to have to get that fence repaired that you knocked down."

"That's not fair!"

"Maybe not. But it's the law."

"You better find him, Feets Patrick. Why in hell should I pay for that fence?"

"Well, our missing friend jumped it. And you crashed it."

"But I was helping you out, Feets Patrick."

"You were over-enthusiastic."

"He would have gotten away."

"He got away, anyway," Feets Patrick pointed out.

Feets Patrick was all for giving it up. He knew he would have to wait for the man to act again. The fellow might not even go after another little girl in his county the next time. Feets Patrick wanted to help Dave Skipton out, but he just could not see how he was going to find that darn high-jumper in a haystack. There were millions of straw-haired little girls, the man could strike anywhere. The Lieutenant needed to get lucky. The little girl's parents weren't pushing for action; in fact, they didn't seem to care one way or the other. They told him they would not press charges because the little girl was unharmed and not upset.

"The man might strike again," Feets Patrick told the parents.

"It's your job, officer, to see that he doesn't," said the little girl's father.

"That's the point," Feets Patrick explained. "If I run him down, I'll need you folks to press charges. Would you do it?"

They did not answer. And Feets Patrick knew it was hopeless. "Well," the father said finally, "he didn't hurt our girl." Feets Patrick had no way of knowing that the little girl's Daddy walked around their house with his pecker hanging out all the time.

"It could have hurt her mind," Feets Patrick pointed out. "A thing like that could upset a child emotionally. Don't you realize that?"

The father—John Penneys was his name—probably thought, *Bullshit!* He was not the kind of man who would put too much stock in emotional hazards, that is, if he had ever heard of emotional hazards. The man said, "My little girl looks none the worse for wear." Feets Patrick sighed. He did not point out that, considering the circumstances, it was a stupid expression.

Feets Patrick had no case, except for damages to the school fence, the injured men's hospital bills, and amends to hurt pride and sentiment. The man did smite Abery's three dogs, and they'd have to be replaced, too, by Dave, he guessed, or the criminal, if Feets Patrick ever found his high-jumper.

What troubled Feets Patrick more than anything else was not that a crime was committed—because whatever was committed was stopped in the middle—but that he couldn't let the thing go. He had spent less time on investigating burglaries in his county than he did on this dumb little event. Was he so upset that an athlete had been involved, especially a track-and-field man, that he could not free himself from the case? What the hell was so sacred about athletes or track-and-field men, anyway?

"Aaah," he said to himself, "screw it!"

When he returned to the stationhouse everybody was talking about baseball. He said to himself, *Damn, you'd think there was no police work to be done. You'd think we lived in a world full of Dagwood Bumstead and Mickey Mouse and Donald Duck. These guys sit around here like there was nothing in the world to do but second-guess the Atlanta Braves manager.* Feets was a fan himself, but he was also a police lieutenant. At least that's what he was supposed to be paid for, he knew.

He listened to the conversation for a while:

"That goddarn rookie of theirs really put it to us. That boy can do anything. He can hit, run, field. He can even jump like a damn kangaroo."

"How come Atlanta doesn't get good young players like that?"

"I guess a player like Potter Cindy only shows up once in a lifetime."

"Yep. He's a sensation."

Feets believed in the principle that a person works for what he gets, especially a cop. "Now, listen here," he told the men in the station house, "I'm a baseball fan, too, but we got a full blotter of cases that need to be disposed of in one way or another. I don't mean to be sassy to you, or a smart ass, but unless you men are totally convinced that talking baseball while you're on the De Kalb County payroll is going to solve some of the crime in this county, I think you ought to save it for when you get home and want to talk to your kids or your neighbor about something other than the weather." Feets felt self-conscious about the lecture he had given his men. He knew he was as guilty as they were on "talking sports."

The men were silent; they had looks on their faces of hushed schoolchildren. "Well, that's all I got to say for now. I'm heading home. I know when I come in here tomorrow," he said with a smile on his face, "you men will have solved all the unfinished police business in De Kalb County."

He started out the door of the station house, when a thought occurred to him about the Briar Vista School incident. He

83

called to a red-headed policeman. "Red, do me a favor, will you? I want you to check the files on child-molestation cases in the Atlanta area. We're looking for a man, black hair, longish black hair, about six-feet-one or two—not the hair, Red—" Red made a face "—about one-eighty pounds, a good athlete, maybe a track star or a football player or something. Check college health services. Maybe they got a male stripper or child-abuser on their psychological records or something. And, Red, get the word out that we're looking for a witness in case the milkman, or the garbage man, or a delivery man saw something."

"That's a big job, Feets. It must be important. That's a lot of checking."

Feets knew it was not important. When Red said that, Feets did not feel very happy about wasting a good man like Red and the county's money on top of it.

"It's a favor, Red, for a friend of mine. If it becomes a big hassle, or frustrating, or a pain in the ass, then drop it." He paused, managed another smile, "You can go back to moaning the blues for Atlanta and talking about how great that Potter Cindy is."

Red made another face.

When Feets got in, his son Corey confirmed his station-house's view of Potter Cindy. "Atlanta lost again, Dad."

"I heard."

"Did you see that Potter Cindy leap to save the day?"

"Nope, didn't catch the series on TV at all."

"Well," Corey filled his father in, "this really great rookie was coming in on the ball while his second baseman was going out and he leaped right over his man, and that's what killed us."

"That's tough luck, Corey."

"That darn Potter Cindy!"

"I guess he's good," Feets Patrick declared.

"He's great!"

Feets Patrick thought aloud. "Sure be nice if we had him here in Atlanta."

A person cannot get very much closer to the truth without having it get in his blood stream, like virulent bacteria. But Feets Patrick had his own special immunity or too tough a hide. Potter was practically laid out before the lieutenant like a laboratory culture. All Feets Patrick had to do was identify the organism. But he just was not the investigator people thought he was at that moment. It was hard for Feets Patrick, despite a revered reputation among his colleagues as a savvy cop, to think of a professional baseball player as being freaky in that way.

Still, nobody ever said that Feets Patrick had extrasensory perception. It would have taken dark and deep magic to have connected Potter Cindy to the events in De Kalb County, a warlock craft beyond the meager intuitions of an Atlanta police lieutenant. There were other things working against Feets Patrick. He had read a newspaper account of Potter Cindy riding around with a "Honk! If you love Jesus" car bumper sticker on a simple working man's automobile and he thought while reading the sports story that the baseball player must be a very nice young man.

For a cop with a good nose for crap, Feets Patrick tended not to be able to smell the evacuations in the sports pages of his paper. In that sense, his sinuses were no different from any other red-blooded American sports nut. Politics turned his nose up. So did the War; he had voted against every presidential candidate connected with the War, except Kennedy.

So if he didn't seem to be watching the TV news accounts of what the governor said, or what the President said, or the Pentagon leaked, or the Joint Chiefs of Staff growled— more, if he seemed restless waiting for the sports report to come on—nobody who knew him would mind. That's the way Feets Patrick was.

There it was on the screen, captured on TV tape forever, for all to see. Potter Cindy destroying the Atlanta Braves single-handedly.

"Here's public enemy number one in Atlanta this week. It was the opening series of the baseball season. The Braves were hosting the bad men from the Midwest, the Redbirds. They weren't very nice guests, as you've heard, especially Potter Cindy. Just take a look at what this Redbird rookie sensation did to our hardball team in the four-game series just ended—thank goodness—this afternoon." The TV station showed film clips of his stealing a base and bunting for a base hit. "Got away with robbery," the announcer said. Films of Potter's three homers were shown. "Sabotage!" boomed the announcer. Potter shagging a long fly. "Watch the stride on this ball hawk. It's something beautiful!... Now watch this. You just have to see it to believe it." Potter Cindy leaping over Bobby Hartman to avoid a collision. "Up, up, and away!" said the announcer. "And he's handsome too, girls."

"Jeeeeeesus!" said Feets Patrick, stretching it out. "What a great play. What a great leap. What a jump!" Then, Feets Patrick blinked, bit softly on the inside of his cheek. He was thinking: *Leap. Jump. Holy shit!* There's somebody that was in Atlanta and could jump that fence at the Briar Vista School. Only thing wrong was that a healthy, young, professional ballplayer would not do something like that. It was far-fetched, he knew, a real long shot, but he made a mental note to go to the TV station and take a look at that leap again at the first free moment he got. If nothing else, he'd get to see the play again.

Chapter Nine

Dave Skipton didn't like the idea that he would have to pay for all the damages. He was willing, or at least thought it was right, that he should pay for Billy's medical tab. After all, he had gotten the guy banged up in that chase. He resented paying for the fence, but what could he do? The pervert had gotten away. He thought it was downright indecent of Feets to suggest that he had to replace the Abery dogs. He didn't do anything to the dogs. Okay, maybe Feets was right when he said, "The fence didn't run into your car, Dave, you and Billy ran into it." But the dogs were a different story. He just couldn't see Feets' thinking on that. He didn't tell the pervert where to run; the man picked the Abery farm on his own.

Dave knew that if the real criminal wasn't caught he'd be out about six or seven hundred bucks. It wasn't that he was broke, or didn't have it saved in the Bank of Georgia. But he had plans for the money. He had promised his wife that this spring, before the Georgia rains hit, he would get the house painted and the roof replaced. Now that was out.

He didn't even have his car back from the garage, not that he could drive it anyhow, with his leg in a cast. *It just doesn't pay*, Dave thought, *trying to be a good citizen*. It wasn't *his* daughter who was being attacked. He was glad he didn't have a daughter. Still, he made himself a promise that if he ever witnessed another wrongdoing, he was going to develop a sudden temporary blindness.

I'm not going to do beans for anybody in trouble. The heck with them! Nobody came forward to ask Dave if he needed any cash to handle the damages. That's the least thing the little girl's father—what was his name?—Mr. Penneys—could have done, Dave felt.

He consoled himself with the fact that he'd get a longer vacation out of the accident, which meant he'd be able to watch the day games on TV, and maybe even sneak in a little catfish fishing in Lake Lucky, that is, if someone would be good enough to drive him. His wife couldn't do it 'cause she worked as an office nurse for a Cobb County dermatologist, Dr. Robert S. Berlin. It was nice of Dr. Berlin to pick her up on his way to the office and take her back now that Dave's car was out of commission.

He wondered if Billy would drive him to the lake; he wasn't hurt all that bad. At least he could drive a car. *Of course,* Dave thought, *Billy'd probably not want to drive me anywhere after what happened when he drove after that pervert.* Dave knew he had caused Billy to ram the fence. Billy didn't really want to go all out once he saw the pervert had a chance of outracing the car.

Dave just couldn't figure out why a fellow, an athlete and all, if he was one, would want to raise hell with little kids. He tried to imagine why somebody would be interested in children, little girls, when there was all that grown-up stuff around. There were a lot of young teachers at school that Dave wouldn't mind nailing, just once, anyway. Dave knew he was all talk, no action, when it came to getting women interested in him. Dave knew that his last great romantic adventure was probably with his wife, but he felt that if a guy is alive at all, he never stops thinking about other stuff.

88

Dave just couldn't believe that there were people who were attracted to kids. He taught little children at school and while they were sometimes cute, they were mostly a pain in the neck. He had two kids of his own, and they were no treat to raise. He knew that. "Children are a lot of care," his wife had once said when both the kids were down with some high fever. "It seems all we're ever going to do, Dave, is worry about them."

Dave had two boys; they were neither of them natural athletes. That was something Dave worried about from the very beginning. But, as he was a gym teacher and a very good athlete himself, he devoted himself to getting them on the right track. He worked real hard to improve their skills. He'd get them out on the field and make them do things over and over, always correcting and indicating the proper way things should be done. He did this with the boys every day that he could. He practiced football, baseball, basketball with them through each season until he finally got them up good enough so that they'd be starters in the Little League and not the last kids to be picked in choose-up football and basketball games.

Dave knew natural talent when he saw it, and he knew that neither of his boys would ever make it as professional athletes. He was smart enough to give up the dream that his sons would be pros before it brought unnecessary disappointment down on his head.

The pervert he chased across the school field was a natural athlete; Dave had seen lots of people run and jump in his time and in his work. He knew how a real athlete moved and how one who was merely well-trained moved. His sons were well-trained; they had acquired smoothness but they were not athletes. No amount of training would give them the speed of that pervert, or his easy, no-effort-like movement, that grace of the exceptional runner who moves like he hardly touches ground.

He hoped his friend would snare the pervert. Maybe the man could be made to foot the bills. It was something to look forward to, anyhow.

Right now, all Dave had was his TV set; maybe the Braves would get rolling, now that the Redbirds had left town. Dave knew, he could feel it, that the Redbirds were going to be fighting tooth and nail with the Braves all season. It would be nice if they only fought with one tooth and one nail, but with guys like Brossi, Mayknoll, and Hartman, and that good rookie, Potter Cindy, in the lineup, the Redbirds were going to raise a lot of hell.

Dave Skipton punched the air. He was cheering on his Braves, silently, hopefully, like the diehard fan he was. It would not hurt him all that much if Brossi or Mayknoll or Hartman or Cindy had a foot in a cast, like he did.

Chapter Ten

Little Miz California Sunshine sat nude, as usual, in front of a huge mirror, which was really more of an entire wall than it was just a mirror on the wall. The mirror and the rest of the walls and furnishings were part of the Los Angeles triplex apartment owned by the kingpin of Atlanta gambling, Scruffy Levinson, a one-time consort of Sissy's, or rather, she had been one of the "neatest little fillies" in his stable. They parted, Sissy and Scruffy, as friends without resentment or grief, when she was claimed by Potter. Scruffy, a generous man, had said that she, with or without her outfielder, was welcome to visit or use any of his places from Atlanta to Los Angeles. Scruffy had never met Potter but he was so fond of Sissy that he offered any of his apartments or houses or properties for their use. Scruffy was set up in Palm Beach, Palm Springs, Frisco, L.A., Boca Raton, Birmingham, Colorado Springs, New Orleans, and Reno.

The mirror that showed Sissy herself was in Los Angeles, where Sissy was staying while she tried to capture a part in a movie, a little part, but one she felt she had a real good chance of landing.

She studied her "bee sting" breasts and wondered what she would look like with a real pair of knockers. She pushed at them, boosted them and, in doing so, became terrified. On the side of one breast she felt a small hard nodule in the soft tissue below the skin. She screamed. *Breast cancer!*

"Shit! If that isn't a laugh on me. I'm going to die of breast cancer. The one thing I thought I would not have to worry about. I hardly have anything to get cancer in. Shit! How can you give me breast cancer, you fuckin' bastards!"

Though she tried to console herself that it was only a swollen gland she was feeling, it seemed to be more menacing and malignant the more she probed and felt. "My life is just beginning, you bastards. I just married Pottsie. I'm going to land a little part in a flick, you sonofabitches."

She picked up the phone and started to call Potter at his hotel in Atlanta. She knew the team was winding up a four-game opening gun series in that city and, what with the time difference, he probably had not left the hotel as yet. The operator asked for the number she was calling and she answered, "Ohh, fuck!" and hung up. She couldn't call Potter. This was his first series in the major leagues. She knew he would be trying his ass off, that he would be tense and the last fuckin' thing he wanted to hear was her whining about a lump in her breast. They just got married. She didn't want him to have to carry this sickly piece of shit around with him till she dropped dead. Sissy, though frightened, decided that she ought to make one gesture in her life at not being selfish; she did not call Potter. She called Scruffy Levinson instead.

"Scruffy, could you come to L.A.? I'm in your place. I need somebody, Scruffy, somebody to help me. I'm dying."

"Whaddaya mean, dying? Where's that jock you married?"

"He's in Atlanta, playing against the Braves. Scruffy, I have a lump in my breast—" She started to sob and cry.

"Whaddaya crying about? It's probably nothing."

She managed through her sobs, "You're not a doctor. What do you know, you stupid fuck?"

"That's a nice way to talk to a friend."

"Scruffy, could you come here and stay with me? At least till I see a doctor. I'm scared."

"Today? You mean today?"

"Of course, today, you stupid ass. What do you want me to do, wait till it spreads to my vagina?"

"I think you're a little hysterical, Sissy. Look. Calm down. I'm going to give you the name of a big breast man in L.A.; he's the best, maybe the world's best breast man. You hear that? He charges a hundred bucks a visit, just to take your name and look at a pair of tits. He gets more money for looking than . . . He treated one of my—how shall I put it?—one of my colleague's friends. . . ."

"I don't want to go to any hundred-buck crook. I want a real doctor."

"This is a real doctor, Sissy, honest!"

"Bullshit! I know you, Scruffy; he's probably into you for a bundle."

"Well, then, that's it, Sissy. I'm hanging up. Call your jock up. Let him find you a better doctor."

"No, wait! What's his name? Will he see me right away, right now? I know those fuckin' doctors. It takes a year to get an appointment and another year of hanging around in the waiting room. I don't want to wait. I want to go right in. I don't want to sit there getting more nervous. I'm nervous enough. I want to go right in."

"Sure, Sissy. I'll fix it up. He'll see you right away."

"How can you be so sure? You said he was a big shot—"

"He is, I promise."

"Big shots have a lot of patients, don't they?"

"I have influence."

Sissy bawled again, like a baby. "I don't want to go to any crooked doctor. I want to see a real breast expert."

"That's this guy. He's the best. Unfortunately, or fortunately, his son is not the best. The kid's into me for twenty-five G's."

"Will you come to L.A., Scruffy?"

"After you see the doctor. Tomorrow, if you still need me."

"What do you mean, *still?* I'm dying."

"Wanna bet? I'll give you 40 to 1 that there's nothing seriously wrong with you."

. Sissy started to laugh, thinking there is no bet old Scruffy would pass up . . . even on death, he was getting to be a regular insurance company. She took the name of the doctor, his address, and waited thirty minutes before leaving for his office, as Scruffy had told her to.

To pass the thirty minutes, she decided to call Potter anyway. But his room didn't answer. He was probably at the ballpark. In her anxiety she forgot that she was going to do something unselfish before she died.

The doctor saw her immediately, felt the lump, and confirmed that it was a real lump of some sort. He determined through a breast scan that her lump was merely a cyst and that she would probably not die of cancer for at least another fifty years, especially from that lump. The cyst required watching but not treatment.

Sissy left the doctor's office, called Scruffy from a chic bar after she downed an extra-dry martini. She told him the good news.

"Oh that's great, Sissy. That's a real relief. You see, even if you were dying, I couldn't get to L.A. today to see you."

"You mean you would have let me die in this city alone?"

"I would be with you in a way, Sissy. You're in *my* apartment, aren't you?"

"You've got a heart of gold, Scruffy."

"Do you owe me any money on that bet with the doctor and your breast?"

"Yep," she said.

"How much?"

"How's my credit?"

"Lousy."

"What was it again, Scruffy—40 to 1?"

"Yeah. That's right."

"Well, Scruffy. I owe you a cool million, 'cause that was my bet."

"Do you have it?"

"Of course not."

"Ahh, chalk it, then. I'll get it from some other dame—one with money—who bets she has athlete's foot."

"Thanks, Scruffy. You saved my life."

The kingpin of Atlanta crime and illegality hung up.

Chapter Eleven

It is said that air travel and war have a way of bringing everybody but American Presidents to confession.

Though the plane ride to Philadelphia had been one of the most uncomfortable Potter had ever taken, it was not the air pockets or bumps or shifting current that produced the discomfort. He hardly recognized that the ride was rough. In spite of Potter's decision to give himself another chance, he was still down on himself about the events in Georgia only a few hours before.

It was a madness, the duster, he saw that. Yet he really did not seem capable of being able to control it. What was happening to him? He was under pressure. But he had been under pressure before. He remembered that last season in the minors he had passed up urges to undress in front of children in Santa Fe, San Antonio, Stockton, Tidewater, or hadn't he? He thought he had but now he wasn't sure. He gritted his teeth in self-disgust and rage. The Beast of Bougainvilla! Jesus!

He would have to stop now. Once and for all. Perhaps there was someone who could help? He considered Hartman and Mayknoll, and Brossi. No. They were out. He had only known them a total of sixty days at best, during the spring for the most part. They were still to be considered fair-weather friends. Whatever friendship he might have with them would have to be seasoned, like a rookie.

Dr. Hardy, the team physician, came to mind. Didn't doctors, like priests, hold confidences sacred? Potter was not a cynical man. But he reasoned, in the skies over Philadelphia, that a doctor who was employed by a profit-making organization, even if the Supreme Court granted it special dispensations, owed something to the company. Didn't they ask doctors to evaluate the physical shape of so-and-so or who's-it before they traded for him? Would Dr. Hardy tell Zarember, or Mr. Heller who signed his check, "Sorry, boys, but any problems this player may have are strictly between the player and myself?" They didn't give Dr. Hardy a healthy retainer so that he could practice the small print of the Hippocratic oath. Potter remembered Zarember telling the doc that.

It would be best to tell Sissy, he realized. But how in heck do you tell someone you're supposed to love and have just married that little girls make you more excited, turn you on? She'd never forgive him. And why, just why should she?

Potter shuddered, perhaps for the third time, when he thought that he had caused two men to get hurt and had killed those animals. And what about that man in the truck who had seen him? He would turn up one day and then, *Swish!* Strike three!

It was not fair to Sissy, the team, anyone. God! God almighty. Help me. Help me please . . . .

It was of no interest to Potter that traffic was heavy over the airport and that the ship would be going into a holding pattern. They would have to hold for at least twenty minutes. The way Potter felt at the moment of the announcement, the plane could circle around forever. A whole lot of folks, he thought, would probably be better off.

The plane came down from the crowded skies and landed smoothly in Philadelphia. He walked quickly out of the airport. If Potter had maintained his cool, it would have abruptly heated up in the Philadelphia airport, near the taxi stand,

97

to be specific. An incident occurred there that had to have an effect of profound importance upon him. There was a man who stood against the wall of the Eastern Airlines terminal, holding a brightly painted cigar box below his waist near his groin. The man beckoned to Potter with one hand, pleading with his expression, a look that asked for help, and Potter in his own misery was charitable. He came over.

"You in some kind of trouble, sir?" Potter asked.

The man's eyes went down to the colored cigar box. Potter followed them. The man lifted the top. And there, resting on a large wad of cotton, was the man's own erect penis. The man had apparently cut a hole in the cigar box and stuck his penis through it for display on the cotton.

Potter was stunned, said nothing to the smiling face and green teeth that looked out at him for a full thirty seconds. Then, he raised his clenched fist to smash that face, but he thought of the chase in De Kalb County, the dogs snarling, the car smashing the wire fence, and in that instant he imagined that the face that would feel his outrage, his clenched fist, would be his own.

"Well," the man said in a high, insane, falsetto voice, "you like El Productos? White Owls? Dutch Masters? No? How about a big Cubano? Mmmmmm. Good."

"Listen, mister," Potter said, his voice hushed by sadness and pain, his own face beginning to show perspiration on his upper lip, "get out of here while you still can. Don't do that anymore, you hear? You're going to get yourself in a mess of trouble. Now...go on...out of here. Now!"

The man laughed the laugh of a madman. "How about a big cigar, buster? He he he he he he...." Potter started to run away. "Who's got the biggest cigar?" The man laughed, flipping his lid. "Cockadoodle-do! Cockadoodle-do! Do I have a cockadoodle-do or don't I?" Potter ran away.

He got into a cab in the next terminal, put his face in his hands and cried or screamed privately, silently.

Chapter Twelve

At night Potter had agonies and thoughts that brought him goose flesh and cold sweat. During the day, he hammered the ball. The records show that he went 9 for 12 in the three-game Philadelphia series. More striking, however, was that the Redbirds won the three-game series having scored only 7 runs, all of them driven in by Potter. His triple in the fourth inning of the first game, behind a walk to Dick Condon, won the game for Mayknoll, 1-0. Mayknoll struck out 12 batters, 8 of them in a row. In the second game of the series, Potter hit his first "hat trick"—a single, double, triple, and homer. With all that, the Redbirds only managed 3 runs, and won the game 3-2. Dick Condon struck out 4 times in a row. In the final game, the feeble Redbird hitting continued, typified by another 4 strikeouts by Condon. Potter collected 2 doubles and 2 singles for the day and, of course, drove in the 3 runs, dragging his team to victory 3-1. In the dressing room a reporter asked Condon, who was ordinarily handy with a bat, "Wha' happened?" Dick Condon spit in his eye. Brossi, the team radical and wit, told the sports reporter with the saliva on his face, "We call that Condonation." But the reporter was in no mood to know whether Brossi was playing with the word *condemnation* or *condensation*, or both. He had a story to file. It was very clear that Condon was in for a year of bad press notices, even if he started hitting like Willie Mays.

Potter was more in Condon's mood than Brossi's. But the rookie outfielder, a gentleman, and afraid, was quiet before the praise being heaped upon him by the sports writers. Though he was a non-complaining person, Potter was also sincere and he found that when asked, "You clobbered some pretty tough pitching in that Philadelphia series. We figured out that there were 16 Redbird hits altogether and you got 9 of them. The rest of the guys were struggling and you didn't seem to have any trouble," he was forced to answer: "There just isn't any explaining it. I'm not feeling well, honestly. I haven't been sleeping right. My sleep has been awfully disturbed. I'm not feeding you a lot of bull, either. I mean, a guy goes 9 for 12 and whines about insomnia, it probably sounds like a lot of horse manure, but it's the truth."

"When you start sleeping, this league is going to be in big trouble."

"I can sure use a good night's rest."

"Why don't you get some sleeping pills from Doc Hardy?" the reporter suggested.

"I might do that. But I just got the feeling that what keeps me awake would keep me awake pill or not. Besides, I don't want to make myself groggy."

"Oh, Sissy's in Philadelphia, then. . . ."

"No, she's in Los Angeles this week."

The reporter winked and Potter tried to take some of the innuendo out of it with, "It's long been a notion of Sissy's—and I guess lots of other folks—that going to sleep is a boon to a head that's brainy to start with. She had heard that the guy who wrote Dr. Jekyll and Mr. Hyde did it after dreaming it."

"He must have had nightmares."

"Yes, sir. I guess some of the dreams were uncomfortable."

"Do you dream of hitting homers?" the reporter changed the subject.

"I know people have been saying I eat, sleep, and drink baseball. But, honestly, I have never dreamed about hitting. Matter of fact, I never dream very much, and when I do it's as dull as dishwater. I was out with Sissy and a Hollywood press agent once, and we were having a similar conversation about dreaming and when I told him that I rarely dream, he said I was a lot like some great writer—I forget the name—anyway the writer said, the poverty of his dreams mortified him, or something like that."

"That Sissy knows a lot of brainy people. Is she very bookish herself?"

"No," Potter said. "I don't think so. She's smart. She doesn't read all that much. But she's got a good memory and if somebody tells her something that she likes, she holds on to it and uses it whenever it seems right, sort of. I guess you've got to say that's using your head, but it is not brainy. I don't think I could be happy with one of your true intellectuals. I wouldn't know what the person was driving at most of the time."

The reporter's story hardly related to the interview. It covered Potter's hitting statistics for the first 7 games of the season. There was just brief mention that publicity or the pressure of the game "was causing Potter Cindy a mild case of insomnia." The writer hoped it would not catch up with him later in the season. Sissy got one line of ink in the copy. "Sissy Lindmore, the outfielder's wife, is in Los Angeles this week and not to be blamed for the outfielder's tossing in bed."

Somebody—guess who?—showed the article with sections underlined to Whitey Knocthofer, the manager. "I don't give a shit if he sleeps with every cunt in Philadelphia as long as he hits like that. He ought to get Dick Condon some of that pussy and the rest of these bums, too."

Zarember said, "One of these days that Potter Cindy's going

to wear out his welcome. I mean wang, in case you missed it!"

"The story said he had insomnia, not a dame!" Hartman complained to the inquiring Zarember. "He's not screwing anybody in the room. I'm in there with him. He just tosses and turns."

"Bullshit!" Remember Zarember said, "I can read between the lines of a sports story. Besides, he lies and you swear to it. Maybe he's giving you sloppy seconds, Hartman, and you're covering up."

"Mr. Zarember, use your imagination," Hartman said. "He's only recently married to Sissy Lindmore, you think he's still running around chasing panties?"

"Never mind!" Zarember said. "Maybe you're keeping him up screwing all night. You're not hitting any better than one of those tramps you guys bring up to the rooms."

"Tramps? Us? Hey! I got one of the 16 hits we got in the Philadelphia series and Potter got 9 of them."

"Yeah. Yeah. Yeah. I know...."

If Zarember thought every ballplayer was a potential alcoholic, drug addict, and sex maniac, his feelings were not shared by many well-known commercial and advertising empires. Business, unlike Zarember, thought a ballplayer's reputation was capital, whether it was that of swinger or square-shooter. That week Potter was given the Life Saver of the Week Award for his all-around efforts. The Double Mint Prize for the Most Doubles in the Majors and the Cap'n Crunch Trophy, for power hitting. Potter turned down the Power House Prize because the Cap'n Crunch people asked him first and he did not think it was fair to accept all the prizes given out for power that week in the majors.

No sooner had he accepted the prizes, trophies, awards, and "small honoraria" (checks ranging from $500 to $1,500 in U.S. currency) which were all presented in New York after the Philadelphia series, when he was summoned to the home office of Heller Bakeries, Inc. The Baron wanted to see him. He was flown specially for the meeting, that is, separate from the rest of the club, who would be playing their next series at home, in the same town that contained Heller's pretzel kingdom.

Chapter Thirteen

"My dear Potter Cindy," Mr. Heller began. Hartman had warned Potter that the Pretzel Baron had occasional spells of long-windedness. He could deliver a lengthy monologue about some obscure point or issue, which had full meaning only to him. It usually meant he felt he was being cheated. It was almost as though Heller believed that if he talked about it long enough the thief or cheat would suffocate under the sheer weight of the verbiage. "For several weeks now the daily news has been dominated with reports of your skills at the bat and in the field. This has apparently attracted the attention of the Goliaths and Beanstalk residents of Enterprise eager to see you beside or hopefully sucking, munching, or crunching their Lilliputian wares. And who, who, my dear young Potter, can blame them? However, most men, given a choice of several little evils, will choose the least. You seem to have chosen all of them. How many stones did David fling, my boy?

"Stones, that is, gems, all look much the same to the layman. Therefore, how are you to decide of those put before you which is the most precious? The answer is that you cannot. You must turn to that stone which will not allow you to leave its presence. That stone is myself. I do believe you have a contract with an organization of mine, a professional baseball team, and as part of that contract you are required by law and gentleman's agreement to fulfill your part of it. I have had my attorneys go over the small print of that contract with an electron microscope to see if they can discover cuckoo eggs anywhere in the document that allows you to be shared by a candy with a hole in its middle, a second-rate chewing gum, or an idiotic children's breakfast cereal. . . ."

"I didn't read the contract, Mr. Heller," Potter said. Potter could feel himself getting unpleasant vibrations. He didn't like the man to use words to make him seem a fool. But he had to practice control, he told himself. Control was important. If he could control himself in these unpleasant face-to-face things, maybe he could control the "duster."

"The human," Heller rumbled on, "I've read in a scientific journal, seems to be unique among newborn animals in being able to be very much aware of its environment even before it has the skill to explore it. You are, my boy, an excellent example of the human beast. In a very short time you have mastered the quickest routes to Madison Avenue and Wall Street. Not only that, we have in the team's publicity department several mail bags containing epistles from fans informing us that they have named their pets after you. You are the namesake, my dear boy, of an Airedale, fifteen turtles, an iguana, eight cats, a boa constrictor, and a rhesus monkey. And an epidemiologist in town is happy to announce that he has persuaded his colleagues to name a virus which causes a new form of foot-and-mouth disease after you, *Potterus Cindis.*"

"That's overwhelming, Mr. Heller." Potter knew he was being taken for a ride in a wagon full of words. He wished this man would stop talking. His right hand formed a fist, but he opened it. It would be out of the question to haul off and poke the owner of the club.

"Overwhelming? Why, my boy, let me quote to you from your epidemiologist admirer: 'Biologically, the new virus is a gut organism which escapes and causes disease in other tissues. At the moment it seems to be attracted to pigs. It remains to be seen if the virus will maintain its exclusive preference for swine or whether it will appear in some other pen.'

"Now, why did I select that particular letter to read of all those which we had to choose from? Oh, I did mean to say that on our club the publicity department screens all the mail sent to players to spare you boys the effort of sending signed photographs to your admirers. We pay the postage. I only tell you that so you will not suddenly feel that your privacy has been invaded. Some players are touchy about that. They still feel that there is a sanctity to unopened letters. However, I can tell you, having had an amanuensis ever since I could clutch a Crayola, that it's a lot of liverwurst. A letter only has meaning if it's from the Internal Revenue, a stock broker, or an attorney. Now, where was I?"

"I'm not sure I know, Mr. Heller," Potter said.

"Not sure you know? Potter, my boy, when you have had time to consider, I'm sure you will realize that we must begin, you and I, to consider our contract and to fulfill its terms."

He held up a pretzel. "I hold in my hand one small pretzel. Note that it is in the shape of a bat. I would be most pleased if you would present this pretzel bat to our customers. Can you bring yourself to please me as you have pleased Life Saver suckers, Cap'n Crunch munches, Double Mint chewers?"

"Wasn't I allowed to accept those prizes?"

"You were not."

"I didn't know that was in the contract."

"You can make a very nice living if you stick to pretzels. Have you ever eaten a Heller pretzel?"

"I didn't take notice of the brand name, sir. But I've eaten pretzels in my time."

"Well, Potter, my boy, if they were very good, we made them. Next time you bite into a pretzel that is as a pretzel should be, you can rest assured Heller baked it. We are the world's best bakers of all things baked."

"Right," Potter said.

"You're a man of few words. I don't admire it especially, I simply acknowledge it. They say you speak with your bat. That has my full admiration. Arrangements will be made for your cooperation on the Heller commercials."

And with that, F. M. Heller dismissed him.

It was only hours before that the Pretzel Baron had managed to control his need to ramble on about every little thing under his barony that made money, or caused money to be lost, squandered, or misdirected. The reason for his aphonia was that he was briefly distracted by a gonadal problem called intercourse.

Mr. Heller once made himself a gilt-edged promise that under no circumstances would he allow himself to consider business or finance during sex. Some pleasures require reverence, silence, total absorption, he had said.

It was only the noises of making sex that could be heard as Mr. Heller and a luscious lady advertising executive, a beautiful young thing who handled the Heller account, were wrapped in a wordless embrace. It would be unfair to say that just because Heller did not think of Dow-Jones averages or pretzel futures while enjoying the thrusts of passion, the woman who clung to the pleasure of his silence was without thoughts of futures of her own. She was, while in the bedroom of F. M. Heller somewhere in the Midwest, on her way to New York, Madison Avenue. It would be Mr. Heller who would take her there, in a moment of passion. Or if not the Pretzel Baron, perhaps some young and handsome superstar of the Redbirds would drive her on the strength of his desirability as a subject for advertising testimonials.

Heller rolled off finally, wheezing a bit from the superb effort.

He looked satisfied, as did the young woman. She was, of course, not so ambitious that she could not find the practiced skills and kindnesses of a rich older man pleasurable. She was only twenty-five. Mr. Heller, after all, had heated many young girls over a slow oven, just as he had ordered his pretzels baked. They were done to a turn, the pretzels and the young ladies, when he finally turned off the heat.

"Samantha," he said, coming from the bathroom where he had gone to empty his bladder, dressed in a toweled robe as thick as a book, "we are in the middle of something wonderful . . . ." My god, Samantha thought, the old fellow's going to get romantic.

"It is time," Mr. Heller went on, "to abolish all that wasteful recording of how my pretzels stay so unsoggy from factory to mouth. The entire world is already aware of that fact. It is important, I grant you that, but it is getting tiresome to our eaters. We must now turn our attention to ways in which we can deliver our unsoggy, crispier pretzels to our kind customers. It is not enough to say that they come to the customer packaged in this easy-open, self-sealing box. We must hand it over to them personally, open their mouths gently with a kiss, put the pretzel in, and ask them to enjoy it. The best way to do this is to collect a team of the most beautiful people in our universe and have them take the pretzels around personally. But as my heirs would curse my soul for such extravagance, we must, Samantha dear, find another way . . . ."

Samantha knew he would finally tell her what he had in mind, but she said, to help along, "Through advertising, F. M., television advertising, it is possible to get the most beautiful people in the world into millions of homes."

"Mirror, mirror, on the wall, who is the fairest pretzel seller in the world?" he asked, a huge smile spreading across his round face.

"We can get anyone you want, F. M.," said the naked Latin beauty on the bed.

"Not anyone, my dear; it must be a person connected to me, to Heller Bakeries. This used to be a family business before I became a conglomerate. It must be a great beauty or great hero and it must be part of the Heller family."

"You have someone in mind, F. M., don't you?" Samantha said without hating herself.

"Indeed, my dear, I will give you three guesses and if you don't get it, I will fire your employers, thereby dumping my advertising agency. You will, of course, lose your job, and that will serve you right for trying to make me out a fool. However, I think I have the power to persuade you to remain as my friend. Now, let's have the first guess—"

"Do I really have to guess?"

Mr. Heller smiled. It said she did.

But Samantha was not a Wellesley girl for nothing. She made her first guess. "Herbert Zarember!" This made Mr. Heller laugh so much it pained. But it worked. He withdrew the other two guesses, thereby sparing her employers.

Her role was secure in any case, or so she thought.

"Do you know who I have in mind, my dear?"

"Of course," she said.

"Who is it?" He got back on the bed, next to her. "Here, my pretty smart little Spanish head, whisper it into my ear."

She whispered something in Spanish, and Heller roared his pleasure. She said, "The old, lame, blind grandmother of Whitey Knocthofer."

"Closer my dear, but still not home. I will spare you. Potter Cindy. He's the one."

"Is he to sell the women, the men, or the kids?" she asked.

"All, my dear. He will sell all. I never order three martinis when one will do."

Potter Cindy, she thought. He will do. She had not seen him in person, but the photos of him were enough. He had very marketable looks: Mr. America, color his eyes blue, suit size long, sexy in a bathing suit, too, no doubt, shy and gentle, nice man. A guy like that, she thought, could take a smart girl to the top. It's probably why that skinny little starlet of his had tied him up to a contract. She must have some sense, thought Samantha Cabodario. Mr. Heller gave him a contract, too, and a bonus of $40,000, but he doesn't get to sleep with him, though she knew F. M. would find a way to screw him on the commercials.

"Perfect," Samantha said, though she was thinking that the American hero bit was old-fashioned, but if F. M. wanted to use Potter Cindy that way, she'd go along.

"What took you so long to say it? What were you brooding about?"

"I wasn't brooding. I was thinking."

"My dear, at twenty-five, you are capable of giving a man pleasure, you are capable of whining, of being irritating, of being fun, of complaining, of rejoicing, of brooding. You are not capable of thinking. Philosophers think. Beautiful twenty-five-year-old advertising executives brood. There is a distinction, but it may take you another twenty years to realize it." Mr. Heller was not angry, he just liked to hear himself express things.

"Do I get to do the commercials?"

"Of course, my child. And you had better do some very good ones or I will relieve those fairy employers of yours, Messrs. Yorktown, Class, and Gently, of the burden of handling my commercials."

"They are not all fairies," she said, unkindly, really.

Mr. Heller showed no jealousy. He was curious to know which of her employers was straight, as none of them seemed firmly committed to displaying overt masculine tendencies. He was too smart to ask or to allow himself to appear curious.

"Gently's not homosexual," she volunteered.

"I did not ask you, but I appreciate the intelligence and your confidence in me. I promise not to tell a soul." Mr. Heller said this with good cheer, at least on the surface. One would have had to know him better than Samantha Cabodario to know he was moderately upset by Gently getting a taste of little Spanish pretzel. The only hint she could have had of his displeasure, if she were an acute observer, was that Mr. Heller always brought up schemes for making more money when he was unhappy.

"You're an advertising specialist, of sorts, Samantha dear. I'd like your opinion of whether or not you think people can be persuaded to bury their dead in mausoleums rather than in cemeteries."

"People can be persuaded to do most things, F. M. You just have to make it seem chic and fashionable."

"I hope you are correct, because you may soon have to get up some chic and fashionable commercials on getting people to give their departed loved ones a vacation at the Holiday Inn of the dead. You see, my dear, I think it will be the thing of the future. I have begun construction in select cities here in the Midwest on high-rise mausoleums. They will contain twenty stories of crypts, which will be able to accommodate up to one hundred thousand loved ones in each and every structure."

"You're not serious."

"Of course I'm serious. Do you realize how much money is spent in this country each year on funerals? Do you have any comprehension of what I would be turning over just in land values alone? Don't bother your pretty head with the figures. Just believe me when I tell you that it takes about fifteen acres to build a hotel catacombs. It takes about one hundred ninety acres to bury one hundred thousand people in the ground. Why, I'll even get government grants from the White House ecologists. There's a man on the President's staff who has assured me that the government will find a tax shelter for me if I turn over some of the land saved to the government for national parks."

"You're not fooling! You mean it."

"Of course, my dear." Mr. Heller peeled off his great robe. "I'll bet I'll make several million dollars." Samantha took hold of his privates. It was not a new experience. Still, she had never held so very much money in her hands.

Chapter Fourteen

Potter was made to feel by the Pretzel Baron that he had done something dishonorable in accepting those promotional prizes. He really had not known that he couldn't take the Cap'n Crunch trophy or the rest. They appealed to him; he wanted them, not for the money, for the gag of it. It was true that he had not read the small print of his contract. He should have asked Hartman or Mayknoll about whether he could or could not legally take the prizes. Why hadn't he? He thought about it a moment with some discomfort. He knew that there was the possibility that he would have been told that taking promos was illegal or scorned upon by the front office. He didn't want to hear that. He wanted the awards. He knew that superstars on other teams took the awards. He knew also that their contracts probably permitted them to accept outside promotions. He was glad that he had not let that car dealer in Atlanta give him that Gremlin. He wondered if he should get himself a good lawyer who could field Mr. Heller's contract knuckle balls. He was probably in trouble with Mr. Heller now. How bad would that be? Oh, screw it. He'd make himself available immediately for the pretzel commercials. That should quiet Big Daddy Heller. He knew the Pretzel Baron was eager to get the commercials done because Mr. Heller had ordered his secretary to be sure and give him the name and address of the advertising agency in town that would be handling the commercials. He had the piece of paper the secretary had given him. He fumbled in his pocket for it. It contained the names of the people and company he would have to work with: S. Cabodario, V.P., of Yorktown, Class, & Gently, Inc.

Though Whitey had called batting practice for early the next day, which meant 11:30 A.M., Potter thought that he could still go to the advertising agency the next morning, get the business part of his contract rolling, and still get back in time to make practice. He had never made a commercial before, but he figured that TV commercials would not be very much different from accepting a promo award. Flash bulbs would pop, cameras would roll, he'd read his lines, and that would be it. He remembered that Johnny Carson had done a commercial live, without preparation, just reading from what the TV people call the "idiot cards." Everything the person had to say about the product was printed in very large letters on big cards and all one had to do was read.

Potter was ready for the advertising agency at 6:00 A.M. He had not slept well again the night before, though he had rested as best he could in between a dozen showers. Sissy was not expected back until the next night. Potter missed her. He needed to see her again, maybe he'd even tell her about his duster, that personal problem that always knocked him down, the "pitch" he could not get away from without having to hit the dirt. Then, maybe if Sissy wasn't too upset, he would have the duster off his chest, and maybe, just maybe, he'd sleep through the night again.

At a civil hour of the morning—at least for Potter—the outfielder presented himself, at 9:01 A.M., to the receptionist of Yorktown, Class, & Gently, Inc. S. Cabodario was not yet in, he was told, but she was expected.

"She, huh? My paper just said 'S. Cabodario.' I didn't realize S. Cabodario was going to be a woman."

"The S is for Samantha," said the receptionist. She was a pretty girl who looked either half-Mexican or half-Pueblo Indian.

"What's your name?"

"Oh, why don't you call me T. Moon?"

"What's the T for, Tomahawk?" Potter asked. He was smiling, showing he meant no hostility.

"No, Tiana. But you're right. I am an Indian."

"I'm from New Mexico," Potter declared. "What kind of Indian are you?"

"I'm from New York," she announced, "Southampton, Long Island. I'm a Shinnecock Indian, at least half."

"What's the other half?"

"Oh, I don't know," the girl said, "Irish or Black or French. My mother gave me different stories, depending upon how it suited her."

"Well, anyway, your mother gave you a nice name. Is Miss Cabodario an Indian too?" Potter inquired politely.

"Samantha Cabodario is a Spanish princess from your home state, Mr. Cindy." She hesitated for a second, and Potter figured he had been rude to ask and she was ruder to answer, but he didn't particularly give a damn. He didn't really care about the Spanish princess or the Indian girl. But the receptionist with the nice name was here and he was waiting for Miss Cabodario anyway. . . . "She was born in Santa Fe, went to some college and was graduated with honors, she says. She is considered very beautiful; she's twenty-five years old, unmarried, and a bitch."

"I guess you don't like her," Potter offered.

"She's all right," the Indian girl said, having already scalped poor Miss Cabodario. "Most people think she's great. The bosses, Mr. Class, Mr. Yorktown, and Mr. Gently, think she's the most intelligent woman they have ever met. The owner of your team has called her a genius."

Potter remembered the battery of words Mr. Heller threw at him yesterday. He thought that the Pretzel Baron's conversation with Miss Cabodario would probably require a translator just to get the gist of the exchange.

Then, in walked Miss Cabodario, and Potter figured that the only exchange worth noting between Heller and the Spanish princess would probably be the grunts of screwing. She was very beautiful, and tall for a woman, about five-feet-seven, Potter guessed, dark hair that fell lightly on her shoulders, green eyes, colored like spring outfield grass, and an upper deck with standing room only. She wore a short skirt that packaged a behind so breathtakingly it was a lethal weapon for a person with asthma.

The receptionist introduced her to Potter.

"So you're Potter Cindy," she said. "You wear number 49. You batted .414, hit 43 homers, 19 triples, and 28 doubles at Bougainvilla. You attended the University of Arizona, and come from my home state." Miss Cabodario was a regular little Guinness *Book of Facts*.

"I guess you've been expecting me."

"I was, but not today, and not in the office. I thought we'd have dinner together and talk about the plans for the Heller Pretzel message. It seems to me, Mr. Cindy, that you have a game today, don't you?"

"It's a night game. I thought I'd spend the morning making the commercial. I hate to have it hanging over my head."

"I hope you're not going to be too compulsive about it. It isn't a thing we can finish in one day."

"Well, how long is the thing going to take?"

"About two weeks of your time here and there, I would estimate."

"If it's going to take that long, we might as well get started, don't you think?"

She smiled at him. "You have a very nice face. Very much more sensitive-looking than one would have guessed from your photographs. You've got the look around the eyes and mouth of a man who suffers, feels."

She was not Potter's type, though certainly few men would

116

have the courage to admit that. So the outfielder was cool and, therefore, said the very thing, perhaps the only thing, that drew her interest, at least more attention than she was willing to commit.

"Funny how you lose a couple of days' sleep and it takes the laughter out of your face. Maybe insomnia becomes me."

She smiled again. She saw he had more to say.

"I can't sleep anyway and we've got a night game so I'd just as soon get started with the commercial."

"Well, we can't really get started, Mr. Cindy, just like that. But, perhaps we could begin with a cup of coffee."

"Would you mind very much if we had the coffee at Heller Park and we talked during practice? I mean, if we're not going to do the commercial now, perhaps we can get the preliminaries out of the way while I'm taking batting practice."

"Mr. Cindy, I have a job here. It's full-time. I'm on the staff. I just can't go out to Heller Park and talk to you while you take hitting practice. I don't think my boss would be too delighted."

"Mr. Heller sent me here, gave me your name, anyway."

"Mr. Heller, Mr. Cindy, is not my boss. I recognize that Mr. Heller is the boss of many things, including a super-rookie outfielder, but Yorktown, Class, & Gently, Incorporated, is an independent operator. We merely represent Heller Bakeries in radio, TV, and print."

Potter saw she was beginning to get her Castilian bull riled up. "I'm sorry. I don't know anything about the advertising business. I was trying to say that Mr. Heller felt he had my services on these commercials coming to him and, if he does, I wanted to get them over with—"

"A commercial is not a home run, Mr. Cindy. Your presence at the bat does not assure us of delivering a big advertising socko, cleanup shot."

"I guess you better call me, then, Miss Cabodario. I apologize for the misunderstanding."

He turned to ring for the elevator, remembering first to

say good-bye to the Indian girl and Miss Cabodario. He got into the elevator and waved so long.

When the door closed, the Indian girl mumbled, loud enough to be heard, "I sure wouldn't mind being caught by him, even in the outfield."

"Miss Moon, mark this day on your adobe wall. This may be the only time you and I will agree on anything in our lives," said Samantha Cabodario.

Potter decided that the only time he got any pleasure was in a baseball uniform. If his face showed sensitivity or suffering, he thought, it probably came from all the damn hours he spent in his life *not* playing ball.

From his meager experience (the Heller swine remarks and Miss Cabodario) he considered advertising an unpleasant business. Actresses were supposed to be sensitive and irritable, but Sissy was as tough as barbed wire compared with the knitting-wool temperament of advertising career women. He was not unsympathetic to Miss Cabodario, he figured she had to deal with the Hellers of the world, as he did. The choice in both their cases was theirs to make. Only he *had* to play ball. If he had not signed with Heller he would have had to sign with someone else. And maybe that person, or corporation or bankbook, would be an even bigger pigpen that kept swine in spike shoes (or so Heller would call ballplayers). Miss Cabodario did not have to be an advertising lady. She could have been anything she wanted, he supposed, what with all she had going for her. Sissy had once told him that she disliked people who bitched about or were envious of other people's gigs.

"Let each guy get his piece," Sissy had said with a twinkle, "and fuck it. It's all set up for the big guy, anyway. If you get your little cut, why should you give a shit? You think this country has gotten big and strong and inhuman worrying about the right of things? That's plain pigshit. Strip a man down and you'll see all the balls are the same. Put the pressure on, the squeeze on, and they'll all go running off making excuses for theft, lies, even murder. Just say 'Gimme' and you're making all the sense you'll ever need in this world."

Potter arrived late at Heller Park, but Whitey pretended not to notice. The manager of a professional team had to look the other way, as much as it might hurt him, when a slugger—rookie or not—was batting over .400. Whitey felt confirmed in his judgment of letting over-sleeping dogs lie when he watched Potter stroke the ball over the fence repeatedly in batting practice. Potter had never been to Heller Park before. It was a big park, a synthetic field, but made for him. The ball was said to carry well, especially in rightfield, the usual landing strip of the Potter Poke. Of course, as the ball always carried well when Potter poked it, the glorious wind currents of Heller Park for left-handed hitters may only have been a lot of hot air, or at least a rumor that could not be proven by Potter.

"How do you like home court?" Hartman asked Potter.

"Not much different from the three other major league parks I've seen," Potter said casually.

"The difference is, the fans love us here."

"Guess so. Hope so."

"What'sa matter? You lost your glow, Potter. You still having trouble sleeping?"

"I didn't get very much last night."

"Sissy back?"

"No. Tonight, I think. Where you bedding down in town?" he asked his roommate; somehow it had never occurred to him to ask Hartman before.

"Oh, I have an apartment out at fashionable Westlake. That's where all the swingers stay. We have lots of little get-togethers. I was thinking of asking you to come over last night, but I know you haven't been sleeping so great, so I thought I better not ask old Potter. If I knew you weren't going to sleep anyway, I'd have had you over. We've got a day game tomorrow. Why don't you and Sissy come over around 9:15? That's when things start to move."

"When?" Potter asked.

"Any night you say that we have a day game," said Bobby. "I'm always ready."

"Remember Zarember," Potter said. He was swinging a bat beside the batting cage, waiting his turn again, as was Bobby Hartman.

"Believe it or not, Zarember is married to a very nice lady and has two nice kids. He never bugs us in town. You can get drunk or smoke pot or jerk off, as long as you do it on home turf. Zarember's too busy here in town being a husband and father."

"Any of the other guys going to be at your place?"

"Oh, sure, Mayknoll, Brossi, Swaps Flattery, Sum Co Kay. . . ."

"Sum Co Kay . . .? Who's that?"

"Oh, that's Mayknoll's Chinese acupuncturist. He brings him along to all the parties."

"Mayknoll's what?"

"His acupuncturist. He sticks needles in him to help Mayknoll control the pains in his arm. Mayknoll says it's better than whirlpool, ultrasound, and aspirin put together."

"Has he got a needle to let a guy get a little sleep?"

"If you fall asleep at the party I'll get Sum Co Kay to stick a needle up your ass. How come you didn't ask me who Swaps Flattery was?"

"I don't know. Sounds like a ballplayer," Potter said.

"Yeah, or a trade," Hartman said smiling. "Swaps Flattery is the swingingest dame in town. That's my girl."

"Why, you little devil. . . ."

"Hey, didya get to see Mr. Heller? He's something special, isn't he?"

"He's long-winded, but he makes his points."

"Yeah, eventually. What's he on to you about? Or is it personal?"

"No. He wants me to stop being a pig and get on with his Heller Pretzel commercial."

"Well, you're in for a treat, boy. You are going to meet one of the most beautiful, intelligent dames in the entire city...maybe even the state...and maybe even all fifty states."

"I met her. I know who you mean, Miss Cabodario."

"Yeah, man. They say she's got a cunt that looks like candy and smells like an English garden."

"She's a nice-looking woman."

"You know, you're the most blasé man I've ever known."

"Except when I sleep."

"I'd swap Swaps Flattery for her in a minute."

"I wouldn't swap Sissy."

"That's different. Sissy's your wife."

"Not much different. I bet you've probably known Swaps Flattery longer than I've known Sissy Lindmore. And I thought you just said Swaps was the swingingest—"

"So what?" Bobby snapped. He was thinking, *Why must this prick point out the right of a situation?* "The whole damn world doesn't have to be good."

Potter was called. It was his turn to swing. "It's my turn to hit, Bobby."

"Big deal. So what?"

"Well, I think I'll park one way out in rightfield for all the poor ladies in the world you've screwed and left, Bobby."

"Why don't you park one up your ass?" Hartman was a fairly healthy boy. He was smiling. He would be hitting next.

Potter drove the first batting practice pitch into the rightfield seats. He called to Hartman. "Bobby, are you watching?" Potter waved the bat back and forth.

"Yeah, unfortunately."

"I'll tell you what I'm going to do for you, roomie. Because

I love you, I'm going to invite the one and only S. Cabodario to your little shindig."

Potter drove the next offering into the stands again. Without looking at Hartman, he said, "Bobby, are you still listening or have you fainted?"

"I'm listening. I'm listening."

"You're going to have two of the hottest numbers in town in your little apartment and you're going to get a chance to romance them out of their shoes."

"Some chance! The place is going to be full of vultures known as Redbirds."

Potter drove the next pitch to deep centerfield. "You are going to have to make yourself stand out, Bobby."

Potter's next two swings were vicious line drives over first base—two two-base hits in any ball game. "I do believe it's your turn to hit, Bobby."

"Get out to the wall, Potter. Because you are going to need a head start to snare my shots."

"If you put one over my head—and I'm not going to play you deep—I'll ask Miss Cabodario if she wouldn't mind going out with my roommate. I'll tell her that she better be careful with you because you're a better runner than you're anything else and if you get a charley horse, it could blow your whole professional career."

"You know, Potter, for a rookie you take a tremendous amount of license with the good nature of the veterans on this ball club."

"I'll be waiting out in short center, Bobby. Try to reach me. There'll be a big prize waiting."

"How do I know you'll deliver?" he called to Potter, who had started his long stride to centerfield. Potter came striding back; he stopped in front of Hartman and whispered in his ear.

"You only have to look at the season's statistics to see that's what I do. I deliver." Potter had the decency to keep the bluster private.

Hartman managed a tremendous drive to centerfield that Potter caught up with on the dead run and squeezed before it hit the ground.

"Too bad!" he yelled to Hartman as the infielder took up his position.

"She wouldn't have come to the party, anyway," Hartman yelled back.

"You'll never know, will you, Bobby?" Potter was pleased; he felt that he was coming out; he saw himself changing.

Potter strode around the outfield gathering in flies, scooping up grounders, pulling down line drives. He was a delight to watch. Even Herb Zarember, who observed from the dugout, had to admit to Whitey Knocthofer, "I don't like that Potter Cindy personally. I get bad vibrations from him. But you got to believe he's as natural out there as stink is to French cheese."

Whitey was revolted by the analogy, but didn't say so. It was enough for him to watch Potter Cindy and thank the heavens over major league baseball that had sent Potter to him. There was nothing stinking about his centerfielder. He's ripe, but that boy doesn't have a stink in him, Whitey knew.

In the outfield, Mayknoll took wind sprints and watched the graceful rookie settle under the ball and take it as though it had been attached to him from the very beginning. Peeve Borkowski, now the rightfielder, watched with admiration. And Peeve was no slouch as a fielder, Mayknoll knew.

"Hey, Potter, miss one," Mayknoll called as he jogged by. "I'd like to give Borkowski something to tell his children."

"He could tell them about your pin cushion," Potter said smiling. "My whole life is snaring these fly balls. I won't drop it if I can catch it, even for a gag."

"What didya mean, pin cushion?" Mayknoll wanted to know. He stopped his wind sprints, puffing.

"Sum Co Kay, that Chinese guy."

"Jesus Christ! Is nothing sacred? You mean to tell me everybody knows about my acupuncture treatments?"

123

"It's nothing to be ashamed of, Mayknoll."

"Doc Hardy's going to be upset. He's worked like hell on my arm. I don't want him to think all of his medical training has been a bust."

"If he can't do the job, Mayknoll," Potter said, mocking Zarember's nuance of speech, his Chihuahua snapping, "we'll have to replace him with a Chinaman." ·

Mayknoll laughed. "How'd you find out?"

"Oh," Potter said, "it was the last thing Dr. Hardy said when he packed his medical kit and bid his final good-byes with tears in his eyes. Defeated, finally, by a needle. You could understand."

"You know," Mayknoll observed, "you're a swinging menace in a baseball uniform. When you die, boy, I'm going to bury you with that number 49 on your back right out here in centerfield."

"Are you coming to Hartman's party tomorrow?"

"Sure. So's my acupuncturist."

"You expecting to pitch?"

"Boy, you don't pitch at that party and somebody's going to stick his wang up your ass in the shower."

"I'm coming with Sissy."

"It don't matter," Mayknoll winked. "Just as long as you do."

"Get out of the way, Mayknoll. Here comes a long hit." Potter bumped him and sped after the fly ball, hauling it down just in front of Tony Baymane, a relief pitcher, who looked relieved.

"Why didn't you catch that, Baymane?" Mayknoll called out.

"What're you, crazy, man? You take that cat's balls away and he might kill you. I don't fuck with fly balls, anyway." Baymane was from Carolina, the rice capital of the East. He was the color of wild rice. "Look it there, Mayknoll, that boy knows how to handle them so that they don't hurt your hand. You see how he jus' glides up to the ball and wraps it in cotton? Now, why would I want to get in the way of anything that pretty?"

Mayknoll only had to look at Potter to see he was enjoying himself. Though Potter was having trouble sleeping, he was an awake, and alert fielder. He caught the ball just the way Baymane described and flipped it softly in the air for the relief pitcher. "Here," he said, "I think you can handle this one, Baymane." Baymane gloved it and handed it back to Potter. "Here, boy, you peg it in. I can't throw that far. It'll hurt my arm."

"Hey, hold it fellows, there's Whitey saying something. But I can't hear him." He yelled to Hartman, who was closer. "What's Whitey saying, Bobby?"

"He said, 'Stop fucking around, and do your wind sprints. Baymane too,' " Hartman told Mayknoll.

"What's he saying about Potter?" Mayknoll wanted to know.

"That he should, and I quote, 'let them cocksucking pitchers do their sprints.' "

"Tell him we're in first fuckin' place and we've won every series we've played," Mayknoll answered.

"Yeah, okay," Hartman said. But he returned to fielding grounders quietly, without delivering the message. He wasn't a fool.

"Chicken!" Mayknoll said, more to himself than to Hartman.

Potter came shooting over to pull down a rising liner off the bat of Phil Brossi. "You dig it, don't you?" Mayknoll asked.

"Dig what?" Potter asked.

"You know, this shit we get paid for."

"What else is there?"

In the night game Potter lined out to the first-baseman and grounded out to second in his first two trips to the plate against St. Louis. In his third and fourth trips to the plate

he ignited rallies with two fiercely driven balls to right that
were hit so sharply he was nearly thrown out at first on one
of them. A slower man would have been caught. The team
broke through for six runs in the last three innings and won
its eighth game in a row. Hartman and Brossi homered. It
was only Hartman's second official major league homer. He
hit homers so infrequently that he actually did a little jig
in front of the dugout, he was that pleased with himself.
When the dance was done Potter got up to shake his hand.
"Bobby, that was a nice shot. Congratulations. You know
who is sitting in Mr. Heller's box?"

Bobby looked up, "Oh, my God, it's her! Miss Cabodario."
She was smiling that smile of hers and looking at Bobby.
He tipped his cap to her. "Potter, you sonofabitch, you did
it. You invited her to the party."

"Not yet. But I will, I promise."

"When?"

"Right after the game."

"Maybe she'll leave before you get a chance," he said anx-
iously, encouraging him to strike immediately.

"Don't worry, Bobby. I'll call her up, then. Relax. We
still got two innings to play."

"Don't forget, Potter, okay?"

Potter nodded.

"Tell her the party is a get-together of friends to teach
the art of making haggis."

"Haggis?"

"Lissen, that's a terrific line. I always tell dames I'll teach
them how to cook up haggis whenever I'm trying to lure
them to my pad. The broads that have heard of haggis or
tasted it are interested in learning how to make it. And dames
who don't know what it is are eager to find out. It always
works. I always make it a rule to have stuffed derma sent
up from the delicatessen, so it's not entirely unfair."

"Stuffed derma—?" asked Potter.

"No wonder you're such a good ballplayer. You've never had indigestion from stuffed derma, I see."

"What do these things taste like?"

"Like a combination of herbs, putty, and cardboard. I went out with a Scotch broad once and she made it for me."

"What do they look like?"

"Like huge poached wangs."

"Sounds unappetizing."

"Still, it attracts the broads. What am I supposed to do, invite them up to show them my jock strap or autographed Louisville slugger?"

"Okay. A haggis cooking party. I'll tell Miss Cabodario."

"Yeah," he said. Then cautioned, "Lissen, don't say 'a haggis cooking party' in an ignorant way. Make it sound convincing, inviting."

"A poached wang that tastes like putty? How am I going to make that sound good?"

"It's the national delicacy of Scotland."

"Big deal."

"Lissen, Potter, take my word for it. It impresses the dames."

"Well, okay. But I think she'd be more likely to come to a regular cocktail party than a haggis roast."

"Don't think, Potter. Just invite her."

The opportunity was there after the game ended, but Potter forgot to ask her. The players had showered and were sniffing around, picking up the scent of printer's ink. With the press huddled around Hartman and Brossi, the home-run hitters, Potter slipped out and headed for his Gremlin, which had arrived from Atlanta and was parked in the players' parking area. The team equipment man had given Potter the keys, which he said had been dropped off by the delivery man. Potter was eager to get back home because Sissy was expected that night. She was probably there already, waiting for him. In the parking lot, he saw Herb Zarember getting into a big coffee-colored Mercedes with Miss Cabodario. Zarember signaled, or waved. It was, Potter knew, his invitation to come over. And as he had promised Bobby that he would offer invitations to a haggis baggis, or whatever, he obeyed.

"Potter, you know Samantha Cabodario, I think." Potter nodded. He could not invite her at that moment because Zarember was there.

"You doing anything right now?" asked Zarember.

"I was heading home. Going to try to get some sleep."

Zarember scowled. "Yeah, well, why don't you come along with me. I'm dropping Samantha off at Mr. Heller's place so that we can go over the campaign—advertising, I mean—I realize the word campaign means a pennant fight to you, Potter." Zarember smiled insincerely. "Maybe we can line up a schedule for the two of you on the upcoming commercial messages."

"I've got my Gremlin over there. I was thinking of driving to my place."

"That's no obstacle. I'll call the clubhouse and get one of the field crew to drive it home for you." Zarember had a smile that was about a millimeter away from a sneer.

"I'm expecting Sissy. She's coming in from Los Angeles. We haven't seen each other for a while."

"You can call her up from Mr. Heller's place."

Potter checked his wristwatch. "It's 11:10 now, Mr. Zarember."

"So what? You're not Little Red Riding Hood, are you? You don't have to be in bed before midnight."

"I think you mean Cinderella," Potter corrected. He thought one of the guys had told him that Zarember stayed home with his wife and kids when the Redbirds were playing at home. Why was he here bothering him?

"Let's not turn this into a children's literature quiz. We've got business to finish." Zarember fumbled in his pocket for his antacids.

"I don't mean to be discourteous to you both, but I'm going to pass up this trip. I'm kind of beat."

"Potter, Mr. Heller wants the arrangements made today. He sent me and Samantha, er, Miss Cabodario, to the ballpark to get the thing rolling."

"Samantha will do," she said. "Potter and I met earlier in my office."

"That's right. And I tried to get things rolling, but you balked, Miss Cabodario, said it would take time, or something like that."

"I did. And it was true. These things do take time. But I have to try harder when the client says so." She smiled at Zarember.

"Right," Zarember said. "That's good advice. Never win an argument with the boss. Mr. Heller wants us to get together. So why don't we sit down and set a date?"

"That's fine with me," Potter said. He waited for them to set a date.

"No, I mean at Mr. Heller's place."

"Why can't we set it right here?"

"In a parking lot?"

"I don't mind," Miss Cabodario said. "After all, it was me who put Potter off to start with. . . ." Then she looked at Potter. "You were ready. I'll attest to that."

"No. That's ridiculous," Mr. Zarember insisted. "Mr. Heller wouldn't want us to schedule a commercial costing millions of dollars in the ballpark parking lot."

"If the commercial is going to work it'll work if we schedule it in the stadium lot, or in the oval office of the White House," Miss Cabodario pointed out.

"Lissen, I don't deal with Mr. Heller on these creative terms," Zarember said. "I happen to know that he doesn't like baseball deals or arrangements settled in parking lots or in the bleachers."

"I'm agreeable to most anything, except tonight. We only met by accident, anyway. If my car hadn't arrived I wouldn't even have been here."

Zarember turned to Miss Cabodario. Looking apologetic, he said, "He's a great ballplayer, even though he's full of a lot of useless observations."

"They make sense," she told Zarember. "Why don't you and Mr. Heller and I fix up something suitable and see if Mr. Cindy can fit his time in?"

"Of course he'll fit his time in," Zarember snapped like a little patent-leather-haired Chihuahua.

"Is that agreeable?" she asked Potter.

"Whatever you decide," Potter answered.

"I'll call you tomorrow, Mr. Cindy, if I may."

"You sure can," Potter said to her, turned, and headed for the Gremlin.

Loud enough for Potter to hear, Zarember told Miss Cabodario, "It's a lousy business, this baseball, especially my job. I'm forty-two and already cooking eighteen ulcers. You have to deal with these young people, these great talents. They're either brainless, thick, stubborn, or resistant. I hate young men. They annoy me!"

"They say," Miss Cabodario offered practical philosophy, perhaps not taught at Wellesley, "all businesses are lousy. People who run nursing homes are fond of the young and can't stand the old."

"Yeah, I guess so," was the last of the conversation Potter overheard.

Potter was handed a telegram from Sissy when he arrived at his hotel. "Delayed, due to fear of breast cancer. Doctor said no. I'm okay. Fine. Don't worry. Hit homers. See you tomorrow night with love and kisses." Later, without Sissy's love and kisses, he tossed and turned in his bed, still unable to put two consecutive hours of sleep together. He sweated,

130

probably from fatigue and irritation with Zarember and Mr. Heller. He was glad that Sissy was okay; he had been so distracted by his own problems that he never even thought to ask Sissy how she was feeling or if she was worried about anything. I've got to start picking myself up and taking a look around me, for Godsake! On that note, Potter fell asleep, at last.

Chapter Fifteen

The dreamer was annoyed by the three barking dogs near the batter's box who were distracting him from the pitcher who was about to throw the ball toward the plate. How could he hit with the dogs snarling, barking, and growling? Who let them into the ballpark, anyway? Why didn't the ump hold up the game and get the damned dogs taken away? He stepped out of the box and appealed to the home-plate umpire. The man in blue did not see any dogs. He asked the first-base and third-base umpires for a ruling. They did not see any dogs. Potter yelled, called them "blind sonofabitches." *Three blind mice*, he thought. *Deaf too*. Couldn't they hear the racket the dogs were making? The pitcher had delivered the pitch and the home-plate ump called him out on strikes. He complained that he was out of the batter's box, that it was not a legal pitch. But the umpires did not listen; they could not hear him. The fans started to shout him down; they called him a sore loser. He was furious and, when the dogs attacked him, he started beating them with the bat, crushing their skulls. . . . He was jolted awake by the police siren in his telephone.

Trembling with the sudden call to consciousness, he heard a voice ask him if she had awakened him, when they could get together to talk about filming the Heller commercial, and if she could apologize for the "destructive" attitude of Herb Zarember.

Still, she had awakened him, kindly it turned out. He answered all he had to say in three, small, sleepy sentences—all that he could manage at that moment. "Yes. Tonight. I'll pick you up."

Miss Cabodario waited for more. Surely, he had to say where he would pick her up and when. Potter said nothing further. How many people in deep REM (Rapid Eye Movement) sleep, unhappily dreaming, abruptly hit with the bucket of ice water known as the phone, or the alarm, would have been prepared to deliver the Gettysburg Address? Maybe she understood. Miss Cabodario was prepared to help.

"But where will you pick me up, Potter? And at what time?"

"At your office. After the game. 6:30? We'll talk at Bobby's place." This time he managed four sentences.

She assumed Bobby's Place was a new swinger restaurant in town. She did not know it. How could she know that this was the way Potter Cindy would invite someone to a party at Bobby Hartman's apartment?

"Have you ever been to Bobby's place?" He didn't think so. Bobby was just too beside himself with the hope of getting his wang into Miss Cabodario. But he thought he would ask her, just to make certain Bobby had not been putting him on about her. He sensed that some of his teammates considered him unsophisticated, probably because of his bumper sticker and because he rarely used profanity and wasn't always talking about "balling" and "stud trips."

"No. What's it like?"

"I don't know. I've never been there either. Bobby's serving haggis tonight. And he's also going to teach people how to make it."

"Sounds absolutely stinko," she joked, meaning the odor of steaming haggis. Potter missed it. "Oh, I doubt that," he said. "It should be lots of fun."

"I think you're still asleep. See you tonight." She hung up.

Potter was not aware that Samantha Cabodario had designs on him more primary than the pretzel commercial, that it excited her to call him, that she got a kick out of reliving the adolescent pangs of trying to capture, if only for a moment, the most desirable boy in class—the four-letter man. He did not know that she was touched by the suffering in his face, and thrilled, even before it thrilled her, by the grace of his body. He had no idea that she thought it would be fun to be chased by him, caught, and gently bifurcated.

Chapter Sixteen

How many people actually believe that just the thought of a person three thousand miles away can produce the body?

Potter was idly soaping in the shower, thinking that he must remember to leave a note for Sissy, reporting Bobby's address in case she got back in time for the party. He missed her. He even wondered briefly whom she was cussing out in old Californayeh.

"What are you doing, jerking off in there...?"

He turned the shower off for it did, indeed, sound like Sissy Lindmore. He cocked an ear. "Wait a min. Don't waste it! I'm stripping down. I'll be right in," she said.

And in she came, sliding a little on the soap, her hand already making the catch.

"My God, it's you."

"How many millimeters is it from soft to firm?"

"I haven't got the slightest idea," Potter said. "But don't let that keep you from finding out."

"We have to establish a base line sometime, Potter." She concentrated, as usual, on her clinical investigations. "Do you abuse yourself when I'm not...?"

"How've you been, Sissy?"

"Hungry. I missed you. You didn't hump anybody, did

you? I don't mind your giving yourself a quick hand job in the shower, but keep it strictly solo or I'll sleep with every-body on the Redbirds on the pitcher's mound in Heller Park."

Potter wished it could all be that simple, that he could have sex with another woman and then get it off his chest, or whatever, by confessing it. His was, he knew, not a problem he could discuss with other men or with women. "The duster" would hardly bring sympathy, or leave a man with respect he could regain if he announced one fine day that he had stopped masturbating in front of little girls.

Men are not prepared to listen to what turns on another man unless it relates to orgies with babes, not little girls. Impotence, at least temporary impotence, would be a smaller hurdle, he was certain. Women, many of them, would be understanding, at least they were on occasion when the pres-sure of a pennant fight or championship left him flaccid. He had never been the kind of man who "knocked off a broadie" during a traffic jam on some superhighway, anyway. No woman that Potter had made a relationship with ever thought he was a super stud. He did what he could, when he could, more or less, and they either accepted it or not. It was usually the woman who was more intelligent than he who was willing to give it a whirl and put up with his occasional failures. Of course, he never told anyone about "the duster." But then, he couldn't really believe that they told him about their per-sonal problems, either.

He remembered reading an item in the newspaper that said most married women, during sex with their husbands, thought about doing it with someone else or daydreamed about being in less wholesome sexual situations. Some women imagined that they were being raped or gangbanged or cornholed and what have you. Potter understood. It didn't upset him. He was, at that moment, in a shower with a sexually easy woman, a wife he loved, who was practicing one of her skills of being able to bring the best out of a man, even if he was not easily aroused.

136

"Potter, without a calipers, I'd say you had the stretching power of 106.39mm. beyond limpness," she offered. She was on her knees looking up and she appeared, with the water beating down on her and an odd smile on her face, like a naughty child. Potter took her to bed and told her that he loved her, and missed batting practice. He had forgotten briefly that he still had that "duster" hanging over his head.

Potter did not play well that afternoon. There was something about the day that did not bring out athletic excellence. It was cloudy, and cold, and it rained in dribbles now and again, like the piss of a poor fellow with an enlarged prostate. Oh, he delivered his timely hit in the third inning to ignite an anemic rally which finally produced a run, but he played uninspired baseball. Yes, the records will show that he cleanly fielded the four balls hit to him in a losing effort. But they were routine flies, and the only way he could have missed them was if someone had taken a high-powered rifle and shot him from the roof of one of the high-rise apartment buildings adjacent to the ballpark. At that, he was draggy getting under the balls, as though the sniper on the apartment roof had missed a vital organ and shot him in the behind instead. He felt as though he had lead in his pants.

Feeling graceless out there in the outfield, uncomfortable, clumsy, Potter began to sweat nervously. He had a horrible thought that his baseball skills were beginning to leave him. Maybe all his old ways were going. His career would be shot, even the old "duster," maybe that would go too. He could not imagine a life in which he was not a ballplayer. The thoughts so terrified him that he found himself running away from the ideas, with nobody at bat and no ball in play.

"Hey! Time out!" Bobby Hartman yelled to the second-base umpire when he saw Potter steaming toward them. "Something's up with Potter Cindy. Probably blew a tire." That was Redbird talk for a broken shoelace or a torn webbing on a glove.

"Hey, Potter! What's up?" Bobby asked the outfielder.

It was only then that he was brought back from the terror.

Potter thought fast, but not intelligently.

"I don't have my sunglasses," he answered.

"Sunglasses? Shit, man, it's raining! They ought to call the game. Sunglasses! You can carry optimism just so far, you know."

Potter smiled weakly and ran back to centerfield. But the outfielder's sudden fifty-yard dash brought Whitey Knocthofer out of the dugout. "What's the trouble?" he yelled in the direction of second base.

"He forgot his sunglasses," the umpire said. Whitey thought he was being put on, but as Potter was back in position and the fans were mockingly applauding him, Whitey returned to the bench, shaking his head.

The bench-warmers wanted to know what was up. "He thought he had to take a shit, but it was only a little fart," Whitey said, while the Redbirds in the nest of the dugout chirped their hilarity. Whitey thought, *What's going on with that kid? He's late for batting practice, comes running in for sunglasses in the rain*. He made a mental note to ask Potter after the game if there was anything bothering him.

When Whitey came to look for Potter later on, the sensation was on the phone with Sissy trying to explain why he could not escort her that night to Bobby's because he had to take an advertising woman, Samantha Cabodario. Of course the explanations were rather fractured and set in a cast of secrecy to throw Whitey off, who was standing within earshot. Potter could only speak in the most guarded sentences, because midweek parties did not delight the organization, especially after losing efforts on the ballfield. Despite what Hartman said about doing anything they wanted at home, he knew no club was that relaxed.

"Sissy, I can't have dinner with you because I have to see this woman about the commercial. You'll have to go to the restaurant yourself."

"What fuckin' restaurant are you talking about? I thought

the party was at Bobby's apartment. And how old is this woman who sells pretzels? And what's she look like?"

"Sissy, what does her age and looks have to do with any of it?"

"Oh, shit, that's why everybody loves you. You're so innocent you're practically a saint. Didn't you learn about the birds and bees at the University of Arizona?"

"I was on a baseball scholarship, but that didn't free me from taking the required courses."

"My darling, I'm not talking about required courses. I'm talking about sex and fucking."

"Sissy, you don't understand. This is a commercial relationship."

"Commercial relationship, horseshit! She's got a cunt, hasn't she?"

"Sissy . . . *Jeez!*"

"Okay, I'll smell her out tonight and let you know if she's in heat. You want me to take a cab to the party? I ain't proud."

"Sissy. Tell me you're kidding."

"Oh, Pottsie, can't you tell I'm just trying to swell your head? You think of yourself as a non-stud. But you're oozing with appeal. I've decided to give you the kind of picture of yourself that you'll need to face the world properly. You can't go around not knowing that a woman is aware of her body and feelings long before you start getting itchy. Why, Potter, what if we bust up, who'll take care of you?"

Potter got nervous. "I hope this isn't one of those long-winded type good-byes."

"No, dummy. It's a long-winded way of telling you that I love you and if I catch you screwing another dame there's going to be hell to pay."

"Good. See you tonight."

Whitey was so engrossed with trying to piece together the conversation, he forgot what he wanted to ask the outfielder when Potter hung up. "Did you want to see me, Whitey?"

139

"Yeah, but I forgot what it was."

"I'm sorry I missed batting practice."

"Oh, yeah, that's what it was. What's going on? Why'd you miss batting practice? And what the hell were you doing running in for sunglasses when we had the lights turned on so that we could see when to swing?"

"Well, I overslept and I guess I was still sleeping out there in the outfield in the sixth inning, thinking or dreaming that I better get my sunglasses."

"Well, let's try to wake up from here on before batting practice. And stay awake till the game's over!"

"I've got no quarrel with that, Whitey."

"Now, I couldn't help overhearing about you and the Mrs. a little while ago." Only Whitey Knocthofer would call Sissy Lindmore *the Mrs*. "And if you don't mind, kid, I'd like to give you some advice, though it's none of my business. Wives can be a pain in the ass. You mustn't let them get you down. Understand? I really believe that my wife was like a chronic sore arm to me. I think she shortened my career. All that nagging and bitching about doing this and doing that, staying with one team, living the right kind of life, and all that other bullshit. It's murder for a ballplayer. Who's got the time to think about all these little shitty things when you gotta play ball every day? So what did I do? Everything she wanted. I even quit playing before I was really ready so that I could prepare myself for a career with the Redbird organization. And what did I get out of it? My kids who had it soft with an old man bringing home good pay, my kids who lived in a nice house and always had money in their pockets, my kids who didn't have to jump from town to town because I made sure the ballclub kept me . . . what did they do? Both of them dropped out of some knucklehead college in their first semester and are bums somewhere—one with the Maoist Legion or something in California, and the other putting out for every jerk-off with a beard and crabs. That's what I got out of it, listening to my wife.

140

"Lissen, I know you two are newly married and stuff—my wife was no slouch in the sack when we were young; she was the homecoming queen of Ashtabula High School, that's in Ohio; she knew how to please a guy. But don't take what they tell you too deep, you know? That's what screws you up and it ain't worth it."

Whitey was not telling Potter this to take the pressure off his star rookie. It started out that way, but by the time he got himself wound up he felt that the kid was too nice to con, and he understood that he told Potter the truth as he believed it, not as a baseball manager but as a friend. "Don't let the Mrs. get you down with any crap. And listen, if you gotta make it on the side, too, then you have to keep it cool. Of course, if she's cheating on you, you got every right to hump whoever you want."

"It isn't anything like that, Whitey. Sissy's just a little upset about that advertising lady, I guess, that Miss Cabodario."

"Yeah, well you can't fault her on that one; she's a good-looking curve. I wouldn't mind taking a shot at that myself. But watch your ass with her. I hear old man Heller's dipping into that."

"You know, Whitey, there's something about a good-looking woman that brings out a whole lotta rumors and guesses and wishful thinking about her sex life."

"Yeah, I guess you're right. Hey, I saw Herb Zarember with her yesterday. You think he's getting it?"

This was the first time Potter saw Whitey as a person and not a manager. He wanted to give him something as a person and as a manager. "I think if they took a poll of the team, 95 percent of the guys would rather see you making her than Zarember, that is, if she was available for making. It's very hard to believe that any woman could actually love Zarember."

"Aw, he ain't all that bad." Whitey said that as a matter of form, but Potter could see he had accepted the compliment to him as a genuine expression of feelings. "Hey," Whitey said, "what about the other 5 percent?"

"Nobody's perfect, Whitey."

Whitey knew he wasn't. He could remember dozens of times that he had yanked a pitcher too soon, or benched players out of irritation rather than for real errors or slumps. Those done injustices might vote against him. He quickly calculated what 5 percent of a twenty-five man roster would be and he came up with 1.25 men, which he took to mean one guy with .25 percent more resentment than the others. But as a manager, he knew that every man on the squad, except maybe Potter, bitched .25 percent more than they had a right to for every damn reason under the sun. *You're not using me enough! You're overworking me! When are you going to take the splinters out of my ass? Why can't I hit for myself? Let me finish the inning, at least!*

Whitey thought about it. And he thought about it some more. He looked at Potter, who waited. He knew that he had been lucky with the club so far. There were no serious injuries. Oh, sure, the club was full of crybabies, complaining about aches and pains, except for Potter, but nobody was out of action. That was important. The sore arms and muscle spasms, the headaches and angry balls, the allergies and summer colds kept nobody out of the lineup. The pitching rotation was in good shape and the guys took their positions each day after Doc Hardy convinced them that their arms, legs, and balls wouldn't fall off if they continued to play.

"I think we're going to win the fuckin' pennant!" Whitey said finally.

"You think so?" Potter asked. It was exciting.

"Don't you?"

"I don't know how pennants are won, Whitey." The possibilities thrilled Potter.

"Well, I do. They are won by a team just like we got. And we're going to do it. We got a good start out of the gate. We're healthy and we can hurt people. We got speed, pitching, and some muscle and the team isn't uptight. That's the formula."

"I hope you told the rest of the club. I can tell you one thing. The guys aren't convinced they're healthy—"

"Aw, crap on that. Nobody's in the hospital. That's what counts."

"Do the rest of the guys know?"

"I haven't told them shit. I want them loose as a goose."

"But you want me tight?"

"No, Potter, I just don't want to worry about you running around looking for your sunglasses every time it rains."

Whitey was back to being a manager. Maybe it was the thought that he could take the club all the way. "I think you might be getting a little too loose." The manager was far away, somewhere beyond, clinging to a thought.

"I've got to leave now, Whitey, if we're done shooting the breeze. . . ."

"Oh, okay, Potter. Sure." The outfielder didn't know that Whitey Knocthofer was having a delusional moment of ecstasy. They were carrying him off the field, a hero in his time. Knocthofer's Redbirds. Manager of the year! The team of the century. After twenty years in the majors, he couldn't think of a better swan song. And then he remembered another thing to tell Potter, a little request from management via Zarember:

"Where's Potter Cindy?"

"I don't know," Whitey said, watching the team work out. "Maybe he got stuck in traffic."

"When'd you ever hear of a rookie missing pre-game practice during the first two months of the season? That Cindy gets away with murder. Every time I want to see him, he's somewhere else. You better discipline him, Whitey. Fine him! Fine the fucker! Otherwise you're liable to lose control of the team."

143

"This is my twentieth year with this club, Herb—"

Zarember interrupted unpleasantly, "What do you want, a set of china?"

"So this is the year," Whitey continued, as though he had merely paused to elucidate his thought. "If I lose, I quit; if I win, I retire."

"Don't forget we've got a three-year contract with you," Zarember pointed out. "We can make you stay after school and write 'I promised to be a good little field general' for two years." Zarember was like a judge who starts out throwing the book at you. Then, depending on the nature of your appeal, he is persuaded to reduce the sentence.

"Herb, you better get off my ass—"

"They pay me to climb up there."

"Okay, Herb, but at least don't jump up and down. Now, is there anything you want with Potter? Or are you just trying to make trouble?"

"We got a call from Our Sisters of Mercy Children's Hospital. They'd like Potter and some of the others to visit the sick kids this weekend. We kind of promised he would. If you see him, tell him he's scheduled there on Saturday morning. It'll be a big deal for the kids. And six weeks from now, we offered his presence to the Golden Slippers Children's Hospital, just out of town."

"Who else should go?"

"Oh, I don't know. Hartman, Mayknoll, Brossi, Condon. Whoever wants to besides Potter. They specifically asked for the kid, so we'd like to produce him. You know, it's good for the children. And, frankly, it doesn't hurt the box office, either."

"Why do you always start out so fuckin' nasty, Herb? Why do you start out blasting everybody?"

"I don't know. Maybe I like it. If I didn't, I'd be in another job, right? I get paid for being what I am. Mr. Heller once told me he wanted the most unpleasant person in the world for his general manager. 'And I chose you, Herbert,' he said. Of course, he was smiling but, you know, I think he meant it."

"If he told me that, I would of spit in his eye."

"Spit in his eye? Mr. Heller probably would of hired you, Whitey. After all, how far is it from manager to general manager? It's at best a psychological difference. And you probably get paid more."

Whitey told Potter, "Lissen, the guys in the front office would like you to visit a couple of hospitals with some of the boys. It's for sick children, okay?"

"Okay. Anytime," said Potter.

"Saturday morning, 9:30. I don't know who else is going but there'll be others. You won't have to go alone. Then in about six weeks the same crew will visit the Golden Slippers Children's Hosptial, it's a place for kids who've had nervous breakdowns. It's just down the road about fifteen miles in a little town called Golden Slippers."

"I don't mind, Whitey."

"Good, kid. Thanks."

Potter felt no concern or nervousness about making the goodwill tours to the children's hospitals. After all, he would have no reason to. He was on top of his problem now. It would be no different from signing autographs at the ballpark for a bunch of kids, a task he had performed for little boys and girls dozens of times without ever having one tiny sexual thought popping into his head. After all, he wasn't a drug addict who had to have a fix no matter who he had to rip off to get it; he wasn't a drunk turned loose in a whiskey bottling plant. What he had was different and he knew it could be controlled. The only other thoughts he had on the subject were that shut-ins, like the children he would be visiting, couldn't get out to the ballpark to see the players and

145

the games. He saw it in part as a kindly gesture of the management to give something to the kids. He didn't mind giving time for that. The other part of it, the box-office crap for management, upset him some. But he let it be, reasoning that the greater good outweighed the bad, or at least in this case.

Chapter Seventeen

In the some nine weeks that had passed since Feets Patrick first entertained the long-shot notion that Potter Cindy was in the vicinity of the "crime" and could leap a school fence, the police officer had dragged his feet about going to the TV station to review the clips. It wasn't that he had dismissed it from his mind for, indeed, at least once every two weeks or so, Feets would think about going to the station to see what he could see. But somehow, whenever he got ready to go, some more pressing police duty would come up.

Feets was in a sour mood. De Kalb County was all fucked up. His department had to break up a demonstration on the campus of Emory University, and one of his overenthusiastic officers had cracked the skull of a second cousin of an important state senator. There was also a burglary on Burton Drive. The local veterinary hospital lost, of all things, a wolf. One of his officers found the animal on someone's property and shot it. Only it turned out to be the people's pet dog, a cross between a Siberian husky and a German shepherd. The only thing that could be said for the cop was that the dog was mean and resembled a wolf.

Feets had his head in his hands when the intercom buzzed.

"Well, what is it now?"

"There's a fellow out here, a truck driver, black man, says

he saw the man who leaped that fence a couple of months back. You know, the child-molester case. Skipton; the Skipton case."

"How long has he been out there?"

"Just a few minutes. Why?"

"Did anyone question him?"

"No, lieutenant."

"Why not?"

"Well, I'll tellya. We were all too busy."

"Get him in here! Now."

Feets questioned the man. He worked for a garbage company. They were picking up around the school area and he saw the whole thing from the cab of the truck. The man was white.

"That's what another witness said," Feets lied. "He was a white man, short, about 150 pounds, blond. Is that the man you saw?"

The man hesitated. "That's the guy you saw, wasn't it?" Feets pressed. The informer looked nervous.

"Well—?"

"No, it weren't," said the black man. "The man I seen was tall and dark-haired."

"What color were his eyes?"

"I didn't catch 'em."

"Was his hair long or short?"

"Huh?"

"How long was his hair?"

The man pointed to the end of his neck with his hand. " 'Bout down to there."

"Was he fat or thin?"

"He weren't neither. He was strong-looking."

"Just what did you see? Tell me everything you remember."

"Well, like I said, I was just sitting there, in the truck, when I seen this man racing across the ballfield. There was a man chasing him, a white man. But I could see that the other man, a big, chunky fellow, wasn't going to catch that

148

first man. I ain't never seen a man moving that fast, so I figured he done somethin' real bad. Then, another man come in a little white car and pick this thick-set fellow up on the field and they start out after the other man. Well, they cut the man's lead down quite a bit, and he was running out of the field, coming dead on a fence. The car was going to get him, for sure, or so it looked. Then the young fellow just got hisself up over that fence."

"You mean he leaped right over a six-foot fence without touching it?"

"It dun seem right, but he did—"

"Could you identify the man if you saw his picture?"

"I think I could."

"It was two months ago. Where have you been for two months?"

"Well, I was scared. It was a white man."

"Okay, you come back here in a couple of days. I want you to look at some pictures."

"I dun know if I can get off from work."

"Come after work, then. Leave your name and address with a policeman outside."

"He dun took it."

"Which one took it?"

"That red-headed man, out on the desk in the front."

"You come back here in two days. Call first. Ask for Red or Lieutenant Patrick. Is that clear?"

The man nodded.

Feets was all set to hustle out to his car and head for the office of the local paper. He needed photographs of Potter. It would be better, he knew, to go to the local TV station that broadcasts the Atlanta games and get the film clips of Potter in action. He'd be able to show the witness action pictures.

The phone rang. Feets picked it up. "What now?"

"Lieutenant, they've trapped that escaped wolf. They got him out in the woods, out near that Baptist retirement home.

They got the woods surrounded. Officer Tommy K. Butler's in charge. Wants to know if he should move in."

"What do you mean, he's got it surrounded? He's only got three men. How can he surround two miles of woods with three men and three Doberman pinschers?"

"Well, he kind of deputized some of the residents of the retirement home. The men, of course. They're out there with broomsticks and shovels and shotguns and rakes all around the area."

"You mean he's got old folks surrounding the wolf? Jesus! Call downtown, Red, and ask them if they'll send a chopper up to spot for us. And let's get our asses out there. If one of them old geezers gets hurt, we've had it."

He dropped Potter, but only for a while. *Shit,* he thought, a wolf surrounded by three dumb cops, a bunch of old folks, and three dumb dogs was a more pressing emergency than a ballplayer who maybe had abused a child.

Red drove, Feets beside him. Red let the siren go full blast. Feets turned it off.

"I thought this was an emergency?" said Red.

"Yeah. But I don't want to scare the shit out of the old folks. Some of them might be asleep."

"I think you're getting soft in your old age, Lieutenant."

Feets ignored the insubordination. He liked Red.

"What the hell is a wolf doing in Georgia, anyway?"

"This vet that runs the animal hospital went on vacation—in Canada, I think, up north, anyway—and he found him up there. The animal was sick or hurt, and the vet took him down here to bring his health back. He was going to give him to the zoo."

"Then what? He opened the cage and gave him to the Baptist retirement home instead," Feets said bitterly.

"It was an accident. One of the handlers didn't lock the cage proper, and the animal just hightailed it."

"Beautiful."

When the squad car pulled up Feets saw the old men hunched over, ready, their knuckles white on their clubs, rakes, broom handles. Some held small-bore rifles, one man had a BB gun. They looked uneasy, nervous.

Feets got out of the car and approached Officer Butler.

"We're ready to flush him out of there, Lieutenant."

"You are, are you? I want you to flush out these old folks. Escort them back to the retirement house."

"We won't have enough men to cover the area," Butler protested softly.

"I've called for a helicopter from downtown. The pilot will radio down to us if he breaks out."

"I think we can use the old folks. They're ready, willing, and able."

"They're shitting in their pants. Take them back and make sure they stay indoors. Where are the dogs?"

"We sent them in." Butler pointed to the woods.

"Alone? Without rifles behind them?"

"Yep. They're killers, sir. They probably got the wolf already. We heard a racket a while back like they cornered him. But it's been quiet for the last ten or fifteen minutes."

"Shit! Get the old fellows out of here, now!"

Feets ordered the two remaining policemen to take up positions on the road adjacent to the wooded area. He told Red to enter the woods a mile away from the spot that he would go in. The chopper was now overhead. The pilot reported that he was in position to see the entire area.

Feets told Red, "I can only give you one piece of advice. If you lose your weapons and you come upon the wolf, try laying on your back and exposing your neck. I read that wolves are supposed to be honorable. They don't kill anything that voluntarily surrenders, unless they're starving."

"Thanks," Red said bitterly. "I can't wait to try that trick."

The two men went in. Feets, moving gingerly, his eyes everywhere, seeing nothing. He had his service revolver tucked into his trousers belt, and a shotgun across the crook of his arm. He picked up a trail of blood in a clearing and followed it, while his head moved like he was watching a tennis match on the ground. He felt strongly that it was dog blood, even though the dogs were specially trained to control their barking. Then, he spotted the body of one of the dogs. Its leg had been broken and its throat ripped out. Twenty feet away was the body of another Doberman. The same pattern: leg broken, throat torn apart. He found the third dog dead from multiple bites of the head and neck. Its legs were intact. Feets saw how the wolf polished off the three "killer" dogs, the pride of the De Kalb police force, terrors to student demonstrators, but lambs to the wolf. The wolf handled the dogs by breaking the legs of two of them first, then killing the third in a straight fight, then returning to kill the two remaining crippled dogs one at a time.

Feets heard a shotgun blast and hustled for cover in front of a tree, facing the direction of the shot. He brought his rifle to his shoulder. Red had found the wolf. From the noises he knew that Red was driving him toward Feets. He was either a smart cop, that Red, or a good hunter. The wolf broke into the clearing. The animal didn't see him. Feets watched him take up a low position, ready to spring. The animal would have an angle on Red if he broke out of the same spot in the thicket. Then, the animal spun fiercely around, growling. The wolf had picked up Feets' scent. The animal charged Feets; it had begun its leap. Feets, without hesitation, blew its head off.

The Lieutenant ordered that the bodies of the animals be taken to the local dump, a land-fill project, and left there.

Feets told Red to get a ride back to the stationhouse with Butler. He was taking the car into town to try to get hold of some photographs. He planned to go to the television station that broadcasted Braves games.

He drove downtown rapidly. There was other work to be done.

Feets was out of his jurisdiction in downtown Atlanta, being a De Kalb and not a Fulton (downtown Atlanta) County policeman. Still, in Atlanta, a police lieutenant is a man of authority. When he asks a question, most people answer without being mean and before they ask about constitutional rights.

So Lieutenant Patrick had no trouble getting hold of old film clips and stills from the sports and news department of the local TV station. What were TV executives supposed do. . . to plead that they had a right to protect old film clips? Even regular newspapermen on the *Constitution* could be slapped in the lockup if they did not reveal news sources to special authorities—*Constitution* or no constitution.

Feets didn't even pressure anyone. He simply let his identity be known and the TV station was "pleased to help in any way possible."

One of the more ambitious TV executives asked, "I hope there's a story in it for us—"

"Well, I can't tell until I study the films," said Feets.

"You're welcome to use our equipment and screening room if you want, Lieutenant Patrick."

Feets accepted the offer. It would facilitate the matter; otherwise he would be forced to go to the police laboratories, make out 431 requisitions, and still have trouble finding someone to man the equipment. His case was hardly what you called priority. It would take him three weeks before he ever got to see the films.

"How does Potter Cindy enter into your investigation? That's a story right there, you know—"

"Can I speak off the record for a moment?" Feets asked him.

"Oh, sure, Lieutenant Patrick."

"Well, then, I have to tell you Potter Cindy doesn't enter

this at all. I'm trying to make a suspect who was in the center-field seats when Cindy played here last. That's why I want to see the film clips on Cindy during that series," Feets lied. *Screw television.*

"I see," said the TV executive, "I hope you make your man." He used the police jargon for recognize, spot.

Feets thought the TV executive was a horse's ass. "Who said I was looking for a man?" He looked at him, blankly.

"I guess I'll leave you to your work."

"That's mighty nice of you."

Feets was taken into a "quiet" room, past three teletype machines, which clattered away many of life's daily dilemmas in between attacks of mechanical, monosyllabic asthma or snufflins.

In the quiet room, after reviewing the film clips, Feets considered the possibility that Potter Cindy could have jumped the fence at the Briar Vista School; the outfielder had the speed to outrun Dave Skipton's Volkswagen on a short haul, and had the power to slaughter three dogs with an ax handle. He would have liked Skipton to take a look at the films, especially the ones shot behind the outfielder, so that Dave could see if the man he chased and Potter Cindy had the same stride. Dave would be able to recognize a running style. Wasn't he a gym teacher and a former track man himself? Cindy seemed to fit the physical description supplied by Dave; he was tall, evenly built, had longish black hair.

There was a hitch in bringing Dave down to the studio—if you told Skipton anything in confidence it was just like putting out a four-points bulletin and simultaneously releasing the name of your suspect to the city editor. Feets wondered if the TV station would be willing to do up a two-minute montage of Potter Cindy running. He'd ask the station to blank out the ballplayer's name and number 49 on his uniform before showing it to the witness or to Dave.

He didn't want to give that much away. Nearly everybody

who followed baseball in Atlanta knew that the only season statistics departments that Potter Cindy wasn't leading in, Hank Aaron was. Dave Skipton was a baseball nut, and a diehard Atlanta fan. If Feets left the name and number on Cindy's uniform, Dave might just say Cindy was the man he had chased so that Feets would arrest him and Aaron and Atlanta would have the statistics and the league lead. Atlanta was trailing the Redbirds by three games with no one else in the division even close. Potter Cindy had become a face on several thousand buttons and tee shirts sold in stores and at souvenir stands at the ballparks. He was, of course, one of the pictures on the bubble gum cards. On the bubble gum trading market, a kid with a "Potter Cindy" who was willing to trade it could get five cards for it. Dave Skipton was not the only person in Atlanta who saw Potter Cindy as the man keeping Atlanta from the championship. It would only be a guess, but many a baseball fan or chauvinist Atlantan would not mind Cindy breaking an ankle or a wrist. They liked him well enough not to want him shot, but they wouldn't mind if he accidentally got a little hairline fracture that took six weeks to mend. Maybe his witness had the same feelings.

Feets was a baseball fan himself. It occurred to him as he watched Potter Cindy on film that he might be fixing on this poor bastard because Cindy could leap a fence, run fast, had power, could hit, field, steal bases, and generally was a painful raspberry on Atlanta's hip. Cindy played his best ball against the home-town hardball club. Feets was disgusted with himself; he had always felt strongly about professionalism. Lieutenant Patrick never consciously let his prejudices interfere with his duty. He would diagnose evidence carefully, judiciously, not letting himself lean the scalpel of an investigation against, say, a black man who was an acknowledged cancer even by his own community but whom Feets knew to be innocent.

One would have to say Feets was a typical red-blooded

American Atlantan. He was thought of as more *macho* than not, if an Atlantan could be so described. He did not play around on the side, but he was active sexually, liked hunting and fishing, had no use for criminals or cheaters or brutal men. He was made uncomfortable by exotic behavior. When he was on duty during the time some of his officers hauled in a hostile, little, square-set redneck who had lured a homosexual to his apartment and then had beaten him up, Feets took over the questioning from his men.

"Just a second," said Lieutenant Patrick, "I want to talk to this fellow." Then he turned to the arrested man. "Are you a fag?"

The man's red neck got redder, but he said nothing.

Feets went on, "I've heard it said that people who beat up on fags are either fags or are afraid of being fags. And I think that describes you."

The redneck started to curse Feets.

"Listen. You listen! If one other word comes out of your mouth I'm going to take you out back and kick your goddamn ass in. You just listen! I know you're a fruity-tootie, a secret one. But that's your business. You go ahead and sleep with anybody who is fool enough to want you. But don't you ever beat up on anybody in this county—man, woman, or child. 'Cause if you do I'm going to stick this gun up your ass and pull the trigger. Now I'm ordering you held till that poor man comes out of the hospital and decides if he wants you put away permanently."

Feets was a professional. He had a job to do and he did it as proficiently and as honestly as he could. He knew Potter Cindy was a professional too. He remembered seeing a game sent back from Heller Park to Atlanta. The Braves were losing 11-3 with two out in the home half of the eighth. Potter Cindy was the hitter. He bunted. One would think he was trying to close out the inning. But no. He flew down the first-base line and beat the throw by a step. That was the kind of ball-player Feets Patrick admired.

Feets looked unhappy in the TV screening room. He knew he was just wishful thinking, hoping by some unprofessional intuitive nonsense that Potter Cindy would suddenly walk into the station house, give himself up, quit baseball, and leave the pennant to Atlanta. *Jeez, am I a bushleaguer!* thought Feets. He returned to police business when the cameraman asked:

"You want to see any of this stuff over?"

"No," said Feets. "Thanks anyway. I'll just take some clips and stills with me if I can."

"Sure; we'll get you copies. Now I guess you want the shots looking at Cindy with the centerfield stands behind him."

"That'll be fine."

Feets drove home, called Red, told him to get the eye witness down to the station tomorrow morning.

Red told Feets that Butler had asked permission to bury the Doberman pinschers out behind the police target range off Briarcliff Road. "I gave him permission. He felt strongly about not throwing the dogs in the dump."

"One dump is the same as the next, I guess," Feets said. "What about the wolf? Where's Butler going to bury him? In the station house?"

"He skinned him, Feets."

"Jesus. Jesus X. Christ."

Feets hung up, kicked off his shoes, plopped down on the couch, and took a nap. He awoke one hour later in a sweat. He had dreamt that he took a high-powered rifle up to the stands of Atlanta Stadium, zeroed in on Potter and, when the outfielder turned to face him, blew his head off.

Chapter Eighteen

Dave Skipton was sitting in the waiting room of his wife's employer, Dr. Berlin. He had said that he would pick her up when she finished work. Dave had to go to see his bone doctor who had an office just down the road from the dermatologist. The gym teacher didn't look too happy. He had been told by his orthopedist all along that the leg fracture was not healing properly and that if the leg wasn't rebroken there was an outside chance that Dave might have a very slight permanent limp. Dave knew it was his fault; he had decided to gamble on the leg knitting together properly. The bone man had suggested that Dave might have lost his bet. Dave asked for the X-rays; he wanted to show them to Feets—not that Feets could make head or tail of them—but he hoped he would be good enough to show the X-rays to the police doctor or maybe the De Kalb County coroner so that they'd confirm or deny what Dave's sawbone said.

Dave was worried enough about his leg to even trouble Dr. Berlin. The dermatologist came out to the waiting room to tell his receptionist something, and Dave said hello when he saw him. It was a glum hello, and Dr. Berlin must have sensed something because he asked Dave if there was anything the matter. Dave told him; then he said that he had his X-rays and wondered if he'd take a look at them.

Dr. Berlin said it wasn't "his area of specialty."

Dave pleaded, and the dermatologist obliged. He told Dave something that sounded like "posterior tip of the medical malice of the haloosus paloosus."

"What's that mean in English, Dr. Berlin?"

"Your orthopedist might be right, but I definitely would get another opinion—not mine. I've only got ranking in the Georgia Society of Dermatologists."

Dave dropped his wife off at home and then headed straight for the police station. He went in and asked for Feets.

Red said he was busy; he'd be tied up for a while.

"I want to leave these X-rays with him. Tell him I'll call him tonight."

"The lieutenant can't read X-rays."

"I know that," Dave said with some irritation, "I want him to ask the police doctor for an opinion."

"The police doctor's busy," Red said, "we can't just hand him your X-rays and say some citizen wants his opinion."

"Why not? I broke my leg chasing a lunatic. I was doing your work—"

"The county salutes you, Mr. Skipton."

"Don't sass me, mister. I'm a friend of Lieutenant Patrick."

"Yeah, yeah, I know. I'll deliver your message, Skipton."

Red personally picked up the garbage man so that he'd be there when Feets arrived to start the day. In the squad car, as Red drove down Ponce de Leon Avenue with the man, he asked, "I know we spread the word around to find eyewitnesses, but it ain't like you people to come forward voluntarily. A black man in Georgia doesn't go out and kill himself to help out the man, does he?"

The man said nothing, so Red dropped it. He was probably in some kind of trouble, thought that if he came forward on this, the police would go easier on him on the other thing. May-be in doing his garbage route, Red figured, he took something else away that wasn't garbage and was worried. Red was a good policeman. He made the witness nervous, but he didn't push him to the point of hostility or resistance.

Feets arrived at the station with an attaché case; it contained the materials the television station had given him. He told Red to have the 16 mm. camera set up in his office. He called the witness into another room.

"I want you to look at these photos and tell me if you think any of them looks like the man you saw running away." Feets had spread before him an array of photos—some were known criminals, others were police officers, others were photos of men picked up for exhibitory acts and child molesta-tion in the Atlanta area. There were also several pictures of baseball players, including Potter Cindy. "Now you look them all over slowly and carefully and tell me when you see the man you saw at the Briar Vista School."

The man went over each photograph methodically. When he had finished, he had selected three photographs of the possible suspect. One had been an Atlanta policeman, killed in the line of duty two years before, the next was a man in the state penitentiary serving ten to twenty years for armed rob-bery. The photo of the last man picked out was Mrs. Patrick's brother, who lived in New Orleans. While the man had not picked out Potter Cindy, each of the photos he did choose bore a resemblance to the outfielder. All of the men had dark hair, blue eyes, and the facial bone structure of the Redbird rookie.

"You didn't look through all the pictures yet, did ya?"

"Every last one."

"There are pictures of other people who look like the three you selected."

"There is?"

"Of course," Feets said, picking up a picture of Potter.

"Here, take a look at this. Doesn't this picture look like the others you selected?"

The black man smiled.

"What are you smiling at?"

The man's face grew serious. "It weren't him," he said.

"Are you sure?"

"Yessir. It weren't him. I know that."

"How can you be so sure? This man resembles the others you've picked out, doesn't he?"

"No sir. That's a baseball player for the Redbirds. His name's Potter Cindy." *Jesus Christ*, Feets said to himself. "Just a minute. How do you know that this man, this baseball player, wasn't the man you saw?"

"He wasn't wearing no uniform."

"Of course not. Baseball players dress same as you and me when they're not playing ball. You don't think they go out to dinner in their baseball uniforms, do you? Suppose he wasn't wearing a uniform. Would he look like the man then?"

"I'm not sure less'n I seen him without one."

Feets got up. "Will you please come with me into this other room? I want to show you a film. Do you think you'd be able to identify the man by the way he ran?"

The man shrugged. It meant he'd be willing to try.

Feets ran the camera. It showed different players on the Redbirds and Braves running.

"Did any of those men run like the man you saw?"

"Them's ballplayers," the man said.

"So what?"

"They all look the same to me. They all runs about the same."

Then Feets remembered a gesture of Potter's he had seen on the TV sportscast. At the end of a run to first base or to home plate—in trying to beat out a hit or in running out a home—he stretched his arms out as though in flight. He couldn't remember if someone else had also told him about that gesture—maybe his son Corey, or one of the men at the stationhouse, or if he had read about it in the newspaper. But he did remember it.

"Now I want you to think back on that man running. Think real hard now. Did you remember him ever stretching his arms out, like this—" Feets demonstrated—"at any time during his running? It's important."

"I just don' remember, sur."

"Think real hard. Did he not put his arms out like that, or do you not remember whether he did or did not?"

"If I don' remember his doing it, I guess he didn't do it...."

"That's not true, mister. He could have done it but you can't recall it."

"I thought that's wha' I done said."

To Feets' mind, the black man had identified Potter. The only thing wrong was that the man hadn't really put it all together yet. The black man would, but Feets had to figure out a way to make it all click in the man's mind. He could see that the case was only going to be resolved with some real leg-work. He had to get to Redbird country, where Potter was, and nose around discreetly. He could make calls up there to the police, but the newspapers would have it in a minute. A police station is a bucket with a hole in the bottom for newspapermen in a big city.

And what if he was wrong? He could be wrong, couldn't he? *Oh, shit*, Feets thought, *for two cents I'd leave right now and give this witness evidence that would clinch it.*

He dismissed the black man, thanked him for his cooperation, and told him he would probably be called back for some further questioning in a few days.

Feets opened the drawer of his desk for no reason at all. He was looking for something, a resolution of the problem, perhaps. He had a box of chocolate Mallomars in the drawer and pulled one out, thinking that if he took a trip to the Midwest he could quietly follow Potter Cindy around for a couple of days, maybe find an answer, a solution. Maybe, if he played his cards right, he could interview some of the players up there. Maybe they'd be able to report on his peculiarities. He popped a Mallomar into his mouth, chewed quickly, and reached for another. He wondered when it was that the Redbirds were due to play in Atlanta again. He got up from his desk and walked quickly out where the baseball nuts, his men, would be able to tell him. Feets went into a coughing spasm when one of the officers said that the Redbirds were scheduled to play in Atlanta in three weeks. It was too long a wait. He wanted the goods on Cindy by then so he could close the case. He expelled whatever was sticking in his craw. He needed the addresses of the Redbirds in their home town.

In better control of his respiratory system, he went back in his office and called a friend of his on the Atlanta police force who was in charge of the squad that protected Atlanta Stadium during games. His friend knew everybody connected with the Braves—secretaries, promotion guys, ballplayers. Feets felt fairly certain that his friend could get him the kind of information he needed—the home-town addresses of the Redbirds.

"If your kid wants autographs, Feets, tell him to wait till the Redbirds come back down here to play us and I'll get him the whole team."

"No, that's not it. I need it for police business. But it's not official. It's kind of my own little investigation right now."

Feets' friend was an experienced cop. "Don't tell me," he said, "that one of these Redbirds knocked up one of our local peaches?"

"Something like that," Feets admitted.

"Who was it? I mean, which Redbird?"

"I don't know for sure yet. That's why I need those addresses."

"You got a description and a name, haven't you?"

"Not really."

"You mean it was rape? One of those Redbirds knocked the dame out and raped her?"

"No," Feets said, "the kid was just too confused to make him. Or doesn't want to say yet who the fellow was."

"Man, the girls nowadays. They'd sleep with anybody in bell-bottom trousers and a flashy shirt and a name. They don't even look at the guy who fucks them. I bet the girl was underage—"

"Yes," Feets admitted that much.

"Well, she probably lied to the ballplayer, told him she was twenty-one instead of sixteen. You know these young ballplayers on the road. They get stiff peckers and sixteen would look like twenty-one even if it didn't."

"Yeah," Feets offered what his friend wanted to hear, "a stiff prick has no time for thinking."

"A stiff prick has no conscience. That's the way I heard it."

"Do you think you can swing the addresses?"

"Yep. But there's twenty-five men on the squad. That's a lot of addresses."

"Start with the starting nine. That will reduce the problem by sixteen."

"I'll call you back real soon."

"When will that be? You see, I'd like to hop on up there and pay the Redbirds a surprise visit."

"Your chief going to let you go sniffing around hundreds of miles away in another state?"

"My chief is in failing health. I thought you knew that. He had a heart attack. I'm running the show in De Kalb till he gets back. I'm Acting Captain. And I think that when he does get back, he'll be on a reduced schedule and I'll be named Captain officially."

"Well, congratulations, Feets. I'm proud of you. But you're working too hard for a Captain, even an acting one. Now, I think I know why you're looking so gray and tired these days."

"When do you think you can get me those addresses?"

"Maybe tomorrow, the next day—"

"Make it this afternoon, okay? I'll really appreciate it."

"Okay, I'll try. You sure do bird-dog a case, don't you?"

"Not every case. The injured party is a friend."

"Do I know the person?"

"No, I don't think so."

"I'll get back to you real quick, Feets. I didn't know it was somebody close."

"Thanks. It will be a big help. It's a ticklish situation."

Feets' friend came through with the names and addresses of the Redbirds that afternoon like a good cop. It was the kind of speed policemen usually gave to one's own chief's request, even if Feets wasn't his Acting Captain. Feets copied the names as his fellow officer read them, only to wind up unhappy.

"Don't you have any others? You only read off the names of eight players. There's one more to go. Their outfielder, Potter Cindy."

"Yeah, well," the policeman told Feets, "he's new this year and none of my sources down here could come up with it, even with connections."

"Why's that? Who's protecting that kid?" Feets asked.

"Well, Feets, everybody is, it seems. Potter Cindy is so popular there that they don't give out his home address. Keeps down the cranks, discourages the nuisances from bothering him. You know, they have some young dames who all but strip a big celebrity of his clothes and give him a hand-job."

"That's unusual, isn't it?"

"Not for a real hot shot, I don't think. Some people can be real pests, ball-breakers," Feets' friend laughed.

"Well, I guess I'll find Cindy when I get up there if I need him."

"Best I can do for you is to call your attention to Bobby Hartman's address. Those two room together on the road, my sources tell me. If anybody can put you on to him, it's Hartman. Hartman's from Atlanta, you know. He's an Atlanta boy. He'll help you out if you get into a bind on anything, I'm sure."

"Hartman's from Atlanta, eh? Well, that's real interesting." Feets set a false trail.

"Yeah, you go to see him first thing and I'm almost sure he'll help you."

"How can you be so sure?"

"Shit, Feets. You ain't trailing Hartman, are you?"

"I don't think so, but you can never tell, can you?"

"You're sure playing it cagey."

"It's only out of ignorance—I can assure you of that," Feets lied, thanked the officer for his help again, and hung up.

Feets already had airline tickets booked on Delta for the flight northwest. He decided, as he drove home, that he would pay Bobby Hartman a visit on his investigation. He might get something out of him. One never knew. His plan was to follow Potter like a bird-dog for a couple of days and hope something good would come of it; then maybe he'd pop in on Hartman.

When Feets got home, he lured his wife to the sack, slept with her slowly, showered, dressed, picked up his bag, and drove quickly to the airport, siren silent. He had told his wife he would try to get back to sleep with her in two or three days, four at the very latest.

Chapter Nineteen

Only Feets and ardent Redbird watchers in the Midwest, where the Redbirds nested, would recall a small item in the gossip column of a local paper that whispered, "Which popular, handsome athlete was seen in a swinging pub with the most sexy account executive in town, rumored to be a favorite of a well-known businessman?" In case anybody missed the references, two paragraphs beneath that item appeared: "Actress Sissy Lindmore, wife of the sensational Redbird rookie, Potter Cindy, arrived in town today to find her slugger not at home because he was preparing a commercial for Heller pretzels. . . ."

The Midwest columnist did not also report that Potter Cindy was at Samantha Cabodario's posh apartment a few minutes after leaving the swinging pub with her.

Potter had no qualms about going into the apartment of Miss Cabodario because the last thing he expected her to do was try to make out with him. She was just too cool and sophisticated and smooth, he thought, to let herself mix pleasure with business.

So when she went into her bedroom to "get the office grime off," he settled into her couch with a bottle of beer and listened to a song called "Rocky Mountain High" and thought of home.

The song was a natural for her to have in her record cabinet because she was, originally, like Potter, a wide-open-spaces person herself.

"One day he got crazy," wailed the singer, "and tried to touch the sun. He lost a friend but kept a memory."

The song made him think about New Mexico—more—it made him long for the silence of its mountains and deserts, where a man, alone, could be free to go crazy and touch the sun, to lose his cool, and afterward remember it not as something embarrassing, but something he did one day without thinking of the consequences and without the newspapers and the thousands of fans there to remind him that he did it. Out there, he thought, with no one watching, you were free to make a mistake, to lose control.

Samantha had showered, wrapped herself in a thick Martex bathrobe, and seated herself beside him. No words were exchanged when she realized he did not wear any underwear. He was grateful that all she really required was to touch him and be touched. He made a note never to let her take that long a lead again.

It was perhaps Potter's instincts for knowing when a base was won and when to hold a throw that kept the game from getting out of hand. It could have been disastrous. Maybe it was that moment in Samantha's living room that led to the creation of the Heller pretzel commercial which introduced to the Redbird home town and the surrounding midwestern states the baseball pretzel bat, the Potter Poker. The commercial showed Potter swinging the big pretzel bat, Redbird fans will remember, and saying, "Drive 'em in with one of these. It's a Hellerva pretzel." It was local but it sold the product. Maybe if other things had gone well, the commercial would have gone national.

It could be that in the commercial which was conceived by Samantha, after plumbing the thoughts of Mr. Heller, she had expressed her admiration for Potter as a sweet, tender human being and a man with a bat.

If Potter only petted Samantha, Sissy almost deflowered her, if that were possible, later that evening at Bobby Hartman's party.

Chapter Twenty

If Feets had caught Braniff flight #135 out of Atlanta instead of Delta #315 for the Midwest, he might have met Braniff head stewardess Swaps Flattery that much sooner. As it was, they met two days later in the lobby of Bobby Hartman's apartment building. Feets saw the tall blonde approaching and, as the regular doorman had conveniently stepped out for a quick beer-and-a-ball at a nearby lounge, Feets opened the door for Swaps in the doorman's stead.

Earlier, using a couple of smooth, softly delivered but well-directed questions, Feets determined from the doorman that Hartman, the Redbird second baseman, did indeed live at the address supplied by Feets' fellow Atlanta peace officer. And, furthermore, that the Redbird infielder was having a party that night and if he stood around, he'd get a chance to see all or most of the best ballplayers on the team.

Feets thanked the man, said that he sure would like to see the ballplayers, and tipped the doorman five bucks. It pained him to have to pay for that kind of information but *What the heck . . . that's how it goes sometimes.*

While he kept the building under surveillance for forty-five minutes, he saw more than the doorman had promised—not only the best Redbirds, but also their chickadees. They all rang bell 6E, labeled Hartman, waited for the buzz of recognition, and went up. He had seen Potter Cindy go up with a real looker, a dark bird that would knock the normal man out of his composure. The woman was not Sissy Lindmore; he had seen her go up ten minutes before them.

Feets was eager to get into the party himself to confront Potter Cindy, but no opportunity seemed appropriate. He gave some thought to the idea of trailing in on the back of some guests, but the tactic made him uncomfortable. So did the thought of just knocking on the door and brazening it out.

The tall blonde seemed like a possible answer to his problem. She was unescorted, and he moved quickly to serve. Feets was lucky. The real doorman's name, which she knew, was Patrick, Patrick O'Ryan, and Feets Patrick just happened to look very much like a certain Ellis N. Mitchell, who not only distinguished himself as the ace pilot of Braniff's mighty fleet, but also as the first flyer in the fleet to have integrated Swaps Flattery into the intimate connections of airline personnel. Their affair was brief and pleasant, and she still had a fondness for Braniff's dashing eagle, though they were no longer lovers. "Well, hi," Swaps said nervously as Feets opened the door for her. She recovered her composure when she realized he only looked like old Ellis. "Where's Patrick?"

"I'm Patrick. Will I do?" Feets asked. He smiled and she saw he was not as witty as Ellis.

"Thanks for getting the door. Are you going to ring 6E for me, or do I have to do that myself?"

"No; I'm at your service, there, too. You see, I was just going to ring that bell myself."

"You were? How lucky. Are you a ballplayer or a newspaperman?" she asked pleasantly, every bit the airline hostess.

"I'm too old to be a ballplayer, but I do appreciate the compliment."

Swaps liked this Patrick's style. He had a soft southern

accent, a mellow voice, and a charming manner. He was a little grayer around the temples than Ellis and maybe a little taller. Ellis was from Boston and he sounded like the Kennedy family.

"I'm from Atlanta," Feets said, "the name's Craig Patrick."

"Nice to meet you, Craig Patrick. Are you with the *Constitution* or the *Atlanta Journal?*"

"Neither, I'm afraid," Feets said, but offered no more gratuitous identification.

Swaps wasn't a head stewardess for nothing. She thought she could tell from his answer that he was from a little dinky paper somewhere around Atlanta and to probe further might be embarrassing to the man who looked like Ellis Mitchell and seemed too nice to insult.

"I'm Swaps Flattery," she said, taking his arm, "let's go up to the bash together. All your stories are up in apartment 6E, but don't write anything bad about Bobby Hartman because he's my boyfriend, okay?"

"Okay. Is Swaps your real name?"

"No. I've adopted it. It's Sharlene—with an S—Wila Alice Priscilla Sheila Flattery. I'm named after my father's five sisters. I call myself Swaps after the first letter of each of my five names."

Feets almost told her he was called Feets and why. She was a nice-looking woman. Hartman was lucky. He could go for her himself.

"Flattery, eh? Are you Irish. . . I mean your folks?"

"My great-grandfolks on my father's side, I guess—"

"I've got the blarney in me, too," Feets admitted.

"Do you cover the Redbirds? It's odd that an Atlanta paper would have a steady reporter to cover a team based hundreds of miles away in the Midwest, or is Atlanta playing the Redbirds here in town and that's why you're covering it?"

Feets tapped into his inherited blarney. "I'm not a sports reporter. I'm in advertising, institutional advertising, with

Coke in Atlanta. I'm here to see if I can get some of the Redbirds to sit still for some promotion for children back home. We're interested in Potter Cindy."

"Everybody's interested in Potter Cindy, especially in this city. He's taken the town by storm."

"He's taken Atlanta by storm, too, in a way," Feets said with ever so faint a touch of sarcasm. "What's he like?"

"I don't know. I'm going to meet him tonight for the first time. Bobby—he's his roommate on the road—hasn't said very much about him, except that he was a terrific athlete and a nice person."

"Well, if you get to meet him before I do tonight, or learn anything about him, I sure would appreciate an introduction or hearing the gossip."

"Oh, of course. That's the least I can do for my favorite doorman."

Feets wished, for only a moment, that he was fifteen years younger and free to try to make this woman, even though, after sixteen years of marriage, he still loved his wife.

"Show me the way to Killarney, Sharlene me-darlin'." Feets' southern accent interfered with his put-on brogue.

"Please call me Swaps, okay? I really hate Sharlene worst of all the names."

"Right. I was just being foolish in my old age. I hope you'll forgive me, Swaps."

"You're okay, Craig Patrick."

He wanted to tell her to call him Feets, but he followed her silently to Hartman's apartment. He had a job to do, even if he was dressed in a dark pin-striped summer suit and a flashy tie.

There was a lot of marijuana around. Indeed, one of the key aromatic ingredients in the haggis, or stuffed derma, Bobby revealed, was pot. Almost everybody but Potter was smashed. Potter drank two bottles of beer and tasted a small piece of spiked haggis.

173

Sissy was, Brossi said the next day, "bombed out of her head and really great." It was true, she was the total entertainer. She had the boys and girls splitting their sides laughing, while she related tales of, as she put it, "certain gentlemen who felt they couldn't go on living without first getting into my drawers."

It was while demonstrating how the Italians make a subtle sex overture that Sissy got carried away and goosed Samantha. Miss Cabodario let go a shriek and said something which nobody heard through the laughter. "That was a real cow bite," said Bobby, who yearned to try one on Samantha himself.

Samantha may have been too dignified to goose Sissy back. It was a good thing, Potter could see, because the general mood of the guests was not tight and the party could have turned into a free-for-all ass-grabbing session, the kind that people would hate themselves for in the morning. Some people seemed to Potter already quite intimate; people who had neither mated nor dated before that night.

A couple of the men threw passes at Sissy, but she fielded them with things like, "Would you please take your hand off my ass now? I want to sit down." And "No wonder you can't hit a curve. You reach for it like an old man."

Samantha, seeing Potter alone, nursing a bottle of beer in the corner of the room, came over to see the man who had brought her to this baseball players' benevolent association bash. She saw a look on his face that was either wistful or unhappy, she could not tell which.

"Hello there, date," she said. "We haven't gotten to see each other all evening, though I did run into your wife."

"Yes," he said. "I'm sorry about Sissy getting carried away."

"Me too. You have a very nice attitude about your wife. I really like that. You don't seem to mind her telling the world about her various sexual exploits. You must be very sexually healthy, very confident."

"That's Sissy's way," he said. "She's an actress, you know, and all the sex gags are part of her routine. She doesn't mean

174

me any disrespect, you see." He sounded quite literally proud.

"You're a very nice man."

"Well, thank you."

Sissy had accidentally come up beside Samantha without her knowing it. Sissy was not listening to their conversation; she was engaged with Hank Mayknoll at that moment, trying to tell him that the reason she didn't do a bit on a black man trying to make her was because she did not know the scene, having never slept with a black man. "But don't get uptight. I would have slept with a black guy . . . only blacks never asked me."

Then Sissy turned and saw Samantha with Potter.

"Did you ever sleep with a black guy?" she asked Samantha.

"How many times are you going to try to get away with goosing me?" Samantha asked.

"Now that is an original line," Sissy said. "I think I may even apologize for goosing you to start with—"

"That would be unusual, wouldn't it?"

"If it shook you up so much, why didn't you goose me back?" Sissy asked.

"*Please.* I thought you were going to apologize," said Samantha.

"Listen, girls," Potter said, "I don't think you started off on the right foot. Now, if you're both willing to back up a little and get a fresh start, it might be worth going on with this conversation. You keep going the way you are, you are going to wind up knocking the heck out of each other. Now, I'm married to you, Sissy, and I have to work with you, Samantha. So you're both going to have to settle this thing for me, okay? I'm going across the room with Hank Mayknoll here and when I come back I hope things will be patched up."

"Oh, bullshit. Don't give us that John Wayne big cock stuff. We're not going to fight. We're too much alike. Samantha may be thirty pounds heavier than me. She may have gone to college. She may use ten-pound words. But we both have to hustle for a living, and I think we're a lot alike, Mr. Cool."

Very much to her surprise, Samantha saw that there really was a lot more to both of these people, perhaps even more than she believed she could comprehend. She could see that Potter ran many fathoms deeper than the exposed portion of his iceberg. "He's not only a great young power hitter," she had read a publicity man's description of him in the Redbird yearbook, "but he gets the job done. . . ." That was hokey baseball writing, she knew, but true. He had actually defused the fight that was about to blow with his John Wayne act, as Sissy had called it. Samantha made herself a promise to find out if he did it for her, for Sissy, or for himself.

Sissy was not just a little vulgar twerp. She was uneducated, but she was quick and instinctively bright. She would be no pushover, Samantha saw. Though Sissy was incapable of drawing truly subtle distinctions between them, Samantha still had to admit that she and Sissy were not terribly different. They were both out in the world trying to make it. They were both scrappers. Sure, a girl can sit back and let some man take care of her—both she and Sissy were expert at that—but nevertheless, they went out there every day and knocked their brains out to please bosses or audiences; it took a different kind of woman. Samantha had a terrible distaste for the kind of woman who bubbled with lethargy. She could not deny that sex appeal was part of the weaponry she used, but so were brains and wiliness and competitiveness and the need to be praised.

"You're right, you know, about our similarities—" Samantha told Sissy.

Sissy did not take up the peace offering immediately. She watched Potter move off with Mayknoll.

"Mr. Cool doesn't like scenes, did you know that?"

"Is he very sensitive?" Samantha asked.

"Sensitive," Sissy said thoughtfully, "I don't think so, unless you call avoiding trouble sensitive. He's a very good person, a sweet person, as you obviously have found out, somehow. But he's not all that sensitive."

"He doesn't seem to mind when you do your sex bit. I think that's very nice in a man," Samantha insisted.

"Listen, Miss Cabdriver, or whatever your name is—"

"Samantha."

Sissy had always been brutally funny with foreign names. She called Knocthofer Knockhockey, Borkowski Boardwalk, an admirer of hers named Katzler, Catsloose, another friend, Fanchetti, Fishnet.

"We understand each other. So I just want to tell you something. I'd like to save you some shit. Pottsie's mine. I found him first and signed him to a long-term contract. You've got more chance of getting a hysterectomy than you have of getting him."

"You tend to put things so vividly—"

"I don't believe in bullshit," Sissy said.

Samantha saw this little girl was fresh in ways that called for closer study. She wanted, at first, to give her a good hard smack in the face, but now she saw there was something appealing about her frankness and vulgarity. Samantha was fascinated by her style.

Sissy had to admit to herself that she was jealous of this Spanish bitch, this tamale with a college education. Then she saw Potter across the room, smiling, engaged in conversation by a tall, thin blonde, who looked like one of the Swedish dames in the shaving-cream commercials, and she realized she was doing something with Potter that she could not remember doing with any other man: she was getting to be a jealous nut. *Shit*, she thought, *being married to him was like that beer-hall song; you shut the windows, the door, and they're coming through the floor.*

She resisted a temptation to go over and recapture her outfielder.

Bobby Hartman resisted no temptations that he could help. He saw Samantha and Sissy alone, isolated, for the first time, and he moved closer to the action.

"Well, what'd you think of the haggis?" Bobby wanted to know.

"Thank you for inviting me to the party." Samantha.

"That was stuffed derma." Sissy.

"Sorry. Haggis sounds better, more exotic." Bobby knew he meant more Gentile. "You two have been brought closer together by that cow bite, I see."

"You said cow bite before, I guess you mean 'goose.' Do you?" Sissy asked.

"Yeah, but not really goose. A goose is done more with an extended finger. What you did to this poor lady is kind of grab her by the cheek. We called that a cow bite when I was a kid. By the way, Samantha, I'm glad you're taking it in good spirits."

"I'm still in a state of shock," Samantha corrected. "One never quite takes being bitten by a cow in good spirits."

"Yeah, well, it's nice of you not to raise a lot of hell and screw up the party. I appreciate it," Bobby said.

Samantha managed a smile.

"I'd like to make you haggis sometime," Bobby said. "I mean *real* haggis. Can I call you sometime to see if you have a free evening?"

"Oh, sure," Samantha said, "but I'm not very often free."

'Well, we'll keep it loose then, okay?"

"Okay," she said.

Sissy asked Bobby who the girl and man with Potter were. An older man had joined the two. He had graying hair and was at least fifteen years older than everyone else at the party. The man was dressed in a pin-striped blue suit.

"The girl is a friend of mine named Swaps Flattery. She's an airline hostess for Braniff. I don't know the guy. Swaps found him looking lost in the lobby of the apartment building when she came and brought him up. She thought he was a coach or a newspaperman, I guess."

"I thought coaches and managers alike were to be excluded from this get-together," Samantha said.

"That's right, Sam. Do you mind if I call you Sam? And I'm very glad to hear you knew the brass was not invited. I'll tell ya, I was a little worried you might tell Whitey or Zarember or someone—"

"Why would I do a thing like that?"

"Well, now that I know you better, I don't think you would, really. But I was worried about it after Sissy gave you that cow bite."

"Aren't you in tight with the brass?" Sissy asked her.

"I'm an independent operator. I work for an advertising agency, not the Redbirds. I can decide when to inform, why to inform, and if to inform."

"That's great," Hartman said, "it really is. I mean, as long as you've decided not to inform."

"You're still worried about me, aren't you?"

"I don't trust anyone," Hartman declared. "Really. Ever since I was lost in an amusement park when I was a kid, and my parents didn't even realize I was missing for hours, I've been suspicious of everyone."

Samantha laughed, but Sissy didn't. The image of being lost in an amusement park, an experience she had separately shared with Bobby, was too unpleasant for Sissy. Samantha had never been lost as a child.

"You trust Potter, don't you?" Sissy asked aloud, though she wasn't sure if she was asking herself or Hartman.

"He's the only one. There's the only guy that I know who wouldn't let me get lost in an amusement park."

"If the guy with Potter is not a coach or a newspaperman, who is he?" Samantha asked.

"He's probably a promo guy trying to get Potter to endorse Philadelphia Cream Cheese or something. Potter's coming over now; we'll ask him. Hey, look, the cream cheese guy's coming with him."

Potter came over with Swaps and the man. Sissy eyed Swaps. She saw that the Spanish grape was infinitely more dangerous. Swaps looked more like a bottle of peroxide than sangría.

"This is Miss Flattery and this is Mr. Patrick," said Potter.

"We were all trying to figure out what you do, Mr. Patrick," Samantha said.

"So am I," Patrick said. He had a soft southern accent.

"I told them you sold cream cheese," Bobby revealed.

"He's with Coke in Atlanta." Potter transmitted the lie Feets had given him.

"I knew he was a promo guy. Didn't I tell you?"

"Well that's sort of right. Mr. Patrick goes around to different schools in the Atlanta area with celebrities to entertain the kids. He gives out free Coke. He'd like me to come out to ... where'd you say you wanted me to visit again?"

"The Briar Vista School in De Kalb County," Feets said, watching Potter carefully again. The ballplayer had shown no reaction the first time, but that didn't mean anything special because he probably didn't have any idea that the Briar Vista School property was the one he was chased across by Dave Skipton. Potter had still failed to connect the name, he saw. Feets thought briefly that he might be staking out the wrong man. He once read an article on people who play the horses and win, and he remembered it said that "sometimes the right horse just jumps out at you and there is no doubt in your mind that you've picked a winner." The trouble was that he had some doubt about Potter being the right one, and he'd have to follow the form and see.

"You think you might visit the school with me next time you're in Atlanta, Potter?" he asked.

"I'll be happy to," Potter said, "but you'll have to clear it with management. I've just been bawled out by the big boss for accepting some commercial trophies."

180

"We won't be giving you any prizes," Feets said.

"Still, you better get it cleared with the front office, Mr. Patrick."

"Yeah," Hartman said, "Potter's right. We're not allowed to help sell Coke without permission."

Feets felt defeated, frustrated. He really knew he had his pigeon but he couldn't prove it. The ballplayer didn't remember where he had been chased. If he could get him out to the spot, he'd recognize the place and break down. He decided to hang around town another day. If he followed Potter around, maybe he'd luck out and catch him with another child. That was a stupid thought and, as Feets thought it, he rejected it. He'd have to bide his time, wait for a break.

"I'll bet you're really with the baseball commissioner's office," Sissy told Feets. "And you're here to see if we do anything naughty like smoke pot or shoot heroin or fuck."

"Why do you think that?"

"I dunno. You look like a cop. And I bet you know a friend of mine, Scruffy Levinson—"

Feets tried to make himself look as cool as Potter Cindy. The boy's wife had a nose for horseshit. She'd make a good cop. Any cop in Atlanta who didn't know Scruffy Levinson ought to have his shield taken away. There was a rumor that a lot of the police officers were on his payroll. He saw his cover about to be peeled off by this skinny little dame. If she knew Scruffy, as she said, she was only a phone call or two away from identifying him. While the king of Atlanta gambling had never met Feets, didn't even know his name, all he had to do was pick up a phone, call one of his people, and he would be identified in minutes. He had not realized that Sissy was a friend of Scruffy's. They must have known each other in Palm Springs, Scruffy's vacation spot.

Feets was upset with himself; he was actually beginning to feel guilty, as though he were the criminal, not Potter Cindy. He knew he had to be cool like Potter. The trouble was that he couldn't because that skinny little dame suddenly had him on the run, ducking for cover. Feets could counterattack, take a chance, confront Potter, accuse him, and hope he'd break. But if he was in the clear, Potter could make it rough for him. Feets was in another state, way out of his jurisdiction. The man was a celebrity and Feets was Acting Captain.

If Feets was mistaken about him and Potter sued the county, the damages would cost De Kalb its whole treasury, practically. Potter would still be a celebrity but he, on the other hand, might be out of work. He was, after all, only operating now on a policeman's intuition.

He looked at Potter. Feets saw nothing but good nature and friendliness. He saw that the man he was trying to arrest was his only friend in this suspicious group of people.

What Feets had not realized was that Potter liked the man called Mr. Patrick. He reminded the outfielder of an older man he had met one winter on a ranch near Las Cruces, New Mexico. They had been hired to run down strays, the man and Potter. He had looked like this Mr. Patrick, what with that graying hair and crow's-feet around the eyes, and those millions of pale freckles on the face. Potter's cowboy buddy was a man dedicated to work; he would rather work than eat, it seemed. While this Patrick had an easier job in selling Coke, Potter saw that, like his cowboy friend, he must work all the time. He never let up on trying to get him to visit that school in Atlanta. Patrick even drank Coke himself, Potter had observed. Potter saw that Patrick was put in a funny position by Sissy, made uneasy. Who could tell? Maybe Patrick had made a few bets with this friend of Sissy's, this Scruffy, maybe he even owed him some money. Potter remembered that Scruffy used to be Sissy's boyfriend. Sissy had said he was the "Gambling Czar of the South."

Sissy had distracted this Mr. Patrick from his work. Potter's cowboy friend would have blown sky-high if somebody distracted him while he was breathing down the back of a runaway. Potter was sympathetic; he understood. He did not like

182

to have his concentration broken when he was up at the plate. When you do that to a man who loves what he's doing, you take away his power. And that was not right.

"Mr. Patrick, they're only kidding you a bit. I tell you what I'm going to do: next time we play in Atlanta, I'm going to go out with you to that school of yours. Now, you'll have to promise me that you don't give the story to the press until I get it cleared with management. But I give you my word—I'll visit the school." Potter extended his hand. Feets took it; it was warm. His own hand was a wet fish.

Jesus X. Christ! Feets thought, *I might just be on to the wrong man*!

Chapter Twenty-One

The party had been a ball for Sissy. She wished that all audiences were made up of ballplayers and their girlfriends. All the routines she had worked out with her agent came easily, like greased shit. She didn't have to split a gut to get that crowd rolling in the aisles. Even Miss Cabdriver seemed amused at times. She didn't have to use her routine that was set up for toughies, those people who sit with their frozen faces, like they were the Justices on the Supreme Court. You can't beat these major leaguers if you're looking for an audience; they came wanting to be tickled; they were holding their sides laughing almost before you opened your mouth.

Well, not all ballplayers. Potter didn't rupture himself laughing. Oh, he smiled; he chuckled; he seemed amused. But he was an overwound watch, except maybe on the ballfield. That was the only place he seemed free. It was painful to her. Potter had such a nice laugh, when he laughed. He looked so handsome when he threw his head back, on those rare occasions, broke up and let himself have a good belly laugh, let himself snap a spring, get out of control.

In the sack Potter was getting there, coming into his own. She remembered being surprised after the party to find Potter standing up as tall as a guard at Buckingham Palace, without even being coaxed by her. Maybe it was that little bit of spiked haggis, or whatever it was, that extra beer he drank. Potter wasn't a pothead or even a drinker. But the night after the party he just sort of took hold of the reins, like the jockey she knew he could be, and rode her out to a lovely finish. Who would have thought it? Potter Cindy a marvelous lover? Marvelous, yes. Love, yes. Marvelous lover, no. It would even embarrass Potter to think of himself like that.

What was wrong with old Pottsie? He was peculiar, that was for sure. There was nothing she could put her finger on, except maybe his niceness, his control, and say that's what's fucked up. She knew he used most of his energy, or a good hunk of it, making sure he was polite, friendly, sweet, respectful. She knew that wasn't good for him, but she could not figure out how to loosen him up. She had tried to get him angry on a number of occasions, but he was always understanding, forgiving, a regular little saint.

"What the fuck are you made of, wood? Don't you ever yell or cry? Did you ever kick anyone's ass in? Did you ever have a fight? Did you ever make a person eat shit so that he would hate you?" She had asked him those questions. And then what did he do? He took her cheeks in his dry warm hands and said, "Sissy, Sissy, Sissy," so softly and tenderly that she didn't know whether to scream, kill, or come in her pants.

"I'm going to leave you, you bastard fuck!" She had threatened that once, testing, just to see if she could get a rise out of him. She wanted to make him do something rash, just anything, even beat her up. And you might know he would say the one thing that would be like a kick in the ovaries.

"If you ever do that, Sissy, I think I might come completely apart."

Come apart, bullshit. He's wound up too tight. He's bolted down, waterproof.

Sissy remembered, or dreamed, that she picked up a lamp

and threw it at him. Guess what happened? The prick caught it and told her to take hold of herself. Then, she thought she threw a bottle of perfume at him and he caught that, too. The only change in him in her dream or in real life was that Potter smelled like a Chanel No. 5 showroom for a day.

Potter didn't know it, but Sissy had decided to leave him the day after Bobby's party, the day after the night that he had really screwed her pants off for the first time in their marriage.

It seemed even to her an odd thing to want to do or a funny choice to make at that time. But she had something to remember him by, didn't she? A good fuck!

She made up her mind that she would never come back to him until he did something crazy—anything, exploded, just something.

She decided to call Scruffy Levinson in Palm Springs to see if he'd let her come there for a while.

"How's your cyst? What's the matter with that jock you married? Is he giving you a hard time?"

"Sort of, I guess. But not the way you think, Scruffy. His trouble is he's too nice. That's almost harder to take."

"What is he, a fag—?"

"Oh, Scruffy, of course not. Would I marry a fag?"

"Who knows? I never try to figure dames out."

"Can I come, Scruffy?"

"Sure. Are you coming for fun or to suffer?"

"Suffer, I guess."

"You mean no rolling in the hay?"

"Not right away. Okay, Scruffy?"

"Okay. Hey! Does your jock love you?"

"Yes. I think so."

"Would he do anything for you?"

"I guess so."

"Do you want to make a bundle of money? I'm talking one hundred thousand bucks."

"I sure do."

"Well, listen, if you could get this Potter Cindy to strike out in a key situation, or lose a ball in the sun at the right moment, we could both clean up."

"Forget it," she said. "He'd sooner cut off his balls."

"What is he, dumb?"

"Oh, Scruffy, you don't understand. He's honorable; he's good; he's straight; he's conceited about baseball, actually."

"Oh, *Jesus!*"

She left Potter a note that she had to go to Palm Springs on business. She left a phone number because she had not yet really decided to leave Potter. She hoped she would figure him out, somehow.

Chapter Twenty-Two

There was something about a tall, slim broad with long legs, nibblable knockers, and blond pubic hair that moved Bobby Hartman to action. Maybe he was especially turned on because Swaps Flattery was such a super *shiksa*. For a Jewish boy, forget that he was a major leaguer, it meant something to put your hand on a cunt that had been blessed by a priest, or St. Christopher. Who knew? It might keep him from getting into a slump. Bobby smiled to himself, at himself.

Swaps was standing by the record player, swinging her behind to some soft rock, listening. Her Braniff flight from Dallas was late, and she was pleased that Bobby gave her the key to his apartment. A lot of men you weren't engaged to would not give you a key. They'd be too afraid you'd catch them screwing. Bobby wasn't asleep when she got there; in fact, he had just gotten in from an extra-inning night game, and was looking forward to an inactive night's rest.

Since she met Bobby Hartman the year before on that plane trip, she had gotten to know lots of ballplayers. They were fun—egomaniacs, crazy, some even quiet. The only one who was really any different was Potter Cindy. He just didn't fit any slot. He was in his own drawer, all by himself. He was calm and quiet and sweet and charming. He didn't show off or make himself out a hotshot like most of the others. He was just a nice person. She tried to imagine what he would be like to sleep with, how much different he would be from Bobby, say, but she could not. Somehow, he seemed to be more like one of those statues of naked Greek gods you see pictures of in travel magazines than anyone's lover. Of course, Swaps didn't know him all that well; she had only met him that one time at Bobby's. He was married to Sissy Lindmore, she knew, and it stood to reason that Sissy did not sleep with a statue.

Bobby came up while she was thinking this and reached for his good-luck spot. She pulled back her hips to take it away from him for the moment, not that she didn't find Bobby fun; she was just caught off-guard.

"What are you doing?" she asked, though she knew very well because he had done that many times before.

"What am I doing? Oh, nothing. I'm just looking for my batting helmet."

Swaps laughed. Bobby was cute; he had a terrific sense of humor. She didn't know very many Jewish boys, but she had heard they were smart and knew how to make a girl laugh. He confirmed that for her, even if he didn't look Jewish at all. Bobby was fair; he didn't have a big nose, and his father didn't run a shop. Some Jews were supposed to be very heavy in the head, very deep, more like Potter than Bobby. Bobby had told her that Potter was an American and "as American as you can get." He was a cowboy on a drive, just like in the movies, said Bobby, no time for bullshitting, no blarney. For a girl whose grandparents were Irish, no blarney meant dull. But Potter wasn't dull; he was mysterious, or something.

"Swaps, you've been in the apartment for two hours. Do you realize that this is the first time, since the party, that we've been together for this length of time and have not gotten undressed?"

"So what? Do you think Potter is so direct? I'll bet he doesn't say that to Sissy."

"Let's go to bed."

"Would Potter say that?"

"Fuck Potter. Anyway, he's got to say something. He's married to Sissy Lindmore. What do you think, they get undressed in the dark by some secret signal and then slip into bed wearing long johns and a granny gown?"

"Why? Do they have a big sexy marriage?"

"Who cares? Who knows?"

"He's your roommate, isn't he?"

"Right now, he's probably enjoying himself. What am I doing? Standing here like a jerk talking to you about Potter's sex life."

"Aren't you curious?"

"There's nothing to be curious about. He's got a pecker like everyone else. That I know because we Redbirds like to measure who's got the biggest in the shower. And since he's got a pecker and a girl who undresses for him at the snap of his fingers, I guess he finds a place to put it."

Swaps challenged Bobby to snap his fingers, to command her.

When Bobby goosed her, she jumped. And when he snapped his fingers, she undressed.

"Do you like Potter?" Swaps asked afterward.

"He's a nice guy, I guess. And a good ballplayer, damn good. He's going to be great! He's Hall of Fame stuff."

"What do you mean, you guess?"

"Well, I've been rooming with him and I hardly know him."

"You mean he keeps to himself?"

"Not really. He talks and kids around same as most guys."

"What do you mean, then?"

"I don't know. He doesn't really relax, I guess. No! That's not it. I mean, he's not quite like a guy who was described in my high school yearbook as a person who 'will stand without hitching.' You know they meant this *schmuck* was a real A-number-one square, a Boy Scout type—honest, trustworthy, not a troublemaker."

"And Potter's like that or not?"

"No. He's not. Potter will stand, *if hitched*, if you know what I mean—"

"I don't really."

"I mean, if you want him to stand, you have to hitch him. I don't think you can count on his just standing there if you don't tie him up."

Chapter Twenty-Three

The pressure of the games, long road trips, pretzel commercials, pennant fever in June in Redbird country, and promotional good-will trips to local civic establishments didn't give Potter much time to consider why he had seen so little of Sissy for about a month. He knew she had been tied up in California, Palm Springs, on some job or other. He had called her when he played in San Francisco, Los Angeles, and again in San Diego. While he was in San Francisco, she told him she might meet him in Los Angeles. When he called her from Los Angeles, she said maybe she could catch up with him in San Diego.

He thought once or twice that maybe she had tied up with another fellow. The thought brought tears to his eyes. When he controlled that, he wondered if he would have the nerve to buy a gun and kill her and her lover. He made an effort to push that thought down. Was Sissy taking advantage?

He felt the top Redbird management, even if the organization had it written in black and white in his contract, was taking advantage of his willingness to help out the team. He was tired of making appearances for the local chapter of Muscular Dystrophy and the Heart Fund; he was irritated by the Redbird publicity department's dredging up cornball features about him as a boy, a cowpuncher, an evangelist. The only thing he liked was the ballplaying. Why did they have to make it secondary to the business aspects? If they offered him the Cap'n Crunch award again, that is, if management would give him an okay to accept it, he would turn it down. He was that fed up. Even if the President of the country asked him to dinner at the White House, he wouldn't accept. He made up his mind that the visit to the Golden Slippers Children's Hospital was going to be the last damn thing he went on. *The hell with you, Mr. Heller. The hell with you!*

What was it Sissy said to him on the phone when he had called her from San Diego?

"Pottsie. I'm sorry I couldn't make it. I would have loved to have had some fun. I just couldn't make it."

"Why not?"

"I was just swamped. I'm reading a part for a movie tomorrow. It's not a big part, but I don't want to fuck it up."

"I would have come to meet you if you asked me—"

"Of course you would. That's you. You couldn't do bad, Pottsie. The whole world's got to love you, don't they? You know, I bet if the manager caught you jerking off on the bench, he'd probably tell everybody that you weren't doing anything wrong, but that you were only doing that because you ran out of oil for your baseball mitt. I wish you were more of a prick, Potter. I think I wish that more than anything in the world."

"I'll tell you something, Sissy. I keep a tight hold on the reins because I've probably got more of a prick under me than you know. And I don't want to give in to those feelings. If I start letting go, all hell would break loose. I can tell you that. I'm maintaining my hold because that's the only way I know how to do it—" Potter had a temptation to tell her about his "duster," but he did not have the courage. He could not face her reaction. He bit his lip and fought back another temptation to cry. Perhaps that was it, that he needed to be loved, to please the crowd. At any rate, he let it go at that; he did not tell her that he was angry with her for being away all the time. He did not tell her that he was finding it hard to forgive her for not meeting him when he had been looking forward to seeing her.

Potter was thinking and fuming about that conversation in his room at home when the phone rang.

"Hello!" he snapped into the phone.

"I'm sorry," said the woman's voice on the other end. "I was calling Potter Cindy, but I think—"

"This is Potter Cindy, damn it!" Then the thought of the anger in his voice calmed him. "I'm sorry," he continued more softly, "I don't mean to be snarling at you."

"This is Swaps. Swaps Flattery. But I see I caught you in a foul mood."

For a few seconds, he tried to remember who Swaps Flattery was and could not. "Swaps Flattery," he said, his voice almost inaudible. She saw he didn't remember. "I'm a friend of Bobby Hartman's. We met at the party at Bobby's."

"Oh sure," he said, but he could not remember what she looked like. At first he thought she was small and cute and thin with a slightly turned-up nose, but that was Sissy. And then he thought she was dark-haired with green eyes, but that was Samantha. It troubled Potter that three-quarters of the time he couldn't remember the faces of people he had met and chatted with at parties. He was so damn wrapped up in his own self, thinking his own thoughts, that he could not fix their faces in his mind a short time after he met them.

"I hate to be disturbing you, Potter. But I'm in town unexpectedly and I was looking for Bobby. He's not at his apartment and I thought you might know where I could get hold of him."

Potter remembered suddenly that she was tall and had long blond hair. "Gee, I don't know, Swaps. We had an afternoon game and everybody just split. Bobby didn't tell me where he was heading and I didn't ask him."

"Oh, okay," she said. "I just thought he might be with you. I'm sorry to be bothering you."

"That's okay, Swaps. I wasn't doing very much." Swaps felt encouraged that the call wasn't completely in vain.

"How've you been? And how's Sissy?" she asked.

"Well, I'm fine and I guess Sissy is, too."

"I love the way you put things." She began to flirt in earnest, with more enthusiasm. She was hoping Sissy was not home because she wasn't really looking that hard for Bobby. Potter fascinated her. She had had a dream that they had made love on a beach and she was exploring the possibility of making a dream come true.

Potter was tempted to ask her up to his place, not because he was attracted to her, but because he was sore at Sissy.

Swaps grew bolder, pushed by her fascination. She took a chance.

"If you and Sissy are free now, would you come and have a drink? I know a terrific place."

"Sissy's not in town, Swaps. Maybe we can get together another time."

"Well, Potter, since we're both kind of stranded, why don't we just have the drink by our lonesome?"

If she wasn't his roommate's girlfriend and if he was sure that his anger at Sissy wouldn't make him impotent with Swaps, he might have agreed. Instead, he said, "That would be nice, Swaps, but I'm kind of beat. I'm dragging my feet. Let's do it another time—"

She made one more try. "I'll come up and make you dinner. I'm a terrific airline hostess. I promise you a smooth, relaxing flight. That's the way we do it at Braniff."

"It sounds real nice, Swaps. But I think I have to hold off the trip for another time."

Swaps shrugged. He had not closed the door entirely. That Potter sure was smooth. He could cancel a flight and not cancel at the same time. She retreated, seeing that she was off course. "Whatever you say, sir. Braniff will be ready when you are. If you hear from Bobby, tell him I was looking for him."

"Thanks, Swaps," Potter said. "Thanks for calling. I'll give Bobby the message."

No more than a half hour later Potter, dressed only in a pair of tightly fitted slacks, went to the door of his apartment to answer a knock. He looked out with surprise and disbelief at Swaps Flattery.

She had had a drink, maybe two or three, for she stood at his door laughing, while telling an off-color joke about the man who took a TWA flight and when asked by the hostess if he would like some TWA coffee, he said no, he'd take some TWA *tea*.

Potter pulled her inside the apartment, not to seduce her or allow himself to be seduced, but simply because he did not think he could stand up to the scandal. He was, after all, supposedly a happily married man.

Swaps said, "TWA tea, get it?" because Potter wasn't smiling.

"Do you want some coffee?" he asked her. He did not think offering her something stronger would be helpful.

She studied him. "What a great body you have!" she observed.

He felt uncomfortable. He knew he should have been the one saying things like that to her. Most guys would have had her in the sack by now and worry about sobering her up later.

Swaps had to get herself drunk to do it, but there she was in the apartment alone with him. It was, she saw, not worth it, and very dumb of her.

"I just wanted to tell you that TWA joke," she said, in jerky explanation. *I must have flipped*, she thought, *to have come up to his apartment.*

196

He felt angry, not at Swaps, for he saw no real harm in what she had done. He thought, *Why not? People can't help their sexual crazies. I only have to look at myself, my "duster," to see that. A person can only control himself to a point. If you're not fighting, holding tight all the time, the defense cracks.* Potter was sore at Sissy.

"Do you have a bathroom?" Swaps felt queasy. She had downed those Campari-and-vodkas too quickly.

Potter pointed to the bathroom. Swaps hurried to it, more to escape embarrassment than to throw up.

When she came out, she was shocked to find Potter had removed his trousers. He was naked and he stood straight and stiff, like a soldier.

Chapter Twenty-Four

Feets, who got the wind knocked out of his sails in the Midwest, came back to sunny Atlanta feeling like he had only the handle of his rudder left. The trip had not increased his enthusiasm for the Skipton case. He let it drag for about a week after his return because he was less sure that Potter Cindy was his man. More than that, he had lost his spirit for the chase. He bet that there were millions of people out there in the world who didn't realize that just because cops chased criminals, it didn't mean that a case can't get boring and tired. A cop, like a ballplayer, could lose "the winning edge." Instead of getting psyched up he could get psyched down on a case.

It was interesting that Potter Cindy, when Feets got him alone at the Hartman party for a moment, or as alone as anyone can be at a cocktail party, was the one who cautioned him against letdowns.

Feets had said he was a baseball fan, had played some ball as a kid, and that he was curious to know what Potter felt like when he was caught off base or stealing.

Potter answered, "Well, you know it isn't a good feeling, Mr. Patrick. You must know that from playing ball yourself."

"I don't know that actually," Feets said, "because you see

we didn't play ball in an organized way. Just a bunch of kids got together and played. We usually didn't have enough guys to allow stealing, or even count balls and strikes. We hit the ball or we wiffed. There were no walks allowed and certainly no stealing. If you hit to the opposite field it was an automatic out. But you, now, you play for real. And if you're caught, it counts. And it can hurt."

"That's the truth," Potter said. "It can be costly to the club."

"What I was asking was how it felt personally. Do you feel as though stealing is a crime? And do you feel guilty?"

"Not really. I feel embarrassed more than guilty. The rules say you can steal, so it's not a crime. But if I get thrown out, or picked off, I feel it's because I have let down. I didn't give the play enough of my attention. Letdowns hurt, all right, but they can also help—" Potter said.

"Help? How's that?"

"Well, there're a lot of guys in baseball who think that a mistake, a bonehead play or a costly error, can throw you off stride. But I don't. They help me concentrate all the more the next time. The things that hurt me more are the good days that I have, because I tend to ease up and live a little on past glories, and I can't do that because it's a long season and there are a lot of games to play."

Feets felt uncomfortable and distressed. The man he was letting down on had told him not to. *Potter may think letdowns are helpful, but I'm not using mine to pick myself up.* Feets saw why, too. He didn't think Potter should be punished, guilty or not.

The policeman had no sooner stopped chasing Potter when the thought occurred to him that the reason the witness in the Skipton matter could not identify Potter was that he had not seen Potter as he had. Feets saw clearly that what was needed was for the man to see him as he had when Dave chased him.

Feets got up from his desk. He was excited but unhappy, a cop on the trail of somebody he didn't want to catch. Red handed him Skipton's X-rays on the way out, explaining what they were and giving Dave's message. Feets threw them on the floor. "Fuck the X-rays!".

Feets drove slowly to Atlanta in his squad car. He was unhappy with himself. He didn't think of himself at that moment as a very good cop.

The people at the TV station remembered him, or at least they said they did. This time they weren't so eager to help without first asking a lot of questions about the purpose behind it, which Feets handled calmly.

"What's this all about?" asked the news editor.

"Oh," Feets said, "it's a big nothing. I just need the pictures of baseball players in civilian clothes. I want to use them as decoys. I've got a guy coming in who claims to be an eyewitness to a crime. I want to use the photos of the ballplayers to see if he's bullshitting or not," Feets bullshitted a little.

"Do you want Potter Cindy? He's been photographed in street clothes a lot on television. He's appeared in civilian clothes on the Carson show. I can't remember, but he might even have appeared on a quiz show with Sissy Lindmore. There are a lot of our own players on the Braves in civilian clothes. Do you want them, too?"

"Sure, that'll be fine. Cindy, the Redbirds, the Braves. Just fine."

While the TV photo laboratory made copies of the stills, Feets waited in the small room that contained the teletype machines. He was feeling depressed. He knew that some crimes really do start getting solved on a hunch, a feeling, a kiss from the good Lord, but he felt at the moment that he was asking for a benevolence even his old Irish great-grandmother in Kilmoganny wouldn't have deigned to pray for.

Praise be the Lord and mercy of mother Mary! Feets, taking a closer look at the teletype machines, watched a story come in that redeemed his faith in the long shot.

GOLDEN SLIPPERS, _____: —SLUGGING ROOKIE BASEBALL STAR POTTER CINDY OF THE REDBIRDS WAS ARRESTED BY LOCAL POLICE FOR "DISTURBING THE PEACE." THE YOUNG OUTFIELDER HAD BEEN VISITING THE GOLDEN SLIPPERS CHILDREN'S HOSPITAL HERE WITH A NUMBER OF REDBIRDS WHEN HE BECAME INVOLVED IN A DISTURBANCE ON ONE OF THE WARDS AND WAS ASKED TO LEAVE BY THE PHYSICIAN IN CHARGE, PSYCHIATRIST JOHN B. MUFUFSKI. WHEN CINDY BECAME INDIGNANT, A FIGHT ENSUED. A NURSE ON THE WARD CALLED THE POLICE, WHO TOOK THE OUTFIELDER INTO CUSTODY. CINDY WAS LATER RELEASED WITHOUT A CHARGE BEING FILED. NEITHER DR. MUFUFSKI, THE DIRECTOR OF THE HOSPITAL, NOR THE POLICE WOULD COMMENT. THE NURSE ON THE WARD, MISS SABRADILLA, SAID SHE UNDERSTOOD "POTTER CINDY DID SOMETHING DISGUSTING." SHE REFUSED TO ELABORATE FURTHER.

NONE OF THE VISITING BALLPLAYERS COULD ADD ANYTHING. THEY WERE APPARENTLY VISITING SEPARATE WINGS AND ROOMS OF THE HOSPITAL WHEN THE DISTURBANCE OCCURRED . . . . NEW LEAD, INSERT, OR ADD TO COME . . . .

Feets took out a cigarette, lit it, blew the smoke straight up in the air, smiled, and waited.

Chapter Twenty-Five

Potter had walked blithely into a wing of the Golden Slippers Children's Hospital; his teammates were doing similar cheer-up efforts in other wings. He had a glove in his hand and several baseballs in his pockets. One he tossed up and caught, saying, "Hi, kids, I've got some balls here and this glove to leave with you, compliments of the Redbirds." A nurse on duty at the desk of the wing came hurrying over. She looked anxious, upset. "I think you've really come down the wrong wing, sir. These children are catatonic. I don't think they're quite ready this morning for a visit from the Redbirds. I must ask you to leave."

Potter read the nurse's name tag, Lucy Sabradilla, R.N.

"Oh, I'm sorry," Potter said. "I thought we were supposed to visit all the kids. What exactly is catatonic, anyway?"

"I haven't time to give you a course in psychiatric syndromes. Let's just say it is a very serious condition, and these children are frozen, locked within themselves. Now, would you please leave?"

Potter looked around. He could see some of the children in their rooms. They looked perfectly normal to him, if a bit somber. He could not believe they would not respond to affection, a baseball. He knew he was no emotional colossus himself. But baseball. . . .

When Potter started rolling baseballs into the rooms, Miss Sabradilla turned tail and growled something about calling Dr. Mufufski and the police.

One child, a girl about ten years old, followed the ball with her eyes. Potter thought he saw her smile and he came forward. She was very pretty with a sad little face and deep-set brown eyes.

"I want you to have that ball and this glove." He held it out for her but she did not reach for it. She did smile. "Go on, take it. It's a neat glove. Look, here, it's got Whitey Knocthofer's name on it. He's our manager." The girl made no effort to take the offering.

"I'll put it on your bed. You can look at it later, okay?" He approached her then to give her a peck on the cheek and to say good-bye. But when he bent to kiss her he felt his organ beginning to swell. And he kissed her again, tenderly. He didn't realize that his hand was on her little body or that he had started to gently masturbate her. He wanted her to love baseball, to have the feeling for the sport become unlocked from her closed-up little body.

"Hey! You!" And when Potter turned, a man in a white coat had hurled himself forward to stop him. "What the hell are you doing!"

"I'm sorry," Potter said. He was frightened. He could think of nothing else to say.

"He's sorry. God almighty, he's sorry. Please come out in the hall with me. This minute, please!" Dr. Mufufski said.

In the hall he asked Potter, "What did you do, Mr. Cindy?"

"I lost control of myself, sir."

He ordered Potter to follow him. The doctor led him into a small room, pointed to a chair that he wanted Potter to sit in. He closed the door. Then he seated himself in a chair, facing Potter. He studied the man, the athlete. He waited for Potter to speak. The doctor could not know that waiting for Potter to speak first might keep them in that room all day. He saw Potter looking at him. The man he had seen with the little child looked both calm and nervous at the same time. Was he worried that he would be exposed, and resigned to it at the same time? The doctor wondered when he would speak, but as nothing was forthcoming, he knew it was his turn.

"This sort of thing has happened before, hasn't it? Probably many times."

Potter admitted that it had. The doctor was surprised by his response; he had expected him to deny it. Once Potter decided to speak, he was prepared to unburden himself.

"Have you been in treatment for it?"

"No, sir. It's been a secret. When I think about it or about telling it, I cannot sleep. I know it's wrong, but—" Potter shrugged; it was a gesture of helplessness.

Dr. Mufufski rubbed nervous beads of sweat from his own brow, then closed his eyes and covered his mouth with his hands. He thought a moment.

"The secret is out, Mr. Cindy. We've called the police. They're on their way."

"Why'd you do that, doctor?"

The doctor was not obliged to answer the question, but he did. He felt the ballplayer was both innocent and guilty at the same time.

"Miss Sabradilla panicked. She did not see you kissing that child, touching her, and doing what you weren't supposed to. I don't think she realizes that you would have masturbated that very sick girl, that ten-year-old, to orgasm and then you would have dropped your pants and masturbated yourself. Isn't that right, Mr. Cindy?"

"I wouldn't have wanted to hurt the child, doctor."

The psychiatrist studied Potter, then he got up and opened the door. He looked into the girl's room. She was sitting in a chair, staring nowhere. One hand was on the ball Potter had given her; in the other she held the baseball glove that Potter had left on the bed. There was, Dr. Mufufski thought, the trace of a smile on her face. She did not seem negatively affected by the seduction. Dr. Mufufski knew the child could not testify against him; neither could he. After all, he had only really seen him kissing the child. Who would squawk about that? Imagine how it would look . . . a psychiatrist beefing because somebody was tender and sweet to a sick child. Dr. Mufufski would not be revered for that complaint. But this kind of thing could not remain the ballplayer's, and now his, well-kept secret. The man needed treatment. Dr. Mufufski knew the ballplayer would resist; he expected as much. How could he convince the man to go into treatment? The police might just provide such a push, he thought. He considered the possibility of using the police as a threat to frighten the ballplayer into seeing a therapist. He walked back to Potter.

"That is a sick child, Mr. Cindy. You are yourself sick. You need therapy. You understand that, don't you?"

"What kind of therapy?"

"I mean, you need to discuss this problem of yours with some qualified person, a specialist who understands what is going on and can help you."

"I don't want anyone else to know. I'm ashamed of it."

"That is your admission that you need help."

"Look, I'm not going to do it ever again."

"At this point, you cannot say that. You have done it before. And you will do it again."

"No, really. I promise. Give me a break."

"I'm afraid I can't."

"Look, I'll pay you. I'll give you whatever you want to keep quiet. Will you take five thousand bucks to keep quiet?"

"No, Mr. Cindy. You need treatment. Money will not keep you from doing this again and again."

"Look, I swear. I promise you. I'll never do it again. I didn't even want to do it this time. It just came over me.

I wasn't thinking about doing it, honestly. I never wanted to do it. But I do it anyway. Suddenly, the sensation is there and I do it. I have never hurt anyone. I swear to you. Please give me a chance . . . please."

"I cannot, Mr. Cindy. Because you have just convinced me all the more that you must have therapy."

"I'm not going to any headshrinker. . . ."

"You don't understand, Mr. Cindy. The choice is mine, not yours."

"How do you mean?"

"I mean," Dr. Mufufski said, "you will either agree to go into therapy with some qualified person, a specialist who understands your problem, knows what is going on, or I will blow it wide open with the police. I will expose you."

Potter saw it would be the end, the end of everything, if he refused. "You're holding a gun to my head."

"The gun I hold to your head, like all guns, can only hurt you if you are stubborn or stupid. Otherwise, it is for your own good."

Potter looked at Dr. Mufufski.

"I'll agree to see you," Potter said.

"Me?"

"I'll pay you whatever you want."

"The pay is standard," Dr. Mufufski said. "Let me think about it."

"You're a psychiatrist, aren't you?"

"Yes, but I'm not certain at this moment if I would be the best person to treat you." Then another thought occurred to Dr. Mufufski. "Do you want to be helped, Mr. Cindy?"

There were tears in Potter's eyes.

"You're not married, are you?"

"Yes, to Sissy . . . Sissy Lindmore. Most people know that."

"I don't follow baseball. I know nothing about your biography. Would you let me talk with your wife?"

"She doesn't know about my . . . my "duster." I'd like to keep it from her."

" 'Duster'. . . . Is that what you call your problem? Does 'duster' have some significance? What does it mean? Why do you call it that?"

"A duster is a pitch that knocks you down, makes you hit the dirt. Pitchers throw them at you to keep you from taking a toehold." Potter gave a longer description than necessary because he saw Dr. Mufufski was not much of a baseball fan. In fact, it was not his game.

"The duster knocks you to the ground. And you get dirty. You have to dust yourself off, is that it?"

"Yes."

"That's very interesting. You think of your problem as dirty or something that makes you dirty."

"I guess."

"Are your parents still alive, Potter?"

"Yes."

"What do you think of them?"

"They're good, hard-working people."

"Do you have any siblings?"

"I guess I'm an only child."

"What do you mean, you guess?"

"My mother had me first. Another child died in the hospital nursery. About two years after that another baby died inside of her. She couldn't have any more children. Why do you want to know, anyway?"

"I have to know all about you, Mr. Cindy, if I am to treat you."

"Are you going to treat me? Have you decided yet?"

The police had arrived. "We'll have to talk more. I'm not sure yet."

Potter had another bad moment because Dr. Mufufski put on a convincing performance with the police, telling them that "that egocentric sonofabitch came into this ward full of

207

very sick young people and started throwing baseballs around. Baseballs! Good Christ! What the hell did he think this was, a meeting of Big Brothers of America or the goddamned Police Athletic League? I want that man arrested. Take him down to the station house and let him take cognizance of himself. Next time, he won't come breaking into a private, off-limits, hospital wing. He can't disregard the rules just because he's a major league baseball player."

"I understand the hospital invited him here—"

"Well, so what?" Dr. Mufufski said. "If I invite you to my home, I don't expect you to go through my dresser drawers. You lock that Potter Cindy up. Teach him a lesson in behavior."

"What can we book him with?"

"That's your business," Dr. Mufufski said. "I'm sure there's a charge on the books that fits this situation."

Dr. Mufufski could not believe the resistance an ordinary policeman has when asked to arrest a superstar of a home-town ball club.

He had known that people were fans, rabid ones, with their nervous systems infected with hundreds of facts about the beloved Redbird heroes. They spoke about ballplayers as if they were relatives of theirs; they knew the year they were born, what schools they went to, and what, if anything, they studied. Never mind baseball statistics. That was nothing. A real fan knew if the player was married or single and, if married, the name of his wife and sometimes his children. Some could tell fascinating adventures about the athlete's boyhood and youth—who got caught putting a dead mouse on the teacher's desk, who got arrested in a peace demonstration, who captured the "peeing for distance" championship, who came out of reformatories for wayward boys, and who could eat the most spaghetti or pistachio ice cream in a single sitting.

At first the police sulked about Potter and hung around

hangdog, unable to perform the simple task of taking a trouble-maker to the stationhouse. Then, in the midst of this inactivity, the local newspapermen and wire-service reporters smelled something baking, bread-and-butter stuff. Potter was in the middle of three unhappy policemen, overcome by a sudden paralysis, and an animated doctor. Finally, the rest of the Redbirds arrived. Now freed of their good-will missions in the hospital wings, some of the players were with the police when they heard Potter was about to be arrested. Dick Condon, the shortstop, for example, was beginning to redden in anger, while he let go some of the strongest language he could remember from the days when he was just another tough, Boston-Irish punk who mugged kids for nickels and dimes and baseball mitts in the johns of Fenway Park. If he weren't a professional baseball player yelling his piss-house grammar at the cops that day, the police would have split his skull open right in the reception area of the Golden Slippers Children's Hospital. As it was, the only blow they delivered was, "Relax, now, Dickie. We don't want to drag Potter down to the station, but we gotta do something. The doc filed a complaint."

"Fuck the doc. We'll knock him on his ass. We got a game to play today." If Condon knew the truth he probably would have tried to knock Potter on his ass.

Finally, the reporters got their story from the cops, the doctor, the nurse, and Potter, and filed it while Feets Patrick sat around smiling and waiting for the tail end of the story in front of the teletype machines in an Atlanta TV station.

OPTIONAL ADD ... POTTER CINDY ARREST .... QUESTIONED ON THE CHARGE, SERGEANT S. B. SAIN, OF THE GOLDEN SLIPPERS TOWNSHIP POLICE DEPARTMENT, SAID THAT NO FORMAL CHARGE WAS FILED AGAINST THE OUTFIELDER. HE WAS TAKEN TO THE STATION "JUST TO COOL OFF THE SITUATION AT THE HOSPITAL. IT'S ALL A BIG NOTHING. CINDY JUST WENT BARRELING INTO

ONE OF THEIR QUIET ROOMS AND STARTED THROWING BALLS AROUND."

THIS APPARENTLY UPSET THE HOSPITAL STAFF. THE DOCTOR URGED THE POLICE TO FIND SOMETHING TO BOOK CINDY ON. DOCTOR'S NAME—MUFUFSKI—M STOP U STOP F STOP U STOP F STOP S STOP K STOP I STOP, JOHN B., PSYCHIATRIST.

THE NURSE ON THE WING WAS ASKED IF TALKING TO THE CHILDREN AND THROWING BALLS AROUND COULD BE DESCRIBED AS DISGUSTING. "NO," SHE SAID. SHE ADMITTED THAT SHE "MAY HAVE USED THE WORD INCORRECTLY." SHE SAID THAT SHE UNDERSTOOD THAT "CINDY WAS IN ONE OF THE ROOMS WITH A LITTLE GIRL AND HAD APPARENTLY UPSET HER SO THAT DR. MUFUFSKI BECAME MOST ANNOYED."

DR. MUFUFSKI WOULD NOT COMMENT . . . .

POTTER CINDY SAID HE WOULD ANSWER ANY QUESTIONS THAT HE COULD. TO THE QUESTION, "WHAT'S THIS ALL ABOUT?" HE ANSWERED, "WELL, HERE I AM IN THE POLICE STATION UNDER ARMED GUARD. I GUESS I WENT INTO THE WRONG HOSPITAL ROOM. THEY DIDN'T HAVE A QUARANTINE SIGN UP, SO I JUST WALKED IN AND DID MY THING . . . ."

Is that so! Well, we'll just see about that. Feets had estimated that the repair of the Briar Vista School fence, damages to Skipton's leg and car and to Billy, the driver, and paying for three new dogs, to say nothing of wounded egos, came to about $1,500. If Potter was his pigeon, he'd get the message to him, and the bill.

Chapter Twenty-Six

Except for the local papers, the story of Potter's trouble with Dr. Mufufski and the Golden Slippers Children's Hospital got no more than a box at best in papers elsewhere around the country. At the Atlanta television station, for example, where the teletype story gave Feets' notion its first hint of credibility, the report was deemed "Not timely" by both the news and sports departments. Feets watched one newsman read the wire and say "Garbage!" Some editor from the sports department confessed that even if the Redbirds were in town, which they weren't, "I doubt if we'd bother with it." He tore the wire out of the machine, handed it to Feets and said, "Here's a present for you, Lieutenant Patrick. Give it to your kids. Show them the kind of crap that's put out over these wires when baseball writers get desperate." Feets took it hungrily, as Exhibit A or B or C—not to show his son the woes of sports writers during a copy famine.

Locally, the incident at Golden Slippers was big, as was anything that could pass as a summer sports yarn. If it fed the egos of the Redbirds, the story was considered worthy of publication. If it had to do with Potter Cindy, the league-leading hitter, they slapped a two-column headline on it and ran it as the lead story. Potter was news. This time he even made the astrology column of the afternoon paper.

"Potter Cindy's 'arrest' today was predicted by the stars. He's a Gemini in his naughty phase, and with Taurus descending and Cancer rising, he would necessarily be pranksterish with children. Gemini are often irritated by children at this time of the month (autograph hunters under eighteen beware). Potter tangled with a doctor who was born on March 21 (we checked the date in the directory of the American Medical Association) and that means the medico was born on the cusp of a water and fire sign, Pisces and Aries, and you know what happens when you mix those two—steam!!!" There was even more steam hissing from the Redbird front office, and if records are correct there is not a Pisces/Aries cusp in the whole organization.

Zarember thundered, exploded, nearly burst a gut. "Holy shit! Can't that sonofabitch Potter even visit a goddamn kids' loony bin without giving me an ulcer?" He said that to nobody in particular. He had just spoken to Sergeant Sain of the Golden Slippers Township police department, informing the policeman that Sunday would be a great day for a doubleheader. "We appreciate the intelligent, cool-headed police work. We'll have a string of box seats at the ticket office. Just say 'Golden Slippers' to the guy at the window and 'Open Sesame!' Heller Park belongs to your entire troop."

This sudden flourish of generosity had followed a long, hot windup by Mr. Heller himself, who told Zarember: "There is more than a million dollars tied up in that young man of yours. I will leave to your vivid imagination how many pretzels will have to be sold before just that much, not half a million more, is returned to its proper coffers. Common sense would dictate that we have placed the money in the hands of a young courier, who, unbeknownst to you, Herbert, is afflicted with palsy. That money is slipping through his nerve-damaged fingers, I fear, even before the

212

last of our promotions is completed. But, as you, yourself, have pointed out many times, and have such miserable, disrupted guts to prove it, baseball talent is unpredictable. Most of the professionals are skilled idiots, or no-good punks, or overgrown children. Baseball is the great melting pot of America's young egomaniacs with the talent for blabbering inanities, getting high on liquor or marijuana or amphetamines, and cohabiting with the prettiest and dumbest cheerleaders or dairy queens in America. I know you can't love them very much, Herbert, for they cause you much grief. That, too, is common sense. But, Herbert, common sense means no more than common prejudice. If something is considered common sense, it has been commonly derived at, and to my way of thinking, it is of little dollar value.

"If you learned to love these youngsters of ours, they would grow closer to you, and you would be better able to predict their moments of capriciousness. You would win their confidence and, Herbert, you would be in a better position to make certain that my heirs will inherit all of the Heller millions, including the million-plus you may have led me to squander on an eccentric outfielder. Now, I'd appreciate your getting the situation resolved—with love and kindness, Herbert, remember."

Zarember interpreted that to mean giving box-seat passes to the police and hell to Potter.

"I mean just what the hell is wrong with you? Can't you even visit a hospital without fucking up the deal?"

"I don't want to talk about it."

"You don't want to talk about it? You keep pulling down your pants and taking a shit wherever you feel like it and you don't want to talk about it."

"I didn't take any shits."

"I know that. It's just a manner of speaking. I mean, you shitted up the situation. It didn't make the team look good. It doesn't sell pretzels."

"Please, Mr. Zarember. Don't bother me. I'm sorry. It was a mistake. I'll make it up to you."

"How are you going to make up for the whole town thinking you're a troublemaker and a flake?"

"The heck with the whole town. Let them start complaining when I stop hitting."

"You stop hitting and I'll send your ass back to Bougainvilla."

"I thought Whitey makes those decisions."

"Whitey works for the organization. He's been doing it for twenty years. He may bitch or act tough or hold up his middle finger at us. But he's a pro. If he quit or we canned him, he'd dig himself a hole right out there in centerfield—your territory—and jump in, hoping someone would be nice enough to cover him quickly."

"I'm sorry. I truly am."

It was not clear to Zarember if Potter was apologizing or commiserating with the plight, and enslavement, of professional athletes. Potter's face bore the look of a person who had just had a nose job and was told by the plastic surgeon that there was a slight error and he now looked like a hyena. But his words were earnest enough, and Zarember softened, on the advice of Mr. Heller, still jabbing at his ulcer.

"Get yourself sorted out, Potter. For Christ's sake. Please do me a favor, will ya, kid? Next time you're going to get yourself arrested, give a guy about a week's notice so that I can arrange to have our devoted press corps visit a massage parlor."

Potter made no comment, as none was called for. He wondered what it would feel like to choke the life out of a man.

"No more shit, okay? Please—"

Potter nodded.

Zarember saw the kid had a pleasant, sweet quality about him. In the old days they used to call it "the honor of manlines." He wondered why he had not noticed it before. Potter was a cut above a lot of the ballplayers Zarember had seen and known, if one could call Zarember's relationship to a ballplayer "knowing" the person. The outfielder wasn't a great brain, but he wasn't a fool, either. He gave the proper weight and respect to a situation, or a conversation. He didn't say dumb or foolhardy things. He was not stubborn, or bad-tempered, or put together with a bunch of wire hangers so that the slightest breeze of criticism made him rattle.

Zarember's stomach was bothering him. He knew ballplayers did not create ulcers. It was the business of baseball, all the goddamned housekeeping chores that did it—arranging bed time, travel, trades, kidnappings from high schools and colleges, grabbing up these gifted young jackasses, hitching them to a contract, and then making them tear up the ground until their bodies wore out. Afterwards, when wracked with tendonitis and arthritic joints, they are released unconditionally from bondage. He was not sure how he had gotten into the work from a major in public relations at the University of Missouri. He suspected that it really was true that he was chosen for his unpleasant personality and his Mediterranean horseshit. The truth was, he had not wanted to become a barber in the greaseball section of St. Louis like his old man. He wanted money and power and a dame he liked. And why not a couple of kids? So he ate up his stomach, severed it on pretzels for that fuck with the bakeries because he wanted real dough and his gonads were behaving normally.

"Potter, Potter. Potter."

"It won't happen again, Herb. That's really it. You got my word."

Zarember's stomach ached so bad he wished he had a bottle of sweet cream. "You are, bar none, Potter, the greatest natural ballplayer I have ever seen. You tell anybody I told you that and I'm going to poison your fuckin' Wheaties." Even love and kindness didn't lessen the ache in Zarember's guts. Everybody thought he was a "no-good greaseball." Well, he was, in a sense. He was a second-generation Romanian pastrami.

Hundreds of miles away, Feets Patrick was feeling no pain in his guts when he picked up the phone, got the long-distance operator to place a call to Sergeant S. B. Sain of the Golden Slippers Township police department, and tell him the Atlanta police were on the phone.

"Who'd you say you was again?"

"Lieutenant Craig Patrick. Shield number 6745, De Kalb County, Georgia, police department."

"How can I help you, Patrick?"

"Well, Captain, I'll tell you." Feets knew Sain was a sergeant, but he never believed in starting out on fishing with a man by telling the guy to call him "sir." It had a way of snagging lines of communication, so to speak. "We've heard on the radio down here that you fellows arrested that ballplayer, that good rookie star, Potter Cindy."

"You fellows heard about that down there already?"

"We sure did. It seems that if Potter Cindy got a case of diarrhea or a parking violation, the news would be all over the country. We see his face on kids' tee shirts, on TV commercials, magazine advertisements. Anyway, the fellows at the stationhouse were wondering what the heck that Cindy did. We figured it was something naughty. I'll tell you why: We had a case down here a while back of a basketball player who visited a Catholic orphanage and tried to bang one of them young nuns—you know, the kind that wear the miniskirt habits—in a broom closet."

Sergeant Sain chuckled.

"Anyway," Feets took his advantage, "the radio report down here was kind of wishy-washy on just what kind of hell your ballplayer raised. Everybody here thought he tried to do a little quickie with that nurse that turned him in."

"Naw," said Sergeant Sain, "it wasn't that at all. Potter Cindy's a clean-cut kid. He's a Christian."

"He is?"

"Oh, sure. He didn't do nothing. The doctor and nurse

just raised a fuss about nothing. We just took him for a ride down to the station and let him go. The newspaper fellows, like you say, turned a traffic violation into a capital offense, you know what I mean? Potter just walked into a room by mistake, and the doctor got all hot under the collar. The doctor looked like one of them little, nervous, edgy fellows, you know?"

"Well, he must of kept something important in that room. Sounds like it was the narco storeroom or something."

"Oh, hell, no. It was just a little sick girl no more than ten years old."

"Potter Cindy just scared the kid then—"

"Naw, he didn't scare her none. He gave her a baseball and a glove. She was one of those very sick children that didn't move or talk or anything."

"Was she paralyzed?"

"No, not paralyzed. But she might well have been."

"How do you mean?"

"Well, they got a highfalutin' doctor's name for it. But what it is, really, is that she just turned herself off from the world. I can't for the life of me think why. She was just as cute as a bug's ear, though she did look like she wasn't entirely tuned in, when you come to think of it."

"What else did Potter Cindy do?"

"There wasn't much else he could do, you see. He couldn't hold no conversation with her unless he felt like talking to himself. He gave her a baseball and a mitt."

"But the nurse called him 'disgusting.'"

"Yeah, well, you can see why, can't you? She was in charge of this wing. And Potter Cindy came marching in there with his high spirits. He's dynamic, good-looking, calls attention to himself, you know? Well, let's put it this way: Suppose you were in charge of keeping a room of hoodlums quiet and some guy busts in and starts stirrin' them up. You wouldn't be too happy about it."

"Well, *disgusting*. That means something different," Feets

pointed out. "I'd be surprised, angry, upset, annoyed. I wouldn't say I was disgusted. Now if someone came down the hospital wing with a hard on, I might find that disgusting if I were the nurse."

"There ain't nobody coming after that nurse with his pecker flying. She's no Raquel Welch, if you know what I mean. Naw, there ain't any similarities between your basketball player and Potter Cindy. But it's been nice talking to you, Patrick."

"Right, Sain," he dropped his rank altogether. "I appreciate your time and intelligence. Listen, if you ever get to Atlanta, be sure and look me up, you hear?"—a matter of formality.

"Oh, I sure will." Sain was about as eager to look him up as Feets was to have him.

The whole damn thing was beginning to get interesting. Feets could not help thinking these kind of coincidences happen all the time. You practically got a gun pointing at a guy's head only to find out you made the wrong suspect. To listen to people talk about the virtues of this damn kid, one would think Feets was the Pharisee and Potter Cindy was a poor little victim of the worst meaning of "Law and Order." Feets had not heard a bad word about him yet, except maybe "disgusting."

He got the operator to call the hospital in Golden Slippers and try to locate nurse Sabradilla. She was off duty. Her home phone number was unlisted. Feets told the operator he was a policeman and the call was official. In Golden Slippers, like Atlanta, the law has privileges.

"Hello. I have a call for Lucy Sabradilla."

"This is she."

"This is Lieutenant Patrick. I'm a policeman. I'm trying to close a file on Potter Cindy and I wonder if I can ask you a couple of questions."

"I answered all the questions already."

"Well, this is just routine to clean up the file." He put it in that impersonal way, as though he was just going to go over the file with a little Ajax.

"No. I don't want to add anything."

"Oh, I know you don't," Feets said, "you've probably been through a lot of questions already. But I'm afraid we have to get this cleaned up. . . ." Feets took a big chance, adding, "Unless you want to do it down at the stationhouse—"

"Oh, all right," she said, though she was annoyed by this obviously transplanted southerner, now a midwest police official, bothering her.

"Good. We appreciate it. Now you said Potter Cindy was disgusting. What did you mean by *disgusting*?"

"I don't know if I meant disgusting, really, now that I think about it. He just burst into the wing and I got excited. He looked very strange in there. His display was disgusting, I guess."

"His display?"

"Well, the way he kind of rolled into the wing. He seemed uncomfortable, nervous, unnatural in some way."

"Did he make a sexual advance at you or anyone?"

"No," she said. "I thought you said you were just going to ask routine questions to close the file."

"Clean the file, I said," Feets pointed out, though he knew he was probably dirtying it. "Were you afraid he would make advances at you or anyone?"

"Now, *listen!* That's enough. I consider your file cleaned up enough." She hung up.

Feets was a little upset with his technique. He knew he had pushed the question too hard. He had to get to that Dr. Mufufski.

The telephone operator informed him that the doctor was not at the hospital, that she would try his office number if he liked. He told her he would like that.

"Dr. Mufufski's office," said a woman.

"I have a long-distance call for Dr. Mufufski."

"Doctor's not in. Who's calling please?"

"Hank Aaron," Feets said, and hung up. He would try him later.

Potter got to Dr. Mufufski before Feets did, or rather Dr. Mufufski got to Potter, thinking the "Hank Aaron" message was really a desperate call for help from Potter. In these days, Dr. Freud was in a bad slump, though he still had some headshrinkers around who—like Dr. Mufufski—had considered him the greatest. The generation that preceded Potter by merely a decade had been convinced to look to Sigmund Freud for answers to all of man's riddles. Maybe millions of highly educated people and even baseball knuckleheads believed that in Dr. Freud's studies and works, his entreaties and imperatives, there would be revealed even the secret guilts and hang-ups of a person who habitually catches colds and fumbles pop-ups. It was part of the game played by all unrecorded closet-psychotherapy-baseball-player patients. Professionals were hired openly in those days to help the players cure failing skills and sore arms with words, rather than with more batting practice and shots of corticosteroids and megaton vitamins.

Later, poor old Dr. Freud—even granting that his genius inspired Dr. Mufufski to call Potter—had failed in too many clutch situations, and they buried him somewhere in the minors with Dick '66' Stuart, Jim Bouton, and Marv Throneberry.

"Hello, this is Dr. Mufufski. Did you want to see me?"

"Well, yes, I guess. I was going to call you for an appointment after Sunday's doubleheader, as you had advised. I didn't remember I was supposed to call you today."

"Why did you use the name Hank Aaron?"

"What do you mean?"

The doctor sensed a deeper trouble in the patient. "I think we should see each other today," he suggested.

"We got a game today with the Mets."

"Are you free after the game?"

"Well, I was going to go the movies with some of the fellows."

"You have a wife, don't you?"

"Oh, she's in Los Angeles, filming a television show."

"I think we should talk about this Hank Aaron business. It might be important."

"There isn't much to talk about. He's just there breathing down my neck in every department." After he said it, he realized that Hank Aaron doesn't breathe down any rookie's neck. It's the other way around.

"Well, that's something to talk about. Come to my office after the game." He gave Potter the address.

"Have you decided to treat me yourself, doctor? Or are you going to pass me on to one of your pinch hitters? You hadn't made up your mind the last time, you know, in the hospital."

"We'll see each other after the game."

Dr. Mufufski had no sooner hung up with Potter when his answering service called and said, "Hank Aaron called you again, doctor. He left an Atlanta number."

"Atlanta? Atlanta, Georgia?"

"Yes, doctor."

"Okay, I'll call him."

Feets Patrick got on the phone, introduced himself as a policeman, not a slugger.

"Lieutenant Patrick, first of all, it's quite childish and probably illegal to misrepresent yourself as a ballplayer. In the second place, I can see no reason to tell you any more about the incident at Golden Slippers Hospital than I have already said and, frankly, you are out of line in many ways. You have no authority in this state and I needn't tell you a blessed thing, nor would I if I knew anything."

"That's up to you," Feets said, but he knew he didn't have a flat foot to stand on. Moreover, his head was probably flat for making those calls to the doctor. "But I keep getting the feeling that there's something fishy about that whole business at the hospital and something fishy about Potter Cindy, too."

"I don't care to explore your feelings with you, Mr. Patrick. I hope you'll excuse me. Good day."

"If you change your mind, I can be reached at this number anytime," Feets told the doctor.

Dr. Mufufski knew no good would come of Atlanta's Lieutenant Patrick.

Feets felt the doctor knew more than he was telling an Atlanta cop. He made a note to check whether doctors in Golden Slippers, like Presidents in the White House and priests in the confession box, had executive privilege and could protect the confidence of patients. He was not sure Potter Cindy was his patient, but the doctor sure sounded to him like he was protecting somebody.

Feets knew, God and psychiatrists willing, that Potter would be in town the next week to play Atlanta. There would be plenty of time to present the Redbird sensation with the bill for $1,500, give or take a hundred. He made another note to call Dave Skipton up and invite him to the Atlanta-Redbird game. In the meantime, he decided to go through the police files for unsolved child-molestation cases in the county for the past six months, just in case Potter Cindy had an extra-special taste for little Georgia peaches.

In all fairness to Feets, let it at least be said that he was still uncertain the outfielder was the one who had taken the fruit from the tree before it was ripe.

He decided to make one more out-of-town call.

Chapter Twenty-Seven

Samantha was most surprised to hear from that Atlanta Coke salesman again. She had almost not accepted the call; she only remembered him vaguely as the older man at Bobby Hartman's party. Still, Coke would be a fantastic account to bring to an advertising agency; it would be a marvelous coup, a great entrée into one of the bigger houses on Madison Avenue. She could not afford to be too snotty and unavailable to this Coke man. Who knew? He might have a more important job than he let on. Although, she would admit that she strove—more—hungered for the big leagues of advertising, she still might not have been sharp enough to take the call. It took Mr. Patrick's cleverness to get her to the phone. He told her secretary that the call concerned Potter Cindy, a man who "might be in big trouble." How super-sharp he was! What could be a better lure than to present to the advertising account executive the possibility that the big testimonial gun in the Heller Pretzel commercial was about to bring down the whole Heller Bakeries and her agency in an eruption that would make Mt. Vesuvius look like a firecracker, at least in the Midwest of Redbird country. Of course, she had to take that call, even if Madison Avenue did not exist as a street she had to own, or at least be recognized on.

Samantha had come to the decision that Mr. Patrick was more than he had made himself out to be. He knew, for example, long before she had, from a point hundreds of miles away, that Potter had gotten into some kind of trouble at the Golden Slippers Children's Hospital. The mental hospital was only about fifteen miles from her office. Mr. Patrick knew what was going on even before it made the afternoon papers, and Potter Cindy was always big news in Redbird land! How powerful was Mr. Patrick that he had such resources avilable to him?

He pretended that he was only interested in the real story behind the trouble at Golden Slippers because Potter Cindy would in some sense be representing Coke at the school, though that was not the expressed purpose of the call. But she had remembered very clearly that he had made a big point to assure Potter that the school visit was not to be exploitative in any sense at all. So what does he do? How does he respond? Coke had to be protected at any cost.

Then Samantha was made very wary by Mr. Patrick's line of questioning about Potter's background, his hang-ups, what in his style of life would cause him to get into trouble at a children's hospital. At some point during the conversation she had the sudden thought that Mr. Patrick was interviewing her on Potter, as though the outfielder was being considered for an appointment with the FBI or the CIA. She thought it must be some very big deal to work for Coke, or the inner chambers of the government. Mr. Patrick was asking questions that bordered on indecency. Why, he had practically asked her if she had had sexual relations with Potter, not in so many words, of course, but the implications were clear. Samantha had told him that he should be asking those questions of his wife, Sissy, who was in a very much better position to answer.

Samantha did not remember when it was she had picked up from unsaid words in the conversation that Mr. Patrick had some suspicion about the sexual preferences of Potter Cindy. No accusations had really been made. Nothing definite had been said, but it was something about the direction of Mr. Patrick's conversation that left the feeling that Potter was not the All-American boy everyone had thought.

What was he, a fag? She recalled that Potter had a way of adjusting his ass when he was setting himself at the plate. Perhaps people might find that a swishy gesture. Also, he carried the bat to the plate across the crook of his arm. It was an odd way to carry it; it was more like carrying a baby. Could that be construed as unmanly? She saw they were just idiosyncrasies no different from that very cute way Potter put his arms out like an airplane when he crossed the plate, a happy Redbird winging in with a worm, or a run, in his mouth. The local papers even carried a story on that, complete with picture, and a caption which began "Big Bird in Flight." Nobody seemed to find that faggy, not even Mr. Patrick, when she mentioned it to him on the phone. Boy, she would love to know if he was a fag. In fact, she had to know. It was, in a sense, her job to find out. It would be important to F. M. to have that kind of intelligence, and she had a responsibility to inform him as the client.

Potter had seemed very sweet and tender with her in her apartment the last time they were together without the company of television crews and script people and make-up men. He had not slept with her. But, then, she had not wanted him to. Still, she could not help thinking if that had been any other ballplayer, he would have insisted on her coming across. Potter didn't. But that did not make him a fag; it just made him all the more attractive. He had that big erection. He didn't wear underwear. She didn't exactly look like a man. He did not have that thing of his ready to stick up somebody's behind.

She decided to make up some excuse to get Potter to her apartment. She would see what his problem was, what that

Mr. Patrick was fishing for once and for all. She told Potter that the first set of commercials was so well liked, so popular, everybody was so happy with them, that they had to rush some more into production. He had to come over that night to look over the script to see that there was no language in it that would seem unnatural to him or cause him not to read effortlessly.

All of what she had told Potter was true; it was just the emergency aspect that she had lied about. Mr. Heller had loved the commercials and even attributed increased pretzel sales to the success of the commercials. Yorktown, Class & Gently congratulated her with a three-thousand-dollar raise. Samantha was only twenty-five and she was already earning, with that raise, more than a thousand times her age. She was also one, and perhaps the favorite, of the mistresses of the Pretzel Baron. If she wanted to she could go to work tomorrow for Mr. Heller; he had asked her many times to join his own advertising staff. She had refused because she had places to go where Yorktown, Class & Gently were only peewees and Mr. Heller was only a very rich man, not a king.

There was still nobody big enough to tell Samantha that she could not try to go to bed with the man most likely to be named Rookie of the Year. The only thing that could stop her was Potter Cindy himself, and that would only happen if, as Mr. Patrick had maybe hinted, there was something peculiar about Potter's desires. Samantha decided, because she wanted to sleep with Potter very much, that she was going to make it hard for him to pass her up.

She was surprised that Potter was not the least bit resistant about coming over. What she did not know, of course, was how lonely, and afraid of being exposed by Dr. Mufufski, Potter felt. The doctor had forced him into therapy. He did not want to make a whole long confession about the many children he had displayed himself to, or tell about those he had touched and those who had touched him. He also came, when Samantha called, because Sissy was not available, had been tied up for weeks, and maybe she was even thinking of leaving him. Maybe Sissy had found someone else. He wondered if she had already left him. He put it out of his mind. He didn't think Sissy would leave him without telling him, and he did not want to believe that she had. He needed someone who was nice and someone who didn't know him. Samantha would be just fine.

They ate at an out-of-the-way restaurant on the road to Golden Slippers Township, of all places, and Samantha paid with her American Express card over Potter's protests.

"It's on the company," she insisted. "It's business, after all. I can't have you paying. It wouldn't be right."

Then he knocked her and her suspicions for a loop when he said, "I wanted to see you, when you called, as much as the company wanted you to see me . . . about the script. So I'd like very much to pay, Samantha, honestly."

Mr. Patrick . . . A lot he knew about a man who knew how to charm a woman into thinking that an aggressive call of hers was his idea all the time. Was this Potter Cindy charming or was he charming, Mr. Patrick? Samantha thought this while she signed the American Express slip. She explained, "If it ever got back that you paid for me, I'd be in trouble with my bosses. It's unheard of to ask talent to pay for dinner."

He drove her back to her apartment building; he was about to park in a temporary spot, for people who were soon leaving, but she told him to park in a space in back of the apartment building.

"That other spot was closer," Potter said.

"Yes. But this one has another advantage."

"What's that?"

"It's permanent. The doorman won't be bothering us to move it."

Potter did not remember having promised himself not to

let Samantha take a long lead on him; he forgot that he said he would not let himself get caught alone in her apartment. He felt, in the middle of all his troubles, very excited by the prospect, very normal.

He put his arm around her shoulders when they walked from the parking spot to the entrance of the building. They rode to the fifteenth floor in the elevator smiling at one another.

She asked him if he wanted a beer or some coffee, and he said, no, that he had all that he wanted. She took his hand and led him to the bedroom.

"What would you like more than anything else in the world right now, Potter?" She was getting undressed while she asked that.

He did not answer right away, because he could not believe she would be asking that question now unless she meant not to give it to him. He was prepared, this time, to demand it.

"I'll do anything you want," she said. She was next to him, already undressed.

He smiled. He had heard about a thing called a "peppermint" from a man he had cowboyed with; a Las Vegas woman had oral sex with the cowboy while wetting her mouth with crème de menthe. He took a chance at having Samantha throw him out. It was not very much of a chance, because by the time he told her what a "peppermint" was they were both undressed and in bed. She laughed sexily and said that if he was very nice to her, very special, she would think about it.

Potter thought about a "peppermint" the whole time that he was being very nice to her, very special. And after she had taken a brief nap, she started to jump out of bed and Potter caught her by the leg. "Don't go," he said.

"Listen, I have to do two things. First I have to pee."

"And after that—?"

"I have to see if I have any crème de menthe."

Potter smiled. So did she. Samantha was thinking, *Mr. Patrick, why don't you go fuck yourself?* She knew there was nothing wrong with Potter that a little dish of paella couldn't cure. Samantha thought of herself as a very sexy woman. It was the kind of confidence, she knew, that takes some people to the very top of their profession. What was it the Redbird yearbook said about Potter Cindy? *Oh, yes, "He gets the job done."*

Chapter Twenty-Eight

When making indictments against a person, an organization, even a way of life, one has to set the record straight, at least to the extent that any mere memorialist can recall, or dig out of the archives of broken dreams or shattered testimony.

"When you are going good, when you're clean and smelling like Brut, there ain't a thing in baseball that can get you, not even the commissioner. But when you are raunchy, man, scurvy, smelling like a Calcutta ghetto, you'd be glad if they just stopped calling you 'shitty.'" Hank Mayknoll said that one season when he got knocked out of the box seven straight times in a row.

"Baseball is a business, make no mistake about it. Athletes are a line of products. You get one fat can that's tainted in some way, and they yank it off the shelf as though it would produce an epidemic of botulism that would decimate the homes of everyone who watched a ball game." Phil Brossi said that two years before Potter had come up to the majors, the year he developed a bit of a gut and a slump and was farmed out for the season to the Class A team in Forgetitville, which is nowhere.

"The culture uses the young and talented and then discards them to make room for its newer strengths. It is on this notion that America became great." F. M. Heller said that at the annual meeting of the Knights of Pythias in Birmingham, Alabama.

On the day before the Redbirds took the field against the Mets, before Potter had his first therapy session with Dr. Mufufski, the outfielder was batting at .384. He had 24 home runs, 6 triples, 26 doubles, 55 singles; he had batted-in 78 runs. He led the league in everything but home runs and singles; he had stolen 27 bases, made only two errors. The players and fans selected him to the All-Star Team. He led all other players, except Aaron, in the balloting, even though he was a write-in candidate.

That's the record, as it is written. If one is willing to play with the cards he is dealt, as most Americans are, and hope for something better in the draw, he would find it unbelievable that someone holding a hand with the case ace would discard it.

Dr. Mufufski had his television tuned to the game against New York and watched with awe as Potter moved after a wicked-rising line drive, headed for the alley in left center. The Redbird centerfielder was stretched out in the air, horizontally, when the ball plunked into his glove. He hit the ground hard with his left arm upraised so that none of the umpires would have any doubts about what happened to the ball. Dr. Mufufski was not an athlete or a baseball nut, but he could recognize a catch that was ordinary and one that took the magic of levitation to perform.

He followed the game for another inning hoping—who knows what?—to see something about Potter that would be helpful in treating him. He saw him smash his twenty-fifth home run of the season high and deep into the rightfield seats. He was greeted by his teammates with a standing ovation. The announcer made a point of the fact that the home run brought the entire bench to its feet, including the manager, Whitey Knocthofer, who led the applause. The announcer stressed, "I just can't recall any other time that Whitey has publicly applauded an individual player, and I've been broadcasting baseball for the Redbirds since Whitey broke in." The home run had tied him with Aaron for that season.

It seems that after that the house caved in.

"I saw you today," Dr. Mufufski said, "you were excellent."

"Thank you. That's good of you to say, seeing as I struck out twice today and made a throwing error."

"I only saw a couple of innings. Do you know someone named Craig Patrick?"

"No. What team is he with?"

"He's a policeman in Atlanta."

"I don't know him. The only Patrick I know sells Coke in . . . ," Potter stopped.

"Did you ever molest a child in Atlanta?"

The question came at him so suddenly, it immobilized him. Potter was tapping off straight pitches and suddenly the doctor threw up this screwball. "I think we both know that you have abused many children, exhibited your genitals before them, masturbated. Did you do this to a child in Atlanta? Can you remember?"

"I guess so," Potter admitted. "It's cloudy, but I can remember doing it in many towns . . . in a lot of places."

"The one in Atlanta may prove troublesome. I think you should be made aware of that."

"I'm never going to do it again. That I know."

"Do you remember the first time you ever had thoughts of doing it?"

"I don't exactly have thoughts about doing it. I mean, I don't plan to do it. It's just that suddenly I'm doing it and I can't stop it. In a way it's like a bad pitch. A fellow throws the ball to the plate and he knows it's the wrong one, but he can't get it back. It's too late."

"When was the first time you remember wanting to exhibit yourself before a little girl?"

"For as long as I can remember. I was about eleven or twelve and I was sort of playing with my friend's six-year-old sister. We weren't doing anything out of the ordinary, but it struck me as very sexual. I think I may have wacked off after that."

"Did you show the little girl your genitals?"

"I guess I did."

"Are you ever impotent with your wife?"

"Well, I'm tired and under pressure from ballplaying sometimes, and we just sort of hold each other and not do anything."

"Are you tired and under pressure often? Are you impotent for long periods of time?"

"Well, I suppose I might be, but I don't get the chance because I'm on the road or Sissy is and we haven't been together that much, or married very long, either."

"I'm really impressed with the ease with which you discuss sex. Most patients find it very difficult to share this information with their doctors on the very first visit."

"Well, I've got to get it over and done with, doc."

"It's a problem that has been with you a long time. We'll have to explore it. It might take a couple of years."

"A couple of years!" Potter shrieked. "I thought we'd be able to settle it up in a couple of months." Potter had an uncle who had cancer of the brain and they bombed his skull with radiation and it only took six weeks. He lived for three years without ever being treated again.

"It's not a problem that one gets under control in so short a span of time. We'll have to work at it steadily."

"I don't think I've got that kind of time to give to it."

"You don't want to be a sexual deviate, do you?"

"No. I'm definitely not going to do those things again."

"How did you feel during your misdeeds?"

"Good, I think."

"What was the most exciting part? The way the little girl looked at you, or masturbating?"

"I suppose then it was masturbating. But as a grown-up, I do derive a certain amount of excitement in watching the children's faces."

"You talk very freely about your problem. Do you also enjoy talking about it?"

"Well, it is kind of a relief getting it off my chest."

"A lot of people, Potter, who have your problem—and it is not uncommon—want to get caught doing it. Did you ever feel that way?"

"Maybe."

"Aren't you sure?"

"I can't be sure. I've been doing this for about ten years or more in a lot of places and I've managed not to be caught until now."

"You are married to an experienced woman, aren't you?"

"Yes."

"Do you perform for her?"

"How do you mean?"

"Straightforward coitus?"

"We do lots of things together besides just straight sex."

"And you enjoy it."

"Most of the time."

"I want to discuss your sex life with your wife."

Potter waited for the question.

"Do you ever masturbate in front of your wife?"

"I don't think I have. But when she's doing it to me I sometimes imagine that I'm doing it and she's watching."

"That's more exciting to you?"

"Yes."

"Do you like people to look at your penis?"

"Yes."

"Why?"

234

"I like them to take notice of it, I guess. I like attention."

"You court it?"

"I guess."

"Didn't your parents pay attention to you?"

"Not very much. They were hard-working people. They were busy and often tired. I don't think they really had too much time for me."

"Was your father affectionate to your mother?"

"They were not affectionate people. They worried about making ends meet and didn't seem to have time for affection, love, or kindness."

"Did you have a bad relationship with your father?"

"More *no* relationship than a bad one. It seems to me that last time we spoke was about four months ago when he asked me to lend him money to go into some chicken-shit business."

"Was the business unsuccessful? And did you feel upset that your father took your money and abused it?"

"Huh? Oh, no, by 'chicken shit' I did not mean that he had made a poor investment with the money. It might be very successful, for all I know. I meant that he really was in a business of raising chicken excrement. They use it for hog feed and things."

Dr. Mufufski was an urban person; he did not think of chicken shit in its literal sense. He returned to pursue his original line of questioning.

Dr. Mufufski had remembered a professor at the University of California, where he had trained, describe the kind of sexual deviation that Potter fit into. He remembered that people with this problem could be found in all walks of life. Still, he was surprised to find someone so frank, clear-headed, and articulate about the problem. In school, the recommended treatment for these patients, he recalled, was a straightforward, direct technique that reveals the patient's basic fear and its origin. The goal, he knew, was to show Potter how he continually recreated the situation in everyday life and to teach him to examine, question, and challenge the fear so that it was controllable.

"When your father asked you for the money, did that bother you?"

"What do you mean? Did I want to give it to him?"

"Did you feel it was yours and that he had no right to it—that it belonged to you?"

"I don't like to spend a whole lot of money. But I don't need much to get by, so it's okay. I didn't mind giving it to my father. Matter of fact, I was kind of pleased to be asked for it, pleased that my father knew I had it."

"It was like showing your penis, wasn't it? You were glad that your father saw you had a penis."

"It wasn't anything like that. I was just glad to help out."

"Are you sure?"

"Of course I'm sure!" Potter said this with some irritation.

"Why are you annoyed?"

"I don't like the idea of you tying up money with the penis."

"Why not? Money and the penis both give pleasure."

"They are not related, in this case."

"They're not?"

"No," Potter said emphatically. "It so happens the one thing that I've always disliked my father for was telling me a story about a man getting his penis cut off by a reaper."

"That was frightening to you, wasn't it?"

"Very."

"How old were you?"

"About seven or eight."

"Why did your father tell that story?"

"I don't remember. I think it was some kind of religious lesson."

"How do you mean?"

"Well, he had no regard for the man. He was a heavy drinker, unsavory. My father said that the Lord didn't want that man to come to Heaven whole."

236

"What did you think of that?"

"In what way?"

"That the Lord made those kinds of judgments. That God castrated the man with the reaper for his sins."

"I was afraid. I was only a kid. I didn't want to have that happen to me."

"What?"

"What do you mean 'what'? What we've been talking about!"

"Say it! I want you to say it," Dr. Mufufski said.

"I was afraid to be castrated."

"Why? Did you consider yourself a sinner at age seven or eight?"

"I was a kid. I did some bad things. At least I thought stealing was bad, or breaking windows, or whatever. When I was yelled at by my parents, I thought I was bad."

"I thought you said they didn't pay any attention to you."

"They didn't. But sometimes they yelled. I remember them calling me a bad boy."

"And you were afraid you would be castrated?"

"Yes. I sure was."

"How were you able to tell, Mr. Cindy, that you were not castrated?"

"I could see I wasn't, couldn't I?"

"Could you? How could you tell you weren't only seeing what you wanted to see?"

"I don't understand."

"How could you prove that you were not castrated?"

"Well, someone else could take a look—I guess—and see that I have a penis and testicles and that would prove it. Even a kid could see that."

"*Especially a kid,* isn't that what you mean? Little girls would be frightened of seeing a penis, might they not?"

"Yes." Potter said this tightly.

"And if they were frightened enough, or touched your penis, or if you masturbated in front of them, or they masturbated

237

you, those things would confirm that you indeed had a penis."

"Yes."

"And if you were afraid that the reaper got you one night like it got that sinner your father told you about, you'd have to go out and display yourself to another child. And then you would be reassured that you were whole—at least for that day."

"YES!" Potter screamed.

"Potter, we all have many things which haunt us. We'll try to get to the things that haunt you. Now, I think our time is up. We'll see each other again next week."

"No," Potter said, "I'll be on the road in Atlanta next week."

"When will you be back home?"

"The following Monday."

"Do you have a game?"

"No, it's an open date."

"Monday, then."

"No, that's it, Dr. Mufufski." Potter did not want to return; he had answered honestly, had told all that he knew. There was no more to tell the doctor. What did he want, all the details, a description of every child's reaction to his pecker?

"You don't understand, Potter. This is only the beginning. We haven't even begun to talk about your problem. We have not even scratched the surface."

"Maybe to you we haven't scratched. But I feel like I've been torn apart."

"That's what I'm trying to point out. I asked you a lot of questions, some of them very painful, but your reaction to them was very flat. You did not seem to be bothered very much one way or the other. Now that is something we must discuss next time. We have to go more deeply into your history. We have to uncover the reasons behind your problem. We've only taken a first step . . . a baby step."

"I don't like it. I don't want it anymore."

"You need it, Potter. Believe me. You have not given one answer, one reaction of a man even trying to control his sexual

238

deviation. You control everything else instead—your rage, your anger, your hate, even your laughter, I'll bet. You also control your sexual energy with women. You do all of these things successfully, so successfully, in fact, that on the surface you perform very nicely with women, with people. And most people admire you for the very control which is destroying you on one hand and making it possible for you to function on the other."

"You're confusing me," Potter said.

"It is confusing, and we have to find a way to make it clear, make you understand it. Is that clear?"

"Yes," Potter said softly.

"You will come back Monday. I want you to call me, Potter, whenever you feel like it, wherever you are. Pick up the phone if you're feeling funny."

"Funny?"

"When you want another little girl to reassure you that you have a penis, that it hasn't been taken away from you."

"Don't you worry. I'm never going to do that again."

"We are going to work together to help you control that one thing in the world you cannot control."

"I swear, Dr. Mufufski, I'm never going to do that again. That's over with."

Chapter Twenty-Nine

Some people in baseball believe that the team that is in first place at the All-Star break will win the pennant. Only two games separated Atlanta from the Redbirds. The Braves would have to sweep the series in order to get that cherished psychological advantage of being on top at mid-season.

Everybody who was interested in baseball in Atlanta knew this, especially Dave Skipton, who was a super-baseball nut. He was overjoyed, tickled silly, that Feets had gotten tickets to this "critical" series. He knew the tickets were a tough proposition to swing, even though they were seated out in the centerfield stands. Never mind, Dave had a good view of the Redbird sensation, Potter Cindy. He knew there was nobody in baseball who played that position better. There was a lot more hanging on the series. Dave's beloved Hank Aaron would be face to face with that Redbird outfielder. They were all tied up in homers and close enough to tell the brand of underarm deodorant each other wore in all the other statistical departments.

Dave was glad his cast was off. He wouldn't want to have to maneuver all those stadium stairs and ramps wearing a cast. It was bad enough having to do it with a cane. He hoped the doctor was wrong about the leg having a permanent fault. He didn't relish walking around with an "ever so slight limp" for the rest of his life. He would love to get his hands on that sex pervert.

Dave looked at his friend Feets, who was watching the Redbird outfielders shag flies.

"Feets," Dave asked, "you get a lead yet on that sex pervert? Remember, you said something about scouring the schools in town for a track man or something?"

"I'm working on it," Feets admitted.

"You're not killing yourself, though. It's been about three months, hasn't it?"

Feets smiled. "A person's got to get lucky and just fall on a needle in a haystack to find one, Dave."

"Well, you're not jumping in any haystacks now, are you?"

"You don't have a forgiving nature, Dave."

"Forgive, hell. I might be permanently crippled 'cause of that sonofabitch. You get those X-rays back from the police doc? Did he tell you what he thinks? Boy, I sure would like to catch that guy and break his legs."

Feets had forgotten about the X-rays. He did not answer Dave on that. "How much you figure that trouble cost you, all things considered?"

"I have to pay for the fence, the car, Billy's medical bills, my own—it'll cost me every bit of seven hundred dollars when I'm finished."

"Is that all?"

"*All!* What do you mean? I had that money saved to have the house painted and a new roof put on."

"Suppose I knew who the fellow was or was pretty damn sure, Dave, and he turned out to be one of our Atlanta ballplayers."

"Come on, now."

"Let's just suppose. Now, would you want me to arrest him now or after the Redbird series? Let's make it better: Suppose the ballplayer was Aaron."

"Well, I know it wasn't Aaron 'cause the fellow was white. So I can't get myself into this little supposing of yours."

"Well, then, suppose he was another guy, a white baseball star, a real superstar like Aaron."

"I'm mad enough to want you to arrest him right on the spot before the series. A crime's a crime, ain't it, Feets?"

"Suppose he paid you the money back—"

"Well, I don't know. I suppose if he gave me back the money and promised not to do that kind of thing ever again—I mean, swore to me on a stack of Bibles—I might let bygones be bygones. He didn't do nothing to the little kid, really, but show her his pecker."

"You'd forgive him, then?"

"I don't know, Feets, what should I do?"

"The law would say blow the whistle on him. The Lord might say be merciful."

"I'd *lean* toward being merciful, even though I'm madder than hell at him."

"Suppose he were not one of our guys but one of the Redbirds, say, Potter Cindy out there."

"That's a different proposition, ain't it?" Dave could imagine what this series would be like without Cindy in the lineup.

"Not in the eyes of the Lord," Feets pointed out.

"Yeah, well, it ain't Aaron or Cindy, so let's drop the little game."

"It's possible, though." Feets led him and then dropped it.

Dave studied Potter Cindy for a long time, watching him run in for liners, chase down flies.

"You know, Feets—"

Feets turned slowly to his friend, and waited.

"This is going to sound unbelievable, but that fellow I chased out at the Briar Vista School was built a lot like Potter Cindy out there."

242

"There are hundreds of athletes with a build like Potter Cindy's."

"Who run with the same stride?" Dave asked.

"Sure."

"Who have the same long black hair?"

"Sure."

"Who can leap fences, Feets? Who can run like an antelope?"

"Come on, now, you're just daydreaming so that we beat the Redbirds."

"Feets, do you think it's possible?"

"He's a religious man."

"That's true. I know he's got that Jesus sticker on his car."

"He's married to a Hollywood starlet."

"And she's a swinger, they say," Dave said. "It doesn't seem to me that he'd be the sort of fellow who'd go after little girls like that, does it?"

"Sure doesn't," Feets admitted.

Potter hit a soaring liner in the third inning that went for a triple and drove in two runs.

"He sure does run like that guy I chased—" Dave grumbled. Atlanta was trailing by two runs.

Aaron homered in the fifth with a man on to tie the score, and he went one up on Potter in the home-run department.

"That sex pervert could have been any number of guys," Dave admitted. Hell, the score was tied.

In the sixth inning, Potter cut off a base hit headed for the alley in right center, and threw an Atlanta player out at the plate, snapping a rally. However, Atlanta managed to push across one run, giving the team the lead.

In the top of the seventh, Potter singled to right, stole second, was bunted to third, and tagged up on a little fly to right and beat the throw to the plate. The throw was on line but Potter got in ahead of it somehow, tying the game.

"Shit," Dave growled.

In the eighth, Aaron homered again with nobody on base, giving Atlanta the lead again. They took a one-run edge into the ninth. Dave quickly reviewed his scorecard. He was relieved that Potter was the fifth man up in the inning; hopefully Atlanta would have won the game before Potter's turn came. The first two men up were quickly retired on ground balls, routine plays. Dave breathed a sigh of relief because he didn't think much of the next two Redbirds as hitters—Hartman and Condon. It looked hopeful, positive. Then Hartman delivered one of his nagging Texas leaguers. It fell in. Dave had a nervous moment. Still, Condon was the hitter. As he expected, Knocthofer sent up a pinch hitter. The Redbird swung on the first pitch and hit it on the ground to third. The Atlanta fielder picked it up, lost it, picked it up again, and threw too late to first. Potter Cindy was going to bat. "Shit!" Dave said. "Can't they handle a routine ground ball?"

"Man alive," said Feets, "I can't watch this."

"They ought to walk him, I wouldn't challenge a hitter like that."

"If they walked him," Feets pointed out, "they'd put the lead run on second base. And it would bring up their clean-up hitter, Phil Brossi."

"I'd rather face Brossi than Cindy. I don't care who is in scoring position. Cindy's leading the league, ain't he?"

"That Brossi's tough in the clutch, Dave. I was reading where he has delivered fourteen hits in late-inning cliff-hanging situations."

Potter took the first pitch for a ball. The next one would have been low, but he swung and fouled it off.

"Keep it away from him!" Dave yelled.

Feets looked unhappy. He closed his eyes because he knew that some things are fated to come out wrong, no matter what. He heard the crack of the bat, and the communal gasp from Atlanta fans, and he knew Potter Cindy had done Atlanta harm. The blow left home plate like a rocket, a typical Potter Poke, and exploded way back in the seats in rightfield.

"That goddamn sex pervert!!" Dave was hurt. There was now no way that Atlanta could be leading the league after the series. The Redbirds would be in first at the All-Star break, no matter what happened in the next two games. There was, of course, still the last half of the ninth, but Atlanta fans were already leaving the ballpark in despair.

Feets got up to go; he was going to the clubhouse to talk to Potter Cindy. There was still another possible score to settle.

"Hey, Feets," said Dave, "we might get hot in the ninth."

"Forget it, Dave. It's over."

Feets told him that he wouldn't be going home with him, that he had some work to do.

"I still have tickets for the rest of the series. You still want to see the games, Dave?"

Dave kind of shrugged a yes.

"Okay, fine. Ask for them at the box office. They got my name on them. Take your kid."

"Don't you want to go, Feets?"

"No. It wouldn't be fun anymore." Feets was thinking that he would have to confront Potter. He knew Dave recognized Potter, even though they were playing a "suppose" game. Dave knew a running style when he chased one. The uniform, the fact that the villain was a Redbird superstar, would distract Dave rather than help him make a positive identification, no matter how hard he hit the ball or murdered Atlanta.

Feets made his way down the ramps with a discouraged crowd, getting by passageways blocked by uniformed guards with his shield. A big cop stopped him at the door of the Redbird clubhouse, but he produced his badge again, said "Official," and was let in. The Redbirds were still out in the field. An equipment man was laying out towels for the ballplayers to use after their showers. They'd be a happy

245

bunch when they arrived. And why not? They came down here and promptly scalped the poor old Braves.

Feets had never been in a major league clubhouse before. He was impressed with the fact that the floors were carpeted and that there was a big table of food set out, a regular smorgasbord, probably for the players and the press that traveled with them, Feets figured. The equipment man nodded at him and Feets nodded back. "Waiting for Potter Cindy," he told the man. "I'm a friend of the Captain."

"Well, at least you're first on line. There's going to be a lotta people wanting to see Potter tonight. Why don't you make yourself a sandwich?"

Feets could do with a snack; he was hungry. He knew it wasn't fair though. You don't steal a man's supper before you kick him in the balls.

"Go on," the equipment man urged, "it's going to be a long night. The stuff is set out for you writers, anyway. You with a local paper?"

"I'm not a writer," Feets said.

"That's okay, we'll still stake you to a bite. What do you do?"

"I'm a policeman."

"Autograph hunter, eh?"

Feets thought Potter did owe Dave some money and in that sense he did want his autograph on a check. "Something like that."

"Eat up. I got to get the rest of these towels put out."

Feets could tell the game was over. The press arrived, went immediately to the food and started wolfing down sandwiches. Feets did not eat, just watched, listened to the shop talk. When Potter walked through the doors, the newspapermen moved like a pack of dogs after him. Feets swore he saw some swallow bites of food without even chewing so that they would be free to ask questions. It was every bit of forty-five minutes before they finally stopped asking the outfielder a lot of questions which didn't amount to a line of type worth printing or reading, to his way of thinking. Of course, Feets was an Atlanta fan.

The policeman was impressed with the young man's infinite patience. Feets did not believe a man could stay still long enough to give all those reporters a shot at asking the same questions.

Finally, they started to drift away, and Potter stripped off his clothes. Feets hated to come up on a naked man pointing a weapon at him, so to speak. Feets had his own sensitive streak—like any cop. He waited for the outfielder to wrap a towel around himself.

"Hello, Potter," Feets said.

Potter placed him immediately. He was the man at Bobby's who said he worked for Coke, whom Sissy accused of being a cop and who Dr. Mufufski said was a cop.

"I'm Lieutenant Craig Patrick of the De Kalb County police department. I'm not a Coke man. That was a lie."

Potter sank back to the bench, his towel fell away from his body. He was naked again. It upset Feets.

"I have to ask you some questions," Feets said, almost apologetically, "but if you'd like to take your shower first, it would be okay."

"Would it be all right to discuss this privately? I mean, not here in the locker room?"

"Sure. I'll wait for you to shower and dress."

Potter thanked him. Feets knew he was suffering, sweating.

Feets was relieved to see that Potter was dressed. The whole deal did not take long. "Where would you like to talk?"

"Anywhere private," Potter said. "I got a feeling I know what you're going to ask me."

"How about in my car?" Feets offered. "It's as private as we can get in the city of Atlanta."

Potter admitted everything, even after Feets told him that whatever he said could be used against him. "I'm in treatment for the problem. I'm never going to do it again. I didn't hurt that little girl. I swear to that. It's a sickness, you see. I don't do it to hurt people. It comes over me and then I can't stop."

The confession overwhelmed Feets.

"You're in treatment, you say?"

"Yes."

"But it's not effective, is that it?"

"Well, I'm banking on the fact that it will be."

"I got the feeling," Feets said, "that you tried to abuse a child in the Golden Slippers Hospital. I'll admit I may be mistaken there."

"You're not mistaken," Potter said, "I did. The doctor caught me."

"And decided to cover for you?"

"No," Potter said. "He didn't report me because I promised to seek treatment."

"But I thought you said you were in treatment?"

"My treatment started with Dr. Mufufski."

Feets saw it all now.

"I've been running hot and cold on you for months. I'd like to blow your fucking head off half the time. The other half of me could grow to like you, maybe even has. I'll level with you. You've been a thorn in my side for months. Once I started after you I couldn't stop. I think I've thought about you more than any other case. A professional policeman is not supposed to do that. So you mean something else to me and I can't put my finger on it. You are a criminal in the eyes of the law, a dangerous criminal because you take innocent human beings off-guard and you hurt them. They think you are okay, nice. Then you hurt them. There have been times in my trying to nail you that I have actually felt as though I were you. That's not unusual; it happens to cops a lot and it happens to hunters. That's where I'm at now. . . ."

"I know that I have caused grief." That's all Potter said. He could find nothing else that was appropriate in the face

248

of what Mr. Patrick had just said. He wanted to say nothing, but he also wanted to indicate how sorry he felt.

"Two men got hurt because of you, a car got smashed, a fence knocked down. . . ."

"I'm sorry."

"You killed three dogs."

"Yes. I'm sorry."

"How'd you manage that? The dogs weren't any pushovers." Feets remembered the wolf in the woods beside the Baptist retirement home.

"I don't remember. I think I got hold of that piece of wood before they set up in their minds how to handle me."

"Then you just knocked them out of the park like you did tonight—"

Potter kept silent, lowered his head.

"You did a lot of damage."

"Yes, sir."

"About seven hundred bucks' worth. Are you prepared to pay for it?"

"Of course; I'm not running . . . anymore."

"I'm not paid to let people who break the law get away. But I believe it's possible to make an exception. Listen, Potter, I don't want to ruin your career. A thing like this could do that if it ever got out. I believe you're trying to control your sexual hang-ups. I'll probably be sorry for it—"

"You won't be, Mr. Patrick."

"Are you prepared to write a check to David Skipton for seven hundred dollars?"

"Who's David Skipton?" The more Feets talked to Potter the better he liked him. Imagine catching a second-story man red-handed and then letting him buy his way out by paying for the broken window or lock. If you asked that crook to make out a check to Jesus Christ, do you think he'd question it?

"David Skipton is the man who chased you, got his car,

249

self, and a friend banged up and paid the bills or will have to pay them for the damage you were responsible for. . . . Does that meet with your approval, or do you want a signed release?"

"Isn't a signed check made out to someone evidence that could go against me?"

"There is lots of evidence against you, Potter."

"What would you do, Mr. Patrick, if you were me?" Potter did not know what to do. He knew that making out a signed check to a stranger scared him. He threw the problem to Feets.

Feets thought, *This guy is not to be believed.* "I'm not a lawyer, Potter. But I can tell you this, if you can't trust me, you can't trust anyone. The best thing to do is give cash, but as I figure you don't carry all that much cash around with you, a check made out to cash would probably be second best—"

Potter thought that he could probably get the cash from that car dealer in Atlanta who wanted to give him free cars each season, who said he would return the money for his Gremlin at any time.

"I can get the cash, I think," Potter said.

"I don't want anything to do with Scruffy Levinson," Feets said. "He's already got about twenty percent of the city's cops on retainer."

"What do you mean, Scruffy Levinson? That's Sissy's friend. I don't have anything to do with him."

"You're lucky. I figured that if Mrs. Cindy knew a big-timer in Atlanta, you could call on him, too. But I'm pleased to be proven wrong."

Potter told Feets about the car dealer, the man with the American and foreign car agency.

"Oh, that weasel." Feets made a disgusted face. "Look, there's a lot you don't know about this town. The car dealer's name is Jim Nebblerman. He's a scurvy little shit who works for Scruffy. You get the picture? It stinks. Stay away from it," Feets advised. "Write the check out to cash."

Potter handed the check over. "I know you are going out on the limb and I appreciate it. I really want to thank you, Mr. Patrick."

"I'm putting a lot of faith in you, Potter. I hope to God you don't let me down."

Feets called Dave Skipton when he got home and said that he had turned up Dave's man, that he was willing to pay all the damages, and that he was in treatment for his problem.

"Whaddya mean, my man, Feets? He's more your man, being that he's a criminal, ain't he?"

"He's a nice person, Dave. He's just got this problem, and he's working like hell to lick it. Are you willing to let it be if he covers your losses?"

"I'm not in any mood to let a thing like this be, Feets."

"Would you be happier if I threw him in the can and you didn't get anything out of it but satisfaction?"

"I don't know, I just don't."

"He's a nice person. He really is."

"Can't we get the money out of him and then hang him?"

"Dave, that's not fair and not legal."

"I'm not sure letting him go is so legal either, is it?"

"We gotta do one or the other. We can't take the money and then clobber him after we've cleaned his pockets. So what'll it be?"

"Okay, then. If he's willing to cover the losses, let it ride."

"I think that's wise, Dave."

"Do I know the guy?"

"Yep."

"You mean he's someone I know?"

"Yep."

"Don't tell me I like the guy now."

"I'd have to say that you probably do, underneath."

251

"Who in hell is it? There ain't no friend of mine that could ever run that fast except maybe you, once, a million years ago."

"It's Potter Cindy, Dave."

"Sure enough?"

"Yep."

"Well, I'll be. . . ."

"Dave, I have the guy's check, so it's a little touchy. I want your word that it's just between us. Okay?"

Dave wasn't listening too well. He was thinking, *Potter Cindy, Potter Cindy*. "Sure," he said.

"Sure what, Dave?" Feets knew that Dave had a mouth like a sieve, but he also knew there was one thing as important as gossip to Dave, and that was money. He had those two boys to send to college who would not be getting athletic scholarships; he had a leaky roof, medical bills, and a pack of money he owed the county which Dave felt was owed to him by the sex criminal. Dave worried about debts; he paid his, and wanted to be paid in turn.

"Dave, I'm going to tell you something. I know you're no different from the rest of us, and you're feeling the pinch of inflation. Nobody's got any cash to waste nowadays. At least nobody like us. Dave, you haven't got a coon's chance of retrieving one nickel of that money you owe the county unless we handle it the way I set down. I can't legally get the money without an arrest, a conviction, and a judgment. I don't think I can even get the first one accomplished within the laws of the state, and certainly not within the articles of the Constitution of the land."

"I see."

"I hope so. I'm asking for silence. Potter Cindy's willing to make a contribution to your financial situation. And I'm urging that it only be between the three of us . . . as much for your sake as his. Do we understand each other?"

"Sure, Feets, I understand you."

252

Chapter Thirty

Feets had slept happily and peacefully in his bed in De Kalb County, and awoke as usual at six in the morning with a smile on his face. He walked into the kitchen feeling that life was worthwhile, that there were good people in the world, after all. When he tuned on the radio to listen to how Atlanta sports reporters handled the exploits of Potter he heard, to his horror, "This is an exclusive report: A local man only minutes ago has accused Potter Cindy, star outfielder for the Redbirds, of sexual perversion. . . ."

Feets fumed. He tried to reach Dave by phone to tell him he was "a cocksucking, son-of-a-whore, no-good shitass fartface." But probably every newsman in the country was trying to reach him. The radio report mentioned Feets as the detective "who got the goods on the outfielder," a Dave Skipton quote, no doubt.

Feets was surprised, angered that nobody had tried to contact him to verify the story. Then he remembered that his phone was always shut down from 2:00 A.M. to 6:15 A.M. (Feets once had insisted that everybody should be allowed to have four hours and fifteen minutes of peace and comfort.) He could only be reached through a special phone hookup from the station house, but no cop on duty would permit that, even if the governor of the state had called personally. There was nothing, except maybe the assassination of a President or the killing of a De Kalb County cop, that could not hold for four hours and fifteen minutes.

He kept the phone off the hook because as soon as he tried to use the phone the automatic shutoff was automatically disengaged. Dressed, not having stopped to shower, Feets drove to the stationhouse.

"Every newspaper and radio/TV station in town and lots out of town have been looking for you. What's this about Potter Cindy?"

Feets ignored the question. "You were a good boy, Red, not letting them wake me," he told the redheaded uniformed cop.

"You taking calls?"

"Only some, Red. Screen them for me and I'll see. And find out what hotel the Redbirds are staying at. And have Potter Cindy brought in for questioning."

"Potter Cindy ain't at the Redbird hotel, Feets."

"How do you know?"

"He called, looking for you. I told him to get out of the hotel pronto and take a cab here."

"Red, you're the smartest cop in the place. I'm glad I made you a detective."

"Very funny."

"That's no shit, Red. I'm recommending you. Oh, Red, arrest Dave Skipton!" Feets thought, *I have such a nice, loyal friend in Dave, I might as well return the compliment.*

"Arrest him? What charge?"

"Disturbing the peace." *My peace*, Feets thought.

"Should I pick him up myself? He's not going to be too happy about that turn of events!"

"No. I want you here. Send someone else."

In his office, Feets thought the one thing he would like to do before he died was kick Dave Skipton in the ass. But he knew that Dave, in his blundering stupidity, maybe in his love for the Atlanta Braves, had done what every good citizen should do, what no cop worth his shield should be caught not doing—blow the whistle on an offender. He had handed the guilty party over to Dave, and now he was bemoaning the fact that Dave was unable to make subtle judgments of character that even he himself had sworn not to make in upholding the law. If the law is indeed just, Feets knew, it was his sworn duty and Dave's moral duty to let the law float free, like they don't let the dollar, and reach its proper value, its true worth.

The phone in his office rang.

"Feets, it's the *Atlanta Constitution*. They want to talk to you."

"Tell them I'm out breaking up a heroin ring." He hung up on Red.

Feets picked the phone up and called the man whose child had seen Potter Cindy's pecker in the woods out near the Briar Vista School.

"Mr. Penneys, I hope I didn't wake you. This is Lieutenant Patrick of the De Kalb County police. Some time ago we were investigating a case of child abuse involving your daughter, remember?"

"That was months ago."

"Right. This is a routine follow-up to see how your daughter is—"

"She's jus' fine, Officer Patrick."

"Same as she was before?"

"Yep. Jus' as happy as a jaybird."

"You don't think she was hurt by the experience?"

"Heck, no. She's jus' fine."

"Suppose I told you we caught the fellow—"

"That's real fine police work."

"Are you interested in pressing charges, Mr. Penneys?"

"I'm a working man. I ain't got time to go to any courts.

255

Frankly, I think my li'l girl would be more upset by the fuss than she was to start with."

"Suppose the man were famous?"

"It don't matter none, famous or not. Jus' tongue-lash him for me and let him be."

"You sure, now?"

"I was sure about it months ago when you first came to see me."

Feets thanked him and hung up. Red called on the other phone.

"Station WBDK wants to talk to you and station WASK wants to ask you some questions."

"Tell BDK I'm investigating a holdup. And tell ASK I'm out breaking up a demonstration."

"And Dave Skipton's just been brought in," Red advised. "He doesn't look too happy."

"Send him in."

Dave came storming into the room wanting to know what the big idea was, why he was taken in instead of Potter Cindy.

"Potter Cindy is on his way in," Feets said, "but we haven't got a case against him."

"I thought you said he confessed and that he gave you a check for seven hundred."

"There's nobody to press charges against him."

"What about me?" Dave pointed out.

"You can sue him for damages if you can prove he was guilty," Feets said. "Or he could sue you for intimidation and harassment. You were chasing him; he wasn't chasing you."

"His check would prove I had a right to chase him. That's a signed confession if ever I saw one."

"The check's made out to cash," Feets said. "It won't prove nothing."

"So what are we going to do? Just let him go?"

"When you called the radio station this morning to blabber like a fool, you did a whole lot worse to Potter Cindy than the law ever could have. You also didn't make me seem too good. I might get in trouble myself. You realize that, don't you?"

"Well, I thought about it a long time and decided it was the proper thing to do. I suppose you don't agree—"

"I don't decide things for you, Dave. That's pretty clear. If someone complains, I look into it. Mr. Penneys, the little girl's father, didn't complain."

"But I did!"

"I got you your money."

"But what about punishing the guilty party?"

"You did that this morning."

The phone rang. Feets picked it up.

"Potter Cindy's here—"

"Send him in."

"Now?" Red asked. He knew who was in the room.

"Yep. Right now."

If you are a baseball nut or a movie fan, there is something very thrilling about seeing a celebrity face-to-face for the first time. When Potter walked in, looking handsome and sun-tanned, maybe taller and stronger and more clean-cut in his haircut than Dave had remembered having chased, Dave was speechless, humbled before the big leaguer.

"This here's Potter Cindy," Feets told Dave.

Potter extended his hand to Dave, thinking he was another cop. Dave was so flabbergasted, he actually went up to him and slapped him on the back. "You played a heck of a game last night."

Potter looked uncomfortable. It was, he knew, no time to indulge fans, even if they were cops. He thanked Dave quickly. Feets thought Dave was going to ask him for his autograph, though he didn't need it—he already had one on the check. Feets knew Dave wished he could take it all back.

"This here's Dave Skipton," Feets said. "He blew the whistle on you, claiming he did his duty as he saw it. I don't think he realized to this moment that you were a real person. But the damage is done. We've got no official case against you on a child-abuse charge. But Dave thinks or thought justice should be served."

"Listen, I'm real sorry, Potter," Dave said. "I don't want to make any more trouble for you."

Potter looked from one to the other, thinking, *What in the dear Lord in Heaven is going on here?* The town was full of people who didn't want to make trouble for him, and here he was in the worst trouble of his life.

"What happens now?" Potter asked.

Dave looked helpless. He shrugged stupidly.

Feets advised, "Well, if I were you, I'd leave town. Try to get away from the news area. I wouldn't try to get out of town via the Atlanta airport because that place is going to be buzzing with journalists and tattletales in the gossip racket. I'd go to Birmingham and fly out of there. We can't take you in a police vehicle because it wouldn't be official or look good. But that's the thing to do. Try to find someone to haul you to Birmingham."

"I'll drive you, Potter," Dave volunteered. It would thrill him to be sitting next to a big star like Potter for the haul to Birmingham, even though it wasn't all that far away from Atlanta.

"It doesn't look so good to leave," Potter said.

"Just to defuse the situation, temporarily," Feets advised.

"We still got two games down here," the ballplayer said.

"You've got a big lead," Dave pointed out. "We can't catch you nohow." Dave did not understand about professionals.

"I'm going to stay," Potter decided.

"You'll have a lot of embarrassing questions to answer. And nobody's going to give you any kisses no matter what you say. The situation calls for some hard thinking at a distance," Feets recommended.

Potter took a deep breath, thought a minute. He wondered if he should call Dr. Mufufski and get his advice. But suppose the doctor told him to come home, back to get his head shrunk. Is that what he wanted . . . to skip out?

"You mind if I make a long-distance call to my wife in California?"

"It's 3:00 A.M. in California—"

"That's only turning-in time for Sissy," Potter said.

He called and found her, as he had expected, just getting ready for bed. He had not awakened her; she was not tired at all; in fact, delighted to hear from him.

"Sissy, I got a lot to tell you. . . ."

Chapter Thirty-One

Potter did not yield to Sissy, who pleaded for him to get out of there and take the next plane to Palm Springs, Scruffy's place. He would not believe that all the little people, like Dave and Feets, fans of his who cherished his autograph and his skills, would not be understanding. He had been warmly applauded in every town in the National League. He refused to see that those who had cheered him would now hoot and howl and boo him, run him off the field. He figured that just looking at it as a strict business proposition, the business of winning a pennant, he was a valuable commodity, leading the league as he was in every department except homers. *How many automobile manufacturers*, he thought, *would stop producing a big seller like the Duster because it had a little engineering flaw?*

Potter did realize that Sissy was wiser about the world than he was; she was a person who knew more about the cruelties of the world. She made her points. "Get out of there, Potter, and fuck them, fuck them all! Come out here to California right now. We don't need those fuckheads. They are going to be cruel; they're going to hurt you. The big guys don't give a shit about anything but money and tax shelters and reputation. They don't know you're a good person, darling. They're going to take their toys and leave you alone, with no game to play. They won't let you play, sweetheart. . . ."

She was crying. She stopped to control herself. "Potter, I promise I'll never let you down. I'll be whatever you want. Listen, I love you, I can be whatever you want, whatever you need. I can be old or young, big or babyish. Don't go back to them. I swear I don't give a shit about anything else. Listen, sweets, we're all fucked up in some way. I'm not upset about what you did, or even about what you will do. Don't you realize that I have hangups, too? Potter, what do I care that you can only sleep with me when you pretend I'm eight years old? Sometimes I can only sleep with you when I pretend you're a water buffalo. Do you understand, darling?"

Potter nodded but didn't speak into the phone.

"Listen, Potter sweet, I'll wait for you at the airport. Take the next plane from Birmingham like the cop said. We'll go away, have fun. . . ." He listened to her sob. He knew she meant it, that she would be an eight-year-old and he a water buffalo.

"Sissy, I love you. Stay where you are. Don't come to the airport. I'll be there as soon as I can."

"When?"

"Soon."

"Oh, shit!"

Aside from some of the gory details, most of the rest is in the records. Potter returned to his hotel room and confessed all. He was kept on the bench for the remaining two games in Atlanta for what Whitey called "his own protection," though protection can be seen from many sides, and part of the world inside baseball and Wall Street saw the benching of Potter as protection of pretzel sales rather than a strong young man's body.

What was not reported was that when the news of Potter's sexual perversion was splashed all over the media, when it reached Redbird territory, the Pretzel Baron's domain, Mr.

Heller called Zarember, with no pleasant thoughts on his mind. He could see housewives everywhere boycotting his products. He saw every mother with a daughter under age eleven yanking her stupid kid away from the pretzel shelf in the supermarket.

"What's the situation, Herbert?" he asked Zarember in an emergency phone call to Atlanta.

"The situation, Mr. Heller, is in a state of flux, without the 'l.' I've heard everything in my time, but this poor bastard Potter deserves some credit. He's spunkier than beef jerky and tougher than a stale hero bread."

"Herbert, *please*!" Zarember forgot for a moment that his employer was a baker supreme.

"The excrement, Mr. Heller, has really hit the fan. But I'm so impressed with Potter's courage I've forgotten to let my ulcer hurt. We've got a real winner here."

"Winner? Herbert, you imbecile. The boy's a freak, a sexual freak. Can't you hear the outcry?"

"Oh, you mean the fans and the players crapping on him, kicking him when he's down?"

"My God, even his own teammates. It's that bad, is it?"

"Some of his teammates. Whitey and the coaches are against him. Hartman surprised me. He's complaining how horrified he is to have shared a room with him. Of course, down here, he stays with relatives. It's Bobby's home town. Jews! Potter wasn't kosher, I guess. We'll have to find him another roommate. Condon said he doesn't want to play on the same team with Potter. Mayknoll's supporting him, though. That's a big plus, because he brings the whole African bloc with him, you know. Did you know we have ten blacks on the squad? It's a good break. Borkowski really hates Potter now. Maybe he's got an eight-year-old daughter. You'd be surprised, Mr. Heller, how much this kind of deviation upsets people. Take Murphy, the leftfielder, he thinks Potter should be castrated. . . ."

"Will you please stop giving me a district-by-district breakdown of the vote, Herbert? Who cares? We're in trouble. That's obvious."

"We still have some commercials to run with Potter in them. What are we going to do there?"

"My good man, I'm dropping those, of course. I'm not going to have people wondering if they will turn into sex perverts if they eat pretzels. Miss Cabodario urged that I continue to run them. She thought it would not be decent to drop them in the middle of his trials and tribulations. But I think she's not seeing the whole merchandising picture."

"I thought you once said he was the best salesman in your employ. . . ."

"Yes, he *was*. Now he's the worst. Does that satisfy you? Must you always remember every insignificant, annoying, or regrettable statement I have ever made?"

"Sorry. I'm in the middle of the fire here, Mr. Heller. And I kind of think we should keep ducking and try to tough it out."

"You do, do you? Well, let me remind you of something, my good fellow. It was you who pressed me to sign Potter Cindy."

"That was a good baseball judgment, Mr. Heller. There isn't a better ballplayer in the major leagues today. I don't think anyone could have anticipated anything like this. Mr. Heller, I think the reason we are in the thick of a pennant fight is because we have Potter on our team. I'm not the field manager, but I think it would kill the team if we lost him."

"You should have investigated him more thoroughly before we put him into commercials. You remember a lot of things, except what you want to forget. You forgot, for instance, that I expressed enthusiastic interest in setting up a security agency for checking on people who appear in testimonial advertising. If we did that we would have avoided this situation."

"How bad is the situation, Mr. Heller? Suppose we lose

some fans to begin with. If we keep winning, they'll be back; they have no other place to go."

"You can't assure me or anyone else of that, Herbert. I want to point out that I not only have fans for this pennant fight this year, but I also have these same fans who are also consumers of bread, cakes and baked goods during the winter when there is no pennant fight. ...Next year, for example, when we are befouling Heller Park with errors and pop-ups and a child-molester. I don't think we can count on simple, everyday people forgiving sexual criminal activities, and I question how much support they would give to the team, or corporation, that succors and protects a sexual criminal."

"What should we do now, Mr. Heller?"

"We have to discuss it. I want you and Whitey in my office tomorrow morning."

Chapter Thirty-Two

So that not a moment would be lost, F. M. Heller spent the next hour reviewing in his mind two possible projects for making more money. The notions were presented in thick reports by Mr. Heller's Indian scouts on Wall Street. He employed a band of very sharp operators who warned him of approaching companies about to float stock. The idea, of course, was that if the scouts got a lead on a good thing, Mr. Heller would acquire a lot of shares early enough to make another fortune. When Mr. Heller was unhappy or depressed, he liked to consider methods of making another million.

Mr. Heller had called a meeting for 9:05 A.M. to review the agonies of Potter Cindy. The team physician would be on hand; he was ordered to bring a psychiatrist with him. Zarember would be there, as would Whitey Knocthofer. Mr. Heller still had every bit of sixteen minutes left to consider whether he should invest in a company that had a patent on a rat poison that killed rats on contact. The poison was placed in an area known for its strolling rats, and the rodents were to be killed by absorbing the poison through their feet. The other company up for acquisition was one that extracted materials from empty seashells, called chitin and chitosan, that could be used to give newsprint extra wet strength, or as a stomach-settler, a food-thickener, or even something that could heal wounds. While the second proposal seemed to have greater long-range possibilities, Mr. Heller leaned toward the first. There was something about a rat poison that suited his mood and blended in better with his feeling about Potter Cindy.

When the gentlemen from two walks of life arrived —medicine and baseball—Mr. Heller gave them a moment to get their behinds settled into seats before he launched into an offensive.

"Dr. Hardy, with all your training, one would think that you would be sensitive to the problems of our ballplayers. Oh, I know that you are not a specialist in witchcraft, in the dynamics of a lunatic, but surely there was a hint, a suggestion that the boy was troubled? It was you, I recall, that approved of another ballplayer we had sometime back who turned out to have an emotional flat tire. That decision cost me many thousands of dollars in bonus money. I hope you haven't forgotten that, Dr. Hardy."

"I don't think Dr. Hardy could have predicted that Potter Cindy had this problem," Dr. Daniel Vestward, the psychiatrist, said.

"Well, is that so?" Mr. Heller asked. "It seems that I read somewhere that these people, people who abuse children, are exhibitionists of sorts. They show off and want to get caught—"

"I don't know that they all fit one mold. For many, probably most, it is a compulsive act; they don't think about it before they are doing it," Dr. Vestward pointed out.

"Are you saying that your colleague here—" he pointed to Dr. Hardy "—had no way of knowing that Potter had this problem?"

"I would say that it was impossible to tell. I don't think a highly trained psychiatric observer could tell. From what I have heard of Mr. Cindy, I doubt that I could tell."

266

"Well, I guess you're in the clear, Hardy. But we're all still stuck with the problem: what to do about him. What do you fellows think?" He included Zarember and Knocthofer in this question.

Whitey spoke up because he had a team to manage and he couldn't waste all this time on a lot of doctor talk. "Look, he's got a bad problem. It's going to hurt the team. He might do it again and kill a kid. A lot of fellows are against him, including me."

Dr. Vestward spoke up. "I think we can rule out the possibility that Potter Cindy will kill a child. That's not his pattern. He shows himself; he doesn't hurt the children, you see."

Zarember got the discussion back to the baseball aspects. "Whitey, I thought you said he was the greatest—"

"He's a damn good ballplayer. I liked him, but a guy who'd do that to little kids is nothing but a creep. I don't want him on the club. I think my coaches agree."

"Whitey, he's not a damn good ballplayer. That's the most unhelpful thing you can say about him. He's the heart of the team, that's really why we're all sitting around here."

"Well, we can trade him, maybe get a good old-timer who can still hit and do a fielding job. Potter's young. A lot of teams in certain cities might be willing to live with the guy. Here, on this club, in this Midwest town, we don't go for Potter's kind of stud. Another place, like New York or San Francisco, they might not mind. Potter's young and he's a good player."

"But does he have a future? People think of young ballplayers, do they not, as being around a long time. Will Potter be around a long time? Dr. Vestward, is Potter Cindy likely to do this thing of his again?"

"Most likely. I think that he may have a need for revealing his penis again and again," said Dr. Vestward.

Whitey made a disgusted face. Zarember felt sorry for Potter, expressing it by rubbing sweat or a small tear from his eye. Dr. Hardy nodded, as though he had the knowledge

267

and training to agree. Mr. Heller was fascinated. In a way he felt that way about the acquisition of money . . . the compulsion. He saw his needs were safer than Potter's; he saw also that Potter wasn't a good investment.

"You see," Dr. Vestward explained, "what he is doing psychologically is demanding that everyone admit he has one. And just his showing of his sexual parts is not enough; he must get a reaction of shock, horror, or something of that nature."

"How long would it take to cure him?" Zarember asked.

"I can't say," Dr. Vestward admitted.

"What do you think, Dr. Hardy?" Mr. Heller asked. "Do you think we should gamble on keeping the boy around?"

"I'm not knowledgeable enough to say in this area."

"That's obvious," Mr. Heller said, "but what do you think about taking a chance on him?"

"I think it might be too late. I think we should admit our mistake and try to find a discreet way out."

"Why?" Zarember asked.

"Just as Whitey said. He's already a disruptive influence."

"But he's a great ballplayer. Why can't we treat him like they used to treat black guys? Isolate him. Let him live by himself. We won't bother with him. But let him stay. Let him kick the hell out of the baseball while he hates us, like the black kids used to do." Zarember was practically pleading.

"Dr. Vestward, do you have anything further to add that might help us reach a sensible decision on this?" Mr. Heller wanted to know.

"No, not really. I would like to say that the problem need not necessarily be permanent. The man can be treated, and maybe taught to keep the lid on his need, if not end the compulsion altogether."

"But that would take years, you think?" Mr. Heller asked.

Zarember noticed that Mr. Heller's verbal delivery had sud-

268

denly turned crisp, to the point. The long questions and explanations, the thinking things out loud were missing. He wondered if that was meant to indicate that he had made up his mind about Potter already. Zarember believed or wanted to believe that Mr. Heller would gamble.

"Yes. A long time," Dr. Vestward answered.

"What are the chances of Potter doing this again in the near future, Dr. Vestward?"

"Potter has said he will never do it again," Zarember put in.

Mr. Heller made a face that said to Zarember, *Don't add your psychiatric ignorance to your poor judgment.* He made a gesture to Dr. Vestward. It said, *I'll take your answer now.*

"The chances are probably very good. In fact, it's likely, with all the pressure he's been under."

"But he might not if he was determined enough not to, right?" Zarember came to fight.

"He might not," Dr. Vestward conceded.

Mr. Heller decided that he really should invest in the company that was extracting materials from seashells. It was a better possibility than investing in a troubled ballplayer.

"What are we going to do, Mr. Heller?" Whitey asked.

"We're going to keep him provisionally. I'm going to try to arrange for a good trade in the meantime."

"But what about the guys, the players, they're down on him."

"Tell them to pretend he's Jackie Robinson the year he entered baseball, like Mr. Zarember suggested. Those who don't mind his being black can accept him. Those who do can shun him."

Zarember did issue a statement that the Redbirds were behind Potter Cindy one thousand percent, and each day of the two weeks that passed before he was traded away, one club spokesman or another would reduce the amount of support. By the time he was acquired by the Texas franchise, the Redbirds were behind him about five percent, and some acute reporter in the Midwest observed that you get a bigger percentage in a day-of-deposit-to-day-of-withdrawal savings account.

It was very clear to Samantha before Zarember's statement that Mr. Heller was closing out the account on Potter Cindy. F. M. Heller had asked her to see him on the matter in his bedroom (they frequently discussed Potter there).

Mr. Heller was in his thick robe, somewhat relaxed.

"Believe it or not, my dear, I really had asked you over to discuss Potter Cindy and get your opinion on whether or not you thought he had any future with the ball club. But, there you were, as irresistible as ever, and I'm afraid I put pleasure before the business of Potter Cindy."

"Does that mean, F. M., that you have decided to give up on him altogether?" She did not tell Mr. Heller, of course, that she found it hard to give up on him after their experimentation with a bottle of crème de menthe.

"Of course. Do you suggest even for a moment that we keep him?"

"I know you don't want him in the commercials, but he hasn't failed you as a ballplayer."

"I beg to differ. He has in fact failed me utterly, my dear. He has darkened our good name, our reputation, our image. He is bad for business. He can no longer be associated with the name Heller in any shape, manner, or form."

"Poor Potter, all that nice style and form, all those base hits and stolen bases and fielding gems. He was so sweet and delicious. Who would have thought he would make people so nauseated?"

"Do I pick up from your rather feeble criticism of my least favorite major leaguer that it does not make you ill to think of how he fooled us?"

"I guess it would have been better if he wasn't the subject of a commercial. But, F. M., he got the job done otherwise. He isn't that distasteful. I just bet there are at least one million women in this country that would be happy to try to straighten Potter Cindy out."

Mr. Heller wasn't thick; in fact, he was quick. "For your sake, and for mine, too, my love, I sincerely hope that the unwholesome, distasteful, and carnal idea you hold concerning Potter Cindy and the lasciviousness of American womanhood is merely a momentary surfacing of a congenital syphilitic strain in your filthy Spanish background and not a desire you hold for yourself. Because, my love, if I thought for a moment that you were not teasing me, I would be made miserably unhappy. . . ." Mr. Heller did not get the chance to finish what he started because Samantha had reached into the opening of his robe and it left him speechless for a while.

Mr. Heller relaxed; he was old and wise enough to realize that there are things better left unexplored. One must endeavor, he had read and held reasonably sacred, not to make life too sad or too shocking.

The saddest and maybe the most shocking treatment of Potter Cindy came from the fans in Los Angeles, during the All-Star Game, where Potter was introduced with a shower of things related to his sexual problem—little girls' panties, lollipops, jacks, and rubber Didee dolls. They hooted and howled and held up a ten-man banner that spread across a row of seventy seats that said, YOU STINK! It is ironic that it should have happened in Los Angeles, of all places, the psychological if not real home of Sissy, the city that contained Hollywood, which publicized sex to the world, the city with a vast cult of rich, smug know-nothings, the city that is said to contain more creeps, heels, and sexual deviates per square inch than any other city in the world, including

271

Sodom, Gomorrah, and New York. There is always an apologist, and one TV commentator explained "the disgraceful display" in Dodger Stadium as being "the first real outlet for the everyday fan to express his feelings of being let down by one of its young heroes."

What the commentator forgot, or did not know, was that Potter did not run away. He stayed in Atlanta and took his lumps, from the players and the fans, from the sanctimonious and the inglorious. They didn't throw any Didee dolls at him in Atlanta, and they did not stick him in a pillory, though he was exposed to verbal scorn and ridicule that first day, the second game of the series. He came back the next day and some in the crowd actually applauded him, at least Dave Skipton did. But maybe people are more polite and gentlemanly in the South. "Even if it's only a surface virtue, it helps when a man can use a little kindness," Zarember said privately.

The only thing that could be said for Los Angeles that day was that television agreed to let Hank Mayknoll and Sissy go on the tube and spew their anger. Sissy hustled her way on. Mayknoll was interviewed because he refused to take the mound for the All-Star Game after what the fans did to Potter. Even the baseball commissioner could not move him to pitch. It looked like the beginning of a gloomy day for the great national pastime with Mayknoll turning the commissioner down. He finally did go out to pitch and mowed down six straight hitters with blazing speed, but that was because Potter asked him to. "Mayknoll, I'd like you to go out there and throw."

"Not after what they did to you."

"It will mean something to me if you pitch, Hank."

"What will it mean to you?"

"It will mean that the thing goes on, that what I've done in my personal life doesn't end it for you because you are a friend."

272

"They kicked you in the balls, man—"

"I kicked them, too. You know, Hank, a fan once wrote me when I was in the minors that he loved me because, while he was only a shipping clerk, I made it possible for him to discuss something with the chairman of the board on equal terms."

"Your fan is dumber than you are."

"The game gives him equality with the big boss."

"The only thing he shares with the chairman of the board is the insignificant fact that they both have cocks. Take that from this nigger boy, Potter," Mayknoll said, before he went out to take the hill.

Mayknoll threw smoke in the post-game interview, too.

"I'm not apologizing for Potter. You go and hang him if that's what you want. What the hell is the difference if you get booed out of a ball park because you can't hit anymore, or you can't get anybody out, or if you are ridiculed and mocked out by a bunch of fans psyched up by you reporters with poison in your veins instead of human decency?

"I know Potter is not going to be a Redbird very much longer. But I tell you he's going to be missed, and I don't only mean his bat and his glove. He was becoming a natural leader.

"He helped the club just taking wind sprints with us. Somebody would get on him about his devotion to the game, or his ball-hawking. Soon we'd all be laughing. We'd be loose. That will all be gone now. I hope you write all that down because I don't sing praises to a white man more than once in my lifetime."

Sissy came on softer to start with on her television interview, sandwiched between the six o'clock news and a rerun of the Flintstones.

"I've always thought of this town as home. There is little that could have happened here that I couldn't find a way to forgive. It used to be a town of Commies, they tell me.

273

It must have been a million years ago, because it's all Reagan now, especially for the big boys. I've known some of them quite intimately, as you've heard. I've listened to them say that anybody who protests or complains is a dangerous radical.

"Potter Cindy never protested or complained. Potter didn't do anything to hurt this town, or our people. He only hurt himself. He was in a way what you always wanted. He was somebody you could adore. But I see this town for what it is now. You need a trained mongoose to survive one day in this stupid snake pit of a city. Potter's not quitting ball. He doesn't quit when things are going against him. So he'll be back in Anaheim or in San Francisco or in San Diego one of these days, hurting your teams like you all hurt him. But I won't be back because I don't want any part of this lousy city where the game is to suck a nice man dry; it's a city that uses talent, wrings it out, makes it sweat. Well, I'm leaving, baby. The last thing you're going to remember about me is my backside. If that doesn't mean anything to you, then you've missed the point."

One TV reporter in the *Los Angeles Times* made the melancholy point that Sissy Lindmore would be missed not for her eloquence but for her vulgarity. "Without one four-letter word, she told people here that they could kiss her royal highness.... She was a bawdy little lady and she'll be missed."

The standings, the final statistics, showed that Potter was missed by the Redbirds, if by no one else in the league. When he was traded away, the Redbirds slowly collapsed. Whitey kept saying to himself that the team was going to take it, take it all, but they were lucky to take third place at the end of the season. Atlanta won it, but Feets Patrick and Dave Skipton somehow didn't feel that the Atlanta victory was a glorious one.

If Whitey was optimistic, it was not all wishful thinking. There was a brief string of Redbird victories following Potter's departure to the American League. Perhaps the flush of success resulted from the players being shocked into action by the news of Potter's misdeeds, or angered for being taken in by the rookie sensation's pleasantness and charm, or freed to express talents, or simply because they were professionals.

The team leaders, before the club sank into third place, were Hartman and Condon, the double-play combination. But as Condon was not the reporters' favorite Redbird—they remembered Condon's "eyewash"—Hartman got nearly all the press.

For a while almost anything Hartman did was glorified, even his drawing a walk. The writers figured out on that particular day that when Hartman reached first on a free pass he was the hundredth Redbird at that point in the season to reach base on a walk, and that the base on balls had led to the only run in the game. The fact that Brossi knocked in the winning run with a long double was almost secondary. Hartman had said to Brossi after the game, "I can't explain it, Phil. Suddenly everything I do turns into a headline. When I take a shit tomorrow, I'm going to check to see if it turned into gold." There was some reason for Hartman's getting all that ink. He had collected 12 hits in 32 at bats during his hot spell. Mr. Heller had decided that it was time for showing "ethnics" in his pretzel commercials and Bobby, Brossi, and Borkowski would be featured.

Mr. Zarember was commanded by his chief to order the publicity department to dig up features on the ethnics of the team, "our great melting pot, our little America on one ball club." Zarember obeyed; he flooded the newspaper guys with what he called "matzo balls, spaghetti, and Polish-sausage yarns about how Redbird athletes grew to become stars on Mama's cooking." Mr. Heller was convinced it would take the curse off the team left by Potter, whose mother probably only "fed him Campbell's soup and peanut-butter-and-jelly sandwiches."

Bobby knew glory, though briefly. One of the incidental casualties of the ethnic campaign was Swaps Flattery. She tried her key in the second-baseman's door only to discover that the lock had been changed. Bobby was in bed with his new girlfriend, Samantha, and he swallowed hard when he heard the door being fiddled with; he knew it was Swaps. But it was not the time of season or the atmosphere for blond things. Those days, that feeling, had gone with Potter. The second- and third-generation Americans, "the foreigners," had suddenly inherited the earth.

"Don't you feel a little sad for Potter?" Samantha had asked the new hero.

"He'll make out," Bobby said. "I don't think we have to worry about him." He stopped to consider if he should say something more generous about his ex-roommate; Bobby was, after all, making out pretty good himself. "Potter's a great ballplayer."

Then, Bobby had another thought. "Say, when will my pretzel commercials appear on TV?"

"Maybe next spring," she said.

"That long?"

"They take time to make."

"Lissen, don't show them on Passover with me in them. My Jewish fans won't like that."

She wondered how far Bobby would go in the majors. She saw, with some mixed feelings, that it would be farther than Potter.

Chapter Thirty-Three

Dr. Mufufski spent the time from the moment Potter's exposure became public, or at least from the time the name of the Redbird sensation's psychiatrist was revealed, till the time Potter was traded, turning down requests for interviews. He had instructed his answering service and the people at the Golden Slippers Hospital that he was available to no one except patients. He would not talk to newspapermen, TV or radio reporters, or baseball people.

The psychiatrist was impressed with Potter's deportment after it was clear he would be coming back to town bloodied and scarred, with little support and encouragement and with fleeing fan clubs and uncomfortable teammates. It seemed to Dr. Mufufski that the events would have humbled bigger and psychologically healthier men. But Potter held on, head erect, with the sticks and stones of unkind comments nearly breaking his bones and the names harming him more than he could let on. Dr. Mufufski knew that underneath Potter had probably wanted to get caught.

He was concerned, after reviewing the material on Potter, that his patient would think that being caught and chastised in some way evened the score, washed the slate clean. He had to make clear to Potter that the score is tied only when he himself had evened it, not by the stupidity or cruelty or folly of others.

Dr. Mufufski was concerned that Potter might have come to place too much responsibility for his problem on fear of castration. The psychiatrist made a note—a mental note—to tell Potter that castration, a theme they had turned up in an early session, was just one idea in a complicated drama, the heart of which was buried late in the last act.

There was so much to do with Potter and not nearly enough time. Each day the papers conjectured on the outfielder's fate. There were dozens of rumors of departure and trade. Dr. Mufufski knew that Potter would be gone after the next announcement, or the next, or the next. And their work together would be aborted, like a traumatic miscarriage.

If they could work together long enough, perhaps he could make clearer to Potter that cure, when it comes, will not be dressed as a miraculous revelation. But, rather, it will be the real face at the end of a gradual peeling away of masks.

Dr. Mufufski did not have to look at his appointment book to know that the patient he was waiting to see while he considered Potter Cindy was the man himself.

"You know, I ought to start banging a few heads together. I mean, what have I got to lose? I've been taking a beating out there. They've called me every damn name under the sun. It's time I struck back. How would you like to get dirty messages written out in baby-talk or Elmer Fudd language? Would you like to receive pictures of nude infants in the mail? Or used condoms, or advertising circulars for male hormones?"

"I get the impression," Dr. Mufufski said, "that you are not all that angry about these attacks. In fact, you might even be using them to absolve yourself—"

"Bullshit! I know I've done wrong. And I know I have to pay for it. But this is more than I deserve, isn't it?"

Dr. Mufufski was not certain how much guilt Potter suffered. Or how deep it went. He thought Potter seemed more embarrassed at being caught than truly morally guilty. But perhaps he was being unfair. He had not seen Potter enough times to make that judgment.

"What do you feel, Potter, what do think after you've committed your misdeed . . . after you pick yourself up from your duster?"

"Well, I feel like a criminal, that I've done something that is wrong—"

"And you are afraid you are going to be caught and punished?"

"Yes, that the police will catch me and arrest me."

"Are you ever afraid you will be caught by yourself and severely punished?"

"I don't understand the question."

"Are you ever tortured or punished by your own feelings?"

"Of course. I've thought about taking my life. I hate what I do so much that I spend nearly all of my time, day and night, except when I'm playing ball, trying to control the problem. Well, this takes a toll on a guy because, in trying to control the problem, I'm forced to control other emotions . . . and, you know, I think now that I've really lost the feelings of anger and love and deep concern for people. I mean, I'm a grown man, and I should have these feelings. I don't think I have them for Sissy, for example."

"Most people speak well of you, or did—"

"Yes. But that's because I went out of my way to be nice so that they could never see what I really was underneath."

"A child-molester—" Dr. Mufufski added to draw Potter out further.

"And that's another thing, you sonofabitch! Don't call me a child-molester. Everybody's making out, or suggesting, that I hurt the kids, or did cruel things to them, or raped them. I never hurt the kids. I never abused them. Mostly I just undressed in front of them. People do that all the time in front of their kids in their homes and it's not a crime. I never had anything but affection for the kids, and all you son-ofabitches are making something ugly out of it."

"You must have thought it was more than just affection and showing yourself. You said you had contemplated suicide—"

"Yes. It was a problem and the damn problem never ended. I wanted to end it. Once and for all."

"Were you afraid you were becoming more aggressive, more sadistic? Were you afraid you would hurt the children?"

"No. I would never hurt the children. I was afraid that the times between children was growing shorter, that I was doing it more often than I could stand."

"The problem was out of control?"

"Yes."

"Why did you decide *not* to commit suicide? Were you afraid?"

"I don't know," Potter answered. "I thought that maybe the problem could be licked. That child in Atlanta was a kind of test for me. I saw it maybe as the beginning of the end, and I suppose gave myself another chance."

"But you failed another test in the Golden Slippers Hospital, didn't you?"

"Yeah. So what are you saying, that I should kill myself? You think I'm hopeless?"

"What do you think?"

"Why are you turning the question back to me?"

"I have to know what you think, Potter, so that I can understand you and the problem."

"And I *have* to know that you believe I can lick the problem. It's taken a superhuman effort on my part to get this far. I want to know that someone is out there, pulling for me."

"That is my function, Potter . . . to help you to get on top of this problem. I thought you understood the point—"

"I thought I did, too, but I can't help feeling that you're pointing the finger at me, throwing up every duster that I have forgotten, reminding me when I want to forget."

"Hiding it, or putting it out of your mind, hasn't helped you before. We've got to take a good hard look at it. We've got to explore its roots, its origins."

"I thought we settled that. I thought we figured out that it was based on my fear of getting my balls chopped off—"

"I'm glad you brought that up again. The fear of castration is merely one of the factors, probably a most unimportant one. Don't fix on that, Potter, or we'll never get anywhere. What we have to do together is peel away all of these factors before we can get at the heart of the matter."

"How many other things will I have to suffer?"

"It's not going to be easy, Potter."

"And the time is running out."

"What do you mean?"

"Well, this will probably be our last meeting, or next to last. It's clear they're getting ready to trade me." Potter took a deep breath and let it out slowly. It was, Dr. Mufufski saw, a sigh.

"There have been a lot of rumors, but you're still on the Redbirds," Dr. Mufufski said hopefully.

"I'm on the official team roster. My name is listed on the scorecard, but I'm not really on the Redbirds. I'm washed up with this club, this town."

The psychiatrist saw the sadness on the outfielder's face, and had to fight down a feeling of distaste for the Redbirds, and the whole business of baseball. Baseball had lived with sadists and drug addicts, psychotics and alcoholics, but it couldn't live with Potter Cindy. He saw that while Potter's "duster" was an exhibitory sexual misdeed, it was the result of a deeply private eroticism, not unlike what might be found in a monk who masturbates. On the surface and in his heart and soul his identity is that of the uniform or habit he wears, but occasionally he cannot control his erotic thoughts or actions —he could not push back gratification for even a moment— and he is forced to show himself, or masturbate. Failure— the surfacing of the duster—required Potter to look for strength and achievement and recognition where he knew he could succeed, and he drove himself as a baseball player until, indeed, his name led all the rest in the records that mark value and worth in baseball—runs batted in, hits, home runs, stolen bases, and fielding average. It was ironic and maybe tragic, Dr. Mufufski saw, that failure made Potter greater—a superstar and hero—and it also defeated him. It made him a villain. Now, Dr. Mufufski sighed. He knew it was true that the time was short.

"How can I help you, Potter?"

Potter looked puzzled. "What do you mean? You're already helping me . . . our talking together and all. It's been a real big help to me. I'm taking a hard look at my problem now and I think I'm on top of it. Not like before where I kidded myself about controlling the duster. This is real. We're getting down to the nitty-gritty, and I'm going to lick this problem. You'll see. I may not be a Redbird, but I'll be a ballplayer somewhere. And I'm going to be the best—"

"You are aware, or should be, that home runs do not erase the other thing."

"I know that."

"You know it with your head, but I want you to know it with your heart. Try to learn it with your feelings."

"I will. I am—" Then Potter thought of something, something important that he had been meaning to ask Dr. Mufufski. "Why do I do it? That's my question. That's how you can help. Tell me why I do it."

"Don't you mean why you *did* it? You said *do* it, which implies that it will still go on, that it is not a thing of the past."

"I meant *did* it. But what I was asking is for you to give me some way to prevent it. Some practical thing. If a player's in a slump or going bad, he's usually doing something wrong; he's got a hitch in his swing or striding wrong or something.

What is the hitch in this problem? How can I correct it?"

"That's what we're here to discover, Potter."

"But I need something now, Dr. Mufufski! Not three years from now. I have to live. I have to do things. Help me, please ... please." Potter wiped his eyes, which had welled with tears.

The psychiatrist considered his answer. He knew the time for Potter was running out. He would certainly be traded. How many more sessions would they have? Certainly not enough.

"Potter, what I'm going to tell you is not a cure or a preventative. I'll make it as practical as we can be in this discipline. What I tell you might sound obvious or stupid, but it is all that I can offer at this moment. Your misdeed is really a very childish one, and you behave as a child. You see yourself underneath as the children you molest and in a sense, you molest yourself. Only children, or grown-ups who are psychologically children, as you are, cannot control gratification. An adult can wait. A child must be satisfied immediately. I believe that you approached your victims in an affectionate and friendly fashion and left them that way. That's positive. It shows that you don't hate yourself. It is also bad, for you, because you don't truly feel, in spite of what you say or think, that you have committed very serious crimes. I don't believe you really have convinced yourself that you are morally wrong, except with the very top of your head."

"If you say I don't feel guilty and that if I did I would be on the right track, how do I get to really feel properly guilty?"

"You may never. But you have to feel some moral responsibility. And that will come when you identify yourself as a man and not a child. You will then understand that it is morally wrong to molest a child because even though you think what you do is not harmful to the victim, it is. It is wrong."

"I know that now, Dr. Mufufski."

"You don't yet, Potter. But I am confident that if you work on it, you will really know it."

"You and Sissy and Mayknoll are about the only people left in the world who don't hate me."

"Most people are ignorant, Potter, but they are also forgiving. Man forgets and after enough time has passed, he tends to let bygones be bygones. A person can only hold so much hate and so much resentment in his head. I think you have more friends out there than you think."

Chapter Thirty-Four

Potter had a friend east of Los Angeles in the Lone Star state. The person was important, most important. He was the governor of Texas. Potter had signed a baseball for the governor's grandson; the outfielder had been warm and friendly and the governor took a shine to him. The governor liked Texas and Texans more than any place or people in the world. He had been elected to office for two straight terms. He once told his grandson that it would be nice if Texas could field a major league team made up of all Texans. If he couldn't have that, the second best thing would be a team made up of all southwesterners. When the news about Potter Cindy and his troubles broke, the governor dispatched one of his key aides to visit the owner of the Texas franchise and try to convince the major league team owner to acquire Potter. The aide's name was Giggin Barewedge and it was said that he, best of all, could communicate the governor's desires. Giggin was a direct man, like his family name; he got his job done, politicians in Texas said, by not only "baring his wedge" but also by driving it right clear through those poor souls who failed to comprehend the real meaning of power.

The owner of the Texas franchise, known to everyone as Uncle Daryl, was not a fool; he understood power for he had some of his own. Nevertheless, he expressed strong reservations about Cindy.

"Giggin, I don't like it. He's bad news that Potter Cindy, bad press, bad everything, just about."

"It's one of the governor's hopes, Uncle Daryl, that the Texas team can field all Texans, but short of that all southwesterners. Now Potter Cindy was born in Albuquerque and he cowboys on the offseason just across the Texas state line, around Las Cruces, not more than 40 miles from El Paso."

"Let me get you straight. You're talking about a whole team made up of what might broadly be called local boys, is that right?" asked Uncle Daryl.

"You're on target now."

"Well, Giggin, I think there's something you want to know. I'm going to read you some of the names of the boys that play for this team. Okay, here we go: we got Al Cappabianca, Frank Melforme and Dom Toscani, our designated hitter, and we got two good, young rookie lefthanders named Marc Sailly and Andy—that's short for André—Vimy. Now, if you stop to ponder those names you can see I can sooner field a team from the southwest of Italy and France than I can from the southwest of the United States."

"Uncle Daryl, you're being difficult and resistant. It's a negative approach to life. May I also remind you that you are signing healthy checks—at least that's what you've been claimin on your corporate income tax statement—to Johnny Monkton, a shortstop born in Yuma, Arizona, Dick Creel, a Dallas boy, Bobby Sparrow, from Anthony, Texas, Cap Harris, Deming, New Mexico, and Harvey Biggs, that catcher from Crescent, Oklahoma. Get the point?"

"Yes. Potter Cindy."

"Right. Albuquerque. Las Cruces."

"That's no way to make the playoffs." Uncle Daryl pointed out.

"You don't deny that the boy has talent, do you?"

"The boy's sick. He needs a psychiatrist. He needs treatment. He needs to stay with that headshrinker of his in the Midwest."

"Now, that's what I'm here to talk about." Giggin explained that the governor was a good friend of the head man at the medical school and that he understood that there would be a nice chair opened up in the psychiatry department for a certain Dr. John B. Mufufski, if Potter Cindy came to Texas.

"Why is this so important to the governor, Giggin?"

"It's special. The governor wants to show the country that Texans can become very charitable to an underdog; we'd be the first to scatter the coyotes nibbling at a hurt animal, especially if that animal had a valuable hide." Giggin said the governor wanted Texas to be thought of as the BIG state, big in size and BIGGER in heart. He told Uncle Daryl that the governor would back him, make it work, if he successfully acquired Potter Cindy.

The rest was a matter of a phone call. F. M. Heller would give up his young slugger, even though he had reservations.

"How much would those reservations cost, F. M.?"

"Three hundred thousand dollars," Mr. Heller said without shame.

"For damaged merchandise? For a sick boy, F. M.? For a gamble and a long shot at that?"

"His hitting's not a long shot. He can help you fellows a lot. I'm not asking you to break up your club and give me another ballplayer for him, am I? It's just money," Mr. Heller pointed out.

"He'll hurt us at the gate." Uncle Daryl was horse-trading.

"That's absurd. He'll help you improve your attendance."

"I hear you fellows are hurting at the gate now, and you're leading the league—"

"The boy's let the town down. The town feels violated. Now, Texans aren't going to feel that way. He didn't do anything to hurt your state. The people will know all about him and they'll come out to see him."

"It's nice to know, F. M.," Uncle Daryl said, "that you think Texans are so charitable."

"Have faith, my good man. The boy will be like a circus attraction at first. People will come out to look at him. Why, wasn't it your state that some years ago acquired a feral boy from India to display in the Dallas zoo?"

"That was different. That was Barnum and Bailey stuff."

"Oh, my dear fellow," Mr. Heller said, "we are all showmen, are we not?"

"I'll give you two hundred and fifty thousand, if I can return him, F. M."

"Once he leaves here, the fans won't ever let us take him back. We're very rigid in the Midwest. I'll take a scalping and give him to you for two hundred, no return bottle."

"I'll send you a check for one seventy-five."

"You want to announce it first or shall I?"

"I want to break the news to our poor fans, F. M."

"That's probably best."

"I've probably just thrown out close to two hundred G's."

If there was something that humbled Mr. Heller, it was losing large sums of money. "You might be pleasantly surprised," he said hopefully.

The owner of the Texas franchise got his first disappointment when he was told that Dr. John B. Mufufski would not accept the appointment at the university. Potter was assigned another therapist, a well-known psychiatrist from the University of Texas Medical Branch in Dallas, to pinch hit for Mufufski. The new psychiatrist's name was Harry Lassington, the author of dozens of papers on the behavioral sciences. He belonged to no special treatment school of psychiatry. He had no more allegiance to Dr. Freud than he had to any of the other geniuses in the field. He told Potter Cindy on the opening visit that it was not sound medicine to lock oneself into any school or fixed idea of psychotherapy. Potter just listened to him. He had never heard anything about the internal squabbles between strict Freudians, the many eclectics and the "other schools" of psychiatry.

"We're going to try to work things out with whatever approach we can think of to accomplish our goal."

Potter thought that Dr. Lassington was a nice enough man. Without realizing it, Potter was feeling "let down" by Dr. Mufufski when he told his new doctor, "I need help. That other doctor struck out with me." Later he would remember that it wasn't so and feel guilty.

"Why do you think he struck out?"

"Well, it's you treating me and not him, right?"

"You're feeling rejected?"

"I was his patient. Now I'm yours. I'd call that a strikeout or rejection or whatever you want to call it." If Dr. Lassington felt anything, he did not express it. He was a professional; he would make no comment on Dr. Mufufski's decision not to come to Texas. But he asked Potter: "What do you expect of me? What do you think I can do for you?"

"Well, I'm coming to a new club. The team is probably going to think I'm some kind of freak. You have to help me through that. It's tough to take all alone. It gets real rough."

"I understand you've met with Uncle Daryl and the manager of the Rustlers."

"Yes, the news travels fast, doesn't it?"

"How did that go?" Dr. Lassington wanted to know.

Potter studied the psychiatrist before he answered. He was a very large man, over 6 ft. 5 in., Potter was sure. He guessed the doctor's weight to be about 260 or 270. He was a bruiser. Potter wondered if he had played any ball before he had gone to fat.

"Was it unpleasant?" Dr. Lassington asked.

"Did you ever play any ball when you were younger? You look like you might have played some football."

"I did here in Texas for a while as an undergraduate.

Why?"

Potter did not tell the doctor that he was looking for a reason to like him. He wanted to know if they had experiences that they could share. He didn't want to be treated by one of those serious-looking, brainy guys again, like Dr. Mufufski. Potter answered simply, "I don't know, you just sort of looked like you played." He did not want to offend Dr. Lassington.

"You haven't answered my question. Did your meeting with Uncle Daryl and the manager go well?"

Potter bounced his head; it sort of said *okay*.

"I think you should tell me about it." Dr. Lassington pressed.

"Well they kind of walked me with two out and men on second and third."

"What does that mean?" the doctor wanted Potter to give more, to express it.

Potter was disappointed with the doctor. He thought that as an ex-football player he would understand another sport's references. "I mean they played by the book. They protected against the bomb. They put in a fifth defensive back. You know?"

Dr. Lassington could not figure out if Potter was stupid or very smart. "You mean they didn't express their feelings one way or another."

"I suppose you can say that. Except if you put a man on base in that situation, you don't want to face him. I suppose they didn't want to talk about you-know-what. It would have made everybody feel funny. They just told me I'd be playing and batting fourth almost as soon as I joined the club, things like that."

"If things get rougher, I want you to talk to me about them. I'll certainly try to support you there."

"That'll be appreciated." Potter said sincerely.

Then the doctor asked, "When was the last time you molested a child?"

Though he might have been asking for it, the question came so abruptly that it was like a blow. Potter felt pained by the words, helpless. He said in almost a whisper, "I think that's all done with because if it's not then I've been through hell for nothing." He would have wanted to tell Dr. Mufufski that rather than this new doctor. He knew Dr. Mufufski had not struck out, he just sort of left the ballgame in the seventh inning.

"We'll see how it goes. We'll try to open a lot of doors to you. There are things we can consider to speed the process along. There are certain shock treatments we can try."

"Shock treatments! What the heck are you talking about? They give those to people in lunatic asylums. I'm not crazy. I just told you I've been through hell. I've walked through hell. Do you understand that?" Potter rose from his seat, his body stiffened by rage, humiliation. His fists were clenched by the cruel realities of his existence. The volcano called Potter Cindy's sense-of-injustice erupted. "You fuck!" he shouted, though he did not mean Dr. Lassington.

For a moment, Dr. Lassington felt fear. He saw tremendous power in Potter's body, strength that could splinter the structure of a jaw with a single blow. Potter was an imposing figure, Dr. Lassington saw, himself a bear of a man who outweighed Potter by more than 60 pounds and who could see the top of the outfielder's head when they stood facing each other.

"I didn't mean shock treatment in the conventional sense," Dr. Lassington quickly explained. "I meant something else. But I see you are too upset right now to discuss it. I know it has been rough for you and I'm sorry. We'll discuss the program I have in mind at another time."

Potter sat back down, embarrassed by the fear he had seen in the doctor's face. He was disgusted by his own outburst. All the crap he had been through was fouling up his control, his sense of balance. "I apologize," he told Dr. Lassington, while he thought life would be a little easier if Dr. Mufufski had come to Texas. He believed that Dr. Mufufski knew where things were at.

The shock treatments that Dr. Lassington had in mind and described in a later session with Potter was a desensitization program for child molesters being tried out on persons with Potter's problem at a prison near Austin, Texas. Three times each week the inmates have their thighs wired up with electrodes. They then lie back on a reclining chair and look at photographs of naked children flashed before them on a screen. At the same time the child molester is given a painful but not excruciating shock. The idea behind it was, Dr. Lassington explained, to discourage any interest in that sexual target. The process is reinforced by showing photos of naked grown women without administering electric shocks to the patients. He told Potter that personality tests on the treated subjects showed a decline in the patients' interest in children as objects of seduction.

"Forget it," Potter told the psychiatrist. "It reminds me of a Frankenstein movie I saw on TV. I don't want any electric shocks to my legs. It might cut down my speed."

Potter was feeling good. He had been with Texas for about three weeks, and had a feeling that the ice was beginning to thaw. No one on the team had said very much to him, no less shown him any warmth. But then he hadn't extended himself very much to try to make friends. He had hit a game winning homer and some of the men came out to shake his hand when he touched home plate but he had just run by their outstretched palms. He knew that he was angry inside after what had followed the Atlanta business and he was taking it out against everybody, even these Texas players who had not done anything to him. On the day preceding the particular visit to the psychiatrist, in which that suggestion was made, Harvey Biggs, Texas' catcher, came up to him in the locker room. "Potter, you gotta minute? I'd like to say something to you."

"Oh, sure."

"I know we've been giving you the chills. I mean the guys. I kinda think the advice we got from the manager and coaches might not have been the best. They told us not to bug you, to leave you alone, not get under your skin. And, well, you know, ballplayers don't do a hell of a lot of thinking once they're told something to do in a strong manner by the manager. So we sort of froze you out."

"That's alright," Potter said, accepting the explanation as an apology, which it was. "I wasn't very giving myself. I don't blame the team, the guys."

"Well, I just wanted to say that I was following the orders like a man without eyes or sense. I think I did wrong. I think maybe I should of chanced speaking to you right out from the beginning."

"It might not of helped, Biggs."

"Well, it couldn't of hurt. I'm a big, thick man, as you see, Potter. I might have provided a nose you could take a poke at."

"You're in your rookie season, same as me, aren't you, Biggs?"

"Yep. But I ain't hitting my weight. I'm 220 pounds. And I'm batting .217."

"But you've hit some homers, I heard that. Some big ones."

"Twelve for distance," said Biggs with some pride. "You might say I had some quality homers but not quantity."

"I appreciate your coming over, Biggs." Potter offered his hand. He had started to say that if Biggs kept his home run pace up he'd have more than 20 at the end of the year, but he thought it would sound stupid and braggy coming from him, who had more than 25 already.

"Maybe, we can have a drink or go to the movies sometime."

"I'd like that," Potter said.

Most professional ballplayers, Potter understood, respected gift, even if, well, the gifted is to them a monster. He saw that a guy could get himself through a lot of crap if he could hit.

Potter continued to get along, still keeping to himself. Other players made small overtures of friendship toward him, and Potter was pleasant in return. He made no close ties, wanted none. He did have a beer with Biggs, and another time went to the movies with him and Andy Vimy, a rookie relief pitcher.

The crowds came out to see him just as Mr. Heller said they would. The fans didn't shower him with unkind objects nor unfurl nasty banners. Neither did they shower him with praise nor hoist any flags of honor. Texas watched with uncommon reserve. *Is that a rattler out there in centerfield or Potter Cindy?* It sure was true. Potter Cindy was a damn good ballplayer. In the three weeks with the club, Potter was a factor in moving it from last place to third from last, or third from the top. The other ballplayers somehow put it together better with Potter in the lineup. It was probably a coincidence, even if it is true that greatness gives birth to emulation of greatness. Potter got very little press for his efforts. The papers reported statements of fact: he went 3 for 4; he made a good catch. The official word to be cool to Potter apparently reached local editors. He certainly deserved more attention. In the grandstand, a lot of fans were privately beginning to feel that the child molester business in Atlanta was a bad, and maybe false, rap.

Texas hit the road on a hot streak. And it wasn't too pleasant for the centerfielder. The fans raked him over again in L.A., in the home of the Angels of all places. Kansas City fans were just as brutal. Texans were told by their newspapers and TV announcers that Potter was getting "the shaft," and was responding with silence, not a whimper from him. Some Texans wondered how the boy could take it. Where did Potter

Cindy cry? Was it in his room at night? That would be a private place. Potter roomed with no one, even though Biggs offered to be his roommate. He even suggested it to the manager.

"Hell, I'll room with him. He's an okay guy. And he probably could use a friend on the road, coach."

"The word is isolate him. It comes from Uncle Daryl. It's the way to go with Cindy."

"But why do they want to isolate him? You ain't isolating him from the lineup."

"There are some things you don't understand, Biggs. You're only a kid. Potter Cindy's got to make it on his own."

"But why?"

"Because Uncle Daryl says he has to win his self-respect back all by himself. We can't hand it to him as teammates, roommates or by getting the press to throw him bunches of roses. Just stay cool."

If there were official orders for chilly isolation, some fans back home were fired up. They did not like the way Potter was being treated. There was even talk in Texas of getting up a vigilante group, a company of riflemen, to go on out to L.A. and shoot off some fireworks.

One day with Texas playing in its own ballpark, a fan out on the field headed straight for Potter Cindy in centerfield. Potter set himself in a defensive position, ready for anything. The man could have been a nut. But he wasn't. He wanted to shake Potter's hand and welcome him to Texas. Potter shook his hand. There followed such a long, thunderous applause and loud whooping, and then such a long cadre of well-wishers heading for centerfield to shake the outfielder's hand that the public address announcer had to appeal to the fans to restrain themselves and let the game resume.

Potter Cindy had tears in his eyes as the applause thundered again when he came to bat. He thanked the fans by delivering a two-run, line drive triple in the gap between center and right. He thought, standing on third base, listening to the appreciation of the crowd that he had, at last, come home. That evening the newspapers carried photographs of the procession of persons who had gone out to shake a man's hand. Potter read the papers and thought fans were like slumps. Sooner or later they decided you've had enough. The fans in Texas, he felt, were okay; they measured him for what he was, and finding him a sum they could understand and budget, they bought him.

A person who bought him with less willingness and understanding, Uncle Daryl, decided it was time to get on the phone to his manager.

"About Potter Cindy, I think the team is isolating him too much."

"But you told me to. You told me to pass the word to be cool."

"I didn't mean to put him on ice," Uncle Daryl said.

"But you said to let him be, let him get his self-respect back."

"How much self-respect do you want him to get? It's time to warm up to the boy, make him feel wanted, that Texas is his home."

"That's a switch in signals. We've been treatin' him like he had B.O."

"Why, a lot of the fans have been saying that he's a sweet ballplayer. And whether we like it or not, the fans pay the freight."

"The fans didn't tell us to isolate him, though."

"Now, listen here, don't give me any of that bunk! When I just asked your opinion of Potter Cindy, you said it was like buying a losing streak, that the guy was fouled up. Now you act like his coming to Texas was your idea, almost," Uncle Daryl pointed out.

"I never said he was a bad ballplayer. I said he could hurt the morale of the club. And that I personally didn't want any

296

part of a man who would do the kind of thing he does."

"I'm told fans are saying that was a bad rap, that Potter Cindy didn't do anything."

"Come on, Uncle Daryl, you know that wasn't no lie—"

"Well, maybe. Anyway, I'm paying for one of the top psychiatrists in the state, and maybe in the country, to keep that part of him on ice."

"Well, Potter Cindy has helped the club. And I was wrong about morale, I'll admit it. Why, I even had a kid come up to me and volunteer to be his roommate."

"Good. Fine. Now if Dr. Lassington does his job, we may make some noise. I'm eager to buy some champagne for the club. What do you think?"

"Maybe next season, Uncle Daryl. But, then, you can never tell if we get the breaks. Remember how the Mets won it, coming from dead last."

Texas and Uncle Daryl didn't get any break one day in early August. Sissy showed up in Texas prepared to become Potter's wife again, to stick close by him and help him. Potter told her that he had appreciated her love and devotion, that she was the finest person he had ever known, that she was the only person in the world he ever really loved, that he would always remember her fondly, that she changed his life in many ways . . .

"Don't tell me you're rejecting me. I really don't believe that."

"I hope we can get together again, later on. Sissy, I need some time by myself. I have to consider all of the things that have happened. I'll come looking for you when I've gotten them straight. We'll start all over, if we can. And it'll be different."

She protested that she wanted to be with him, that he needed her.

"The time will come Sissy, you'll see," Potter said.

Sissy went back to California, a place she had said she

would never return to. She arrived with swollen eyes and a forced smile on her lips.

From the lips of Dr. Lassington, came the question:

"Why'd you turn Sissy away?"

"I didn't," Potter said, "I just took a raincheck."

"I don't interpret it that way. And I don't think she did, either. Is there something about Sissy that throws you off stride?" the doctor asked.

"No, I'm not ready for her yet. I don't know why. Maybe I pushed into marriage too soon. I think she's a fine person. But I think for now it's better this way."

"For a person who wins so many laurels and is so often cheered, I think you secretly enjoy chastisement. I think you enjoy punishment."

"What are you talking about? Nobody enjoys punishment. I've been through hell. Nobody likes that."

"Some people thrive on that," Dr. Lassington told him, "they look to catch hell. In fact, being in hell is the only way they can reassure themselves that they are alive."

Potter considered the words. "Dr. Lassington, I am only really alive when I'm playing ball. Everything else is just life. Sometimes it's fun and sometimes it's not, and that's about it."

"Some day you will not play ball. Every ballplayer's career comes to an end. Then what will you do?"

"I don't know."

"I'd like you to answer. What will you do?"

"I really don't know. I've always done this. I suppose, when I'm old, like forty, I'll become a cowboy full time, maybe buy a ranch or something."

"What about a family life?"

"I don't like kids all that much."

"Don't you?" Dr. Lassington asked sagely.

"What are you driving at? I told you lots of times I'm all done with that. That part of my life is finished. Why I haven't done anything like that in—" Potter stopped himself there because he realized that the last time he touched a child was as recently as two months ago at the Golden Slippers Hospital. It certainly had seemed longer than that, years, a lifetime.

"What were you going to say?" Dr. Lassington pressed.

"It wasn't important," Potter answered. "You know, doc—" Potter stopped to consider what he was going to say, "You know, maybe you were right. Maybe when the season is over, I'll try those shock treatments."

"I'm glad you changed your mind, of course. But it might be helpful if you could tell me how you reached this sudden change of heart."

"I don't know," Potter said. "I guess it just seemed to be worth a shot."

"Is that all you want to say about it?"

"Yes. I guess . . ." Then another thought occurred to Potter. "I think I got this problem pretty well licked, don't you?"

"I think you're going to lick it, Potter. And I think the program I outlined is going to help. We don't have to wait for the end of the season to begin."

"Okay," Potter said. Then he smiled, "You think I can sue you for malpractice if those shocks slow down my speed in the outfield, or on the bases."

"Don't worry about them, Potter. They won't hurt you."

The outfielder thought of one more question: "Do you think those shock treatments can cure a bank robber by showing the crook pictures of holdups and shocking him?"

"I can't say," Dr. Lassington answered, "I don't think they've tried it at Austin prison. There are no studies on it one way or another. But why did you ask?"

"I don't know. Just curious or thinking out loud, I guess."

"Don't worry about the treatments," he said. "Take my word for it. They'll help."

Potter never did take the shock treatments, the medical records show, because of the strange and eerie thing that happened to him in Lubbock, Texas, where he had gone with his ballclub to play their top farm team in an exhibition game.

The game was scheduled for the evening. Potter remembered being in a hotel room, waiting out the long hot Texas afternoon. Had he gone for a walk or only dreamed that he had?

He thought he remembered taking a walk around Lubbock—up main streets and down side ones. He was killing time so he wandered far from the heart of the town onto roads of far lesser vitality. He was on a street with nothing on it but one long hedge that stretched out for about two hundred yards or so.

It was most unusual for him, because he had always held his water well, but he suddenly had to urinate. There were no bars or stores or even a house he could pop into, and if there were he was not sure he could make it; he had to go so badly. He looked around. There wasn't anyone in sight so he opened his fly. He didn't see the little girl come out from an opening in the hedge until he started to urinate. She was about fifteen yards away and he hoped he would finish before she was in sight of his penis. He knew a freak accident like this could get him into a mess. He just had not realized that the long hedge had walled-in grade school property. And suddenly the little child was squealing in fear or excitement. "Look, calm down," he told the child. "It was an emergency. I suddenly had to go. You can understand that, can't you? Don't you have to go sometimes badly and can't hold it in? That's all it is." The little girl held her mouth and stared at Potter, below the belt. "Was the child giggling or crying? Was she horrified or pleased? He looked down at himself; it was only then that he fully realized that he had an erection. A passing motorist had seen it too. When the car came to a screeching halt, Potter zipped up and cut out on a dead run back to the hotel and up the stairs to his room. He threw himself on the bed and cried in anguish. He had, it was true, lost control again. He prayed that this time the whole thing was just a frightening dream of incontinence. He begged God not to let it be the duster . . . for surely this would be the pitch he would never recover from. God. PLEASE. . . .

Potter was quietly picked up at the ballpark by plainclothes local Texas peace officers. Only the team manager was told.

People did want to know why, of course. But what is the good of *why*? Potter confessed that it probably was not an accident after all, that perhaps underneath he knew he was near a school and that he hoped a little girl would pass. Perhaps it was not possible to prevent it. He was sorry. Perhaps it was pressure, a new situation. Maybe the new psychiatrist upset him or Sissy. Maybe he didn't believe the shock treatments would work. If he was forced to point his finger to one thing that set him off it was the knowledge that only two months had passed since he had handled that child at Golden Slippers Hospital. Perhaps he knew he was lost at that moment.

Uncle Daryl could hardly catch his breath when he heard. He thought he would have a coronary. Everything had been going so well. He called Potter's psychiatrist. "You sonofabitch, Lassington, you blood-sucking maggot. What the hell was I paying you for? Were you too damn busy to take care of the boy? I paid you to look out for his welfare, but you were too damn busy giving nipples to a bunch of neurotics whose only problems were worrying about whether their mommys or daddys loved them."

"When you calm down, Uncle Daryl, you'll realize the boy is a chronic case. There wasn't enough time. He struck too fast."

Uncle Daryl hadn't yet calmed down when he called Giggin Barewedge at the state house in Austin. "I say that it was through your pressure and over my dead body that I got into this mess. You made me take—buy for nearly two hundred thousand dollars—a chronic child molester."

"The governor wants to make amends, Uncle Daryl."

"Amends? When this news breaks I ain't going to have three paying customers to rub together."

"The governor's going to clean it up, Uncle Daryl. We got word from Lubbock before anyone. The hush is on."

"What hush?"

"Well, you see, my nephew is the District Attorney in Lubbock."

"So what?"

"Well, we convinced my nephew to drop charges. The governor agrees on the condition Potter Cindy leave the state and never return to it."

"What about the child's parents?"

"That's going to be taken care of," he reassured him. "Trust me."

"What about my own players?"

"You'll take care of that end. I suggest that you tell them that for the good of the team Potter should remain a family secret, a skeleton in the closet. The cover story for the press is that Potter disappeared. Leave the suggestion that he was mentally fatigued from his trials and tribulations in Atlanta and in the Midwest and disappeared, like old Indians do when they go off on their own and die."

"What about my money?"

"Shit, Uncle Daryl, there's just so much the governor can do."

"Where's Potter Cindy now?"

"The Lubbock police escorted him in a squad car across the State line, governor's orders. Or at least that's the plan. I'd say that just about now he was in a squad car somewhere between Seminole, Texas, and Hobbs, New Mexico."

Uncle Daryl felt a certain, inexplicable sadness, or maybe he hated to see all that money slip through his fingers so quickly. "Didn't anybody from the team say so much as a goodbye to him?"

"Only the manager and it wasn't a very nice sendoff."

302

"Yeah, I know he was hopping mad last night when he called me. Hey what about the press?"

"Lucky for you the Dallas papers didn't cover the exhibition game."

"What about the local papers in Lubbock?"

"Well, there's only one and my nephew, the DA, is a close friend of both the editor and publisher. In fact, he's the controlling stockholder in the paper."

"Sounds tidy."

Giggin took it as a compliment. "Thanks. I thought so myself."

It is said that from Hobbs, Potter disappeared into the vast scenery of New Mexico. He was never heard from again in organized baseball. Harvey Biggs claimed he caught sight of Potter in a carnival during the annual *Fiesta del San Judas el Apostol*, the patron saint of lost causes, in Mesilla, New Mexico. Biggs happened to be in the area visiting a teammate, Bobby Sparrow, who lived in nearby Anthony, Texas. Sparrow could not confirm Biggs' report. It was hard to tell because the man Biggs thought was Potter was wearing jeans and boots and a cowboy hat, and sporting a beard. The ballplayers never did speak to the man who looked like Potter.

Who knows? Potter did his cowpunching in that area in the off-seasons. He liked Mesilla. It was quiet. A man could get rid of his cares there. Perhaps it was only coincidental that Mesilla was one of Billy The Kid's safe havens, one of his hideouts.

Anyway, a man who could have been Potter's twin stood in the carnival during the fiesta of Saint Jude, watching one of the main attractions. Perched on a platform was a short, thin blond man who urged the crowd to throw balls at him. He was protected by a wire cage so that he could not be hurt by the pitched baseballs. It was a good thing, too, because the man in the cage baited the crowd, often unkindly. To draw quarters, he said things like come on fatso, or peewee or ugly or pimple-face, try to dunk me. The only way one could get back at him was to hit a small target dead center about sixty feet away with a baseball. If struck, the target would trigger a mechanism that split the man's perch and he would fall into a huge tub of water below his seat.

Dozens of people had thrown at the target to dunk him and missed, and with each miss his comments at the throwers would grow bolder and unkinder. Finally, he saw the man who was Potter Cindy's twin in the crowd. "Hey, cowboy, come on. Step up. Don't be cheap. It's only a quarter for three balls. Shake the dust out of your wallet. Let's see if you can throw anything but bull." The man who was Potter Cindy's twin seemed to be amused, maybe enticed. He plunked down a quarter, and threw a blazing fastball dead on target, dunking the loud mouth. The man who was like Potter had two balls left. When the loud mouth's perch was re-established, the thrower drew back his arm again. Loud mouth said, "Hey, this bull-thrower looks like he played in Little League ten years ago." On hearing this, the cowboy who was Potter flipped the remaining two balls impotently to the attendant who was collecting the quarters and walked out of the carnival. The cowboy either got something in his eye, or he was crying.

NORMAN KEIFETZ has been sports-medicine feature writer for a leading weekly medical news magazine and is now director of a number of clinical medical journals in New York City, where he lives with his wife and two children. *The Sensation* is his second novel.